SINGLE

Single

A NOVEL BY
Harriet Frank, Jr.

WARNER BOOKS

A Warner Communications Company

WARNER BOOKS EDITION

Library of Congress Catalog Card Number 77-6481

ISBN 0-446-81543-8

This Warner Books Edition is published by arrangement with
Houghton Mifflin Company.

Cover design by Gene Light

Cover art by Elaine Duillo

Warner Books, Inc., 75 Rockefeller Plaza, New York, N.Y. 10019

 A Warner Communications Company

Printed in the United States of America

Not associated with Warner Press, Inc. of Anderson, Indiana

First Printing: September, 1978

10 9 8 7 6 5 4 3 2 1

FOR MY HUSBAND
WITH LOVE

"I'll face the unknown.
I'll build a world of my own.
No one knows better than I myself
I'm by myself, alone."
from "By Myself," by Howard Dietz
and Arthur Schwartz

Single

1

THE END of the affair seemed clearly in sight. It was plain when one's postcoital thoughts turned to hot buttered toast and strong black coffee. She longed for both, although the man asleep beside her had wonderful legs and beautiful muscles running down his back. Toast with jam. Thin toast. Strawberry jam with red perfect berries still tasting of the sun and sand they grew in. She yawned hugely and shifted away from Cass. He ground his teeth in some remote sleep-drenched confrontation. She sat up naked and chilled to study him. He did look charming, she gave him that. Dark hair, dark lashes, greedy face, stubborn mouth... boring, boringly young.

She slid from bed without waking him. She found her shoes and panties by the door and her dress draped over a chair. She smiled a little at the hasty carelessness of it all. She reached for her glasses on the bedside table and swore aloud as they eluded her blind groping.

"Where *are* the goddamn things?"

She found them, thrust them on and made for the bathroom, scratching absently.

She hated his taste in wallpaper. Some kind of an ethnic horror in black and brown. And the vanity of the little cub. She squinted at the vast array of lotions, the silk bathrobe, the English hairbrush, the water pick, the fistful of toothbrushes, the stationary bicycle, weapons clustered to defeat even the first feathery touch of age.

She was brutally indifferent to her own image in the glass. Large clear eyes, yes, woefully near-sighted. A long nose, straight, rather distinguished. A mouth hinting of appetite—men looked at it first and lingered on it. Too strong a chin, a jutting chin that warned of strong opinion strongly expressed. The body was nothing much, tall, flat, robust. She had warned lovers on occasion that sex for her was largely in the mind. She knew a hundred and fifty witty dirty limericks. She had read yards of erotic Japanese literature. She was curious, inventive, athletic, tireless. What they heard whispered in the dark often startled them.

She selected a toothbrush at random, scrubbed, spat. A fling of cold water, her fingers raked through her short hair, a cigarette butt plucked from an overflowing ashtray completed her morning ablutions. She lit the stub, her eyes narrowing against the sting of the smoke.

"Nell?"

"In here."

"It's five-thirty, for Christ's sake."

"Six."

His tone was hostile. "Aren't you even going to take a goddamn bath?"

"At home."

"Why do you always light out of here like you'd stolen the silver?"

She walked back into the bedroom, crossed it with rapid strides and hunkered by the bed.

"Go back to sleep. If you still feel lousy, if you're still coughing, come into the office and let me look at you. Drink some orange juice."

He raised himself on one arm and looked at her, smoothing his hair, devoted to his appearance, preening. "Where are you going?"

She was soothing and patient. "Where I go every day. To work." Her hand went out and touched his face. "A little fever, maybe. Take your temperature."

He pushed away from her fretfully. "I'm sick."

"Not very."

"I'm sick of this fucking affair."

"Ah," she said mildly, "that's something else again." She stabbed the cigarette out neatly.

"You're a crazy woman in the dark, and in the morning—cold haddock."

"Mmm." She was struggling into her jacket. "Well, at night I'm in heat, and in the morning clear-eyed and surfeited."

"Nell, come in here."

"Take some aspirin. Two. Three. Can't hurt."

"I don't want aspirin. I want a stud fee."

She was at the door. "I'm your doctor. You don't pay your bill. I'm taking it out in trade."

13

She was gone.

She drove too fast with the windows down. The smog already smudged the sky, dimming the California sun. She listened to the news briefly, switched to the delicate melancholy of a Schubert sonata. She was reminded again of the pleasures of being alone, of letting her thoughts spool lazily like threads unwinding. One had to be eccentric or old to respect that profound inner quiet she found so delicious. That was the joy of living with William. Her grandfather had a positive mania for stillness. Long, silent meals. Evenings washing over them as they sat side by side in the garden, the old stone wall tangled in grass and ivy, the final night call of a dove pulsating just before dark. Then when the conversation came it was heated, spiced, a fencing match.

Well, it was peace no longer. He had shattered it. She put the thought aside, vowing to deal with it later and to deal with it harshly.

It was then she saw the apartment. I hope it's bloody expensive, she thought. I'll make him pay for at least half.

It was a ridiculous building, all jutting corners and glaring glass, set in a contrived crush of trees and flowers, but there was the smell of the sea in the air and beyond a stingy strip of beach. She parked her car and approached it cautiously, peering into the huge courtyard. Three swimming pools steamed into the morning air, all shaped like kidneys and all a poisonous blue. And be damned if there weren't waterfalls spilling from hidden pipes into concrete troughs. It was an amusement park Eden, the hibiscus grossly enlarged, the fir trees pitifully stunted. Above her a banner waved in the breeze, promising nirvana: MARINA ONE. SAUNA, TENNIS, POOLS, HAWAIIAN WATERFALLS, PRIVATE PATIOS, THE GOOD LIFE, SINGLES ONLY.

He was sitting in a deck chair, a dog asleep on his chest. He was unshaven, his skin deeply tanned. She ticked him off instantly: lazy, likely to run to fat, lecherous. She deduced the last by the long, nimble look he gave her, stopping short of her face.

"You have an apartment for rent?"

"Yes, ma'am."

"I'd like to see it."

He unwound himself from the chair, hoisted the pup under his arm. "You ever live in a singles apartment before?"

"No. Never before."

She was already poised on the edge of displeasure, sniffing the insistence of next-door neighbors, the pressures of intimacy with no possibility of escape; life without the blessed dignity of the closed door.

"They're a mixed bunch. I've got 'em divorced, I've got 'em dumped, I've got 'em suicidal. The noise level is high, the turnover rapid and the atmosphere unbuttoned. You sure it's your dish?"

"We'll see." She shoved her glasses up into her hair. "Are you the owner?"

"Jake Cooley," he said.

"Do you live here yourself?"

Doubtless he did, in a welter of dirty shorts, dog-eared books, crushed beer cans and the faded scent of someone's perfume on the pillow slip. Would there be something singular?—a bust of Lord Byron, a collection of Baudelaire?

"Top floor," he was saying. "The rent's six

hundred and twenty a month, first and last in advance."

"Fair enough," she said. "I'm Dr. Willis. Good morning." She held out her hand.

"Pleased to meet you, doctor. It's upstairs, next to mine."

The tiles of the kitchen were a shade of pink she particularly loathed, the insistent color of dime-store nail polish, English pastries, the nervous rose flush of menopause. She let him precede her through the apartment; he kept the little dog tucked under his arm and its tail thumped against his stained and worn chinos. He had not shaved. He had the look of a castaway prepared to be amiable to the natives and to survive at all costs.

She paused to rap on the wall. "Paper thin," she observed. She passed by him into the bathroom. One glance sufficed.

"The toilet bowl is unspeakable," she said pleasantly, "and the stain on the bedroom wall is unmistakably semen."

He shook his head. "He was an untidy fellow. People don't have much respect for the places they live in. They mostly rut and eat and relieve themselves and call it home."

"Apparently." She made for the window and strained at it, but it was jammed shut. She slammed her palm against it until it gave. "A little soap would help," she suggested.

"Never thought of it," he told her complaisantly.

She thrust her head out. There was only the merest wedge of blue visible from her vantage point, as if someone had torn a scrap of cloth and let it fly like blue silk into the wind. But the air was

16

salubriously full of salt and foam, the landscape recalled Antibes and a large white sail suddenly floated by, a stately swan on a pond, its canvas flapping and cracking loudly, making her throat tighten with its spank and flair.

She turned back into the room. "It's not a generous view but I like it." She paused a moment and studied him. "Now about me, Mr. Cooley. I'm not convivial. I don't want to meet airline pilots. I'm neither predatory nor frustrated. If you'll paint this room white and put a dead bolt on the door, I'll take it."

"Well," he said, "you should lend a note of class to the place." He rocked on his heels in front of her. "Doctor, huh? What kind of a doctor would that be?"

"I'm a medical doctor. I practice internal medicine. My specialty is gastrointestinal problems. Gut aches and the like."

"My Aunt Fergus was a veterinarian. I guess that's as close as we come to medicine in my family. A very determined woman, my Aunt Fergus. Unmarried and hell on bores, deadbeats and mankind in general."

"She sounds very sensible to me," Nell said.

"When will you be moving in?"

"Tomorrow."

"I'll get right on it. White paint, you said."

"Pristine white."

"There's one other thing."

"And what's that?" she asked, jingling her car keys impatiently.

"I'm an insomniac. Every once in a while I'll be cooking myself ravioli at three in the morning or playing some Beethoven on the record player. If that doesn't work I do a couple of laps in the pool. It could be at any time of the night."

"I'm not easily bothered," she said, "and you might try some calcium for sleep."

She started down the stairs. He called after her, leaning over the balcony. "I have a poker game every Monday night. The boys drink a little beer. Sometimes they raise a ruckus if the cards aren't falling just right. Nothing mean, but they cuss and break up some of the furniture."

She stopped on the landing and looked back up at him. "I'll be out Monday nights."

He wasn't talked out. "My Uncle Tyler, that's my uncle on my mother's side, used to say look before you leap. It wasn't original with him but he sure as hell said it often enough."

She smiled. "And did he?"

"No, ma'am. He just put his head down and rammed on ahead."

"You have interesting relatives, Mr. Cooley. I'll see you tomorrow." She waved and went. He pulled his nose thoughtfully and watched her go until she was out of sight.

His house had a dry, sweet smell as if someone had crushed lavender in its dark hallways. Her room on the third floor was shabby and old-fashioned, the walls faded to the color of honey, the bed narrow, lumpy and virginal. She had never tired of the delights of it, the sagging bookshelves, the painted furniture, the chair broken to suit her posture, the smell of ink drying in a pot beside a pen that scratched fiercely, the mirror dim and scored with age cracks, the bunch of pinks or geraniums she had jammed into an empty pickle jar.

18

Here she had lived, slept, studied, nearsighted, gnawing on her glasses. Here she had wept, raged. Here she had fantasized, stuporous, on long summer days: a man's mouth, a hand between her legs, her own mouth moving, roving.

He sat in a chair and watched her. She searched his face for any sign of regret and saw that it was as remote and composed as always.

She stripped the room methodically in her mind's eye, angrily removing every trace of her long stay there. What would it look like with the books, the Daumier drawings, the Chinese vase, the scrap of Oriental carpet, the tennis rackets all flung without care into boxes and cartons and hauled away? She fought down the annoying sting of tears and opted instead for anger.

"You're a bastard, throwing me out like this. You really are."

He folded his fine, delicate hands and remained silent, heavy, preoccupied.

"You're the only man I ever loved."

His voice when he spoke was dry. "You've been in a dozen beds, my girl."

"Two dozen. Anyway, where's your sense of responsibility?"

He remained silent. She emptied her drawers in an untidy flood, tangled the clothes and dumped them into a suitcase. "Besides," she fumed, "you *need* me. How are you going to live without me? You're chronically absent-minded. You don't balance your checkbook. You dribble cigar ashes on your shirt. You smell like a zoo unless I remind you to bathe. Ugh. You're disgusting."

"Not entirely."

She turned on him, studied his face with desperate intensity. "You'll fall down and break a

19

hip," she threatened. "You'll become reclusive. You'll eat candy all day long and become diabetic."

"None of these things."

She floundered for a weapon. "You'll be lonely."

He closed his eyes to ward her off, a trick of his that maddened her.

"I warn you," she said, breathless for battle, "you'll turn to religion."

"Unlikely."

He rose then, a tall, spare figure, fine head, white hair. It seemed grotesque to her; he looked like a young man fresh from the hands of a make-up artist, made up to resemble an old one. For one moment she felt what it would be like to lay her head against his chest, to feel his hand heavy on her head.

"Turn loose, Nell," he said. "You're too long in the tooth to be sequestered with an old man. It's unnatural, it's regressive, and besides you wake me when you roll home, damp and still tumescent from your current lover."

"I'll give him up," she said promptly.

"Mama's girl—possibly, if she were still alive. Daddy's girl—absurd at your age. Grandpa's girl—totally neurotic, my dear."

"But you sweet old cock," she murmured, "I love you. I like talking to you or even being talked at by you. You're sensible. You're undemanding. You're witty—quite often. You're even handsome, in a desiccated kind of way."

"I want to live alone," he said stubbornly. "I want to prepare for what must be my imminent end. I want you to go forth."

She slammed a suitcase shut. "I'm deflowered.

20

I'm independent. What more do you want from me?"

"I'm very old. You need to let go. Anyway, you're moody. Untidy. We have political arguments. You avenge yourself on me for every man who bores or annoys you."

"You'll take up with a Pasadena widow, damn it! You'll leave all your money to someone else." She bit her lip to stop a sudden childish tremor.

He picked up a silver-framed picture of himself she had thrown into a cardboard carton. "That was taken fifty years ago, at the peak of my virility. Leave the damn thing behind."

She snatched it back from him. "You have no family feeling. Your arteries are hard. *You're* hard."

She was being rancorous now. He disdained it. "This place you're moving to. You say it's by the sea?"

"It's one of those damn fool singles places where I'll undoubtedly drown in the tears of the divorced ladies wailing through the night."

"You're single," he said flatly. "You belong there."

"You don't draw blood that way. Better try something else."

"You're overbearing."

"Better. What else?"

Long afterward she would remember the concern in his voice. "You're incomplete, my love."

The barb landed. She gathered up her coat and glanced once more around the room. She made up her mind there would be no further outbursts.

"What final word of wisdom?"

"Come back Saturday night. We'll play chess."

21

She grabbed him in a crushing embrace. "Stay alive," she commanded, and ran before he could deny her.

Nell attracted strays. Ellen, her office nurse, was first among them, a thin frantic woman given to head colds and girlish crushes. She was a model of efficiency in the office and the lab, one of life's victims otherwise, defensive of Nell to the point of obsession. She knitted Nell scratchy afghans, put a comic valentine on her desk and presented sugary fudge at Christmas. She blushed deeply and frequently. She carried a wad of damp Kleenex clutched in her hand. She was a cross to bear.

"Dr. Steinberg's waiting for you. He's been on a rampage ever since he got in." Her voice was a wet whisper. "He's already fired the new lab girl and he called a collection agency—a *collection* agency—to handle this office. He said if the patients didn't start paying their bills he'd haul their . . . their . . ."

"Asses," Nell prompted gently.

". . . into court."

Nell put a comforting arm around the woman's shoulder. "I think that's dandy. Let's give him a list of my deadbeats, too."

"You wouldn't do a thing like that, Dr. Willis. Your patients adore you."

"Where is he?"

"In his office. With Mrs. Katz."

She walked toward Amos' office, led by the rancid smell of his cheap cigars. She heard his voice raised through the closed door.

"Take off the goddamn weight. Stop telling me it's your thyroid. Your thyroid is the only normal thing about you. You're fat because you eat like a pig. Go take those piss shots those phony Beverly Hills doctors give you. Pay through the snout. But don't come whining to me about palpitations. I've got really sick people to deal with."

She waited outside, lounging against the wall till the wave broke over Mrs. Katz.

"Stop crying, for Christ's sake. Minnie, stop, or I'll tweak your tit. Now, listen. Eight hundred calories. No strudel. No chicken fat. No little nosh during Johnny Carson. I want to see you in six weeks. If you haven't lost that lard by then I'm sending you to a shrink. He'll ask you how you and Marvin shtup, Minnie. He'll talk about oral sex. You won't like it, Minnie, so do what I tell you."

Mrs. Katz, a tremulous, tear-stained mountain, stumbled out. "Dr. Willis," she said, grasping at Nell, "your partner's crazy. He's a crazy man. If shouting and yelling were malpractice you'd be in plenty of trouble."

Nell clucked and soothed. "It's only his manner. Another visit or two and you'll be used to him. We've all had to go through it."

"My daughter's marrying a ballet dancer next week. A skinny nebbish with long yellow hair. A boy in tights with cotton padding you know where. Who wouldn't eat? Of course I eat. I'm nothing but nerves—*hungry* nerves."

"Get in here, Nell. I want to talk to you." Amos loomed upon them. "You still here?"

"I'm going, Dr. Steinberg. Maybe I'm going to another doctor."

"Go. In good health."

He grabbed Nell and pulled her through the door, slamming it in Mrs. Katz's astonished face.

Nell took out a cigarette and perched on the edge of the desk.

"Don't smoke in my presence."

She lit it nonetheless and expelled a long stream in his direction, studying him.

He was a bear of a man, hairy, pugnacious, solid as a house. He had the dark, angry look of his parents, patrician Jewish refugees who lived in Oriental splendor in Bel Air. They took tea in the afternoon under the brooding gaze of a Rembrandt of dubious authenticity. They played chamber music together and grew monstrous mauve orchids and battened on their only son. He remained unmarried, dutiful, enraged.

He slammed into a chair, thrust his feet up on his desk and glared at her.

"You fucked your brains out last night, didn't you? I can tell. You only get that pinched look when you've gone down on somebody."

"You're charming this morning."

"Tell me about it." He put his fingertips together and bared his teeth.

"Amos, what's on your mind?"

"I've got a problem."

"Like what?"

He began to hook paper clips together. He stared at the ceiling. He got up and walked to the window.

"I got you through school. Right? I pushed you. I hammered facts into your head. I cut up your cadavers. I gave you beautiful lecture notes. I held your head when you puked on rounds. I fell in love with you."

"All of that and more."

She remembered him as he was then, hollow-eyed, brilliant, erratic. She remembered the long

24

Sunday dinners, with his mother seated regally at the head of the table, his father docilely at the foot. She remembered the table gleaming with silver almost too heavy to lift, the room dark at noon with rose velvet drapes, the funereal bouquets hinting at death approaching. She remembered Amos carefully placing her in his life.

"My best friend, this clever little shiksa," he had told his parents. "Very smart for a goya. Top of her class. Behind me. But *just* behind."

"Not married?" That had been a little tug at the oedipal string from Mama.

"Not married."

"A lovely young woman like you."

"He only wants to sleep with me, Mrs. Steinberg," she had told her. "Not to worry."

His father had hidden a nervous laugh in his napkin.

He had never taken her there again. Later, when they'd opened their office together, his mother had come bringing an exquisite Georgian inkstand. She had even conferred a dry, powdery kiss on her cheek. It had been a gesture of alliance. Two practical women, one to nurture his work, one to bind him close with delicate, age-spotted hands.

His voice interrupted the reverie.

"Nell," he said suddenly, "I've been messing around. With a sixteen-year-old girl yet."

"As I recall," she told him, "you graduated cum laude. Messing around? Surely you can command the language with more accuracy than that."

"All right, I'm involved with a nubile, silken, rather vicious brat, a nymphet, if you will, a half-ripened peach. Daphne fleeing an overheated Apollo. A child of the times, avid, expert, oh, how

25

expert, with just the merest touch of venereal disease."

"Are you telling me you have the clap?"

"Lower your voice," he said, "and be supportive for a change. I'm coming into your office for a shot."

"You're *not*."

"Well—I can't reach my own left buttock—and I'm sure as hell not going to the Free Clinic."

She clucked censoriously. "Congress with minors? At your age?"

"It would never have happened if you'd let me into your bed."

"No excuse, Amos."

"Are you going to help or no?"

"Certainly. I'll paint your balls as blue as a Mediterranean sky."

He was suddenly meek. "I'll take your night calls for a month."

She regarded him thoughtfully for a moment. The fact was he could easily give himself the shot, attend to himself quietly and discreetly, with no fuss. But it was necessary for him to let her know that he had a life independent of the one they shared in the office, that he slept with young girls, allowed them to infect him. It was perverse, altogether like him.

She held out her hand. "Come on."

He yelped with pain at the needle. "Christ, woman, all that training and you haven't learned how to throw a shot without maiming a man?"

"Consider it penance."

He sat on her examining table with his pants drooping forlornly at his knees, piteous, Chaplin without comedy.

"What do you know about passion?" he accused her. "You're a cold cunt. I know how you live. You hunt the pack like a hound, cut one out, cut one up, and you're gone."

"Not so. My intimate friends remain my friends. Cry on my shoulder. Borrow my money."

"You want to know how it happened?"

"No."

"She looked like you must have at that age."

"She certainly didn't behave like I did at that age. At that age all I did was read Virginia Woolf and masturbate to Mozart. It's spoiled me for everything else since, too."

He pulled up his pants and marched to the door. "I want to be around when it happens to you."

"When what happens, Amos?"

"When someone hits a vital nerve. When someone melts the ice."

"I expect I'll make an absolute spectacle of myself. Witless, defenseless, depraved, despondent. Everything you could possibly hope for."

"Now you're sore." He came back and draped his arms around her in a brotherly hug.

She broke free of him and opened the door, waving him through it. "Kindly go to work," she told him.

She refused a heavy patient load for herself. She insisted on having enough time for each case. The speed with which most medical care was given offended her deeply. The most endearing thing about Amos was his total support.

"No factory medicine. No assembly line medicine. I don't have to drive a Jaguar and you don't need charge accounts at Saks. No unnecessary lab work, no thirty-dollar vitamin shots, no placebos.

27

But keep up, Nell. Read the journals. Burn the midnight oil. I'm going to know if you goof because I'm a very hotshot doctor."

They had been in partnership for a month when they went a hundred thousand dollars into debt, sued successfully by a middle-aged woman with greasy yellow bangs and a mild case of anemia. Nell had administered a few iron shots which had caused some yellow splotches on her buttock and had, her attorney told the court passionately, repulsed the woman's husband, leaving her rejected, crying out in the night, pleading for sexual sustenance; vainly, vainly, for he, the husband, revolted to the very depths of his being by those rust-colored stains on that (already) wrinkled ass, refused ever again to perform his marital duty, could not, in point of fact, your honor, with the best will in the world, get it up anymore.

But Amos remained strong in those early days. "Never mind, we'll get 'em," he had told her with his arrogant German Jewish confidence. "Word'll get out that we make house calls. Where are they going to find medics like that, Nell?"

"On the soap operas," she told him.

They had located under the freeway near the old soldiers' hospital in Sawtelle. There are plenty of specialists in Los Angeles and Westwood and Beverly Hills, Amos told her; we're needed here. So they had settled in a low stucco building among the Japanese truck gardens and the Japanese nurseries and the Shinto temples north of Sepulveda Boulevard, and they drew students from U.C.L.A., pensioners from the large English colony in Santa Monica, beach people from Venice, the shy, elderly ones and the dazed hippies, the runaways, the junkies and winos. The nucleus of their practice remained the demanding, querulous friends of Mr. and Mrs. Steinberg, Senior, with their fading memories of Vienna and Berlin and Budapest, flickering out as the years passed in this new, barbarous, unlettered country.

She faced one of them across her desk.

"Pacemaker? I don't understand." Mrs. Lowenthal laced her fingers together tensely.

Nell came around and drew up a chair beside her. She untangled the old woman's hands and held one firmly in hers.

"Did you go to the Horowitz concert, Eda?"

The woman was diverted, her face glowing. "The man is a poet. Sublime."

"And you? You practice every day?"

"No more. I can't. These days I'm helpless. Exhausted. You know."

"That's why we're talking about a pacemaker. To give you back your music."

"Where does it go?"

"Into your chest. A wonderfully skilled team of doctors implants it. Your heart will beat normally again, you'll have your strength back, and you'll play beautiful afternoon concerts for me and everyone who loves you."

"A mechanical doll. I'll be a wound-up toy."

"You'll be a woman of sixty-five with a future. You won't be tired anymore. You'll buy me a very expensive present and tell everyone I'm a genius."

"I know a lawyer who is just forty and very well off. Come to tea. He's looking for a wife."

"I've already had a lawyer, dear Mrs. Lowenthal. I'm looking for a tinker now, a tailor, a cowboy, a sailor."

Mrs. Lowenthal was confused. Nell abandoned her slight joke.

"Bring George with you next Wednesday. I'll arrange with him about the surgery, about your care."

"George. George sits in the garden by the summerhouse, reading Balzac. If I die, he'll look up with his finger still on the page."

"We'll do it without him."

Mrs. Lowenthal bent a pale, probing gaze on Nell. "You stay alone. Unmarried. By your own choice. What is it like to live like that?"

"I hesitate to inflict," she told her, "and I don't want to be afflicted. There's some pride involved. Some regret. Some gloom. An occasional triumph. It's I who read in the garden without looking up."

Mrs. Lowenthal nodded. "The lawyer I was speaking of, he's not interesting enough for you. I'll look further."

Nell laughed. "If you do, I like the kind that come out from under the rocks."

"Pardon? Pardon? I don't understand."

"I don't either." Nell linked her arm through the woman's and guided her to the door.

"I was alone one summer in Paris," Mrs. Lowenthal mused. "I sat under the trees in the late afternoon. I drank wine. I let a very young boy take me home. I never saw him after that night. I didn't care. That one night was enough. They're afraid to let you know how nice that is—to do what you want, to surrender, without guilt, freely." She patted Nell's face. "I'm not afraid of that thing anymore, that pacemaker. Thank you." She was gone.

Nell went back to her desk, pushed the clutter of papers aside, swung her feet up and folded her hands behind her head. She felt agitated as she always did when confronted by the frailty of what she dealt with. A mechanical box in the chest, and if it didn't work a sudden stabbing pain, a dark murmuring somewhere in the body, and all that vibrated and defied would be stilled.

She decided to prescribe for herself. A long walk, a hot fudge sundae, the expensive Watteau drawing she coveted in a Rodeo Street gallery. She shrugged them off impatiently. Cass's head between her legs, a healthy smell of warm skin, her own mouth offering feverish service. That was better, better, best.

She gave in to caprice and reached for the phone.

He was slow to answer but she waited him out patiently.

"You were lying out by the pool, naked as a jaybird," she told him, "and now you have a warm groin from all that sun and a mind full of obscene conjectures."

"What the hell!—is that you, Nell?"

"If I were there right now," she breathed, "what could I do to you if I were there right now, my randy friend?"

"What you're doing *now* is a helluva thing to do to me. I've got an erection so big it's knocking this phone off the hook."

"My new address is Marina One. Apartment

twenty-three. I'm moving in today after we close the office. Come over tonight. I'll have the pictures up and the bed made."

"We'll do something dirty," he said jauntily.

"I doubt it," she countered. "You have such a paucity of imagination."

"And what's that supposed to mean?"

"It's youth, mostly," she sighed. "Never mind. I'll think up something for both of us. Don't come before nine unless you want to line shelves." She hung up.

At the big house she was ruthless, a rampaging Genghis Khan. The moving men stood in awe as she prowled through the rooms ticking off what she wanted. Her grandfather's housekeeper, Mrs. Keitel, watched, her stern bony face wearing the look of a woman suffering rape. Nell had never liked her. She had the fussy possessive air of a nanny. She warred against dirt, disdained aesthetics (flowers shed petals, sunlight faded carpets) and she talked to herself and God in a harsh New England twang.

"Those things are your grandfather's," she snapped as Nell waved the George the Second table, the blue delft jar, the Victorian armchair into the brawny arms of the waiting men.

"All too good for him," Nell said. "All he requires is a narrow bed, a bowl for gruel, a Gregorian chant and your nasty cooking to be completely blissful. I'm going into the kitchen now." And she stalked past the hapless woman.

"I'll take the Crown Derby, too." She opened the china cabinet and scanned the delicious porcelain like a child at a candy counter. "Two plates from the Lowestoft. That heavenly blue. And all the

Meissen dessert plates. And the Baccarat crystal, and the plates from Provence for breakfast and the Sabatier knives and the French copper pots and the Peking glass for roses. Now, linens!"

The woman pursued her, her face flushed and frantic. "You're not leaving us a thread!"

Nell paid no attention to her; she was now focused on the linens. "Let him sleep on nails. Porthault? No. Vulgar." She pushed a pile aside. "I'll take the Irish with the crochet edging. I like linen that crackles when you make love on it, don't you, Mrs. Keitel?"

She heard the little gasp and she grinned. "Clearly, you're repelled by talk of the flesh, but I'm moving out, Mrs. Keitel, so now it can be all New Testament and leftover lamb soup in this house."

"Running off and leaving him," the woman muttered darkly.

"*Thrown* out. But never mind. Now, listen. If anything troubles him, the slightest cough, the smallest pain, you call me. I'm leaving him in your care, but reluctantly, and only because he insists. But you *watch* him, do you hear?"

"Your voice is loud enough. Of course, I hear."

"And pray that nothing happens to him, because if it does, the first thing, the *very* first thing I'll do is throw you in the street, and your Bible and your wretched baggage after you."

Alone, she looked about the drawing room, the room that held so much of her history. She remembered being brought here long ago. Her grandfather had come to the funeral wearing a black suit and a look very far removed from melancholy. Surely he grieved for her departed parents, but he seemed instead like a man putting aside a fettering role.

"You'll like living with me," he had told her. "I'm extremely permissive, enlightened and modern and I will treat you like the adult I see you are."

"How soon can I smoke?" she had asked him promptly.

"Is that the only vice that occurs to you?"

"I bet you know about all of them." She had put an arm through his then and walked from the cemetery without a backward glance.

"I do know all the vices," he had told her over tea, "but I choose mine carefully." He hovered over a tray of pastries presented by the waitress. "Just as I choose a little cake. The one which pleases me. The one that will just suffice but not surfeit. Do you follow?"

"I'm glad they died," she had said suddenly.

"And why is that?" He was grave but not shocked.

"They only loved each other. Mama told me once that my father came first...and he said the same thing. Do you have anyone else who will come first?"

"Not a soul."

"Then *I'll* be first." She was positive and assured.

She had commanded him from that day to this but now, powers failing, he had begun to turn away. Damn him. After she had spent so many years beguiling and entertaining him.

Well, she had thoroughly looted the house, realizing all the while that she held a forlorn hope he would pursue his goods and chattels. Grasping at straws. Asinine waste of time.

"Be careful of that vase. I intend to put my own ashes in it one day."

The moving men stared at her in horror.

She fled the house.

Marina One in the late afternoon bustled in anticipation like a beehive, murmurous, swarming. Already some of the tenants leaned over their balconies, glasses in hand, shirts wrenched open, ties askew, as if they had all survived a peril-torn journey home. Smoke rose here and there from stoked barbecues; blood red meat and charcoal assaulted the air. Somewhere a wind chime evoked a gentler garden and in the pool a pretty girl swam, her hair spread around her like a golden flower.

Jake Cooley watched Nell direct the movers, a curt general with no time to waste.

"I see you got here all right. Give you a hand?"

"No, thank you, Mr. Cooley. I'm paying thirty dollars an hour for the brawn you see."

"Well, if you want a cup of coffee, the pot's always on the back of the stove. I polish off about twenty cups a day myself."

"That's nineteen too many. Think of your nervous system, Mr. Cooley."

"Steady as can be." He lingered for another moment. "I'm putting a steak on about seven-thirty, nicely marbled and weighing two pounds. Cut you off a slice if you care to stop by."

"I plan to be too tired to eat. Thanks just the same."

He was unoffended. "You don't have to be neighborly in a hurry," he said. "Or at all. Everybody can graze their own piece of range. But I'm getting tired of cropping the grass by myself, so I thought I'd ask."

He looked at her amiably. She found that she liked his lazy good humor. "Ask again," she said, and hurried up the stairs after the two lumbering men, warning them that anything they broke, they would have to pay for. They said something profane and she answered in kind. By five o'clock they were gone, leaving a cigarette butt ground into the carpet and a bill of startling proportions.

She dispersed her possessions as quickly as she could unpack them, with her easy flair for things in their proper places. The small sang de boeuf vase near the large Sung bowl, a drop of blood against the snow. The leather-bound books were stacked carelessly on the table, three drawings grouped beside them, another standing on the floor just because she liked it that way. Let the lamplight strike the worn upholstery of the Directoire chair. Worn things had a kind of grace that pleased her. She would wax the table tomorrow. None of those nasty quick polishes but a slow sensuous rubbing with English wax. She would buy flowers, white narcissus and white tulips and bugger the cost. She would buy everything for a finicky, fastidious dinner, trout, endive, Vouvray because Colette had mentioned it once in a favorite novel. And cleansing powder and ammonia and a stiff scrubbing brush for that elemental sense of order in her soul.

"Very elegant. Very tasteful."

She turned to see a man lounging in the door she had left ajar.

He was small and thin to the point of emaciation. He wore a waistcoat which immediately delighted her; it was Edwardian and flowered, a fantasy waistcoat with embroidery and gilt buttons. He had a long slim throat like a ballerina's and balanced on it a hatchet-sharp face and strange dog-brown eyes.

"Devon Scott," he said. "Peeping Tom and neighbor."

She wavered between good manners and a sense of outraged privacy. Crouching on the floor, surrounded by books, she was put at a disadvantage. It was difficult to stand on one's dignity kneeling.

"If you leave your door open around here it is taken as an invitation to drop in."

"Well, if those are the rules of the game—"

He advanced, ferreting out the best chair and settling in with a satisfied air. With a slight groan Nell rose to her feet and made a tidying pass at her disheveled hair.

"Am I intruding?"

"Not at all—but as I haven't been to the market yet, all I can offer you is a glass of reconstituted orange juice or an apple with one bite already taken out of it."

"I'll tell you what brought me. I saw the movers bring in all those beautiful things and I had to see who they belonged to. Childish curiosity but I always try to satisfy it. Are you nosy at all?"

"I sometimes read other people's mail if they're foolish enough to leave it lying around."

"The fact is we all huddle together in this place. We wander around like spirits any time of day or night, scratching on doors, making tribal circles around that barbecue pit out there, having intimacies over the washing machine, passion in the Jacuzzi, borrowing booze, sharing beds. Have you ever seen starlings perched on a telephone pole

37

at dusk? No song, no flight, just a silent gathering? Well, welcome to the wire. Welcome to Marina One. We'll all move down one and make a place for you."

"I hope I don't frighten the flock," she said.

"You can always pound on a wall and someone will come running. We lend money to each other on demand, dry tears, remember birthdays."

"Mine's next month—but I don't celebrate them anymore."

"You needn't mingle if you don't care to. Instant friendship is like instant pudding, synthetic, tasteless, artifically flavored. But no one makes the real thing anymore."

He was obviously a nice little man, living on the fringe of things, needful, speaking to people at bus stops, at concerts, at monuments, holding doors ajar, assisting with packages, terrified at being anonymous—no need to fend him off.

"Come visit again," she said. "As soon as I'm settled. I'll make a great effort."

"You won't regret it," he beamed. "I'm amusing, a superior cook and as faithful as an old dog."

She called Cass and put him off, suddenly desperate for sleep and solitude. She was enclosed and lost in a dream of Roman streets and extravagant Italian glances with men in pink shirts floating after her with cries of "Bella, bella, Signora," when the pounding on the door awakened her. She put on the light, squinted at her watch, saw that it was approaching four and groaned aloud.

"Doc? Doc? You in there? You awake?"

"What is it? Who in hell is it?"

"Jake Cooley."

Crossly she stumbled out of bed, tangled

38

hopelessly in a robe which seemed to have seven sleeves.

"What in God's green name?" She thrust a pugnacious face out into the dark.

"I got an emergency."

"My partner is taking my calls," she said fuzzy with sleep.

"I'm sorry to bust in but I've got a tenant in a little trouble."

"Do you know it isn't four yet?"

"Yep. It's early and it's cold, but this little gal is in some kind of a fix. Her roomie called me. She's doubled up and hurting."

"Why don't you roust out her own doctor at this ungodly hour?"

"She hasn't got one. Aren't you up to the Hippocratic oath this early?"

"Just barely. Let me get my bag."

She followed him out into the fog and chill of the dark morning. Lights still burned throughout the building. Unaccountably she noticed that Cooley's bathrobe had the legend "Swanson's Gym" across the back and that his legs, visible beneath it, were strong and hairy. She was conscious of her own utilitarian flannel and the messy flopping of her worn-out mules.

"I see you wash your face before you go to bed," he told her, as though reading her thoughts. "I like a clean face on the pillow, myself."

"You'll forgive me if I don't make small talk," she said. They cut across the tennis courts and past the kidney-shaped pool.

"It was just a passing observation," he said. "Doesn't require any comment if you don't care to make one."

They raced across the grass side by side. It was soaked with dew.

"These two women live together," he told her. "Hortense and Eunice. Black and white. Nothing complicated—they just split the rent. The black woman's head is where it ought to be. The other one lives in a tree."

He pounded along the walkway. She had to run to keep up. Somewhere a window was flung open and a complaining voice ordered them to "Button your lip out there, for Christ's sake, I'm trying to get some sleep!"

The woman who opened the door to them was all bone and angle and towering height. Close up, Nell saw that her face had the planes of a Congo Kinshasa tribal mask, strong vertical lines for brows, a downward slash for the mouth, skin the shade of dusky blue plums. Her voice was deep, sure, flat.

"Everything's coming unglued in here. She's sick as a dog."

Jake indicated Nell. "It's okay, Horty, I got an M.D. right here. She's going to patch things right up."

"You a doctor?" Hortense sounded doubtful.

Nell nodded. "S.C. Medical School, class of sixty-nine."

The black girl shook her head in disbelief and gestured toward a bedroom inside. "She said something about a party. She ate some chili or something. That girl loves junk food."

"All right, I'll take a look at her. Her name's Eunice?"

"Eunice Forrester."

"How old is she?"

"She'd sooner cut her throat than tell you."

Jake waited outside. The room she was ushered into was a tangle of disorder. There was a jumble of plants on the windowsill, a horde of carefully collected rocks and stones, a Victorian porcelain doll with a staring countenance, a brooding black and white photograph of Garbo as Camille and a rainbow of dresses, dangling like soft scarfs from every piece of furniture. The cover on the bed was a network of cigarette burns, which had been whimsically embroidered around, as if they were the hearts of some unusual garden flowers.

They found Eunice hanging over the side of the bed, lifting a putty-colored, sweating face as they entered.

"God," she cried, "am I sick. If there *is* a God. It's coming out of every end of me!"

Despite her woes, Nell saw that she was a jaunty little blonde with a slightly out of date prettiness, like a calendar face from the thirties.

"Whoever you are—do something—or I'm going to ruin this rug right here and now." She gagged violently.

Nell stood by the bed, took her pulse, spoke quietly. "Chili, huh?"

"Oh, God, don't say the word. I'll whoops again!"

"Just breathe through your mouth. How long ago did you eat it?"

"At eight, at nine, who remembers? Oh, shit, you're like one of those damned nurses—you go in to have an abortion, they want to know when you had measles. Give me something, anything, *everything!*"

"Did you have any liquor tonight?"

"I don't drink. Lots of sex but no alcohol. Oh, Jesus."

Nell opened her bag, moving swiftly. "I'm going to give you a shot of Demerol for the pain, and a shot of Compazine for the nausea, and some Lomotil for the diarrhea."

"I don't like needles. Horty, tell her I don't like needles."

"Just shut up and do what she says!"

"There's nothing like a loving spade friend." Eunice gasped and groaned and flopped back on the pillows. "She's like a Southern mammy, my Hortense. Horty, you're my mama."

Nell prepared the needles, swabbed the girl's arm, injected her. Eunice howled at the first one, howled again at the second, looked at her resentfully.

"Don't you leave me until this works. I feel terrible. I know I'm going to feel worse."

"You'll feel better in a minute. Just try to relax."

Eunice made a disbelieving face. "You sit down. You too, Horty. Nobody leaves this room. I'm so *dizzy*."

"Are you ever," the black girl told her. "Shut your mouth now. Try and go to sleep." Hortense put her hand on Eunice's forehead, brushing her damp hair back. "I told you not to go over to his house, didn't I? You ever going to listen when somebody smarter than you tells you what to do? Huh?"

"God," Eunice said woozily, "that was some little party. Not very big but very busy. Just the three of us. Do you know how many arms and legs there are in a bed when three people get in it? There were only two when I walked in on them but they

42

moved over and made room for me. I don't know, I was just delivering him his birthday present, a super body shirt that cost me the moon, and there he was, the shit, in bed with her. I was so sore at him. But she was nice. Pretty, skinny and pretty. She said, 'Darling, he's a prick, but I'm not.' Hah. Never be taken in by a pretty face, my friends. What that lady did to me, I mean, Vaseline and a broom handle, honestly! It got crazier and crazier. I'll tell you this, it's a good thing they didn't climb into the ark three by three." She gave them a pale, unfocused smile. "That's how we got to the chili. It was so damn athletic in that bed we all worked up an appetite, and he had chili sent over and we all put it in one big bowl and ate it with soup spoons. It was either spoiled chili or spoiled cock, I don't know which, but here I am. *Whoops.* Oh, my God."

Hortense looked grim. "It's that bastard director she works for. He's been fucking her over for months. I told her to quit him."

"She sounded right at home." Nell's comment was uncritically offered.

Eunice had closed her eyes. "I heard what you said," she said. "Well, it wasn't always like that. I'm a small-town girl, Kelso, Washington. I bet you never heard of Kelso, Washington. It's right next to Longview, which is fifty miles from Portland in the rain. Clean, open country. That's me, Eunice, the country girl. Some time back, of course, though it isn't all that goddamn innocent in the country either. I knew a boy, Kelly Frasier, he 'd things with sheep and his daddy's horse. So there you are. I mean, *I* stay with the human race. At least I think they're human to start with." She suddenly sat up. "Doctor, I've got to go to the bathroom again." Her eyes were wild, she dangled rubbery legs over the side of the bed.

Hortense and Nell supported her across the room. She pushed them away at the bathroom door.

"I'd like some privacy," she said loftily and shut them out.

"Privacy," Hortense snorted. "She's in the sack with two other people and she wants privacy."

Groans and curses sounded from Eunice through the closed door. Hortense sat on the edge of the bed and looked at Nell.

"I don't know about that one," she said. "She's had five abortions, and every time she comes home like a squeezed lemon and says to me, 'Horty, I'm going to join a modern dance class' or 'Horty, I may turn Catholic,' or 'Horty, lend me money for a shrink.' And I do, and she spends it on an Indian rug or fake pearls or megavitamins. It's all crap."

"She seems to depend on you."

"She puts those skinny arms around my neck and hangs there till one day I'm gonna turn black in the face—or at least blacker than I am." She sniffed. "She's a baby. If she wasn't around I'd probably get one of those shivery little hairless dogs and make a baby out of that." She dragged a blanket off the foot of the bed and wrapped herself in it.

"How long you going to be in there?" she shouted.

"I'm out." Eunice wavered in the doorway. "I want to be cremated and my ashes scattered on his breakfast food."

She fell across the bed. The two women settled her into it and covered her. She groaned once or

44

twice and then she slept. Her breath came and went in little sighs, as if breathing at all were pointless.

"Want a cup of coffee?"

Nell nodded. The two women tiptoed into the kitchen.

They were silent while it was being made and sat silently a while over their cups.

"What do you do, besides look after her?"

"Me, I teach school. Before that I worked as a fry cook, with a book propped up above the stove, conjugating verbs while I fried bacon for cowhands. I come from Texas, forty miles from Lubbock. She's not going to die on us, is she?"

"No. She'll be all right. She's going to sleep right through tomorrow."

"She's crazy."

"Well, neither you nor I can cure that."

"Amen."

Nell got to her feet and yawned widely. "I'm off, then."

Hortense walked her to the door. "You going to send a big bill?"

"No bill. This one's for the sisterhood. But tell your friend not to make a habit of it."

"Thanks. Good night."

Nell paused at the top of the stairs to appreciate the drama of the thin moon hovering low over the sea. She was both weary and wakeful and began to regret Cass, when Jake came out of the shadows and stood beside her, an unlit pipe in his mouth.

"Everything tamped down?"

"All quiet."

"What's the tab for the house call? I'll take care of it."

"It's on the house. But in case you feel I'm your resident physician, disabuse yourself. Blood can flow into your heated, lighted, filtered swimming pool before I'll lose sleep again."

"Want a couple of eggs?" he asked easily.

"If you do them in butter."

He waved her into his apartment. It was antiseptically clean and in perfect order without the blank look which usually accompanied such meticulous care. It was like a room in a New England house where neatness is a part of tradition and things preserved are the marks of thrift and character. She watched him as he moved around his kitchen and tried to place him in the lexicon of the men she had known. Recounting the list to herself she was a trifle startled at its length and variety. Men, she realized, were an indulgence she allowed herself the way other women gave in to cravings for fine French furniture or chocolate creams or massage. That predilection for male company explained Cass. She amused herself with the thought that had she seen him in a shop window she would have tapped the glass and told the proprietor, "That one, please, the one with the sleepy eyes. No, I don't want a talking doll, just wind up all the essential parts and I'll take him home."

It hadn't happened that way, of course. She'd met him sleeping on the grass of his Bel Air house when she'd called to attend his father. Amory Belwright, relentlessly successful since the age of twenty, his letters already published, his wastebasket emptied for posterity, had been felled by a stroke which had pulled his handsome mouth awry and retired him from the movie business and the beds of a dozen famous ladies.

46

She was the last to see the expiring gleam in his eyes flare as he died in the vulgar grandeur of his plaster palace. She had been the one to seek out the son with the news of the death and offer a consoling embrace, which led in short order to another, and another, and still another on the very day the old man had given up the ghost. A particularly delicious bonbon in a particularly fancy box was Cass, but it appeared now that that craving had been satisfied.

Before him? An icy surgeon who had thawed to the extent of suggesting that he give up his Pasadena wife, his ancient Packard, his seat on the Board of Regents at Berkeley for her. He had lasted as long as his considerable bag of sexual tricks astonished her. When they came panting and exhausted to conversation, her interest lagged, and she sent him a book on abnormal psychology with the words "Thank you" emblazoned on its flyleaf for having so extended her repertoire. And then the silent poet who dabbled strangely with his toes, and the bitter politician who could only get it up while John Chancellor was intoning the evening news, and then memory balked and what difference did it make anyway? Her attention, her passion, her true grit belonged to her job. She thought it pompous to call it a career—it was a job that took her time, her temperament, her tears, her sweat, one in which failure caused lacerations of the mind that no man had ever elicited from her.

Jake was back with breakfast. The eggs were sunny-side up and parsleyed, the toast was hot, cut and buttered, coffee was in flowered Danish cups. He proffered a napkin of damask and sugar in a heavy silver pot.

"You do yourself nicely," she said, holding the cup aloft.

"I treat myself to the best I can get."

"I see that."

He sat opposite her, spread his napkin with a flourish and tucked into his food with gusto. "I built this place," he told her. "It's my own rabbit warren. I used to keep rabbits when I was a kid, rabbits and pigeons and a red ant colony, which didn't go down too well with my mama. I got a great kick out of seeing how they organized themselves, how they ran their lives. Now I'm doing the same thing with people. And here we all are, backing and filling, pushing and shoving for a spot at the trough. Enlightening and sobering. Yes, indeed, enlightening and sobering."

Nell studied him over the rim of her cup. "You make me uncomfortable, Mr. Cooley. I'm not sure I want to be under your watchful eye."

He shoved his plate aside and lit a large black cigar, puffing smoke in her direction. "Nothing to worry about. I'm an ordinary kind of fellow. I allow for other people's lapses and hope they do the same for me. It's to my credit, I think, that I read Emerson and change my underwear daily and make a full disclosure to the Internal Revenue Service. I share my dinner with anybody who comes to my door. If a woman passes through my life, I give her breakfast in bed and any other consideration I can think of. In matters sexual, I'm affectionate, leisurely and properly grateful to my partner; without undue immodesty, I think I can safely say that I'm experienced and innovative. I never argue religion or politics. I write my old mother once a week, although she has disowned me publicly for drinking, swearing, gambling and other offenses. I throw back undersized trout. I've never been known to cheat the phone company."

Nell said, "When can we embark on an affair?"

"At your convenience," he said promptly.

She laughed. "I'm going to enjoy your company, Mr. Cooley. I can see that."

"I'm always on the premises. Drop in any time." When she looked at him, he added, "There's no other lady around at present. That is to say, nobody has put a toothbrush in the glass next to mine. There's a nice little waitress who drops in some rainy nights, but she's got a husband in San Dimas and she's just sheltering, you might say." He paused. "Would anybody jump for his trousers if I knocked at your door?"

"It's not likely."

"Well, fine," he said. "We'll be running into each other."

2

THE WORDS appeared on the clapper board for the twenty-seventh time:

> The Right People
> Director... Alan Leonard
> Cameraman... Loren Mitlin
> Take... 27

Eunice, seated at the rear of the projection room, slipped out of her shoes and wriggled her toes like a child paddling in its bath. The figures looming large on the screen before her played out their dramatic pas de deux: close shot, medium-close shot, over the shoulder, her POV, his POV—the scene was repeated over and over. The exorbitantly paid actors found no nuance, no shading. At a million dollars apiece they went through their paces, a theme without variations, mechanical, plodding, low-key. Eunice yawned loudly, opening her jaws until they creaked.

Alan, blue-jeaned and Gucci shod, whirled in disbelief and scanned the dark room. "Who the fuck is making that noise!"

"It's me," Eunice said. "I'm the only one in here besides you and Roy."

He pounded up the aisle with search-and-destroy rage in his face. When he found her he hauled her upright. "Serious work is being done here," he said in a choking voice. "How dare you impede the serious work that's being done here?"

"It's boring, Alan," she said, pulling herself free from his grasp. "It's very, very boring. I think since I'm your personal secretary and friend that I ought to tell you the truth, that's all. And the truth is, it's boring."

"Putting aside your atrocious judgment," he snapped at her, "you are here to take notes and telephone messages, period. You are not here as a colleague, a critic or anything beyond the dumb cunt that you are."

There was an uneasy stirring in the dark and the cutter spoke with a perturbed Texas drawl. "Take it easy, Alan. Come on, now."

Alan's finger stabbed in the direction of the rebuke. "Watch it, my friend," he warned. "You're here on sufferance. There's a smart young twenty-year-old kid breathing down your neck right out of S.C. Cinema School who calls my office fifteen times a week."

The cutter got to his feet, a cigarette glowing in the dark. "Listen, pricko," he said. "I worked for

52

Wyler and Minnelli and Ritt when you were jacking off in the mail room. I own a condominium in Bakersfield and my house is paid for, so simmer down or I'll walk and leave you sitting with this turd."

Alan grinned. "I love you, Roy," he said.

"Yeah, you love me. I don't love you."

"How many films have we done together?"

"Movies, not films. And the answer is too many."

"Roy, trim a little off the front for me. Use the second take, it's the only one in which she doesn't sound like she's stoned out of her mind, and let me see it after lunch." He snapped his fingers. "And you, Eunice, come on, we'll take a ride."

She followed him out into the bright sunlight, blinking owlishly. He walked ahead of her with his bantam cock strut, compensating for his being closer to five feet than six. She trotted after, her silver bracelets chattering. Two men in black suits and silk ties hailed him. When they were close enough they draped arms around him and stood in a conspiratorial huddle. Eunice leaned languidly against a tree, waiting. Alan's ready grin flashed, he ruffled one of the men's hair with impudent good humor, he patted a buttock close at hand. But in another moment the bodies stiffened, the arms dropped, the voices in the hastily convened meeting on the sidewalk under the spreading pine tree grew louder, Alan's loudest of all.

"I want you to realize that I'm not being willful or obstreperous. I've put eighteen months of my life on the line with this picture out of a deep conviction that it says something worth saying about the human condition. Now I'm not going to

53

fuck that up, and with the utmost respect, gentlemen, I'm not going to let you fuck it up with haste born of sheer panic. I'll have an answer print for you as soon as I feel the picture is right. Not later, not sooner. It's in my contract, boys."

There was an angry hum as if a hive had been struck. Alan's voice rose above it.

"You'll have a festival picture, gentlemen, and without vanity, I suggest you might even have a prize picture. Let's all work toward that end." He closed his eyes as if some swelling chorus were chanting a sonorous Amen and then he walked back to Eunice and swept her toward his Jaguar.

"I want to be sucked from Laurel Canyon to the end of Mulholland Drive," he said, sliding under the wheel.

Her mind flashed to the time she had been strolling home from school and a car had pulled up, a smiling, handsome young man offering a ride, and though warned often enough, threatened with horror stories, murder, mutilation, white slavery, sexual perversions too terrible to recount, the day had been hot and she was tired, so she slid in beside him, grateful for the air conditioning, the soft leather seat, had sat up prim and proper, her schoolbooks and notebooks, triangle and ruler arranged neatly in her lap, her feet tapping to the music coming from the radio, such a big, luxurious car, the ride so smooth, gliding so effortlessly; when he had turned to her with that nice, crinkle-eyed smile and asked:

"Do you blow the bugle?"

"What?" she had said.

"Do you blow the bugle?" he had repeated.

She had no idea what he meant, was about to

reply that she had no competence with any instrument, was on the gym team, not in the band at all, when her startled gaze was captured by the thing that grew from his lap, that stood up so suddenly and immensely from his open fly. She dimly began to perceive what he had in mind and she had begun to cry. He had pulled over hastily at that, brakes squealing, lunging past her, had almost fallen out of the car himself in his scramble to get the door open and deposit her safely on the sidewalk.

Did she blow the bugle?

Well, yes, she did, as a matter of fact, had learned how. You could hardly get through life, hardly go out on a date, without taking a man in your mouth.

What she didn't like was the necessity to assume the abject posture, to bow her head, bend her knees. The submitting thing bothered her. Something symbolic there.

Alan was finished and still panting. She glanced up at him, at his handsome, pouting face.

"I don't like blow jobs."

"That's an infantile, repressive attitude," he said smugly.

"I want to get into a nice bed with Lady Pepperell sheets and have somebody kiss me on the mouth and tell me he loves me. Then I want to lie on my back, not on my stomach with my fanny in the air like a dog, but on my back, so he can see my face and I can see his. Then I want him to come into me and not grunt or say anything mean but just melt into me and call me a sweet name and last and last so I get to come first for a change. I don't want to be tied to a bed, or peed on, or hit, or crawl

55

around on all fours with a man on my back yelling giddy-up! or suck somebody off driving around the greater Los Angeles area."

"Find a fourteen-year-old high school kid with pimples and you've got it made," he said. He stopped the car, zipped his fly and lay back with his eyes closed. The sun beat through the windshield of the car. A meadowlark sang three liquid melodic notes.

"Are we just going to sit here?" she asked.

"Yep." He pushed his sunglasses up on his forehead. "You know what I want?" he said suddenly. "What I'd rather have than the biggest come since King Kong? A good picture. Just let John Simon compare me to Fellini and my cock will stand up like a soldier. I don't want cunt...I want Cannes. How do you like them apples, Eunice baby?"

"Then why did you do that rotten thing to me with that woman last night?" She looked at him with accusing eyes.

"Because I'm fucking impotent where it counts," he shouted. "Scorsese is a young pisher...Spielberg is still a kid...I'm forty-five, for Christ's sake. My bones are already bleaching on the goddamn beach. I've had three wives. I've given sixty thousand dollars to a shrink. I've read a hundred great books and slept with my tennis pro and I still have nothing to say. My father did a million dollars a year in the rag trade. My mother raised seven hundred thousand dollars for Hadassah. My brother's a brain surgeon. *I'm promising.*" He slammed his hand on the steering wheel and yelped in pain.

She leaned over and patted his cheek. "You can go down on me if you want to."

He groaned. "Big deal. A mercy fuck from a goyish basket case. Jesus, why didn't I go to Harvard like my father wanted me to?"

She slid back to her own side of the car and stared out the window, her eyes welling suddenly with tears. "That's the trouble," she said, "I don't ever make anyone feel good."

He whirled on her. "Make *yourself* feel good, dummy! Shit, you're hopeless. You've got no self-image! Stop seeing yourself as dog do-do for a change. Listen, I'll treat you to my shrink. No strings."

She sniffed disdainfully. "He's suing you for his fees. I've seen the lawyer's letter."

"Okay. I'll send you to *est*. On the picture."

"I don't want to go. A friend of mine went and they started off by calling her an asshole. I get enough hostility in this life."

He grinned. "Well, then, I'll eat you. But I'll say something nice first."

The birds sang again. Little did they know. Eunice lay back and closed her eyes and told *herself* all she wanted to hear.

Alan kept her working late. He snarled over a typing error, swore abusively when he learned he was overdrawn at the bank, smoked a joint in preparation for his return home to wife and family and left shortly after eight o'clock.

She sat at her desk, sunk with fatigue, feeling too inert to move. The cleaning woman came in, a pretty Mexican girl who smiled brightly and waved a greeting with a dirty dust mop.

"You stay late?"

"Hello, Maria. I'm going to water the plants and then put on my dancing shoes and dance out of here."

"He work you too hard, maybe."

"That's right. And how about your husband letting you work like a dog with five kids at home?"

"He very handsome. I like him. You married, Miss?"

"No," she said bitterly. "I have to fill in my silver pattern before I take the great step."

She got up, took the watering can and went into Alan's office. She had made a lush jungle bloom there. She talked to the plants as she misted them. The cleaning girl shook her head and clucked behind her back as if she were watching the antics of the insane.

"Turn out the lights before you leave, Maria. We've been getting hate mail from management about waste. And dust his desk. He checks to see if you do every morning, the prick."

She went down the echoing empty corridor. The studio was still. She paused for a drink at the water fountain. It ran dry. One day, she thought, it will all dry up and blow away.

At the far end of the corridor a lone writer emerged from his office, his face the gray color of the interned.

"Hiya, baby," he called. "Want to grab a drinkiepoo around the corner?"

"Hello, Mr. Stacy. No, I've got to get home and we both know your wife is waiting for you."

"Wrong, honey, she's in some motel somewhere

with a lady masseuse. But never mind. I'll ask you again."

She walked down the stairs, beginning to feel the dull throb of a headache. Hortense was teaching late. She'd have to make her own dinner. The thought of a fried egg sandwich made her mouth sour with distaste.

Outside the night air blew cold and wet. The gate guard, shirt buttons straining over his girth, was the bearer of bad news.

"You've got a flat tire, girlie," he said sucking his tooth.

"Oh, no."

"Flat as a pancake. Got a spare?" He ambled toward her.

"Yes. Bernie, I know you're going to be a darling angel and change it for me, aren't you?"

He shook his head. His jowls trembled with the back and forth motion. "No, girlie, I can't do that. I've got a weak back." He laughed. "A weak back and a strong mind. You call the auto club."

"I don't belong."

"I've been a member for twenty years. Best money I ever spent."

"Well, I don't belong and I'm in trouble." Her voice slid high, went frantic. "What am I supposed to do?"

"Lift up your skirt and stick out your thumb. Somebody'll stop for you." He guffawed.

"Let me use the phone, you oaf." She squeezed into his glass cubicle. He gave no ground. She was aware of her backside being pressed by his protruding, billowing gut.

"Lissen," she said hotly, "no feeling up, you

hear? I've had *enough* today!"

He heaved his bulk out into the driveway, his face aggrieved. She remembered that Devon Scott was working on the lot. He often stayed late, reluctant to face his empty apartment.

"Scotty, it's me, Eunice."

"You're working late, pet."

"I have a flat tire. I didn't get any lunch. Alan's been shitty all day and Hortense is out with her boyfriend and..."

"...and the stock market fell and three urban guerrillas bombed a bank and Chicken Little says the sky is falling and I'm coming right away." He was soothing and fatherly. "Go sit in the car and wait for me."

She flounced past the guard and got into her car, huddled miserably in the corner. She was wearing a 1930s voile dress which she had bought with cries of joy in a thrift shop a week ago. In the penetrating chill of the California night it seemed symbolic of all the kitsch of her life. She slid down on her spine in the boneless adolescent slouch of her girlhood and raged at herself. Here she was, alley-cat miserable in fabled Hollywood watching an Exxon sign flicker on and off, tasting stale, smelling of faded Norell, hampered by the day that had passed, wretched at the prospect of tomorrow.

"Oh, Mama," she said aloud, imploring that faded weary woman long in her grave. "Oh, Mama, why'd you go and die on me?" She tried to sort out her sudden grief. It couldn't be for that bony silent woman whose only maternal gesture had been a dry kiss of farewell when she'd left home.

She thought about her mother sitting at the

kitchen table with its dreadful oilcloth cover, it's ketchup bottle oozing like clotted blood, the smell of cat pee which never left the room; her mother's pale myopic eyes looking ahead to her early death. Home. The frame house with the broken concrete steps and a dusty lilac tree making a brave seasonal show. Her father had promised to mend the step and died the Saturday after he rented the concrete mixer. She had always been secretly convinced that his death had been a purposeful avoidance of work. For years her mother had murmured "bad health" in explanation of his presence on the front porch, slumped, inert, overall clad, the cat resting eternally in his lap.

"He took a bad chill working over to Weyerhaeuser," her mother had said long ago. "He never threw it off, I guess." And there he had sat while her mother ironed for neighbors at fifty cents a basket and blushed as she produced food stamps at the grocery store. Eunice remembered how the minister had searched and floundered for a eulogy and produced, "He was a kind husband and father" as he had been laid to the perpetual rest he had not earned.

It had all been her mother. Her music lessons bought in exchange for housecleaning, her graduation dress purchased with saved pennies, the sugary pink cakes baked from mixes for her birthday. And finally, her benediction and sad blessing when she had decided to go.

"You ought to leave if you don't think there's anything here for you, Eunice." She heard again the sound of her tired voice like a dry stalk rustling. "I'll give you enough for the Greyhound. And my winter coat."

"It's sunny in California."

"Is that where you're going?"

"They have oranges growing on trees in the front yards."

"Is that right?"

"After I get a job you could come on down and stay with me. I'll get a place with a wall bed. Wouldn't you like that?"

"You'd be better off on your own, I guess."

"You don't have any spunk," Eunice had cried with youthful contempt. "Are you just going to live and die going to the A and P and those damn church meetings?"

"What would you do with me if I was to come?" Her mother smoothed the apron in her lap and sat with downcast eyes.

"Well, first I'd give you a home permanent. Then we'd go to Grauman's Chinese Theatre. We'd eat out in Mexican restaurants. We'd go to Disneyland. We'd paint our toenails red. We'd eat shrimp cocktails. We'd buy black underwear. We'd have our fortune told."

"You go along. You can send back postcards."

She had packed that very night with anger she did not understand. She had stuffed the worn Gladstone bag with her worn sandals and flowered jersey dresses. Her mother had helped, silently folding her slips and adding the torn nightgowns without comment.

"I went to Chehalis on my own once," her mother said.

"Chehalis. It's a *cow* town, like this one."

"I met a man there."

She had dropped the sweater she was flinging into the bag and regarded her mother with surprise.

62

"*You* met a man?"

She nodded. "I went up to get my teeth fixed. Your father said he couldn't stand my front teeth bucking out like they did. He said to go get them fixed so I went up to Chehalis to the credit dentist."

She sat down on the bed and leaned back, brooding, garnering scraps of the past.

"I remember I got off the bus and it was raining. I was supposed to go straight to the dentist but I didn't."

Eunice sat beside her. "What'd you do?"

"I went and had a vanilla ice cream soda in the drugstore. Then I went for a walk down the main street. I looked in the jewelry store window and saw a pair of little gold earrings for pierced ears. They were the prettiest things. I had the money for the dentist in my purse. I went into the jewelry store and asked to see the earrings. The man in the store was very nice. Polite. He asked me did I have pierced ears and I said no. And he said, 'Well, those are for pierced ears but we do that for you on the premises without charge and it doesn't hurt a bit.' I don't know what got into me. I said, 'Well, how much are they?' And he said, 'Thirty-two fifty.' I had fifty dollars for the dentist so I told him to go ahead and get them out of the window and fix my ears so I could wear them."

"Was he the man?" Eunice wrinkled her nose, already disappointed in the adventure.

Her mother went on, straying in a more pleasant place. "He took me in the back room and sat me down in the chair. I remember it started to rain very hard then. You could hear it come down cats and dogs. He asked me what my name was and I said, 'Mrs. George Wilson,' and he said, 'No, your first name,' and I said, 'Helen.' And he said,

'Helen, you have ears like little pink shells from the sea.'"

"You do, Mama."

"And he took my ear lobes in his hands and petted them like I do the cat. And then he pierced them and put in little studs and he wrapped the real earrings up like a present. Then he asked me to stay until the rain stopped. There weren't any customers. So I did."

She touched her mouth with a tentative finger. "We talked and talked just like we'd always known each other. He told me how he'd wanted to play the violin in a symphony orchestra but his father owned the shop and wanted it to stay in the family. He said he'd gotten married when he was seventeen to a girl his father picked out for him. She had chronic stomach trouble and couldn't eat anything but boiled food. He said he took violin lessons by mail. I told him I loved the violin and he asked me would I like to hear him play. I said yes and he got it out and played a piece. To tell you the truth, it sounded pretty scratchy to me but I said it was just lovely and I enjoyed it very much. Then he asked me was I a happily married woman and I said I had been married a long time and he said that isn't the same thing. Are you happy? I said I'd been very happy when I was a child. And he groaned right out loud. He did. He groaned. Then we just sat there and looked at each other. The rain stopped and he gave me my package and walked to the door with me. He just said one thing."

"What?"

"'I'll never have another afternoon like this one.'"

"That's *all?*"

64

Her mother stood up. "If you'd like to take those earrings along with you, you can."

Scotty drove up alongside her in his 1935 Studebaker. It was burnished brown, waxed, the glove leather soft and redolent. He leaned out the window and called to her.

"Lock up your car. I'll get it fixed for you in the morning."

She grabbed her purse and slid in beside him, shivering in her thin dress. She pawed for a cigarette and matches, scattering coins, chewing-gum wrappers, a sprinkle of old tobacco.

"My house is in Mars," she said darkly, "so everything is shit."

"Your problem is not astrology, it's disorder." He tossed her his jacket. "Put that on." Then he glanced at her critically. "Eunice," he said sternly, "what are we to do with you? You're not a Southern deb, so there's really no point to this loony, demented way you carry on. Did you have dinner? Probably not. Did you have lunch? Have you been to the bathroom in the last twelve hours?"

"I'm a camel," she said.

He nodded. "Do you have money in your purse for muggers and such? I venture not a sou. If I hadn't been working late you would've probably stood on Ventura Boulevard and hitched a ride with Charles Manson."

"Scotty," she said, "you're so nice. You're always there when I need you. I wish you were my brother."

She snapped on the car radio, put on the heater and closed her eyes, fragile and submissive. She had a child's habit of surrendering to someone else's care; a door held ajar for her, a salesman's practiced smile, her hairdresser's caressing hands, even her dentist cupping her chin made her feel singled out and protected.

"I think I might lose my job," she said suddenly.

"I'm not surprised. Your typing is atrocious, your spelling is illiterate."

"I do other things."

He grimaced. "You fall to your knees on command. You can hardly put that in a job résumé."

"So do you," she said. "I've peeked through your window."

"I'm old and lonely. You're young and pretty."

"Fat lot of good it's done me." She shrugged, turning an offended back to him.

"If I were your brother," he said firmly, "I'd have a great deal to say to you."

"I have a brother," she said resentfully, "and he lives in Grand Rapids. I went there once after I had an abortion and got anemic. He put me in a back room on a lumpy old bed and gave me a Bible and five dollars a week to live on. He poured my perfume down the toilet and threw out my lipstick and told me to take cold showers. He's only thirty-eight but he has white hair and halitosis and I *hate* him."

"My mother," said Scotty, "wept when I was born and said she wanted a girl. She dressed me in a ballet tutu and never cut my hair. My father put me up on a table one evening and made me dance in front of his cronies who had come in for poker. As a result I bugger boys and you sleep with the world at large. And neither one of us has an adequate excuse."

"I'm twenty-five years old, do you know that?" she said angrily. "With my luck if I had a baby it would probably be a mongoloid. I've tried everything," she wailed. "I go on water diets to stay thin and enroll in charm schools and hang around in singles bars and go on Pacific liner cruises and sleep with waiters and say prayers in three different religions—and here I am, in nowhere city." She stabbed her cigarette out fiercely and jabbed an accusing finger at him. "You're no better off. I've heard you crying through the walls. I have, lots of nights."

"I weep easily," he said. "I was probably watching Bette Davis die."

"Why don't we take up with each other?" she said airily. "A friend of mine married a gay boy and she's happy as a lark. He picks out her clothes and decorates the house and buys her gorgeous antique jewelry."

He paused at a stoplight and shook his head in disbelief. "Eunice," he said, "I have never rolled a sailor in a hotel room, I've never chained anybody to a bedpost, I've never looked at a boy under eighteen or accosted anyone at the urinal in a men's room. What in God's name makes you think I'd fuck up your life by moving in with you?"

"At this stage I'd try anything."

"Not with me, you won't."

There, she thought, as they rode on in silence; that's what always happens. Little screen doors slide down between people. You can see through them and even press your lips against the wire mesh, but you are still separated.

"I'm tired of sex anyhow," she told him.

"Not a moment too soon," he retorted.

"Are you satisfied with your life? Do you want to get up in the morning?"

"Satisfied?" he sniffed. "When one is a vampire, my love, the diet is blood."

"I wish I'd taken a taxi home," she said. "You depress me."

"That may be a good thing. You need shaking up. Try getting off your back for once, Eunice. You might find that your feet will hold you up."

"I'm sorry I asked you. Maybe I'll have a thing with a girl. God knows men have been a big nothing."

"Try abstinence."

An old man crossed the street in front of the car, bent double, his face turned to mold by the green light washing over it. For a moment she saw her father lying in his cheap coffin, his features pinched by death. She blinked rapidly, but death was still there.

"I don't want to go home just yet. Hortense is out and the canary is at the vet. I know what will happen. I'll get into the refrigerator and gobble everything in sight. I'll gain pounds by the minute. I'll have to stick my finger down my throat. Couldn't we just ride around for a while?"

"No," he said. "There's an old Susan Hayward movie on. If you want I'll stop and get us a quart of ice cream and two spoons and you can come in and watch."

"Pistachio," she said and sat back, content.

3

THE WINDOW SHATTERED, hurling glass into the room. The kids slouching behind their desks like flowers wilting emitted an enthusiastic war whoop, suddenly free of the torpor that sun and lessons had produced. Yips, cries and catcalls rose in a chorus. Hortense was on her feet in one fluid motion and pounding the desk with her fist in another.

"Knock it off," she snapped. "And I mean right this minute, people!"

"Hey, it's war, man!"

"We gettin' hit from outer space."

"It's the Fourth of fuckin' July. Yeah, yeah."

She approached the window warily. In the playground below she saw belligerents, one huge and white, the other small, quick and very black, writing and struggling, panting, sweating, swearing.

"You two," she yelled. "You down there, I'm talking to you!"

The struggle went on, unabated. She whirled back into the room.

"Not a peep," she commanded, "not a sound. Now I'm leaving this room and I want to hear the silence of a grave. *That's* so quiet I can hear the worms crawling, you understand?"

"We gotta *study* while you down there?" drawled the largest, the most insolent boy, lounging over his desk.

Hortense disdained an answer. She turned to the blackboard, snatched up a dusty eraser and approached the rebel. With one decisive motion, she balanced the eraser on the top of his head. The other kids watched with curiosity.

"Now, big mouth," she said coolly, "this eraser better be just where I put it when I get back or it's going to be your tail in the principal's office. What I'm saying is, don't budge, don't fudge, don't even let wind or you're in big, big trouble. You listening, *mouth?*"

An awed silence fell over the room. The large boy began to sweat. He remained frozen, the eraser trembling, as Hortense stormed out without a backward glance.

She crossed the playground on a run and got between the antagonists just in time to take a fiercely knotted fist slammed into her ovary. She yelped and slapped in the same moment, swinging her hand back in a wide, emphatic arc. She was in the middle now, smelling sweat and blood and possibly even urine released in the hot anger of the moment.

"Stop! Stop! Damn you little pissants, I said quit it!" Panting and heaving, elbows out from remembered street fights of her youth, she pried them apart and held them squirming and squealing at arm's length.

"Just what the hell is going on out here? Just what the hell do you think you are doing? *Answer* me!"

The little black snuffled and blinked away tears. "He...he said my girlfren' got crabs. He said he been in her pants and *knew*—so I tromped him...and I'm gonna tromp him *some more*."

Hortense waggled him back and forth in her fierce grasp. "Your *girl*friend, you little snot? You're *eleven* years old...*what* girlfriend?"

He groped for dignity. "I got one."

She shook the other boy till his head rolled. "Is that what happened?"

"Naw!"

"Then lemme hear right quick."

"...it was nuthin'."

"You damaged school property and knocked each other cockeyed and you've got the brass to say it was nuthin'? I'll nuthin' you!"

"Lemme go."

She turned him around and booted him ahead of her with a shoe planted firmly against his backside. "March," she ordered. Bumping and colliding, kicking one and dragging the other, they made for the building.

The bigger boy assumed outrage. "You can't shove me around...you can't lay a hand on me, it's against the law."

She laughed, her grin splitting her face. "*I'm* the law right this minute, little boy, and I don't see any lawyer in your corner. March!" she repeated.

She herded them through the hall, past a group of giggling girls.

"Give it to 'em, Miz Washington."

"Lookit Mr. Big Shot, with his ass in a sling."

"Yoo-hoo, Fred Kolenkamp, you gonna eat shit, man..."

At the door of the office she let go and stood regarding them.

"You got a comb in your pocket?" she demanded.

The little one looked at her sullenly and whipped one out.

"Use it."

He dragged it through his hair, his eyes never leaving her face.

"You got a hankie?" she said to the other.

"No."

She took one from her pocket and thrust it toward him. "Blow." He honked loudly into the handkerchief and started to hand it back.

"Nuthin' doin'. You get that washed and ironed and bring it back."

"Yes, ma'am."

"Miz."

"Yes, miz."

She shooed them through the door.

Harry Saul looked up from his desk in the principal's office. He had dark, sad eyes and an exhausted, hapless air.

"What have we here?"

"Muhammad Ali and Joe Frazier. We've also got a broken window in my classroom, twenty minutes of my class time wasted and sexual precocity which will curl your hair. They'll tell you.

Also, I may have sustained internal injuries but that's par for this course."

Harry's fingers snapped at the two cowed boys. "Get into that office and sit down, fifteen feet apart, and wait for me."

They slunk past him into the next room. Harry sighed and shrugged.

"Why didn't you let the little bastards kill each other, Horty?"

She grinned. "I love a fight. Seriously, Harry, come down tough. My kids are getting too big a kick out of this kind of thing. It's like having a ringside ticket at a heavyweight match every day of the week."

"I'll hang and quarter 'em."

She nodded and turned to go.

"Horty?"

"Yes?"

"Can I ask you something?"

"Make it short. I've got thirty-five monkeys loose up there."

"How do you cook a pot roast?"

She turned slowly to look at him. "What did you say?"

"I asked you how do you cook a pot roast?"

"Who the fuck do you think I am?" she said coldly. "Aunt Jemima?" She stared at him, her hands resting on her broad hips.

"What are you sore about?"

"I teach English. You want recipes, haul your ass to your home economics department." She turned again to leave.

He sagged against his desk and rubbed his hands over his eyes.

"Horty," he said, "my wife walked out on me two

weeks ago. She left me with an eight-year-old boy and a six-year-old girl. She isn't coming back. She didn't leave a forwarding address, she didn't leave a phone number. She didn't say any goodbys. We've been eating tuna fish for fourteen nights. I'd like to try a pot roast."

"You've been dumped, huh?" Her tone changed, softened.

"I feel like I've been hit by a ten-ton truck." He looked at her with despairing eyes. "How could she do that, walk out cold like that, two kids ... ?"

"A man does it every day," she said. "Hell, in my family there wasn't *anything* but leftover women. No, sir, there wasn't a man over ten in the whole cottonpickin' bunch of us."

In her mind she ran over the list again. Aunt Jody, hot-blooded and good-looking, left to wait table in a soul food joint. Aunt Essie, with six children and six dollars in a fruit juice can. Aunt Tacey, with cancer in the right breast who died alone in a charity ward. It was with something of an effort that she continued to listen.

"Fourteen years," he said. "I never missed a birthday or an anniversary. I bought her a new car every three years. I never looked at another woman."

She interrupted, holding up a staying hand. "I'm hearing you tell the story, Harry. She must have had something on her mind."

He was abrupt, harsh. "You girls stick together, don't you, no matter what?"

"Honey," she drawled with exaggerated sweetness, "we ain't had too much help from you guys. Look. Maybe you're kinky in bed. Maybe you're tight with a buck. Maybe you zig when you're supposed to zag. How do I know?"

He was stiff. "I'm sorry I brought it up." He began to arrange papers on his desk with fussy particularity.

She regarded him calmly, easing off.

"...You take a bunch of carrots, a bay leaf and three onions," she began, and then broke off. "I'll type it up and stick it in your box."

He retreated into formality. "I'd appreciate it very much," he said.

She was at the door. "And, Harry," she crooned. "All that crap about not lookin' at another woman—you've been lookin' at me for six years and today was the first time you got to my *face*." She laughed and threw a farewell wave over her shoulder.

The showers were out of order, the gym was closed, so the teachers' washroom had to do. It smelled of pot. Hortense, standing by the dirty sink, a black hair curled like a snake in its grimy depths, the soap a jellied sliver, wondered who had sought the consolation of cannabis before her. She pulled her blouse over her head; naked to the waist, she began to wash like a field hand, scrubbing under her arms lathering her strong neck, digging into her ears with soapy fingers. She worked up a real sweat after a day with the kids—bellowing, cajoling, exalted, fed up. But then labor was nothing new to her. She had swung a hoe down a corn patch with the same vigor. She had herded pigs at the top of her voice. She had pulled a foal from a mare, cleaned the shit from the outhouse in the backyard, awakened at dawn to milk cows, scrubbed the kitchen on her hands and knees, the water stinging with ammonia.

The door behind her opened as she scattered

water off her body, shaking herself like a doused dog. A woman edged gingerly into the cubicle, giving her a critical look.

"I would have knocked if I'd known you were going to be nude in here."

Hortense's eyes were mischievous. "I've got tits, you've got tits, all God's chillun got tits. Don't be a damn fool, Mildred. I've got a date with my man. I don't want to go dirty, because he gets up close."

She put her shirt on again. "And you're teaching sex education to your kids." She shook her head; Mildred was hopeless. She sloshed cologne down her arms, between her breasts, behind her ears. The smell of jasmine filled the room.

The other woman stared at her, strong, glowing, fragrant. "That smells nice," she said slowly.

Hortense tossed her the little vial. "I buy it by the gallon."

"Well, thank you."

Hortense brushed past her, "Put it between your legs," she said brashly. "It'll change your whole life."

She came upon Booker asleep in his car, his face upturned to the sun. She paused to admire him, the blue black sheen of his skin, the big thighs, the large humorous mouth, a line scar left over from childhood which gave vulnerability to what would have been arrogant good looks. All that was butting and violent in the man was stilled. He slept like a child, legs splayed wide, hands unfolded. She leaned down and blew softly into his ear.

"Don't sleep on my time."

He woke with a start, grunted, hauled himself upright.

"Hey, woman..."

The top of the car was down. The children still swarmed out of the school building, straggling home. She did not kiss him. He put a hand on her thigh, squeezed.

"Cut that out. I got half my class walking by here."

"They oughta know you're a lovin' woman." He left his hand there.

She tossed it off. "I do what I do in *private*. Let's go."

He put the top up, sulking, and then swung the car with tires squealing down the street. The school out of sight, he reached over and hauled her close with a powerful arm. She pulled free and examined him head to toe. He wore tennis whites, the shirt tight against his big chest.

"I thought you were taking me out to dinner at the beach. And there you are in those togs lookin' like a black and white ice cream sundae. How come?"

She folded her arms across her chest in a gesture of displeasure. "How come, Booker?"

A car cut in front of them. He blasted his horn and swore. He stuck out his lower lip, a trick she knew he did when he wanted to evade her. "Drives like an asshole," he muttered.

"If you stick your lip out like that," said Hortense, "a bird'll sit on it." It was what she had said to him when they were kids. He sucked it back and grinned.

"I've got a five o'clock match in Bel Air. A guy named Teddy Todson. Nice guy. He's got a big ad agency he runs with his brother-in-law. So we're stopping by there first." He was innocent, ingenuous. "He's got a big house. He's got a big tennis

court. He's got a beautiful wife. He's got a beautiful
kid. He's got a beautiful job opening in his outfit."

"The spade who came to dinner," she said flatly.

He wrenched the car over to the curb, tromped
on the brake, pulled the key and exploded.

"Goddamn it, don't black-mama me, Horty. I
had my mama wearing those floppy overalls and a
man's hat, tellin' me what to do since I was five
years old. 'You go to school, Booker.' 'You talk nice
to the Reverend, Booker.' 'Don't pull your joint,
Booker, you'll go to hell.' Kneel down. Wash up.
Keep straight. Boss, boss, boss!"

Hortense snorted impatiently. "You big fool,"
she said. "Your mama broke her ass for you. She
had a tumor in her as big as a watermelon but she
kept digging that old dirt farm with her two hands
till she died. And where were you," she flared,
"dancin' around on the high school tennis court,
making all the little girls' panties wet with your
big black beautiful bottom wagglin' around." She
cuffed him on the shoulder. "Take me home."

"I won't. You're goin' with me."

She sighed and ran her fingers through her hair.
"Booker," she said, "I'm gonna sit there with my
mouth like a prune. You ain't gonna like it."

"They're nice people, and you're gonna *act*
nice."

"I don't see how you're going to play tennis and
keep an eye on me at the same time." She had a
combative jut to her jaw which he knew all too
well.

"You wanna fuck me," he said shortly, "don't
fuck me."

"I can live without," she said stiffly.

"I ain't noticed it."

They stared at each other, hot-eyed and angry, and then Booker reached across and tugged her hair. "Say uncle," he cajoled.

"Uncle Tom," she retorted. They did not speak again till they arrived.

The house, Hortense noted with irony, was a Southern Colonial. The lead figure in the front flowerbed was a jockey with a white face and pert features. The maid who opened the door was black.

"Hello, Sally." Booker was a smooth-mannered familiar. "Where's the family?"

"Hello, Mr. Brown. They're down at the courts. They're expecting you." She regarded Hortense warily. Booker ushered her past the girl with his arm under her elbow.

The rooms they crossed were cool, polished, bland. The paintings were reproductions, the flowers artificial. There was no wit anywhere, no eccentricity; everything was costly, cumbersome, uncomfortable, controlled. The very temperature was regulated, there was no sense of spring light, of spring air. Nothing was communicated, no pleasure was expressed, no evidence of family life was to be extracted.

Booker waited for her reaction. She sniffed and muttered, "White bread." Then they were outside, walking down a mile of manicured grass to the courts. Two players were warming up lethargically. Two figures in pale dresses lay back in deck chairs, watching without interest. Booker approached them, the potency of his smile preceding him like the sun's rays. He held his racket aloft and waggled it in greeting.

The older woman rose from her chair. She had a deep tan, deep lines, narrow, intelligent eyes. Her voice was flat, crisp.

"Hello, Booker. He's been watching the clock for you all afternoon."

She turned and smiled at Hortense. She was a woman with large white teeth, an angular body, a springing, electric mane of hair. She thrust out a warm dry hand.

"Who's this handsome lady?"

"Mrs. Todson, Miss Washington. A friend of mine."

"Come sit with me," she said, "and we'll drink while they kill each other."

Hortense found herself relenting, her defenses ebbing. The woman had a kind of candid and unaffected air which pleased her.

They settled into chairs. Her hostess was all boneless grace, folding onto the cushions like a ribbon, loose and limp. Beside her, on a table milky with dust, stood a pitcher of lemonade. A bee circled it, settled on the rim, wobbled there a moment, fell. For a moment the women watched the battle, the sodden flutter of wings. On the courts the men called jocularly to one another, danced on the balls of their feet, contended. The bee thrashed feebly. Hortense plunged her hand into the pitcher, fished it out and held it on her open palm. It staggered drunkenly back and forth in a weaving trail, circling on itself.

"Fly off," Hortense commanded, "and remember who saved you."

It was a ritual of childhood for her. It had been spoken a hundred times to ladybugs and housespiders, to caterpillars inching sinuously up her brown arm, to red ants and even to black cockroaches found in her bed.

"I hope you were finished with that lemonade," she said blandly, "because I think you are now."

"No problem. I'm drinking vodka." Mrs. Todson lifted a bottle and squinted at it. "It would appear I've been drinking a *lot* of vodka." She seemed mildly surprised. "Can I fix one for you?"

Hortense shook her head and slumped down; the chair was too small for her. Her knees jammed against her chest.

"You're too big for that chair," said a high sweet voice. The girl was young and bruised-looking, like a peach a moment past its prime. Her eyes were intensely blue, her mouth bloodless.

"Try this one."

"My daughter." Mrs. Todson waved with a disinterested gesture. "Stacy."

"You Booker's friend?" The girl stood in front of her, peering like a curious five-year-old.

Hortense offered a slight nod in assent.

"Are you shacking up?"

Mrs. Todson's sigh was less dismay than disbelief. "Christ," she said, "you're sixteen years old. Hasn't that fancy-shmancy girls' school taught you *anything*? Next you'll be picking your nose. If I were Catholic I'd throw you to the nuns." She appealed to Hortense for tolerance. "There are no social graces left. If they think it, they say it."

"I teach school," said Hortense calmly. "I'm used to sassy kids."

The girl laughed. "Booker's been giving me tennis lessons. He's a tiger."

Hortense wiped the perspiration dewing her upper lip and snorted. "He's a tiger, is he?" She sat back in her chair and bent her stern gaze on the girl. The girl returned the look, meeting Hortense's black velvet stare with one of her own.

Mrs. Todson felt the constraint in the air. "Stacy still sleeps with a teddy bear," she said.

"Well," drawled Hortense, "I sleep with Booker, so now we got it all sorted out."

She lay back in her chair, looking up through the green filigree of the trees surrounding the court. She stretched her long legs out in front of her, raised her arms above her head in a good muscle-easing stretch. Somewhere in the grounds a power mower cut grass. Her nostrils widened, pleased with the scent. The two women preserved a respectful silence, as if some glossy exotic bird had come to perch among them.

On the court the action was fast and aggressive, both men ripping their shots. There was no slicing or cutting, no hanging back at the base line, instead clean, flat strokes, each of them hitting hard and all out, and the rhythm of the game was a satisfying metronomic thunking of the ball on the green asphalt surface. Nor was a point ever very long; the two men played the same kind of game, the big game, serve, return, volley, serve, return, smash. They seemed extremely well matched, with the swift, easy movements that only first-rate players have. Hortense sat up to watch. The men ranged from one side of the court to the other in what seemed to her two or three quick steps, bounding from the base line to the net in a blur of speed. She concentrated on Ted for a while. He was very good, his strokes flat, hit with pace every time, low over the net and deep in the corners. Then her attention went to Booker. She had watched him in dozens of matches and she knew how duplicitous he was being now, how cleverly and

82

artistically he was throwing the game. He was missing just a bit too often, his key shots grazing the white lines, skidding just beyond them, the lobs, the cross-court volleys, the overhead smashes, missing the lines again and again by the merest fraction, by a hair. He didn't hit into the net—nothing that obvious—he simply hit the ball out. A little. It's a game of inches, he had told her; today everything seemed to be half an inch out of the court. If confronted, he could shrug it away, claim his timing had been off. But she was certain he was playing "client tennis."

Yet he made Ted work for his victory. The two sets ended with identical scores, 7-5, 7-5.

"Two points the other way," Ted said happily as they came toward the chairs, toweling off sweat, "and you'd have won."

"Timing's off today," Booker grumbled.

Ted, energized and ego-stroked, preened in front of the women. "Not bad for an old man," he said.

Mrs. Todson stuck out her tongue and dipped it delicately into her drink. "My darling," she said, "we have a five-thousand-dollar sauna, a thirty-five-thousand-dollar country club membership, a Norwegian masseur and two complete physicals a year to make you the man you are. But you were splendid." Her voice slurred slightly. "Perfectly splendid." She looked up at Booker, who was gathering up his can of balls and his racket.

"I think we're having roast beef for dinner. I never know, my cook's on the take, so it may be hamburger, but do stay."

"I'd love to, Mrs. Todson, but Hortense and I have a favorite place at the beach. The chef's gotten something special going for us tonight, and

83

he's a friend, so we can't let him down."

Hortense felt a hand on her upper arm. Ted leaned over her. The ghost of his cologne still lingered on his wet torso. He had a finely shaped head, like the portrait busts of Alexander, and the eyes were just as blank and cold as the stone.

"I know he threw the game," he said in a tone too low for the others to hear, "and I know you don't like it. Stay for dinner."

She rose to her feet, brushing off his hand.

"He's on to you, Booker," she said. Then she turned to Mrs. Todson. "You've got a lovely garden. I enjoyed sitting in it."

Hortense started up the grass hill, her stride long and easy. Stacy looked after her and whistled between her teeth. Booker wavered between fury and urbanity. After a long moment he found a smile.

"She spent a lotta time in Sunday school," he said. "It took."

Ted picked up his wife's drink and drained it. He had the certainty of a man never questioned. "I can take you without any edge, Booker. I'll demonstrate that next time." His voice was cool, kept its neutral tone. "I fancy-dance a lot in my business," he said. "I can give you lessons in that, too."

Booker rebounded with ease. "My mama always told me, 'Booker,' she said, 'if you put your finger in the jam pot, you're gonna get caught.' Next time I'll beat your ass."

"You got it."

They did not shake hands. Booker followed Hortense, swinging his racket and humming boldly off-key.

At the end of a cul-de-sac overlooking the freeway traffic snarling through the San Fernando Valley, Booker laid her on the back seat of his car. She had one leg out the open window, the other up under her chin. Her orgasms were quick and repeated—she hit like a slot machine paying off, spilling, flooding, profitable every time. Her hands clutched at his buttocks; they patted, they applauded, they approved.

As for Booker, he made love like a boy, ardent for pools and tides, jackknifing off a log into a stream and coming to the surface again, dripping and grinning, calling out raucously, weedy, drenched and joyous.

"Sweet Jesus Christ, God Almighty." He burrowed his face into her belly and nuzzled ferociously. "Gimme some of that every day and I'll live to be a hundred."

Hortense heaved him to one side and groped for her purse, abandoned on the front seat. "Well," she said, "you do that better than you do anything else, I'll say that for you."

He hugged her back to him, unwilling to be finished. "One more time."

"You didn't even have the ticket for this ride," she said tartly. "I'm sore at you."

He cupped her breast and gently traced the nipple with his mouth. "You didn't *act* sore."

"I've been balling with you since I was twelve years old," she said. "You know just what I like and how I like it but that's just being *used* to each other. We're not twelve anymore, Booker. At least I'm not." She dragged a comb through her tangled hair and found a candy mint, which she crunched ferociously between her strong white teeth.

Piqued, he clambered out of the car, adjusted his fly, picked up a rock and pelted it at a tree. He waited to be invited back. He waited on Hortense's pleasure.

"Now I want to talk to you." She stuck her head out the window. "Turn around and get back in here."

He glared at her. "The only way you're any fun at all, Hortense," he said thoroughly riled, "is when you've got your legs open and up on my shoulders and your big fat bossy mouth shut. If you think I'm gonna get in there and get chewed out by you, you got another think comin'. Anyhow, I know what you're gonna say."

"I'm waitin', Booker."

"Piss off, Hortense."

They were children again, cuffing and spitting at one another. It had always been that way between them. She remembered sitting next to him on a sanded wooden church bench, her hands twisting the thigh under his smelly cord pants, pinching and pinching while he fought not to cry out. She remembered the first time they'd made love, on the bank of a dried-out stream, she on her back among the cow pats and flies, he manfully mounting her, yelling, "Where, tell me *where*, I can't find the hole!" They had wrestled in a barn on rainy days with the calves watching them with round wet eyes. She had fought him like a virago, biting his ear, kneeing his groin, until she made him say girls were as good as boys any old time. And this was after they had been lovers, sleeping sweetly in the hay. Kiss or kill. Sometimes both at once.

Now he sat down on a rock and chewed a stalk of grass and showed her a stony profile. She got out, slammed the car door, shoved him over to make room and plopped down beside him, legs wide, her hands hanging between them. She nudged him with her shoulder.

"I've always been smarter than you," she said, "and you know it. Listen for your own good."

"Shit."

"My mama's dead. Your mama's dead. All we've got is each other. I've *always* told you what to do."

He shoved her off her perch. She thumped into the dirt and looked up at him disgusted. "That's pure childishness, Booker."

She stood over him. "You're gonna hear it because I'm gonna say it. If you keep on the way you're going, you're gonna end up wearing black and white shoes, a diamond pinkie ring and making phone calls for a nigger whore. You're hustling, Booker. That's what you were doing this afternoon and that's what you've been doing ever since we came up north."

He was on his feet and fairly hopping with rage.

"I'm the tenth-ranked tennis player in Southern California," he shouted. "I've played exhibitions with movie stars. *Movie* stars!" He thrust his face close to her. "Dinah Shore, Charlton Heston, Dino Martin, Efrem Fucking Zimbalist! Old Blue Eyes himself had me down to Palm Springs for two weeks. Whadaya mean, *hustling!* They wait in *line* for me!"

A small dog appeared on the rise before them yapping shrilly. Hortense whistled the dog to her side, ruffled its coat and murmured to it while Booker thrashed in front of her like a gaffed fish.

"I don't need no righteous Baptist to tell me how to cut it!"

She'd had enough. She rose, marched over to

him and clapped a hand firmly across his mouth. "Shut up now. Hush," she said. "I've got more to say. You've got five more years and then you're going to be too old for what you're doin'. You can't figure to make it forever with that tennis racket or even with that bulge in your pants. I want you to go back to school. I'll help you. That don't mean silk shirts from Eric Ross or a fancy pad or a Mercedes-Benz Four Fifty SL. That means one room and a lot of grind and the fuck of your life once a week if you keep your grade average up." She let go.

He wiped his nose with the back of his sleeve and glared at her. "You got to be kiddin'! One year from now you can call my secretary in Beverly Hills for an appointment." He snorted derisively. "I don't have no house key tied around my neck anymore. I don't have holes in my shoes. I got *charm*, honey."

"A black cock's no different than a white cock," she said flatly. "What're ya gonna do when they find that out?"

He grabbed her and snapped her head back and forth. "Whada *you* know about white cock?" She had lifted weights in the gym all summer and he felt the results as she shoved him. Flat on his keester in the dust, he was still wild. "You gettin' it off with whitey?" he demanded.

She grunted in disgust. "I should have left you in Texas," she said. "You could've stood with your back against an adobe wall and sucked your teeth for the rest of your life and dug the cooties out of you with a penknife."

She started for the car. He loped after her.

"Booker, come with me," he taunted. "Booker, I can't make it up north without you." He mimicked

88

her voice with perfect accuracy.

"I was fifteen and foolish," she countered. "Now I'm twenty-eight and smart. You gonna drive me or do I have to hitch?"

4

STELLA CARVER could see in the dark. She could peer through her almost empty apartment and into the recesses of her soul. Of the two, she preferred the monastic simplicity of the apartment. It was a plaster box, nearly empty, containing not much more than a metal cot with an often-washed white coverlet, an oak rocking chair of surpassing ugliness, an enlarged snapshot of a man looking at her with a brooding worried stare, fading away now to the blur of an old daguerreotype. In the corner were three-dozen empty whiskey bottles lined up in neat rows. Beyond, in the kitchen, a carton of cottage cheese bloomed with mold, an apple shriveled and rotted, an empty birdcage swayed beside the open window, the bird long flown.

She appeared to be sitting idly in the chair, a large writing pad across her lap, but her face, in the dim light, had a ferocious and imperious air as if she were commanding something into being. After a moment she scrawled a word or two on the paper, crumpled it and consigned it to a growing pile beside her. She got to her feet and walked back and forth across the room through the welter of balled papers like fallen leaves at her feet.

She was a tall woman, formidable. Cadgers gave her a wide berth. Children withheld their smiles. She heard no small talk, she indulged in none. She was forgotten at Christmas, and other anniversaries went unmarked as well. Her whole persona warned the world to mind its own business. She went about hers as secretively as a closed clamshell, asking no quarter. Her work was sacred; she was a poet, the rest of life profane. She drank with monumental thirst but in a solitary way. A fraternal arm about her shoulders in a bar would have elicited a stream of vivid abuse couched in the language of a truck driver. There was no one to share her kind of loneliness. It was a force she bowed to alone.

Her large gray alley cat sat on her sweater and watched her with cautious gray eyes. They did not like each other, but he was a presence she felt she needed. Words addressed to another living being were a release for all the others dammed up inside her, obdurate and heavy like stones in her mind.

"Move, you great fat thing." She shoved the cat onto the floor. He arched his back and spat. "Give me back my sweater." She sniffed at it as she shook it out. "Cat hairs and randy." She struggled into it. It had a hole in the sleeve. The pockets sagged from her constant thrusting. It was an unflattering color. She hauled a squashed cigarette pack from its depths, thrust a broken cigarette into her mouth, lit it and let her gaze stray to the bottle-filled corner.

"Well," she said aloud, "the wellsprings are dried up and the booze is gone. Must see to that." The cat ignored her. She went to the closet and took down a floppy black hat which she clapped onto her springy gray hair. An old purse followed, turned upside-down and vigorously shaken to disgorge a candy wrapper and a fine linen hankie, beautifully embroidered.

"Not even a bus token. And me with sand in my mouth." The need to scavenge seemed to infuse her with life.

"Who haven't I put the bite on this week yet?"

There had been the airline stewardess in the laundry room, a silly sentimental girl who'd thrust a dollar in her hands with an embarrassed but virtuous smile; there had been that little butterfly of a man who lived above her, Scotty or Dotty or Potty, she couldn't remember his name, who had produced a lovely bottle of Scotch and a warning. "Watch the liver, Stella, when it's gone it's gone, love."

And the black girl with the striking eyes and the acerbic manner who had parted with a six-pack.

"But that's only for watching baseball games," she had objected. "I'm a serious drinker."

"Honey," the girl had said, "you been living next door to me for a year, I *know* what kind of a drinker you are. But that's all I've got and I probably shouldn't be giving it to you."

She had taken it. "It's an inelegant drink, but you're very kind."

There was, of course, always Jake. Jake. He

created an unnatural anxiety in her. Doubtless because she was beholden to him. Jake, who gave her an apartment in this tacky, dry-wall Shangri-la rent-free because he had been one of the hundred and seventy-two people to buy her thin volume of poetry bound in green vellum the color of lettuce. "Cultivate and Harvest." He had even read it. He had even understood parts of it. Behind that doggedly male face was some hint of excellence. If she had friends she might have allowed him to be one. As it was he could be called a patron. Rich as bloody hell, too. A wad of bills like a boxer's fist stuffed into his pocket, bound around with a rubber band. Jake it would be.

She came out on the landing of her apartment. Below, Marina One pulsed with early evening life. It was the time of showers and pissing, shaving and primping, priming and hoping, that strummed through the compound like a throbbing pump. In the picture window across from her a man naked to the waist chopped onions with great tears rolling down his face.

"Hi." His greeting belied his swimming eyes. "How goes it?"

"Do I know you?"

"Benson. American Airlines. I'm in and out."

Jake was in the swimming pool. He swam till he was brute-tired, surfacing and submerging like a dolphin. As he hauled himself out on the coping he saw her ridiculous shoes planted close to his nose. They were brown, scuffed, disgraceful. One of them was untied.

She hunkered down until they were face to face.

"Five dollars would see me through the night very nicely," she said without preamble.

"For food or drink?"

94

"Drink, of course."

"I don't think so." He hoisted himself out, grabbed a towel, working over his dripping body with careful attention.

"Have you gotten tight all of a sudden?" she said rancorously.

"You can come up to my place. I've got a two-pound steak. Sirloin. Prime."

She shuddered. "Blood meat. Grain's the thing, my boy. Barley. Rye. Not slaughtered cow." She held out an insistent hand. "You can spare it. Come on." She was not wheedling. It was more like a command.

"I don't think so," he said again. He looked at her with distaste. "You haven't washed your hair in a week, Stella. You're beginning to get gamy. You'll give the place a bad name."

"This place? Steaming with fornication and frenzy. I don't see how I could. Consider the money a loan then."

"You don't pay back loans."

"I'll dedicate my next book to you. I'll make you immortal with a kiss." She grinned without mirth. "I'm going to the Dead Duck Bar with or without money. If they present the bill and I stiff them, they'll call the police. You'll have to come and get me out of jail. It'll cost you more. Surely, you can see that!"

"Hand me my pants."

"Ah, good."

"I'm not giving you the money. I just want my pants."

"Prick. Bastard. Asshole."

She gathered the dreadful sweater about her shoulders.

"I'll be up late," he said pleasantly. "You can

drop in for a sandwich if you're still on your feet."

She stormed past him. "I am always upright in every way," she said, "looking down on the verminous world beneath me."

On the television set a row of dancers offered a view of crotch and smiles of dazzling whiteness to the watchers standing at the bar. It struck Stella as she elbowed a place for herself that the hand of the Creator was as unsteady and erratic as her own. Look at the odd shapes and sizes human beings assumed; two skinny girls exposing their jagged hipbones and rounded navels, a snout-nosed fellow with merry blue eyes, an old woman with the ruin of her life tracing its lines across her face. At the end of the bar was a tall young fellow with damp, slicked-down hair and a guileless look. He had a cut scabbing from too close a shave, a sweet, full lower lip, the high color of a child. His hands were big and raw with grease making half-moons under his nails. He stood looking into his half-filled glass with infinite sadness, his bony Adam's apple bobbing in his throat as he belted down one drink and then another.

She made for him. Standing close, she caught a whiff of naphtha soap and cheap bay rum. She knew his sort. He would wash his dog on Saturday morning, his car on Sunday. He would replace the toothpaste cap and hang his tools in neat patterns on a garage wall. He would know how to repair a watch, how to get a kite smoothly airborne. He would sail one in a public park on a windy day. His teeth were doubtless without cavities, his soul without stain. She watched him tossing his drinks back. He winced at the sting, coughed into his fist. She made a clucking noise of disapproval.

"A pleasant drunkenness is achieved slowly, young man," she said. "The sun is going to come up tomorrow morning. You needn't rush to meet it."

He turned sea green eyes to her. "Ma'am?"

"That grain ripened slowly under a bountiful sun in Scotland. It gentled in beautiful handmade barrels. It recalls peat fires and bogs. And you're guzzling it like a hog."

"Well, I don't know anything about that. I just want it to hit me, is all."

"A thirst can be slaked at the water tap. A need has to be nurtured."

He squinted at her uncertainly. "Lady, you drink your way, I'll drink mine, if it's all the same to you."

She inched in beside him and pulled off her hat, stuffing it carelessly into her pocket. "I have a problem," she began.

"Ain't we all?"

"Mine is pressing. I haven't the price of a drink on me."

He turned back to his glass. He had been hustled before. But not by the like of her. She tried again.

"Well, then, could you spare a dime for the ladies' room? They've put pay toilets in there for some barbaric reason. If you won't help me with one call of nature perhaps you'll help me with another." Her smile was bold; she had a pirate's audacity. The young man shook his head, bested, dug in his oily jeans and handed her a dime. She threaded her way through the tables with a purposeful stride, jabbing with an elbow to clear her way.

The ladies' room bore a sign reading "Little

97

Girls." She snorted at that and passed into the candy-box pink cubicle. A torpid black woman, eyes closed, sat beside the dressing table. On it, in a saucer, were a handful of coins and a two-dollar bill. A small handwritten scrap of paper thanked one and all for gratuities. The woman groaned aloud, shifted into a deeper dream. The room stank of Lysol and face powder. Stella stood for a moment, then scooped the contents of the saucer into her hand. She hesitated over the bill, but not for long. She snatched that up too.

At the bar she scattered the money in front of her and rapped for the barman's attention.

"Glenlivet. No water. No ice. Full measure, please. Fill the glass till you wet your finger."

The gloomy young man was still there, nursing his drink.

"What'dya do, rob a piggy bank?"

She was serene. "I stole it," she said comfortably.

He swiveled around to give her his full attention. "You're kidding."

She saw that in his innocence he would leave his front door open, his car unlocked. He would point out mistakes to a bank manager, file an honest tax return, return a lost watch, give honest change to the penny.

"You must be far gone, lady."

"Very far indeed."

He was suddenly on to her. "Hey, I bet they got an attendant in the washroom. They keep a little plate out for tips. That's what you lifted. That's right, isn't it? Poor old lady's probably got five kids somewhere."

"Yes. It's dreadful to be driven to such behavior." The barman set a drink in front of her. She let it sit there. She was like a gambler turning away from the crap table while a stack rode on a bet with bad odds.

The young man appraised her a moment. "Hell, I ain't standing next to you. You'll probably lift my wallet off me." He took it out of his pocket to assure himself it was still there. As he flipped it open he saw the picture of a girl with pointed features and long hair. The sight of it seemed to agitate him.

"I've been tryin' for an hour to get drunk and I'm sure not there yet. When I was in the navy all it took was two three-point-two beers and I was pain-free. Yes, sir, two beers lying on Waikiki Beach in Hawaii was all I needed. Hell, you can get drunk on the air over there, on the frangipani blossoms. I wish I was back right now—I'd do another hitch in the goddamn navy to get there. I'd trade this whole state for Hawaii. They got everything we got, only better. The girls are better. They don't put their hands in your goddamn pockets. You don't have to buy 'em a nine-dollar steak. They just sit on the beach with you and rub Man-Tan oil on your back and treat you like you were a fucking king."

Stella began to sip her drink. "Be quiet now," she said.

He wouldn't have it. "Bars are for company," he said angrily. "Why don't you just get a bottle of wine and sit on a curb huggin' it between your legs. That way you can *roll* home when you're all finished."

"You're looking for a fight, aren't you? Well, there's a great beefy-looking clod down at the end there. I'm sure he'll oblige you."

She turned to the bartender, pointing to her

change on the counter. "There's enough there for another, isn't there?"

"No, ma'am, there isn't. Even if you don't leave me a tip...which you don't."

"When my ship comes in," she said smoothly. "You're sure there isn't enough? Perhaps you miscounted."

"You're two cents short, lady."

"For want of a nail the shoe was lost." She sighed deeply.

The young man was still there. He stepped in. "Give it to her. I'll pay."

"I misjudged you," she said. "You're a prince of philanthropy."

He shifted back a little so he could study her. "You're something else," he said. "You don't even say thanks."

"I don't say please either." She was busy watching the glass being filled. "Short measure there, my friend."

The barman scowled at her. "If they were all like you I'd lose my job. The boss says *when* in here, lady."

She took the glass and made for a dark corner. The bar was for single patrons. She watched a deeply tanned man bite the ear of an underaged girl at the table next to her. She heard the buzz of conversation made cheerful by Old Grand-Dad and Miller High Life and bar Scotch. She found the young man standing beside her, drink carefully balanced in his hand.

"Can I sit down?"

She relinquished her privacy crossly. She was edging toward that moment when her mind moved swiftly from image to image, leaving a rush of words boiling in their wake. Damn. He persisted, his hand already grasping a chair.

"You have my attention until the glass is empty. That seems fair since you paid for it."

He scraped the chair and settled his thin frame onto it. She saw a button missing from his shirt cuff. She saw freckles trailing in a golden pattern up his arm.

"I gotta talk to somebody," he began abruptly.

"You can train yourself not to," she said flatly.

He paid no attention to the sarcasm. "My old lady took off tonight. Just like that. Took my navy skivvy bag, stuck her transistor and her hair dryer in it and took off."

"Your mother?" she queried. "Is that who you mean? Your mother left you?"

"Not my *mother*. She died in sixty-seven. My wife. Julie. I've only been married two years. Two years Valentine's Day. That was her bright idea. She even got herself some of those red bikini pants with hearts all over 'em, you know?"

"No. I'm afraid I don't know. Mine are plain white cotton."

"They said 'Happy Valentine' right across the ass."

She burrowed into her glass, gulping deeply. He seemed impelled to further intimacy. "By the way, my name's Ben D'Agostino. I'm of Italian descent."

"Molto bene."

"Yeah," he grinned, pleased. "That's it. Italian. You got a good accent."

"Those are the only two words I know." She paused. "I know two others in English. Good night."

He gestured to her drink. "You still got somethin' in there. Stick to what you said. I talk while

101

you got somethin' in the glass."

She honored the bargain. "Very well. Did you beat your wife? Is that why she flew the coop?"

"Beat her?" He was indignant. "Listen. I painted the kitchen twice for that bitch, once green, once blue, because she changed her mind in the middle. I did all the cooking. Tortellini, spaghetti with clam sauce... nothin' bought, nothin' frozen. I washed the goddamn windows. I built her a doghouse for her little yappy dog and cleaned up the turds he left on the floor, too. Shit, I even rung up curtains on the Singer because I got taught to sew in the navy and she didn't know how. Six pairs. She didn't have to lift a fucking finger."

"You're a man among men, Mr. D'Agostino."

"Ben. You're fucking A." He jabbed a finger at her. "I been ten years on my present job. No sick days, no goofin' off. I got a triple A credit rating at my Security Pacific bank. Car's paid for. Television's paid for. Appendix which I had out four months ago... paid for. I made my service insurance over to her, I give her a solid gold heart for our second anniversary present plus three pairs of black pantyhose... I held her in my lap like she was a kid when she had bad dreams. And she ran off."

"You tell a sad story," Stella said, and drained her glass.

"That's all? That's all you gotta say? A sad story?" He was outraged.

"Not *Oedipus Rex*...not 'All in the Family.' Perhaps somewhere in between." She dragged out her hat and clapped it on her head, preparatory to rising from her chair.

"Boy, I don't know. You're tough as nails. I don't

102

think I can talk to you, lady."

"I'm a realist," she said. "Plain-spoken. Harsh, perhaps. But bracing. It's lucky you ran into me instead of some great soft pillow of a woman you could blubber into."

"I don't know," he said again, shaking his head. "You're a real dingbat." He peered through the half-light at her. "How old are you, anyhow? I can't see with these twenty-five-watt bulbs they got in here."

She picked up a match, struck it and held it up to illuminate her face. "Take a good look."

He studied her, grasping her hand until the match burned her finger and she quickly shook it out.

"You're not bad looking. I had an English teacher once, looked like you. She flunked me. But you're salty. I like you."

"That's up to you."

"Why don't we take a walk on the beach, huh?"

"For a host of reasons," she said. "You're a stranger. The night air gives me asthma. My shoe has a hole in it."

"It's nice on the beach tonight. Hey, the grunion are running." He tilted back in his chair, suddenly buoyant and enthusiastic.

"The question is," she said carefully, "where are they running to?"

"Come on. You know what grunion are?"

"Little silvery fish. Slithery, slippery, slyly salaciously silver."

He stood up, pulled her up. "You talk too much. Let's take a walk."

She was too bemused and too drunk to be afraid. "All right. Lead away."

She awoke to the sound of the sea and the scratch of wet sand on her back. Somewhere, foggily, there was the recollection of an amorous tussle on the beach the night before. There was evidence of it in the beach fire dying away in the daylight, in the limp condom draped over a stick, in a denim jacket which did not belong to her hung over her shoulders. Yes, there had been some goatish revelry, of that she was quite certain. She recalled a cock as big as a hockey stick and waved around with the same reckless abandon. She'd been struck in a heap by the saucy redness of his pubic hair. Who could have guessed at a bush so flaming God himself might have spoken out of it in a stentorian voice. He'd been at her rump and at her front like a great friendly collie dog, all tongue and blister, and he had even, in his transport, cried out a cheer which sounded like a salute to his high school football team. Of that, she couldn't be sure. Perhaps it had only been, "God, Stella, I'm coming," but it had seemed to her that there was a "rah, rah, rah" in there somewhere. Seduced and abandoned? Neither? Both? Never mind. She hoisted herself on an elbow, hairpins springing from her disordered hair, and looked at the scene before her.

A city truck trundled along the sand, combing it like a fussy mother, digging tracks with its steel teeth. Up came pennies and wedding rings, bottle caps, fragments of sea-smooth glass and finally a woman's shoe. Had the woman fled? Had she drowned? Was she a limping Cinderella somewhere in the city?

Out on the swells a boy rode his surfboard, seal black, seal slick, in his wet suit. When he saw her he saluted with a jaunty wave. On this morning she felt impatient with the young. He waved in vain. Damn foolishness, wandering off with that youngster from the bar. Could have gotten her throat slit for an encounter so brief she could not remember the taste of his kiss or the look of his backside.

She debated washing her face in the cold saltwater, shuddered, decided against it. A cruel rumbling in her gut reminded her of the many hours she had gone without eating. She thought about a glass of wine, darkly red, sweet Jewish wine perhaps, as breakfast. She was not likely to come by it. She hauled herself upright and massaged the small of her back.

On the boardwalk, a little man, swaddled in a huge prayer shawl and skullcap, opened the doors of a storefront synagogue. It was a lovely sweeping motion he made as he threw the doors wide to welcome the Sabbath and the presence of a God who did not disdain the Orange Julius stand abutting His shrine.

She turned away from him to see her hat and her bag lying on the scuffled sand.

My God, she thought, it looks like a rout, a thorough rout. She stooped, groaned, retrieved them. She took a cursory glance in her pocket mirror, searched for signs of lechery lingering in her face. None. A purple bruise on the neck was all. She grinned, knowing for certain he had a mark on him somewhere, too. Give as good as you get. She lived by that.

It was then she saw the woman running, a Diana jogging down the beach toward her. The figure hesitated, swerved, made toward her. It was

105

that doctor from the Marina. She vaguely remembered her. Now she pounded toward her with vitality so forceful it made Stella recoil.

"Hello there." Nell stopped beside Stella.

Stella noted with some resentment that despite the run she breathed with ease. She would have been bent double herself.

"Yes, good morning," she said vaguely.

"You're out early."

"I am taking an early-morning constitutional," Stella said with elaborate dignity. She smoothed her hair by wetting her fingers in her mouth and patting it into place.

Nell pulled a towel from her neck and mopped her face. "Well," she said, "you've left your panties behind you, if that's the case. She indicated a rather scruffy pair of briefs blowing away in a sudden gust. "Are you all right?"

Stella watched the panties flapping across the sand with no discernible embarrassment. "My old mother always said, 'Air your private parts and you'll never have a sick day in your life.' She said other things just as foolish. Yes, I'm all right."

"I'm Nell Willis. We live in the same apartment building."

"Delighted to make your acquaintance." Stella sat down suddenly on a stump. "Whoopsie-daisy," she said. "All that roistering has taken the stuffing out of me."

Nell watched her, then made a casual offer. "I've run a mile and that's enough. I was going to have coffee on the boardwalk. Join me."

"If you pay. I haven't a red cent—or a blue one or a green for that matter."

"Be my guest."

Nell tucked into eggs and bacon and toast and

cereal with gusto. The same food steamed untouched in front of Stella. She broke a roll into little pieces and made pellets of them, arranging them in a pretty pattern on the tablecloth.

"You appear to me," Nell began, "to be an intelligent woman. Is there any reason for you to be a suicidal one as well?"

Stella made more bread pellets.

Nell cleaned her glasses and adjusted them on the bridge of her nose. "You see, you'll get D.T.'s sooner or later. Probably sooner from the look of you. Not eating. Lying around in the night air. Lapping up liquor. You won't expire in a lovely swoon saying something epigrammatic, you know. You'll get penumonia. Your lungs will fill with fluid. You'll drown. It takes a long time, dying like that. You struggle. You choke. You wouldn't like it."

"My God," said Stella, "but I'm sorry I ran into you. Who asked you to speak to me?" She put her elbows on the table and leaned toward Nell. "People have a way of taking me up. I don't really understand why."

Nell shrugged. "They adopt dogs from pounds. They help the blind across the street. Probably foolish, I agree."

"I'm a poet, you know."

"Yes, I've read you. You're quite good."

"Good!" Stella snorted. "Read me again. I'm far better than that, my girl."

"You don't write 'pretty' things...nothing lyrical...nothing very hopeful either."

"I choose the commonplace, the plain, the ordinary, even the ugly. Those are my subjects. That's my meat."

"Are you famous?"

"No. Not famous. Decidedly not. I've had very little attention from the professional and the academic critics. I've never been nominated for the National Book Award; the Bollingen committee, year in and year out, do a very consistent job of ignoring my existence. No matter. A prize from them is like a dog accepting a bone, up on its hind legs with its paws in the air, for doing a trick. I have no loyalty to any literary clique; any literary theory that tried to swallow me would have to disgorge me again in a hurry. I'm not an imagist or a cubist, an objectivist or a social realist, I don't belong to the Black Mountain or the San Francisco schools of poetry." She paused, shrugged. "I live a poet's life. They can take me, they can leave me—I move in my own orbit."

"That should make us great friends."

Stella shook her head. "I don't muck around looking for friends. I have other fish to fry. Are you rich?"

Nell beckoned for the bill. "Not very."

"Too bad. I'm writing a book of verse and I'm looking for a soft touch so I can keep mind and body together while I do this very important work."

"Look further." Nell rose to her feet. "Why don't you put that egg on that bread and eat it in the car while I drive you home? I think it's a crime to waste food. Also, if you don't eat you'll keel over on me and I'll have to give up my Saturday looking after you, which would be a nuisance."

"It looks like a cold yellow eye," said Stella, but she slapped the egg onto the bread and followed her benefactress.

Stella enjoyed riding in the taxicab. She enjoyed the darkly shaded streets with the heavy trees inclining toward one another to make a somber arch of green. She delighted in the jumble that had Tudor mansion jostle New England saltbox, stately Colonial abut a steel and glass box. Oh, how the rich played with their money. Here stood a small Versailles of potted orange trees, there sprawled an acre of grass untroubled by weed and as close cropped as if sheep had been at it; beyond was a cupid wrenched from its French garden, boxed and crated and hurled across the world to gaze into a smoggy California sky.

And there she was in front of Henry's house and it was best of all. It reproached its neighbors with its gentle faded air. Buttermilk had been mixed into the paint to produce an age it had not earned. There were ancient trees of great size and greater cost that had outlived generations. The dog on the lawn was old and cranky, his coat in patches, his gaze milky, his tail bedraggled. Yes, indeed, Henry had made tradition where there was none. He had forced roots into sandy soil. Nothing belonging to him was transitory.

An ample Irish maid answered the door. Her apron was crisp, her expression matched.

"Yes?"

Stella indicated the cab waiting at the entrance to the drive. "Kindly pay him," she said. "Mr. Dillon is expecting me."

She swept past the woman into the hall, pausing for a moment to get her bearings. The furniture was old and gleaming with wax. A bouquet of roses, old-fashioned and pink, shed their petals in a fragile shower on the chest before her. There was a Pissarro on the wall, not one of the best but close to it, and a Renoir lady, plump and pearly, on the opposite side. Old Henry had made no mistakes.

Beyond were glass doors, brightly, brightly washed, leading into the garden and there, under the spread of an avocado tree, one plonking into the grass even as she approached, sat a family group. Henry Dillon, playwright extraordinaire. He might have been the paterfamilias of a New England primitive painting. An untutored artist would have delighted in the benign face with its plumped cheeks (did he conceal hazelnuts there?), his narrow nose, the foxy shrewdness of his eyes. And Alice? Artist, record Alice for posterity. Two round spots of color which nerves of delicate sensibility caused to blaze in her cheeks, dark brown eyes widened to assay the world around her, quick sparrow movements of the head bobbing away from imagined blows. Alice, taut and clever, whose mouth had pursed from years of blowing on Henry's flame. There was a quiet little boy, as well, spoon clutched in his fist, dreamily eating vanilla ice cream. There was birdsong. Dappled light. A tree house perched above their heads. Yes, paint them on a barn board in strong true colors. Immortalize them in all their probity and sweetness. They have posed for the portrait all their lives.

"My dear." Henry rose from his chair and came forward, arms outstretched. "My dear Stella." His kiss smelled of Sen-Sen and tobacco. "You look wonderful, wonderful."

Alice rose and kissed the air above her ear. "Stella, you haven't changed a bit."

The child was introduced. "Our grandson, Willie."

He put his sticky hand in hers and then hid behind his grandmother's knee.

"Sit down. We were just having tea."

Stella took her place in the arrangement, immediately disordering it. Her sprawl was ungainly, her dress food-spotted, her gaze harsh. Where did she fit in among the flowered teacups and the whisper of sprinklers sighing over the asters and begonias, the peonies and roses?

"It's nice of you to see me," she said.

Henry's reply was a soothing murmur. "My dear old friend," he said, "it's been far too long. You've stayed well?"

"I've stayed alive." She waved away the cup of tea Alice proffered. "I don't take tea."

Nothing else was offered. She might as well have something. "Well, a drop then." Her eyes swept around the garden, came to rest on the tree house beautifully balanced in the branches above them. "Is that yours?" she asked the little boy. He shook his head, dropped ice cream on his shirt front.

"It's mine," said Henry. "That's where all the work is done. A childhood dream fulfilled."

"In spades, considering the money you've made. Tons of it. My God, they must have backed up trucks, it must come in over the transom. You shimmy up a tree and the world's your oyster. Sixteen plays," she said, "and not a flop among them. Not a single stiff. English companies, French companies, Rumanian, Swahilian. It's awesome. Stupendous. Mind-boggling."

Alice sniffed criticism. Her voice rose. "Henry works harder than any man alive," she said.

"Alice," said Stella roughly, "I love Henry. I've known him since he was a humorless, good-

111

natured, sturdy little boy. He lived next door to me. We drank lemonade out of the same glass and showed each other our genitals in the garage. He took me to my first dance and left the print of his hand in sweat on my silk dress. I gave him German measles. I visited his rooms at Yale. I saw him off to war."

Alice drained her teacup as if it contained hemlock. "You've stayed away a long time for such an old friend," she said caustically. "We had one Christmas card, I believe, and a telegram from Mexico asking for funds. You can't blame me for feeling that perhaps the ties that bind aren't all that tight."

"Girls, girls." Henry was patient, avuncular. "Pax. Stella's a gypsy, a wild gypsy. She can't be expected to toe the mark. I wouldn't know her if she did."

Alice retreated, eyes blinking with the fervor of her defense. "It's just that I get sick of it," she said. "Henry's work has given pleasure to millions of people all over the world. They *lose* themselves in his plays. They laugh and cry. But there's always someone *carping*. They're not above taking from him. Oh my, yes. Just make a plea and out pops the checkbook. They don't carp about the writing when it's on a signed *check*. No, indeed. And there are plenty and plenty of those, I can tell you." Her cup chattered against the saucer. She set it down.

"Well, we're not here to talk about that." Henry hitched his chair closer to Stella. "You still write?"

"Yes."

"You've never sent me a copy, not a line. Shame on you."

"No."

"Why not? You know how proud I am of you."
He patted her hand. "Really proud, Stella."

She regarded him for a long silent moment.
Henry, standing on her doorstep with a gardenia
in a cellophane box, Henry asking her in the dark,
on the porch swing under a pale moon, what made
a girl love a man and how to go about it. Henry,
white as ashes, waving to her, gawky in a military
cap too big for him, as his train took him away.

"You've always told me that you wanted to be
an important writer," she said. "Well, you've been
very successful. The whole world knows your
name. But I'm the writer, Henry. That's why you
haven't seen my work. I spared you comparisons."

"I'm going in the house." Alice stood abruptly.
"I have a headache." She turned to Stella. "You
can let another ten years go by," she said, "or a
lifetime. Come with Grandma, Willie."

They were alone. Henry stood up and jingled the
change in his pockets. For a moment the set of his
shoulders was stiff; then he turned back to her,
shaking his head in wonderment.

"'My big brother is bigger than your big
brother,'" he chanted. "'I'm a better writer than
you are, Henry.' Still the same arrogant, blunt,
rude, marvelous Stella you ever were." He took his
chair again, carefully hitching his trousers
against creases. "I can't afford to agree with you,
Stella. You were right not to send your work. I don't
want to see it."

She stood up, knocking over her chair. "I've
made a mess of this," she said. "I'd better go
home." She stopped in her tracks. "I *can't* go home
till I get what I came for. Damn, shit, hell," she
raged.

"Sit down, sit down. You're digging up my turf with all that clumping around. What do you want? Tell me."

"Money, money, money, money!" she yelled at him.

"Nothing simpler. How much?"

"You'd give it to me? After the way I've dumped on you?" She struck her forehead with the flat of her hand. "Now I could tear out my tongue."

"Baloney," he said. "You meant every word of it. You think I'm a hack and you're a genius."

"I could kiss your hand," she said gleefully.

"You'd kiss my hand or my ass or my anything else to get what you're after. You don't have to. I've always loved you, Stella. Not sexually. You're too raw for me that way. But it reassures me to know you're around somewhere, swilling and swindling. I won't give you much this time. You'll drink it up. But enough to get by for a while." He reached into his pocket, extracted a battered wallet, peeled out some bills.

"Cash," she said with some awe.

"I have tubs full," he said dryly. He thrust the money into her hands. "Dedicate a volume to me."

"I won't," she said. "I consider that lickspittle."

"Then come and visit again."

A jerk of her head indicated the absent Alice. "She won't let me in."

"I will. Always." He approached to give her a farewell hug, then paused.

"Stella, don't you ever take a bath?"

"Kiss me anyway," she said, and threw her arms around him. Then she broke free. "Keep churning 'em out, Henry. I'll be back."

She was gone.

5

MRS. LOWENTHAL died on the operating table at two o'clock in the afternoon. At five minutes after two Nell sat in the cheerless waiting room of the hospital on a bright orange Naugahyde couch and told an old man with a terrible tremor in his hands that his mainstay for thirty-five years was gone.

Mr. Lowenthal's eyes implored. It was a mistake. It couldn't be.

"It was an atypical myocardial infarction," she told him, as if the weight of the words would convince him of the reality of the event. "She went into shock. George, it was very quick."

He got to his feet, his hand clenched into a fist. "Quick!" he cried out. "Quick? Her whole life was quick. Sixty-five years. Sixty-five, only. What is God thinking of? Let Him take someone without

115

her talent, without her brains, let Him take me."
He shuffled back and forth in the narrow little
windowless room, stumbling against a table leg,
bumping into a lamp. "You know what we lived
through already in our lives, the hiding, the
running? When we got to this country she weighed
ninety pounds. Her hands like claws. She wouldn't
put them on the piano, she refused, she couldn't
look at them playing. Eda, liebchen, liebchen."
The tears splashed onto his bravely figured tie; one
hung from the end of his nose, somehow reducing
his dignity, mocking his grief.

They had gotten married at sixteen, he went on;
they had been two children in her mother's garden
in Vienna, she with a crown of flowers in her hair.
But Nell was not to think of her as a little angel
made of spun sugar, oh, no, she was to disabuse
herself of that notion. For during the very service
itself she heard the organist make a mistake in the
wedding march and she scolded him for it
afterward. She had her standards, she was stern,
with herself as well as with him. And now, he was
a vine without support, a tree bent. He sat, his long,
thin hands hanging between his knees. "I can't
make myself a cup of coffee. I can't keep a
checkbook. I don't know where my collar buttons
are. She drove the car, she spoke to the maid, to the
lawyer..."

Nell waited in vain to hear more, to hear praise
for the woman's spirit, hosannas for her mercurial
temperament, a cry for lost lasciviousness, an
amen for wit and beauty. But there was only the
melancholy catalogue of domestic inconvenience.
Her own eyes filled with tears. Lovely Eda
Lowenthal, whose vitality promised that age could

116

be graceful and stylish. A lost friend, a lost light. Thieving Death.

"I'll drive you home," she said, "but let me have a word with Amos first. I'll meet you downstairs."

He blew his nose; he mopped his eyes. "Yes, that would be good. I came in a taxicab. A neighbor called it." He stopped in the doorway, stagnant in his grief. "Her things? Her wedding ring?"

"I'll bring them along."

"Bring the candy boxes also. I have a sweet tooth."

Amos hugged her to him in the hallway, glaring over her head at a student nurse who showed too much curiosity by turning to gawk at them. "I'm sorry as hell," he said. "She was a fine lady."

"I promised her she'd be all right. So much for promises."

He patted her. "Why don't you go home for the rest of the day? I'll mind the store."

"Would you? I feel I'd just like to sit down and think about her. George will cry a little and take a nap and watch some television, and by tomorrow be on the lookout for a plump widow who understands the care and feeding of diabetics and is willing to float her dentures in a water glass next to his." She turned her coat collar up, dug in her purse for her car keys. "If I lived a lifetime with a man I'd want to mean more to him than nursemaid and chambermaid. Yes, I'm going home."

She left George to the long-faced neighbors gathered on his front porch, carrying Pyrex dishes of macaroni and cheese and chocolate cakes and strudel.

A light rain began to spatter. The ocean turned gray.

117

At Marina One the sun umbrellas flapped damply in the breeze. A light aluminum chair toppled into the swimming pool and bobbed like a life raft with no survivors. Stella's cat curled itself under a balcony, nursing his ill will toward the world. Somewhere in the far reaches of the complex a daytime soap opera played out its dolor. The fire pits were smokeless. The sails on all the masts were furled. The ladies had been driven indoors. They were even now being comforted by the hairdryers in the beauty salon, warming their hands in sudsy manicure water, watching with too excessive an interest their own reflections in the long pink-tinted mirror.

Nell passed Jake Cooley's door. It stood open. He was sitting under the light of a Tensor lamp, an embroidery frame in his lap, sewing, his hand describing a graceful arc of needle and thread. He looked up at her. "You're home early."

"Yes."

"Anything wrong?"

"A friend died."

His cool blue eyes lingered on her. "Want to be alone?"

"Yes and no."

"Sit here for a while." He stood and beckoned her in. She walked into the neat apartment. He surrendered the best chair and she took it. The air was perfumed with vegetable soup, steaming in the kitchen beyond.

"I cook soup on rainy days." He put aside the flowered panel and stuck the needle like a careful housewife into a strawberry pincushion.

She sank back and closed her eyes. Some of the physical discomfort of wet and cold left her. As

118

often as she had seen death she had never become reconciled to it. A close look bred fear. Fly blithely when you are not the pilot. Live boldly when you don't know the hundred different ways the body shuffles off its coil, hemorrhage and shock, blood clot and cardiomyopathy, kidney failure, pulmonary edema...The list stretched on—miles of tombstones. On bad days she saw her own. Here Lies Nell Willis...Beloved of Whom?

"You're a long way from it," Jake said suddenly.

She opened her eyes. "A long way from what?"

"Your own end. That's what you're looking at, isn't it?"

"You're reading my mind."

"Some of my friends have gone, which makes me thoughtful. A thirty-five-year-old forester, a fifty-year-old professor. The wind chill factor at those funerals was seeing myself in their overpriced coffins, seeing the worms at me. It turns your bowels to water to confront mortality at my age...at any age."

"It makes you examine your books," she said. "Debits, credits, miscalculations. You see all the mistakes, all the ink blots. You see the total."

He began to sew again. A spray of lilac began to bloom beneath his clever fingers. "Well, I guess it behooves us all to live with a flourish. The part I always like best in Will Shakespeare is 'Enter with Drums and Trumpets.' A man might well advance with trumpets clearing a path for him. Don't know anyone who blows one, but I hear 'em in my head...I've stepped off a lot of curbs to that sound. Want some soup?"

"Yes," she said, "I would. Let's have it for dinner. Bring it upstairs. I'll make a pie."

"Set out some bowls if you've got them and I'll be up with the kettle."

She hurried upstairs. She heard no threatening footsteps or chariot wheels at her back.

Nell sat with a cognac warming between her cupped hands while Jake cleaned her kitchen. He dug into the corners like a Dutch hausfrau while she lay back, eyes closed, listening to the efficient swish-swish of his dishcloth. She was amused. She had half expected to be lying with her face crushed into his hairy chest by now. Her fingers were almost alive with the tactile possibilities, rough, smooth, warm, hard. Could it be that his erotic fantasies included an Ajaxed sink, a floor swept and scrubbed? My God, the man was even wiping down the stove. She leaned against the back of the couch and watched with delight. How far would he go? He ran a sponge against the windowsill, rinsed the dishcloth, snapped the towel and hung it with an accurate toss. For some unaccountable reason she saw herself naked in a bathtub while he stood over her with a soaped cloth. He'd find every crevice. She broke into uninhibited laughter at the thought. Not dildos, not whips, not chains, but a darkly handsome man subduing her with soap and water.

She was tempted to drag him into the bathroom and put it all to work, right now. She put aside the liquor. Strong drink always made her randy and reckless.

"Can I hire you to come every Saturday?" she asked. "You don't have to do windows or ironing."

He sprawled into a chair opposite her and lit a large cigar. "It's habit," he said. "I was on a P.T.

120

boat in the navy. They're small—there's a slot for everything and everything in its slot."

"True," she said. "True of the entire natural world."

He studied the ash forming on his cigar. "Winston Churchill could get a two-inch ash on a stogy," he said.

"Well, great men are capable of anything." She sat upright, brushing back her hair impatiently.

"I'm waiting for greatness to be thrust upon me," he said. "It's a little slow in coming."

It was her habit to question bluntly, professionally—"Are your bowels regular, do you sleep through the night?"—and out of female curiosity. "What do you do with your life, besides sit in a chair and sew a fine seam?" she asked him.

He slumped comfortably on his spine. "Well, I started out working for my daddy, who was a marine colonel and a building contractor. He felt if a building he put up lasted ten years, it was a monument comparable to the Parthenon. In essence, he was a cheap son of a bitch, but he's dead now and he left me money, so I try to speak kindly of him. He bought me a bulldozer when I was eighteen—I rampaged around in that thing like a demented hot rodder, tearing out hundred-year-old trees, slicing off hilltops—there wasn't a rabbit or a bird or an earthworm left a hole or a nest within a fifty-mile radius. Between us, we just about wrecked the look of this country, all the way from Torrance to Torrey Pines, putting up dry-wall condominiums and no-frill tracts. My daddy's motto was build 'em with spit, shit and speed; he lived and died by it. I'm living off those ill-gotten gains with some sense of shame—but not much."

121

"Were you ever married?"

"Yes, before I came into my maturity I had a fling at it. Care to hear it? I come off as a horse's ass—but you'll see that for yourself."

She did want to hear about it, kicked off her shoes, cupped her chin in her hand and gave him her uninterrupted attention.

She had been a high-tailed little Texas girl who wore white duck pants with nothing underneath. She spoke with a lisp which made him concentrate on her mouth and wonder, in the comparative innocence of his youth, what many, many things she might do with it. She had long curved nails which he felt like the lash of pure lust down his back and she fell open like a disintegrating flower whenever he put a hand on her. She grieved over John Garfield's death and voted for Dwight David Eisenhower because he looked like her daddy. She kept a cheerleader's pompon pinned over their bed with streamers that blew in the wind and reminded her of the one year she'd spent in high school in Waco. She loved the big Rexall drugstore with its racks of gothic romances and its pink douche bags. She would sometimes spend a whole afternoon there with one strawberry soda spilling over onto the counter in front of her. She read every religious tract left on her doorstep by Jehovah's Witnesses and other peripatetic evangelists. She felt her role in life was to make her bed with flowered sheets and striped pillowcases and lie on it, her pubic hair white with Cashmere Bouquet bath powder, her perky breasts pointing to the ceiling. His penis had gone limp, his mind dark. It lasted three weeks.

"Did it sour you?" she asked.

He chewed on the cigar stub, working it from one side of his mouth to the other, and reflected. He was judicious, not to be rushed into an answer.

"On balance, no," he said. "A good marriage has a lot to be said for it. I've seen a couple that have worked just fine—my brother Adam, my first cousin Jonas. A little forbearance, a healthy mutual passion, some money, a reasonable sense of humor—all glue to hold it together." He cocked his head at her. "You ever try it yourself?"

"No, I seem to stay with short-term arrangements. Going to bed isn't a very complicated business; marriage is. Besides, I'm a handful. I've been told that I'm cold, perfunctory, spoiled and willful."

"All by the same man?"

"Different men, same criticism. So it seems wiser to just come and go, before the charm wears off."

He dipped the chewed end of his cigar in the remains of her drink and tucked it back in his mouth. "It's a funny business," he said. "You pick your friends after you know something about them. What their golf handicap is, how they hold their booze, what they think of Karl Marx, what they'd do if the house caught fire. But we head into our love affairs catch as catch can, two bodies on a collision course. It's a shame. Tell you what," he said to her agreeably. "Let's start out friends and see where it gets us. Put the building up on a good foundation. Care to do that?"

It was a new tack. The unfamiliar had always appealed to her. Intimacy and coolness, they made for interestingly defined boundaries. Familiarity before fellatio—why not?

"You're on," she said. "I play poker, skeet shoot, understand football, trawl for bass. I can build a campfire, I can Indian wrestle."

"Oh, I'm sure there's more to you than that, and all of it of considerable interest. Spend a little time with me. We'll take a walk in the woods or read some Shakespeare or wash the dog—whatever. I'm a handy fellow to have around in case a light bulb burns out or your toilet doesn't flush. The passage of time, no display of ire, no rancor of any sort, no payment on demand might very well bring us to a pleasant conclusion."

"It's as good an offer as I've had all year." She held out a hand and he took it and raised it to his lips.

"To the buddy system," he said, and he grinned at her.

The phone rang insistently. He got up to go but she held up a detaining hand. He lingered at the door.

A Mrs. Scheinbaum was on the line. Her voice was loud and apologetic. She was sorry to disturb the doctor but she was becoming a little alarmed; her tenant, Mr. Solomon, was running a temperature, had been for most of the day. He had spurned her boiled chicken, he loved boiled chicken; it struck terror to her heart. Nell was soothing; she told the woman to keep him warm and covered, she would arrive within ten minutes.

She hung up. "I've got to go to Venice to see a patient."

"I'll drive you."

"I don't know what I'll find. I may be a while. It could be the whole night."

124

He shrugged. "I've got it." He held the door for her.

Venice, California, was no kin except in name to that other lovely, fabled city. The loop of lights stringing this shore glittered over taco stands and addict shelters, Chicken Delight stalls and men's and women's urinals standing like fetid little houses on the beach. There was a small amusement park, the steeds on its merry-go-round prancing to a scratchy amplified record. Girls with short flowered skirts and fine legs rode them like Valkyries, hair flying, minds stoned. There were photograph booths with strips of film on the outside showing pimply adolescent boys and winos wearing their battered hats at rakish angles. There was a fortuneteller, a gassy old man who cursed his hemorrhoids, his hard chair and his hard lot while he promised sailors and spinsters love and marriage, fertility and futures for a buck-fifty a throw. And all around was the sea rolling forward in foam-edged waves which stank of oil and sewage.

Mr. Solomon lived above a family grocery store. Its stock was sparse, its aisles dotted with rat droppings, unswept and unnoticed. His apartment at the front had two salt-crusted windows overlooking the beach.

Mr. Solomon's zealous pursuit of life, God and Mammon were to be seen in the prayer shawl draped like a sheik's tent, in the Shabbat candles melting to greasy stubs in tarnished holders of some beauty, in the racing forms strewn across the floor.

Mr. Solomon, sunbrowned and skeletal, sat in

his bed, his thin white hair bristling over a high domed pate. He held the bedclothes up under his chin and looked at Nell and Jake warily.

"A house call costs more than an office call. That nosy landlady sticking a thermometer in my mouth—let *her* pay the bill."

Nell sat on the edge of the bed and placed a stethoscope against his chest, prying down his protesting fingers. She listened, she probed, she palpated. He wiggled under her hands like a recalcitrant child. "Who's your gentleman friend?" he demanded.

"Just that. My gentleman friend."

"He's new."

She ignored him. "You have the flu, Sam. You're underweight. You have high blood pressure. And you're no spring chicken. I think I want you in the hospital and have a pretty nurse rub your back."

"I'll die first. I'm staying here!"

"If you do you'll have to let Mrs. Scheinbaum go with you when you go to the toilet. You understand that."

His old head waggled, his eyes went sly with pleasure. "She's already seen my thing on other occasions."

"Do tell."

He looked at Jake. "If you don't use it, you can't use it," he warned.

"That's right, friend." Jake was an instant ally.

Nell wrote a prescription, tore it off and put it by the bedside table.

"How old are you, Sam?"

"Seventy-five." He tapped his nose and winked at her. "You're asking yourself am I a liar about Mrs. Scheinbaum. The answer is no. I join the

126

company of Picasso and Toscanini, Rubinstein, that Senator Thurmond with his babies and Bertie Russell—he had women till he was eighty and *he* was a philosopher!"

You and me, Sam, she thought, I know it's curative powers. Better than two Alka-Seltzer tablets, more soothing than wine.

"Stay in bed. Lots of fluid. Light diet. And keep your hands off your crotch and off Mrs. Scheinbaum until your temperature is back to normal." She tucked him in. She didn't wish him sweet dreams. If anyone had them he did.

They came out into the nearly deserted walk fronting the beach.

They were hit from behind. She saw Jake throw his hands up in the air and then twist into what seemed to be a slow endless collapse to the ground. Two arms clamped her, one around her waist, lifting her from the ground, the other around her neck. She felt the blood pulse behind her eyes as her wind was cut off. She felt the heavy, irregular thumping of a man's heart. Her hand still clutched her medical bag, which flapped against her legs as he whipped her one way and then another in a ferocious, punishing, jolting motion. Then she was being dragged away from the limp figure on the sidewalk. She felt a concrete wall scrape her knee. She tried to make herself go limp, to fight against the impulse to claw and scratch. She felt his slippery hands. A spray of his sweat hit her in the face.

His breath was wrenched from a heaving, overtaxed chest. He set her down, grabbed her hair and pulled her face back. She saw blank green eyes, a broken nose. There was a knife in his hand.

"I was afraid you'd be old," he said. "They're all old around here. Old Yids."

He held her out at arm's length. "Won't do no good to yell. They don't come out anyhow. Scared."

"I won't yell," she said, hardly able to talk, her mouth dry.

"What's in the bag?"

"Medicine."

"You carrying any money?"

"No."

"I'll get it off him. Later. You know what we're gonna do now?" He suddenly stuck a grimy finger into her mouth, forcing it open. "You're gonna suck me and then I'm gonna pee on you and then we're gonna make it right here in this alley with the garbage for a pillow."

She didn't let a fraction of a second go by. "All right," she said. "We'll do what you say. But I have to tell you. I have syphilis." She spoke very distinctly. "Syphilis. Advanced. Virulent. Contagious."

The green eyes blinked. "You're shitting me."

"It's true. I'm very sick. I'm running with pus." She didn't move a muscle, returning his hard look without blinking. "You're going to be sterile. You're going to have a fever and a rash. You're going to feel as if your balls are falling off every time you have to urinate."

"You dirty cunt," he said.

"Yes."

He hit her with the flat of his hand. She felt the bag wrenched from her and then heard him running, running down the alleyway as if pursued. It was then a terrible palsy overtook her. She let it rattle through her frame as she tried to keep from passing out. Head down. She directed herself as if she were apart from the scene, looking on. Head between the legs. Then she was on all fours, then on her feet. She had wet her pants. She stopped to pull them off, leaving them sodden on the street.

When she got to Jake he was doubled over, his head in his hands. She knelt beside him, ran her fingers through his hair. There was a fast-rising bump but not blood. She pried his eyelids wide and turned his head to the light, examining his eyes.

Recognition flooded into them. He put out a hand to her. "You?... What happened to you?"

She told him, letting him rest his head in her lap. He struggled to rise. "Which way? Where'd he go?"

"Never mind. He's gone."

They were arm in arm then, supporting each other as they staggered for the car. Once inside she turned to face him, her teeth chattering. "Well," she said, close to hysteria, "if we're not friends now, we never will be."

He pulled her close.

Impatience with fear, Nell decided, was a good remedy for it. She elected not to lock her car door on the way to the hospital in the morning, or to buy a gun or to go looking for an attack dog. There were other strengths to go to. After all, she told herself, she was a Willis. A stalwart bloodline, staunch and stubborn and combative. There had been a sod-buster from Montana and a labor organizer in the lettuce fields of Salinas. There had been a renegade priest, a hanging judge, a San Francisco madame rarely acknowledged in the family and a clever felon who had never seen the inside of a jail. Rapists, leary lovers, her own goblins—she could handle them all.

Her tire went flat. She burst into angry tears.

The boy at the station gave her a lift to the hospital. He was a Mexican youngster with a soft deferential air and when she told him she was a doctor he became even more ceremonious, delivering her to the door as if she were a nun returning to a convent. She pressed a tip on him, which he held in his hands as if it were a talisman, staring at her with dark, brimming eyes.

"I fix your car for you, doctor. Myself."

"Thank you, Carlos."

"My mother is a midwife."

She saw now that she was in celestial company. Women who nurtured and birthed and bossed.

"Sixty-five babies." He volunteered the number proudly.

She was out of the car. "Don't you add to it," she said. "Viva zero population growth."

"But I'm Catholic. An altar boy at Saint Joseph's by the Sea."

"Fudge a little," she advised him, and added another dollar to the one he held.

The young man who accosted her in the hallway was Protestant, vasectomized and frantic.

"Dr. Willis—you got a minute?—"

"One." She paused in her forward motion. The intern was pale, his collar wrenched open, flecks of blood on his white coat. "I'm in trouble," he said urgently. He trotted alongside her as she strode down the hallway.

"Where's your resident?"

"Off today."

130

"What's the problem?"

"I've got a sixty-year-old woman oozing white foamy stuff from her mouth. I'm not talking about a trickle either. She's gushing."

"Let's get there." They were almost at a run now. "Have you got a history?"

"I didn't have time. I shoved a suction tube into her."

"Did you get a stethoscope on her?"

"Lady, I tried. I'm not sure what I heard. She was pounding away like a jackhammer, I can tell you that."

She took hold of his arm. "You're Vincent, aren't you?"

"That's right."

"All right, Vincent, what orders did you give?"

He was sallow, young, with an unruly cowlick standing up like a coxcomb. He seemed close to tears. "Uh...uh...aminophylline, to be given I.V."

They were at the door of the room. She gripped him by the shoulders and shook him. "Pull yourself together. A woman in paroxysm is not likely to be cheered by that face. You're an airline steward, Vincent. When the plane is crashing, you smile. Smile, Vincent."

A grimace twisted his face. "I guess that'll have to do," she said, and went in ahead of him. The nurse stood aside for her as she approached the bed, moving quickly, snapping out orders.

"Adjust that oxygen mask. Turn it up. Get tourniquets on her legs. Get me some injectable digitalis and a sixth grain of morphine. Also get out of my way." This last was aimed at Vincent, who stood helplessly in her path. She grabbed the

131

tube and jammed it deep into the woman's lungs. The flood of mucus and blood hit them both.

"Oh, *Christ*." The young intern turned away and gagged.

The big black nurse grinned at her. "Looks like they sent a boy to do a man's work."

"You just sweep your own corner," Nell told her coldly. "I see where you tried to get that I.V. into six different places. This woman looks like Swiss cheese."

"They're hard to find on her," the nurse said sullenly.

The patient's color had returned, her breathing was easier. Nell beckoned the intern into the hall.

"Get an EKG later this morning. If you're not sure when you've read it, I'll take a look."

Vincent sagged against the wall. "I was scared shitless."

Her glance flicked off him. "If this scares you, sonny, you better get into dermatology."

"Can I buy you a cup of coffee?" he asked.

"You can buy me bacon and eggs and coffee."

The cafeteria smelled as damp and soggy as a Chinese laundry. Her food was expensive, cold and unappetizing. She ate heartily nonetheless while he watched like a seasick traveler.

"This is a lousy life," he said. "If I had it to do over I'd have gone into Beverly Hills real estate."

Nell sipped the bitter coffee. "You may yet," she said, looking at him over the cup.

"You love the life, huh?"

"Some days."

He tilted back in his chair. "I noticed it in med school. The women were hell-bent. I mean they didn't take time to change their Kotex pads."

"Listen," she said to him flatly, "you're not going to push me into delivering you a diatribe on women and how they won the West. I can only speak for myself. I wanted to be a doctor. I waited tables, tutored assholes, went sleepless, hungry and mostly unlaid for the better part of six years. I missed concerts, theaters, holidays and home life in the process. I'm unmarried, in debt, harassed and cynical, but I'm here. Like old Harry said, 'If you don't like the heat get out of the kitchen.' And thanks for breakfast." She got up.

"Want to see a movie Saturday night?" His grin was engaging.

"No, and neither do you. Stay home and read some medical journals. You're sloppy."

She left him slamming his napkin into her egg-stained plate.

"Oh, God, oh, God, Dr Willis—?" Ellen met her at the top of the stairs as she approached her office.

"What is it?"

The girl stood before her, wringing her hands, mouth opening and closing as if she were choking on a stone.

"For Christ's sake, girl, speak up. Is it my grandfather? Has there been an accident? What is it!"

"The office—somebody—the drug cabinet...it's a robbery—"

She pushed past the girl and into the waiting room where two patients looked up idly from their magazines. She smiled stiffly at them and muttered a good morning. Ellen followed hard on her heels, her hair damp with sweat.

"Where's Amos?"

"He hasn't come in yet."

133

She went into the lab on a run. The drug cabinet was wrenched open, one door hanging by a broken hinge. She could see at a glance that all the hard stuff was gone, the morphine and heroin, the Demerol, the amphetamines; bottles and capsules spilled out onto the floor, broken glass syringes crunched under her feet. She checked the shelves, sweeping the debris out of her way. The two lab technicians, Sally and Mavis, sat on a bench against the wall, their faces totally devoid of color.

"Who found it like this? Who was the first one in?"

"I was." It was Ellen. She was leaning against the wall with the glazed look of a soldier about to be shot. Suddenly she sighed and slipped to the floor in a dead faint. She fell like a rag doll, revealing bikini panties and an ugly purple bruise on her thigh—a love bite or the sharp edge of a kitchen table? One of the other girls gave a little squeak of dismay and started to rise. Nell motioned her back.

"Just stay put!" She crushed an ammonia capsule between her fingers and thrust it under Ellen's nose. The girl rolled her head from side to side to escape the fumes. When she opened her eyes, tears filled them.

She grabbed beseechingly for Nell's hand. "I had nothing to do with it, Dr. Willis. I swear on Saint Anne and the Mother of God!"

Nell pulled free and rose to her feet. She exploded at them.

"An enormous quantity of morphine and Carbrital has been taken from the drug cabinet in this office. Only the staff and Dr. Steinberg and myself have keys to the office." She began to pace back and forth in front of them. "The cold facts are

134

that someone here is hooked, a thief, a liar, a junkie! Understand me," she went on harshly. "We're not talking about rifling a purse or stealing a credit card. We're talking about hard drugs. I'm giving you fifteen minutes to come in and tell me who is responsible. And whoever it is who walks through my office door had better know this. I'm not going to throw an understanding arm around you and ask you how come. I'm going to call the Santa Monica police and have you arrested. If the other two know who it is and don't speak up in the same time limit, they're out of this office and on the street by six o'clock tonight. No references, no paycheck. Just gone. That's fifteen minutes." She slammed the door furiously behind her.

Her office was stifling. She turned on the air conditioner and then sank into her chair, her head in her hands. Where the hell was Amos? She needed him to handle this. She went back over the past weeks, digging into her memory. Who had seemed jazzed, intense, hyped-up? Who had been careless at work? Who had stayed late or arrived early?

She saw Ellen's red-rimmed eyes wide with fear, swearing on her protecting saints. Ellen, who lived alone and went to night and morning Mass. Had she found that the pretty little wooden statue was just that? Had she prayed in vain?

The other two. Mavis, a Wisconsin dairymaid, plodding, efficient, humorless. Married. No children yet. Working so she could afford them. She suffered from migraines. Nell had treated her and finally suggested a psychiatrist. It had been her mother-in-law nagging her, she had told Nell. She lived in the same house, slept in the room next

135

door, listened with her ear to the wall. She couldn't make love to her husband for weeks at a time knowing the old woman was there, sleepless, avid, listening.

And Sally. She was fairly new. She was clever, quick, crocheted bikini tops while she ate her diet lunch. She joked with the patients; she had a sure gentle touch with a needle. Had she used one on herself? Damn Amos for being late!

A sparrow lit on the windowsill. Another joined. They swirled around each other in a mating flight. A boy whistled off-key in the street below. The air conditioner hummed its one monotonous note. Nell snapped a pencil in two and waited.

She got to her feet, leaned out the window. A woman in a blue police uniform ticketed a car, her blond hair spilling from her crash helmet. An ice cream wagon cruised by, its bells jangling. She sat down again with her back to the door.

When she turned Amos stood before her. He had not shaved. He was coatless. Sweat ringed his armpits—she caught a whiff of him all the way across the room, a stench.

"Poor Nell," he said. "Poor Amos."

She stared at him.

"I was going to tell you, Nellchick. Some day."

He collapsed into a chair, his hands hanging limply over the arms, his legs spread wide in front of him. He tipped his head back, closed his eyes. She might have been looking at his corpse. She saw the dark rings under the eyes, the heavy pulse beating in the throat. When he spoke again she recognized the tone. She had heard it at the scene of an accident when someone was led, bleeding and dazed, away from the wreckage. She had heard it in hospital corridors when pronouncement of death was made to someone who had gone sleepless for days.

He spoke listlessly. It had started in medical school. All that white hot brilliance had come from a needle used in the back seat of his car, in a toilet cubicle, once even near a city dump with the garbage steaming and smoking like an inferno. It had begun with arrogance. Wanting his brain to race ahead of the others, wanting insights and perceptions and visionary truths ahead of the others. He had been a man enmeshed in the dark memories of his family, bound and held in the horrors of their past. His mother still wore short sleeves so that her concentration camp number could be visible to all. His father took scraps of bread and meat to conceal in his bed, until the putrescence revealed them to the disgusted maid. He had been afraid to be without food.

The melted bones of an incinerated family had been the ashes of his youth. To be a Phoenix, to rise through that powdery dust, took help. He had found help.

The raid on the office had been made to look like a robbery. Ordinarily he simply picked out a phony name, wrote out a prescription in triplicate, presented it at a neighborhood pharmacy. But in the early hours of the morning he was a man in despair, a man without alternatives. His face was waxy, his head sagged, his chin resting on his chest. A hanged man, a dead man. "What are you going to do with me?"

Her throat closed. There were no words. She bolted from the room.

His straw hat had been battered into a shape that pleased him by being left in the rain and the sun and to the ministrations of a teething puppy. It rode low on his brow, a white fringe boiling from beneath its brim, giving him the look of a beneficent impoverished monk. She noted also that he was sockless in his worn, English, handmade shoes. His thin anklebones were visible beneath the cuff of his pants. The hat, the shoes, the trousers he considered old and honorable extensions of himself. He never threw anything out.

She remained on the verandah watching for a moment. He was scattering bread crumbs for the birds, speaking aloud in the voice of a martinet.

"Territorial imperative, if I ever saw it. Get off her, you predator." This last was to a swooping blue jay. "There's enough for all. Don't crowd. Observe a pecking order. Be reasonable."

The birds fed voraciously, clustering, chattering, darting at each other. He was not pleased by the disorderly scene before him; he believed that both man and nature must come to terms. He flung the last of the crumbs and picked up the book that lay beside him in the grass.

Nell approached from behind and dropped a kiss on the bristly back of his neck. He turned. He saw in the look of her face and the weary way she sank into the grass at his feet, hugging her knees and staring away across the garden, that she suffered in some way.

"This is a nice surprise," he said, letting a hand rest on her shoulder.

"It's a crisis."

He knew her to be sensible. She was not given to

138

hyperbole. A cloud passed over the sun. He saw a shadow fall on her from within and without.

"Well, what is it?"

She buried her face in the rough cloth covering his knees. It was an attitude she had taken as a child when a confidence had appeared to her to be too horrendous, too private, too chilling to be told face to face.

First she had been stunned, then angry. How dare Amos have betrayed his monkey-clever mind, his jocular spirit, his talent for medicine? How had he dared to turn his back on their old astringent, knowing, forgiving relationship and have hidden this dirty secret? She appealed to her grandfather. Didn't he remember how it had been with them? Amos lying on her bed, crumbs from chocolate cake scattered on the cover as they lay there, heads bent over the open texts, studying till morning? Hadn't he witnessed Amos in the library of this very house, striding back and forth, whacking his thighs with a folded newspaper, making her a learned Galatea as he chanted facts at her in a sonorous, professorial voice? Hadn't she listened to his siren song, calling her to attention from stuporous hours of study: "You can, you will, you must."

And all the other fragments in the mosaic of their friendship...the birthday flowers, hideous spiked gladioli in a hideous beribboned basket, the concert tickets given to applaud a pass mark in chemistry, the box of fudge which they consumed to the point of nausea in the hope of jogging their exhausted minds with sugar, the sweat of their hands intermingling as they peered anxiously at deans' lists and honor rolls. Who was this

139

unknown man with the dark guilty face, with whom she had had impromptu pleasures and binding links?

Her grandfather heard her out silently and remained silent. She knew of old that he came slowly to judgment. He fished for a pocket handkerchief, snapped it open. The suggestion of lavender rose in the air. There were sachets almost as old as herself lying in the drawers of the house. Her grandmother had put them there and they remained undisturbed, with only a ghost of their scent remaining.

"I think," he said slowly, polishing his glasses, "that you are more dismayed for yourself than you are for him."

"Not true." She was on her feet, defensive.

"How is it that you didn't know till now? Could it be you weren't paying attention, Nell?"

A chipmunk ran along a bough above her head, flicked a tail and disappeared into the tree. Then its face reappeared, framed by a clump of leaves. He waited. Her grandfather waited.

"We're not children anymore. He had to know what he was doing. He's grown-up. I'm not his caretaker."

"Friend." The word hung on the air. It reminded and accused. She saw his standards raised before her like a bar high off the ground. She was expected to take its measure, to fly over it, to land unharmed on the other side.

"Stop trying to soften me up."

"Am I?"

"He's got track marks on his arm," she shouted. "Like any other hophead. He's practicing *medicine*, for Christ's sake. He has to rely on his judgment, make evaluations, use his goddamn head."

She marched back and forth in front of him, digging her heels into the grass, ruining it.

"I can't countenance it," she said flatly. "I won't."

"What will you do?"

"Throw him out."

"Then why did you come here?"

"To hear what you had to say, if you ever descend from that fucking Buddha calm and *speak*."

"Please put that divot back in the grass. It's unsightly."

She dropped to her knees in front of him. "I hate him for being weak. He was always larger than life-size to me. Now he's Tom Thumb. What the hell do I do?"

She walked away from him to the end of the garden. "You're making me wild," she said across the intervening space.

He rose stiffly from his chair, the last crumbs in his lap spilling on the ground. "I went to Yale," he began, "with a fellow who killed his wife. She ran her car into his greenhouse and destroyed all his bedding plants. He came to me the night he did it and I called the police. Afterward I found an attorney, a sharp fellow who got very high fees, to represent him. He lost the case but they later judged the man insane. I went to see him twice a week at the asylum until he died. He said I reconciled him to life. I intend to use that statement to get myself into heaven."

He started for the house. She ran after him, caught him at the steps and followed him into the

141

gloomy hall. "You want me to stand by him. Is that the point of your story? To help?"

"Have you any other good deed to your credit?" he asked, looking at her sharply.

"I'd have stood for anything but this."

"That's up to you. Are you staying for lunch?"

"Do you take lunch?" she said acidly. "You're so spiritual I'm surprised it isn't a communion wafer and wine."

"It's lamb cutlets," he said, "and I'd be glad for your company."

Amos was not in the office when she returned. Ellen fluttered in to tell her Dr. Steinberg had cleared everything up. He knew who the culprit was, a young patient of his, a badly disturbed young man. He had taken steps to the have the boy sent to Synanon. The hen roost was soothed, the barnyard quieted to its customary clucking, the fox, with its bloodied muzzle, driven off.

"He said we could all go home early. Will that be all right?"

"He told all of you to go?"

"Yes."

"Who's left for me to see?"

Ellen was puzzled. Dr. Steinberg had said she was to cancel all of Dr. Willis' afternoon appointments.

The news made Nell uneasy. She felt all her muscles tightening, coiling, as though in defense against an attacker. "Well, run along then. Tell the other girls."

"I saw a darling two-piece knit in the mall. Blue with a kind of yellowish piping on the jacket. I told the girl to hold it for me." Ellen was like a child let

142

out of school. "I never wear blue. What do you think, Dr. Willis?"

"Yes, by all means, buy it." She was abstracted. She saw the office empty, late afternoon sun streaming through dust motes. The girls would leave everything in order; there would be neat piles of paper on her desk, manila envelopes, all the histories for tomorrow's patients ready for her. There would be a hospital gown draped on its hanger in the examining room. The scale resting at zero. Blood shining like dark wine in specimen bottles. The calendar from the insurance agent heralding spring. There was nothing whatever to fear.

"Put the calls on the service," she told Ellen.

"Dr. Willis..."

"Yes?"

"I heard Dr. Steinberg crying in his office."

She sat behind her desk without replying for a moment, her hands in her lap. Then she stirred. She knew she could manipulate the girl with a word. "The toilet makes that noise. It's been driving me crazy for a week. We'll call a plumber in the morning."

"Oh—"

"Be on time tomorrow. Big day."

"Of course. And doctor?"

"Yes?"

"Am I too washed out for light blue?"

White's your color, my girl, she thought. Virginal white, sacrificial white, shroud white. "You'll look very nice in blue," she said.

Ellen was gone, clumping down the hall in her sensible shoes, calling to the others to turn out the lights and lock the back door.

Nell remained very still in her chair; she felt blank, oddly suspended. The phantoms of childhood seemed to be in the room with her. They had not been fear of the dark, or solitude or the faces of strangers. No. They had been formless, shapeless, the rushing of black water, the white flash of lightning, spaces that converged and crushed, noises that deafened. Her mother and father had died in a car, rolling over and over to rest in a deep river. They had tumbled together, pushed into a final, fearsome embrace. There had been the rending of steel, the last bright flash of sunlight, then death. She knew the shape of the stakes driven into her heart.

"Stop it," she said aloud to herself.

Footsteps sounded in the corridor outside her office. She swung her feet up on her desk, pushed up her glasses and presented a demeanor of complete composure to Amos as he opened the door.

He had shaved and changed his shirt and he didn't smell any longer but it only seemed to intensify his diminished look. She was reminded of the cadavers they had studied together, bodies on slabs with the gray hue that spoke of finality and terrible conclusions.

"Come in, Amos." Her voice was matter-of-fact and flat. He advanced into the room, but he did not take a chair or look directly at her.

"This is the end, you know," she said. "I'm throwing you out."

She waited for protest, explanation, appeal. He rocked back and forth on the balls of his feet and stared over her head as if he were witnessing

144

someone else's fate. Another man was confronting a sheer cliff, an impossible barrier.

Struggle, she demanded, thrash, answer for what you are.

"You're a cold bitch."

She sighed. He had no center to go to—the only weapons at hand were sticks and stones. Jack and Jill went up the hill. They had done that, she and Amos, and now it was Jack falling, sliding, flat on his ass.

"You're not the first to have noted it. You probably won't be the last."

"I've always been in love with you. That's what I tripped over."

It was a false turning, the wrong key. She was suddenly furious.

"Hell, don't lay this at my door. You're a spoiled brat. I'm not your German governess promising *Liebchen* a *Mandelbrod* if he eats his spinach like a good boy or goes potty like a big boy. If you came unglued you did it without any help from me!"

He dug into his pocket, came up with a handful of change which he jingled absently. It went back into the pocket. His hand followed, hangdog, caught.

"There's no appeal in this court, I see. Friends for fifteen years, partners, colleagues, but it's guilty as charged."

"You're right," she said. "I don't trust you anymore."

He gave a little laugh, a small, dry, mirthless attempt that died away into a nervous cough. Nell clasped her hands in front of her, rather ugly hands, she thought, ringless, scrubbed, freckled.

"It'll be best for both of us if we go our separate ways. You'll get your fair share of the money and the practice and the furniture." She made him meet her eyes by the unblinking directness of her own.

"Get some help, Amos. Get some good professional help. That's for old time's sake..."

He shuffled his feet but remained standing before her as if he'd grown into the carpet. An almost playful expression passed across his face, transforming him from culprit to gamin.

"What'll you do about the music of a German band?" he asked.

"What are you talking about?"

"We used to go folk dancing to the music of a German band. And you got flushed and thirsty and drank beer out of a stein and hung around my neck with both your hands. And what will you do for dirty limericks which make you laugh and for long talks on the telephone in the middle of the night? And where, Nellchick, will you get a dose of bitter truth when you need one?"

"There are lots of comics around," she said, "and fancy dancers. And as for the truth, bitter or otherwise, I don't think I would have gotten it from you in any event."

"Oompa-pa, oompa-pa, oompa-pa!" He waltzed in a circle, his arms flung wide till he bumped into the door. "I hope you're always right about everything," he said, and like a performer he bowed himself out. She heard his crazy singing in the hall for another moment and then it was quiet again.

She picked up her purse off the desk and dug for

146

a mirror. She stared at the face reflected there; a severe woman with cold blue eyes stared back. Who had been sacrificed in this encounter? She allowed the question, put off the answer. Some day she would probe it, yes, some day she would have to know why it had been so easy.

6

THE BARMAN at the Glass Slipper was named Harold; he made lovely tongue sandwiches on thin buttered bread which he kept under the counter for Eunice. When time allowed, he clumsily carved a radish rose. There was always parsley.

He charged her fifty cents more than the same sandwich would have cost at the delicatessen down the street, but he steered her right nine times out of ten and the four bits covered the time away from other customers.

"Mustard?"

"If you've got that yellow kind. Like you get at the baseball games."

"Brown mustard. You want brown mustard on a sandwich like that."

Eunice twined her legs around the barstool,

149

daintily lifted the bread and rearranged the meat. "So?" she said looking through her false eyelashes. "Who's who?"

Harold brought his face close to her. A dozen small veins had broken under his skin, making a bloody freeway across his nose.

"See that guy down the other end of the bar? The one with the Harris tweed jacket?" His breath, stale beer, wafted toward her. He kept a glass at the ready under the bar.

"Yes. I saw him when I came in. He's got hair growing out of his ears."

"What about it?" Harold was aggrieved. He had hair growing out of *his* ears.

"He doesn't look special."

"Beverly Hills lawyer. Tax lawyer. House in Newport Beach, house in Encino. Royal Oaks. Doesn't booze. One martini with a twist and he makes it last an hour. He's not in here for action. I figure what he wants is to meet a nice lady and buy her lobster tails and French fries. Okay?"

"What're you gonna do," asked Eunice resentfully. "Slide me down the bar into his lap?"

"You know better'n that. Don't I always introduce you? Don't I find a topic of interest to get you started? What's wrong with you tonight?"

Eunice chewed on a hangnail and wondered why she felt lighter than air. Alan had told her she was putting on weight so she had gone all day on black coffee and a cheese Danish. Or maybe it was a dismal sense of déjà vu. Here was Harold with his beer breath computerizing her life. That one's a dentist. This one's a cartoonist. Look over there. He's a pilot. He's a piano player. This one wants to talk. That one bites. The one in the corner is borderline psychotic—or maybe already there.

"A lawyer?" Lassitude made her slump on her elbows.

"Big lawyer."

She craned past a woman in a large hat to look again. "Is he tall or short? I can't tell when he's sitting down."

"What's the difference?" Harold became mildly threatening. "You wanna go home alone, go home alone. I'm being mister nice guy but if you don't want any, you don't get any."

She pushed the sandwich aside. If she went home she would straighten her drawers and wash her hair. There was a whole lemon pie in the refrigerator. She'd eat that. All of it—and the Oreo cookies and some graham crackers and dry corn flakes and soda crackers and butter. She'd eat until she sat with a mouth full of food and her gorge rising behind it. Hortense would be at Booker's, lying in bed with him, flowing over and under and around him like a spill of chocolate syrup. There were all those long empty hours to fill. Alan had been too busy to boff, as he so elegantly put it. Well, she knew the taste of lemon and defeat. What did the man at the end of the bar taste like?

"Bring him on," she said. "But not till I finish my sandwich."

His name was Harvey Medford. He spelled it for her, first name and last. He spoke slowly, as if he were controlling a stammer, but he had a nice smile and very white teeth. She told herself that must mean something. He took the time to get them cleaned or perhaps he rubbed peroxide on them before he went to bed. He was very pleased that she was free for the evening. And it was interesting that she was a Dodger fan. He had been a Dodger fan ever since the team had come out here from Brooklyn. Of course, he'd lost a little of his zest for the game after Sandy Koufax retired, but it was a great team and he had great hopes for it.

"Harold says you watch all the games. That's unusual for a woman."

"He just told you that to get us started. I don't know first base from second. He thinks you have to *launch* people, like satellites." She focused her attention on the white teeth. "Otherwise we might just float by each other."

Her retort gave him a desperate moment. Whatever they had in common was going. "Well, that's all right," he said. "I go to the games with my next-door neighbor."

She knew instantly that he was not a lawyer, he was a bookkeeper in Studio City. She knew his house was redwood with a birdhouse perched on the roof. She knew he opened a can of Campbell's Manhandler soup most nights for dinner and ate it lukewarm from the pan. She knew that he went to the laundromat on Saturday morning and measured out the soap in a cup, that he had just begun to let his hair grow when everyone in his office was now beginning to cut his. He would have his license in his hand before a cop got off his motorcycle. He would stay off the grass and observe the No Smoking signs in elevators.

Shame extorted a confession before she had turned a single screw.

"He told you I was a lawyer, didn't he? I'm not. I'm a store manager for Safeway. The one on Laurel Canyon and Riverside. Do you know it?"

Go home, she told herself, take a warm bath and

put on some perfume and get into bed and make yourself come. Otherwise it was going to be a long night short on talk and a dry kiss just wide of her mouth and maybe dinner at the Tail of the Cock, soup and salad included.

"Well, that's a good job."

"What do you do?"

Tell him, she thought dully. Tell him you go down on a vain little peacock of a movie director who talks on the phone while you're doing it. Tell him how long it takes for you to climax because they've sucked so many fetuses out of you with that little vacuum cleaner they use now. Tell him about Yoga and Zen and *est* and needlepoint and exercise classes. Tell him about psychiatrists who fuck you and make you pay the bill and gynecologists who fuck you and won't take Blue Cross. Tell him about Harold who wants to hear all about it the next time you come into the bar with his big pouty mouth hanging open at every word. Tell him not to be afraid of performing for you. You'd welcome the missionary position as a change from all the variations that make your lower back ache.

"I'm a secretary. Just a secretary."

"Most of the guys who come in here say they're doing some kind of important work. I didn't mean to put you on or anything. I guess there's nothing wrong in managing a grocery store. I came up from box boy."

"I'll buy my milk from you from now on," she said restlessly. "You might as well have the business." He was going to sit on the barstool for the rest of the night, eking out his confidences, one at a time. She fought a yawn by patting it daintily to death with her hand.

153

"There's a nice little smorgasbord restaurant up the street," he said. "It's clean and not too crowded. Could you have dinner with me?"

"I'd love to."

The peroxided smile flashed brightly. "That's great. And you don't have to worry. I can talk about things besides baseball. It's getting over this first hump..." His voice trailed off. She saw him make a tentative move toward his left hand as if to twist a ring. A white line circled it where the gold had been.

"How long have you been divorced?"

"Oh. Well, it's a couple months now. Fifty-four days."

She picked up her bag and swung herself down from the barstool.

"I fuck like a rabbit," she said. "You'll feel better soon."

They made love three times during the night in a little bedroom with daisy-strewn wallpaper and two scratchy Hudson's Bay blankets on the bed. The third time Harvey's transport stained the sheet. He sat up, a flush dyeing his fair skin, and muttered something about how sorry he was and how happy he was and would she excuse him a minute—he'd get a wet washrag and clean it up. She watched him as he scrambled from bed. Something about his small tight buttocks, the thin line of blond hair downing his stomach made him seem like a boy.

His gulping eager response in bed was not dissimilar to that of a gawky young newsboy she had once had in Seattle when she had gone there to try to get an Avon line of cosmetics to sell. He had

154

been standing in front of the Empire Hotel in the rain and she had bought all his papers and the rest of his afternoon for twenty dollars and for a cup of hot cocoa she had sent to the room; he had gobbled her up like a bag of popcorn.

Harvey, in his sad maturity, had gone a step further. In the dark middle of the night he had whispered his gratitude. He had begun to envision a monkish abstinence in his life. He was afraid no one would see anything in him. He had even thought of placing an ad in one of those newspapers or magazines that carried them, advertising the few virtues he could summon up. He ticked them off for her. He was, he thought, of good character, average height, unquarrelsome disposition. He hesitated to include a passionate nature, but he would mention intelligence and kindliness, and last but not least, solvency. He had kissed her nipples with pride at being the sole and only owner of the ranch house they slept in. Now she heard the sound of his electric toothbrush and a discreet hawking as he cleared his hay-fever-ridden sinuses.

She looked around the room and knew why there had been no vice in the night. The woman who had furnished it came clearly to mind. She was probably small. The slipper chair was undersized, the ornaments on the dresser itsy-bitsy Japanese shepherdesses and little dogs with gilt ruffs around their foolish faces. The curtains had had the life washed out of them. They hung at the window, stiff with starch and shrunken, two inches from the sills. Eunice sniffed. Doubtless the lady of the house had marched poor Harvey into the bathroom and washed and scrubbed him until

155

he too had shrunk into the man who called out, "Oh, golly," as he spilled his seed onto the bed.

She scratched her thigh and blew a strand of hair away from her face. She thought idly about washing herself but she knew it wasn't necessary. She always woke in the morning with a sweet breath, as though the sex act scented her through and through. She ascribed it to nature. Your hair either curled or it didn't. You had clear, healthy skin or you didn't. You had head colds or you never had a sick day in your life. Eunice was all clover and rainwater and regular bowels.

The bedroom door opened cautiously. A small boy stood there regarding her with solemnity. She drew the rough blanket up to her chin and stared back.

"God Almighty, who the hell are you?" It was not said with irritation, but it was not friendly either.

"Archer."

"Archer *who!* It's seven-thirty in the morning."

"Archer Medford." He had the rabbity look of prepuberty, large green eyes, long legs, short torso.

"Is my father up yet?"

She nodded toward the bathroom and the noises coming from within.

"My grandmother sent me home to get some clean underwear before I go to school." He stood for a moment and then edged toward the bathroom door. He looked over his shoulder at her while he knocked politely.

"Yes?" The voice came from within. "I'll be out in a minute, honey."

"Daddy. It's me."

156

The door was flung wide. Harvey stood there, stark naked and dashed to bits. "Archie? What are you doing here?"

"Grandma says I have to have decent underwear to wear to school. Today's gym day and everybody will see it." He spoke with poise and clarity.

Harvey ducked back into the bathroom, groping for a towel to cover his loins and an explanation that would suffice.

"Didn't you have some shorts and stuff with you?"

"Yes, but they've got holes. She said they were disgraceful and I couldn't wear them. She said I should walk home and get some without holes or I couldn't go to school. I have a test today."

"This is Eunice, Archie. She missed a bus and stayed all night." He bobbed his head in her direction. "Eunice, this is my son, Archie."

"Archer." The boy amended it formally.

Eunice plumped the pillow behind her back. "Have you got a middle name?"

"Wayne."

"Like John Wayne?"

"For my Grandfather Wayne. He was a minister at the First Congregational Church."

She asked him then if he would kindly go out of the room for a minute so she could get up and get dressed and make everybody a nice breakfast.

"I can make the breakfast. I take cooking."

Harvey excused himself. He would just climb into his clothes and then they would sort everything out. He left the two behind him taking stock of each other.

"What can you cook?"

"French toast. Blueberry muffins. Jell-O chocolate pudding. Blueberry muffins."

"You said blueberry muffins already."

"We had to make them twice. They didn't come out right the first time."

"Make French toast," she said. "Not too brown."

"How many pieces do you eat?"

"Three."

He walked slowly toward the door. Eunice did not intend to lose an opportunity. "Archer—where's your mama?"

"In Glendale. Working things out."

She was not sure she had heard him correctly. Was he being sage beyond his years or smart-ass or parroting what he had heard?

"What's she doing there?"

"Working things out. She's doing it in Glendale and my daddy's doing it here. I'm staying with my grandmother till they're finished."

"Swell. Well, get cracking on the toast. I'll make the coffee."

It seemed perfectly equitable to him. He left her without a backward glance.

Harvey came to the table in a tie and jacket. Eunice and Archer sat across from one another nicely washed and combed. They might have been the family from a Cheerios commercial, so bright, polite and sunny were they to each other. Harvey made appreciative noises over the French toast and interrogated his son like a kindly but nagging schoolmaster. Was he all right at his grandmother's? Yes, he was. Did he have enough allowance to get by on during the week? Yes, he did. Was he cutting down on sweets, did he say prayers before bedtime, did he still wet his bed? This last was offered as a gentle admonition. The boy turned fiery red to the tips of his ears and looked imploringly at Eunice.

"I peed in bed till I was thirteen," she said promptly. "It's nerves and you outgrow it."

"Well, of course, it's not his fault," Harvey said. "Things have been pretty upsetting for him. It's just that his grandmother is quite old and..."

"*I* change the sheets," Archer said in a small voice.

"There's got to be something else to talk about at the breakfast table," Eunice told them firmly. "This French toast isn't bad."

"I did it better last time," Archer said. "It doesn't always come out the same."

He slid from his chair with an apologetic sideways glance at his father. "I've got to go to school now."

He picked up his jacket which was dark green and dusty looking and a brown paper bag containing respectable underwear.

"Well, so long," he said.

"Hey?" Eunice's voice stopped his progress toward the back door. "You like to go swimming?"

He thought it over. "I don't know how."

"You don't know how to *swim?*"

"No."

"What if you got swept down a storm drain? What if you fell in a river?"

"There's no water in the Los Angeles River," he said patiently. "And there's no storm drain anyplace around this neighborhood."

Eunice wouldn't have it. She wanted him

imperiled and part of the drama. "I know a man," she began darkly, "who fell asleep in his bathtub, slipped under the water, and glub, glub, he was gone."

"My grandmother sits on the toilet seat in the bathroom with me when I take a bath." He had a lawyer's neat and methodical logic.

"You're too old for that. Lock her out." A thought dawned. "I'll tell you what. This Saturday you get on the Olympic Boulevard bus with forty-five cents exact change in your hand and ride it all the way out to the Marina. You get off and walk one block to the big apartment building that's staring you right in the face. At ten o'clock in the morning you'll find me by the swimming pool, ready to teach you to swim and save your life from any accidents that might befall you."

He looked to his father, who beamed. "Well, Archie, that seems like a generous offer. What do you say?"

"I'll try it."

Eunice was in high spirits. "We'll go off the deep end together," she said exuberantly.

Doubt and fear instantly shadowed Archer's face. She saw it and she grinned. "We'll start out in two feet of water. I'll hold you up by your bellybutton."

Sensing that something untoward, something bristling with possibilities had overtaken him, his face cleared, his head bobbed, and he went out the screen door running, allowing it to slam behind him.

Harvey hardly knew how to let her see what was flowering in his heart. He had been loved all night, his son had been nurtured in the morning. She evoked sunlight and madonnas at his breakfast table. What could he say? She divined sentiment in the air and banked the fires before they could catch, let alone burn.

"I've got to toddle off myself. I'll be late to work." She sipped the last drop of her coffee and rose, stacking the dishes on her arm like a harassed waitress.

He protested that he would clean the kitchen. It was his daily and accustomed task. He rose to help her, paused to kiss the soft nape of her neck, causing her to spill syrup on her blouse.

She pushed him off and blotted the stain. "That's enough now, Harvey," she said as if she were fending off a nipping puppy.

"Eunice, Eunice, Eunice." He sang her name in concert with the birdsong outside, his chant the more piercing of the two. "I can't believe any of this."

She peered under the sink for soap and splashed it over the piled dishes. "You're almost out of Tide," she said.

He was not to be put off.

"I'll pick you up tonight. We'll ride out to the beach. I have a blanket in the car."

She envisioned sandy carnality under a pier and winced.

"I have a Spanish lesson tonight." She turned to face him and saw the hopeful light in his blue eyes. "Not true. I haven't got a Spanish lesson, Harvey. I just don't want to get all clogged up before I think this over."

Harvey martialed his forces right and left. But she had gone to bed with him, right off the bat. They had made love only one hour and fifty minutes after they had met. And the beauty of it. She must consider the beauty and the rightness of it. Hadn't it been as if they had always known each other? Hadn't they been in perfect harmony, perfect rhythm? Why, he had been married half a lifetime and never spent a night like the one he had just passed. No, his wife had taken hot milk and aspirin tablets on those rare occasions when he sought her under her Sears Roebuck cotton pajamas. She had come out in bright red spots like giant hives, which made her look like a victim of measles and brutality at one and the same time. He had tugged, she had thrashed, and all the while she had grown blotched and bellicose. How often he had closed his eyes and conjured a milk white nymph, naked as a jaybird and pliant as silk. How often had he turned away from her nightclothes puddled on the floor like discarded Dr. Dentons and wished for her death and his. But now all that was at an end. He caught Eunice's hand, brought it to his lips. She was beneficence, she was balm in Gilead.

"Goddamn," said Eunice. "I'm in a hole *again*." She pulled free and started for the bedroom. He followed, cracking his shin smartly on the table leg in his haste.

She was already making the bed as he entered, flinging the blankets about and plopping the pillows by crushing them against her bosom. She had been in many beds and never left one unmade. It was a matter of pride.

"Stand on the other side and grab hold," she said. Meekly, he complied. "Somebody hand-crocheted the lace on this sheet. My mother did that stitch."

"Eunice, please, I beg you. Don't just walk out of

my life."

"Miter your corners," she directed. "Otherwise they pop out in the middle of the night and leave your feet cold."

"I won't get in your hair. I promise you that. But I can see that you need care, Eunice. I can *see* that."

She gave a final smoothing pat to her side and took her coat off the chair.

"I know how to balance a bank statement, Harvey, and change a sparkplug. I left home when I was sixteen with twelve dollars and a hatpin with a jet knob on top of it in my purse in case I was accosted in a bus station. I never spent the twelve dollars and I never used the hatpin. So it's as plain as the nose on your face that I can look out for myself."

He used his last weapon as she trotted toward the front door.

"What were you doing in that bar then?"

She took a deep breath. The question had been asked before. "I was saving somebody the waltz," she said flatly.

"I won't call till the weekend. If you just want to go to lunch that'll be fine..."

"You'll find lots of girls at scientology or folk dancing," she suggested. "You'd probably find just what you're looking for."

"I've found her, Eunice, I've found her."

She took out a lipstick and swept it across her mouth expertly. "You don't know how crazy I am," she said. He paid no heed. She gave in then. She always did.

"I'm at Burbank Studios. We can eat Chinese across the street."

By some kind of common unspoken consent the men stayed away from the damp, warm cauldron of the laundry room on Saturday mornings. They sat around the pool reading newspapers or worked out in the gym, grunting and puffing with the unaccustomed effort. They courted hernias and heart strain as they lifted weights, rowed machines on mechanical tracks and pumped stationary bicycles on long trips to nowhere.

The ladies of Marina One had the room to themselves, and the oversized glass-walled dryers tumbled with bras and panties and machine-washable knits. They came wearing their bunny-rabbit slippers and pink plastic curlers and terry-cloth robes, faces free of make-up, mouths without lipstick, giving some an air of innocence, others the denuded look of age. It was a gathering that reached back in time to riverbanks and rushing streams. Pursuing cleanliness, eschewing godliness, they let their hair down.

Stella was the earliest arrival. She sat on her bundle of disgracefully dirty sheets, a beer-stained sweater, an unraveling nightie, and, cigarette drooping, she bided her time. Someone would show up with two quarters for the machine and she would insinuate her laundry together with her victim's.

She was surprised and discomfited by the sound of sobbing. It was a scale of woe rising from a high note to a low one and then to a rush of shallow sobs much like a drunk in the throes of hiccups. Stella heaved herself upright and peered into the far reaches of the room. The weeping Niobe was an airline stewardess she remembered vaguely as a cream-slathered, inert figure browning in the sun, navel, loins, and the faint hint of pubic hair for all the world to see.

"You sound like a cat with it's tail in the wringer. What is the matter with you anyhow?"

The girl's face dripped tears. She was a bloody leaking faucet.

"Oh," she sobbed, and, "oh," again and that was all that was to be had out of her.

"I don't want to know anyway," Stella said. "You're making a hell of a racket considering the state of my head this morning."

The girl inched back further into the corner and wept on.

Stella hunkered on her pile of clothes and smoked gloomily.

Hortense and Eunice came through the door carrying a plastic wash basket heaped high. They gave the snuffling figure a curious glance, and then began sorting their wash in neat piles on the floor. Stella gave them a decent amount of time to organize and then she descended upon them.

"As is usual with me," she began, "I'm out of money. I've gotten as dirty as I can without becoming disgusting to myself and I need a load of wash done. Perhaps you'd throw my things in with yours."

Hortense lifted her head. She knew Stella's cadging ways.

"It's sure all hand to mouth with you, isn't it?" She knew the answer but a mild irritation caused her to pose the question.

"I never think about it," Stella said. "The ravens have always fed me and I trust will continue to do so. Will you take my wash?"

"Throw it in." Hortense turned to Eunice.

"Plenty of Clorox. She's been in those duds for a month."

Eunice made a shushing motion at her friend. She felt that Stella, despite her granite, had feelings which could be hurt and nothing could have dissuaded her from that view.

"It's all right," she said. "Just toss the stuff over and we'll get you nice and clean."

Stella had no further use for the steamy intimacies of the washroom. "You can bring them up to me when they've run through," she said.

Eunice was about to acquiesce when Hortense stopped her.

"Just whoa up," she said. "We don't mind doing you a little favor but neither one of us is your maid. You just wait and take up your own bundle."

"I've left important work," Stella said.

"It's not gonna run away while your undies wash. You're one funny lady, you know that? It's always, 'Get me this' or 'Give me that,' like you were born to it." She was not chiding so much as probing into the source of Stella's colossal nerve. She was never grateful, never suppliant, never apologetic. Hortense marveled at her.

"I must put first things first, it's as simple as that," Stella replied. "I've always known my order of priorities. I just follow it." She scratched her ear and looked complacent. "I don't know why it makes people bridle. Not you, Hortense. You've always been very helpful. Yes, I've got you marked down as a helpful one."

"I'll bet." Hortense was mild again.

The girl in tears blotted her damp cheeks and sidled past them to the door, hugging her pile of neatly folded towels. Something in her pale, woebegone face spoke across the room to Eunice. She had begun many a morning with wet eyes and a bitter mouth.

"Is something wrong?" she asked. "Are you late with the curse? What's the matter, honey?" She searched for other possible disasters. "Are you knocked up? Has someone died?"

The girl looked at the others. The lure for her was the sympathy in the voice, the eyes wise with understanding, the shoulder to lean on. There was the memory of pajama parties and sorority sisters and best friends and maids of honor. Wasn't there always a woman across the chicken salad sharing your agony and the check? Didn't the manicurist hold your hand and the secrets of your heart? Hadn't your mother brushed your hair and hushed your tears? It came out in a rush.

She had received her final divorce papers in the morning mail along with an advertisement for a sale at the May Company and an appeal from a day-care nursery. It had been a terrible marriage. Not sexually. It had been all right on its back but on its feet, God, on its feet. She had never gotten a single cent from him that wasn't meant for the grocery bill. She had had to ask her mother who was seventy years old to send her clothes and Kotex and even postage stamps. She had never been able to offer a gift or walk into a store or buy a flat of pansies to plant in her front yard. He made good money. He wore nice clothes and drove a BMW. But he cut the phone pad in half to make it last longer and bought chickens in the downtown Central Market that were old and blue and hairy and made her eat them for a whole week at a time.

"The first paycheck I made," she said, "I spent

167

every single cent in one day. I bought ice cream and lipstick and a red setter puppy and sling pumps in three colors and..." She stopped abruptly. "I'm crying," she said, "because it took me ten years to get the piece of paper that came this morning. Ten years," she said dully. "They say everything that goes wrong in a marriage is sex. It isn't. It's money. It's fighting about money."

"It doesn't come as any surprise to me that men are worms," Stella said. "Of course they'll take advantage if you let 'em. Nothing new in that. I'd say blow your nose and forget him. Spilt milk." She rose. "I'll come back for my wash. It would be convenient if you folded it." She started to go and looked back at the girl. "You should have shoved his bankbook up his ass." And she loped out, banging the door behind her.

"Amen," Hortense said.

"That woman's always drunk," the girl said with lofty disdain.

"She's got craw."

"I think she's crude," said the girl.

Hortense bent a sour look on her. "I say she's right. I say if you eat shit there's no good wailin' 'cause it ain't caviar. I ain't ever gonna beg from any man 'cause his hangs out and mine's tucked in. Not this girl."

"Tote that barge, lift that bale," Eunice said. "Miss Independent."

"It beats sniffing around the garbage pails like you do."

"*What* garbage pails?"

"The *men*, honey. The men you dig up out of the banana peels and the tomato juice cans!"

The washroom conviviality was suddenly gone,

a wrangle erupting, caused in Hortense by the tides of the moon, in Eunice by her needful alliance with losers.

The stewardess beat a retreat. Cat fights were her daily diet; she could do without the one shaping up before her.

"Some people can't be big, black, strong, make-it-on-your-own types. Some people don't want to end up with a teacher's pension and a dildo for company. Some people want to love and be loved. I'm prepared to take chances."

"Child," Hortense said, "you've taken more chances than a Chinese lottery, and so far zilch, zero. Don't forget I've stuffed cotton between your legs when you were bleeding and cleaned up puke after you were sick. I know where you're at and it's trash city. Now if I ain't earned the right to say that to you as a friend, I want my door key back and goodby, whitey."

"You're one mean nigger today," said Eunice.

"Go clean the bathroom," Hortense told her. "It's your turn."

Eunice pranced past her, spirits restored. Horty on the boil was as good as a dose of castor oil, nasty but cleansing.

She spotted the moldy green jacket clear across the pool area. He was standing stiffly, staring straight ahead as if his head had frozen to his neck.

"Yoo-hoo!" Her raucous call caused him to turn around. He raised a tentative hand and gave it a tentative waggle.

She beckoned him to her side. He came slowly, scuffing his sneakers along the coping. She saw

169

that his jacket was zipped to his chin, a ratty quilted cocoon concealing the butterfly beneath.

"Hi, Archer."

"Hi."

"Aren't you too warm in that jacket?"

He shook his head.

"I see you got here okay."

"Yes."

"Well, where are your trunks? You can hop upstairs and climb in 'em and we'll dive right in."

"I didn't bring any."

"How come?"

"I don't have any."

She looked at his solemn face. "Well, if it was just you and me and God in his heaven we'd go in starkers, but since it isn't we'll go into Santa Monica and buy you something zingy at Henshey's."

"I haven't any money."

"Honey, till Master Charge catches up with me, you're with the last of the big-time spenders."

He sat silently beside her in the car, rivulets of sweat pouring down his back. His heart hammered in his chest and in his ears. Eunice whistled through her teeth while she drove. He wondered if a gap between those fine white teeth produced the sound. He was afraid to look directly at her.

"Take off that damn jacket," she said. "I'm roasting just looking at you in it."

He tugged manfully but the zipper stuck. She reached across and whoosh, the jacket fell apart, revealing his Mickey Mouse shirt.

"Whatcha been up to all week? Have you gone to the movies? Have you fallen in love with anybody? Have you grown a mustache? What's new?"

170

"I pasted Blue Chip stamps in for Grandma." It was the best he had to offer.

"Uh huh. Well, that didn't take you all week, did it?"

"I watched *Stella Dallas* on television."

"With Barbara Stanwyck?"

"I don't know."

"Did you cry?"

"No."

"How come?"

He wanted to tell her that all his tears had been used up with the departure of his mother. Emotion now produced only a stinging between his eyes and a dry heaving. Sometimes he curled his toes inside his sneakers until they ached. Sometimes he bit the inside of his lip.

"It wasn't too sad," he said.

"I'm a big crier myself. I believe in it. I boo-hoo-hoo at least once a day."

He wondered if he should commiserate.

"Most girls cry," he consoled her.

"They've got plenty to cry about, believe me, baby."

He nodded. He didn't know what he was agreeing to, but it seemed friendly.

They drove in companionable silence to the store.

The saleslady measured his waist while he stared at the ceiling in an agony of embarrassment. His stomach roiled with gas and excitement. What if he let wind and she smelled it. He tightened his buttocks and submitted to the will of God.

"You're a little fellow for your age, aren't you?" She was an old woman with glasses dangling from

171

a black cord and a sprinkle of dandruff on her rusty black dress.

"He's twenty-one," said Eunice, winking at him. "Hey, I like that red satin number. How about you, Archer?"

"I guess so."

"Well, whip into the dressing room and let's see 'em on you."

He went off clutching the trunks. The curtains of the cubicle thrashed and billowed as he struggled into them, wondering desperately where he should put his wienie. Ah. There was a little knitted pouch. He stuffed it in with both hands and then peered into the glass to make sure there was no bulge. There was none, but there was goose flesh clearly visible on his skin from the air conditioning.

He rubbed at himself in the hope that that chicken look would leave him. He needed to blow his nose, but there was nothing at hand. He snuffled and then used the back of his arm. He'd been in here for at least five minutes. He was expected to come out. He cleared his throat and emerged like a man on his way to the firing squad.

Eunice sat on a counter swinging one brown leg. She did not laugh or whistle or catcall. He swallowed the spit pooling in his mouth and advanced further. Her steady regard made him forget to suck in his stomach. He was sure that it swelled in front of him like a basketball with his bellybutton protruding and ugly for all to see.

"Archer," she said, "you've got a swell build."

He loved her from that moment on.

He was rocked in the cradle of the deep. He was rocked in an ammonic womb. He gulped water, he thrashed, he made it across the pool and turned, a drowned rat, wreathed in smiles.

She clutched him by gathering up a handful of his swimming trunks. He bumped into her breasts, grabbed at her neck.

"I opened my eyes," he said.

She hoisted him up on the coping, where he sprawled panting. She was beside him, shaking out her wet hair, the water spattering his heaving chest.

"Did you like it?"

"Yes."

"Next time we'll go in the deep end."

"Sure," he said. He was as bold as brass. Hadn't he seen her through the veil of water as a mermaid shape beckoning him on and on? Hadn't he felt her encircling arm? There was no depth he feared; no perilous height either. Could he have grown an inch or two this afternoon? He felt if he stood now he would tower over her.

The late afternoon sun fled away, cooling the pool area with shadows. There was the stinging slap of a breeze off the ocean. Eunice hugged her knees and felt a bud of melancholy open slowly inside her. This was an empty hour. Others stretched ahead.

"Hey," she said. "Do you have a date tonight?"

He thought of sitting over a plate of cooling creamed tuna with his grandmother sitting opposite, teeth clinking like a tiny metronome as she ate. He thought of early bedtime with the summer light still washing over his bedroom walls

173

and the sound of a ball game being played in the lot next door.

"We go to bed early on Saturday so we can get up for church on Sunday." He watched her like a kitten about to pounce on a string.

"Let's eat hamburgers and go to the pier and get our pictures taken and see a double bill. Let's do that instead."

"I'd have to ask." His mind raced ahead to possible refusal. Nails whacked into a coffin. The earth split. The sky fell. His knees trembled visibly.

"I'll call." Eunice was on her feet. "I'll say I'm a distant relative of your daddy's. I'll say you might inherit a fortune if you play up to me. I'll say I'm blind and you have to lead me across the street. Leave it to me."

They went up to the apartment. Hortense had propped a note on the coffee table. She was out for the night with Booker. Eunice should not get into bed without bolting the door. She should throw out the crab meat in the refrigerator. It was doubtless toxic by now. She should sleep well and alone. There was a scrawl of x's across the bottom of the page and a round face drawn with a down-turned mouth as a signature.

Eunice dried Archer off with a beach towel, stripping him with one yank on the red trunks. He felt a shock of surprise and then pleasure. His skin tingled. He jumped as her hand approached his groin but the swipe she made at it was practical and purposeful. He was warm and dry in a jiffy and sitting on the bed in her bathrobe while she showered with the door open, yelling to him above the rushing water.

174

"Look in the *Times* for the Venice Theater and call for when the show comes on. One's mushy and one's roller skating. I want to see all of the mushy one."

He pawed through the paper and squinted at the print. He had only been allowed to see G-rated pictures. Now he saw the sprawled and licentious figure leaning out of the ad toward him. His nose was pressed to a shelf of bosom. He made a quick and sidelong comparison with Eunice as she emerged from the shower. She kicked the door shut, but he had decided in her favor during that instant she had been in view.

He thought of strawberries crushed sweetly against the roof of his mouth and the down of peaches furring his tongue. He thought of the warm underbelly of his cat when he put his face against it and the disturbing lurch of his heart when he lay, belly down, in his bed. Oh, he was happy.

"We are proud to present a double feature starring Raquel Welch and..." The tinny, recorded voice foretold the delights to come and the scheduled showings as well.

"It's eight o'clock for *Kansas City Bomber*," he told her as she emerged tugging a sweater over her head.

"Do you like chili on your burger and onions and Russian dressing? Do you like French fries and a root beer float?"

His mouth watered. His grandmother served lumpy mashed potatoes and string beans floating in greenish water. His palate roared to life. Panic followed. He only had bus fare home. Did she mean for him to pay his share? He could say he wasn't

175

hungry. He could have a stomachache.

"My treat," she said.

"Thank you very much."

She sat on the bed next to him. "Are you ever going to call me by my name?"

"Thank you very much...Eunice."

"You're welcome...Archer."

She tossed his clothes at him. "Hurry up. I want to be there at the beginning."

It was after midnight when they came out under the starry sky. Little belches arose in Archer, recalling onions and Hershey bars and cherry drink and bubble gum. His head ached dully and his bladder sloshed with liquid. He thought of the long jolting bus ride home and groaned inwardly. He'd have to sit with his legs crossed all the way and what of the walk to the house when he got off? He would go behind a billboard and pee a stream that would wash away the ground under his feet. He hardly heard what she was saying.

"Listen, it's too late for you to go on the bus now. You'll sleep at my place. I'll call your grandma again."

That was a bad plan. His grandmother awoke cranky, he told her. Her teeth floated in a water glass by her bed. Her glasses with their thick lenses glinted beside them. Her hearing aid rested on the bureau. She was helpless, lurching, groping, bound to be unfriendly.

"She's afraid to be alone in the house," he said. "We lock up right after supper. She's afraid she'll die in the night from her emphysema."

"Then I'll take you home."

A bad plan again. He saw his grandmother

peering through a cautious slit in the door at Eunice in her tight blue sweater with a gold chain separating her high breasts. She would smell that scent of cloves and cinnamon and see the red-painted toenails poking through her sandals. She would drive her from the door, shrieking Jezebel in her wake. His grandmother spoke of Sodom and Gomorrah more often than San Francisco or San Diego.

"I'll just catch the bus."

"Aren't you scared?"

How did he know? He had never been on a bus at this hour of the night. And what were his defenses? He had a pocketknife with a snapped-off blade and a Christian prayer learned at Sunday school to fend off the devil. Neither seemed enough. He swallowed hard.

"It's okay," he said with a squeak of fear in his voice.

She saw that he had made a test, a crucible of it. He had laid his undersized balls on the line.

"Well, you're not a little kid, are you?"

"No." He was both grateful and appalled. She was going to let him go alone.

She gave him an approving whack across the shoulders. "I bet you would have hopped on that bus, but I'm not going to let you. I'm going to dump you right down on your doorstep. But you know what's plain to me, Archer?" she added. "What's plain to me is that you've got a steel rod right up your spine from your ass to your hairline, and I'm proud of you."

She hugged him to her and they walked to the car, bumping hips all the way.

Alan waited until she brought him his coffee, black, with two sesame wafers and some honey; waited until he ate them to the last seed; waited until he sucked his tooth clean. Then he looked up from *Variety* and fired her.

He moved around the room gesticulating like a Turkish rug merchant, bowed over by the weight of it all, alert with cunning. The thing was, he told her, rubbing his hands together, they had put the screws to him. Somebody upstairs had gotten righteous and closely questioned the charges he had put on his last picture. They built houses for executives and put in sprinkler systems and raised walls of old brick, but they were pissed off by a side trip he had taken to Mexico City. That and a bill for a new motor in the Jaguar and a little tailoring done by a rip-off limey on a couple of suits. They figured he could use a secretary from the pool until he checked off the lot. She should look at it this way; if his days were numbered, so were hers. Get off the *Titanic* before it sank, right?

Eunice stood in front of his oversized desk and felt her face stiffen into that cold wet mask it became before she fainted. Her mind raced wildly through dunning letters and lawyers' threats. It sorted stacks of bills—the antique dealer who let her pay off the amethyst beads because she pretended not to notice that he was rubbing his erection against her hip when she bought them, the Saks charge, the Standard Oil charge, the goddamn Spanish boots she had snapped up on impulse. Christ, she even had an unpaid tab at Art's Deli. She tried to slam the Pandora's box shut, but it was overflowing. The florist. Her masseuse at the gym. Horty. She owed Horty fifty

178

dollars for something or other.

Alan was droning on about references. A dirty grin accompanied his promise to describe her various services in glowing terms.

"You little prick"—she cut him off short—"stuff your references. I've been with you for five years! I've taken your laundry and called your chicks and blown you under your goddamn desk! I'm going where you go, buster!"

He leaned back in the leather chair and stroked his stubbled chin judiciously. "Sweetheart," he said, placating her, "I'd say yes in a minute, but it isn't good for *you*. You're the best. You've been the crème de la crème, but what's happening here isn't good for you. It's not healthy." He was a physician, solemnly prescribing a necessary tonic. "You know how you are. An arranger walks through the door, you're going down on him the next night. I use a talented English writer, you ball him till he can't write his name. Even the mail kids aren't safe. Sweetheart, you need a quiet backwater. A nice insurance office, a nice real estate office. Out of trouble. Eunice"—he was paternal now—"you're getting older, baby. It's settling-down time."

She stared at him in disbelief. This little crumb with his sexual itches furtively scratched was telling her how to live?

"I want the rest of this week's salary. In cash. And I'm leaving as soon as I can clear out my desk." She moved stiff-legged with fury toward the door. "One other thing, Alan. Your picture stinks. They're saying it all over the lot. That house you just bought? It'll go. The new car? They'll pick it up for payments. That little cunt at the Château

179

Marmont? Bye-bye. I'll see you at the unemployment window."

She slammed the door and leaned against it, shaking. Then, as if pursued, she ran to the phone. Scotty. Scotty knew thousands of people. She broke a nail dialing and shouted at the girl who told her he was out of town on location.

"Give me a number. I've *got* to reach him."

He didn't leave a number. He'd be gone for a month.

She sat tapping the desk with the pencil. Horty. She'd call Horty. No. Horty had laid down the law about being called at school. Only an accident would make it permissible. And that meant her head through the windshield, not rear-ending or anything minor.

Alan burst through the door, his face aggrieved. "I am not able to pay you in cash. If you'll accept my check?"

"You're overdrawn, shit-heel!"

"Eunice," he said with a pained look, "I think we should try for a dignified parting. After all, we have been something to each other. I think I may have been instrumental in broadening your view of life, culturally, humanly. You've seen me at my best, and, yes, at my worst. You've been a confidant and a friend."

"Get the cash up," she said, emptying her drawer onto her desk.

"Listen, cooze, don't threaten me!" He edged toward her, an ugly flush suffusing his face.

"I take karate lessons three times a week," she said holding her ground. "If I kick you where I'm thinking of kicking you, you're a disabled veteran."

He winced. "Charming." He took out his wallet and threw some bills at her. "Don't keep in touch."

She went into the washroom to cry and changed her mind. She phoned Harvey at the store with just the hint of an ordeal in her voice. She hated to take him away from work, but after what had just happened she wasn't feeling very well or thinking straight. He would be there, he promised her fervently, in twenty minutes. They would go to his house. He would give her some sherry. She would tell him all about it. The comforting net he threw settled around her.

The house was stuffy and hot and smelled of the morning's fried bacon. She sat on the vinyl couch with the springs twanging under her and took tea and sympathy. The tea was too strong. The hand patting hers was too hairy and freckled. She tried to compose herself by closing her eyes and going limp. For a moment, boredom with him and her own plight almost tipped her into sleep. He waited patiently.

"Well, I'm broke," she said loudly. "Fired and broke."

"You know what I think?" he said. "I think it's all for the best. You've got shadows under your eyes and you're pretty nervous. You've been working too hard."

She thought of the long afternoons at the office while a picture was away on location when she yawned over a book and did her nails. She'd even brought an afghan from home and napped on the army cot in the ladies' room.

"He expected a helluva lot."

"Eunice," he said, "I don't know how to put this

so it won't offend you. Look. I'm doing pretty well right now. Why don't you let me take care of you for a couple of months till you get settled? You know how I feel about you..."

She sat up and took life. She debated naming a figure and settled for a look of profound gratitude. "You're very sweet, Harvey."

"You could move in here."

Her eyes swept the twelve-by-eighteen-foot room. The abyss yawned wider. She saw herself tamed, penned, bundled into domesticity, condemned to one bathroom. "You have to think about how it would look, Harvey. Let's just leave things the way they are. The time will probably come when I'll have to call on you. That'll probably be tomorrow night at the latest." She put a gentle hand on his arm.

"I'll try not to be a burden, Harvey."

He was a conservative politically with a strong sense of fiscal responsibility. He nodded approval.

"I'll make you an allowance," he said. She wondered if it would be more than Archer got.

"Thank you." The next question followed without a beat. "How much?"

He cleared his throat. "What do you usually spend for pocket money?"

She hadn't heard that expression since she'd left home.

"I'll leave it to you, dear."

He named a sum. It would take her and Archer to the movies a couple of times and leave enough over to buy arsenic to poison him.

"That's a beginning," she told him sweetly. "I'll take in ironing to make up the rest."

Booker told her a story that made her laugh. It was an old joke and she'd heard it before, but she laughed anyway. It was either that or scream.

He sat on the kitchen table munching an apple, dressed in his tennis whites with a towel knotted ascot style in the deep opening of his shirt. Eunice noticed his dimples for the first time. She had a passion for dimples. She had once slept with a button pressed to her cheek for a month trying for those delicious little hollows.

"It's a bitch, your getting fired."

She was fascinated to see that he ate the core of the apple and all the seeds as well. She sat in front of the boiled egg she had fixed for her own lunch and looked at its runny interior with disgust.

"Fat troubles and lean pickings, that's the story of my life." She dabbed at the egg and then threw down her spoon. "I should have stayed in Kelso and gone to work in the salmon-canning factory. I'd have married a lumberjack by now and had a houseful of kids."

He turned a chair around, swung his long legs over it and rested his head on bent elbows. "You've got the glooms, baby," he told her.

Harvey came to mind, with his milky glance and his milky kindness. She saw herself being led into Chamber of Commerce dinners on his arm. She saw herself serving coffee and Ralph's coconut cake in his neat kitchen to his neat friends as they planned camping trips and compared sleeping bags. She saw him preparing for bed with an extra wash under his armpits and a careful gargling with Listerine. He would lay a towel under her hips to save the mattress and turn out the lights to save on the electric bill. He would take out the garbage and repair alarm clocks and recount the news she had already read in the daily paper. Harvey was the prize in the Cracker Jack box. Harvey was her fate. She sighed.

"You've got it made, Booker. You climb into those white shorts and that Izod shirt and zap around the courts and drink Gatorade and suck up to the ladies..."

The dimples disappeared. The friendly smile, white teeth and porcelain caps, was gone. "You been listening to Horty? That's the shit she lays on me all the time."

"I wish I was a man."

"You ain't, baby."

She ignored him and rambled on. "I'd be somebody's son-in-law living the *good* life. Yes, sir, I'd grow a *Viva Zapata* mustache and hunt for a bucktoothed dentist's daughter. I'm surprised you aren't in that slot right this minute, the way you look and all."

She cocked her head to one side and studied him. "I guess Horty keeps you in line."

He corrected her coldly. "Maybe Horty tells you what to do, girl, but *nobody* tells me!"

"Uh huh." Eunice twisted a lock of her hair and stared at him. He went to the refrigerator and rummaged through it noisily, looking for a beer. There was none. He drank a whole quart of milk from the carton, head thrown back, throat glistening with drops of sweat. She followed the course of one in her mind's eye. Down the throat, down the muscled chest, down the groin, down, down, down. She had spent an hour lying in a hot bath before he got there and now everything seemed warm and loose and open.

"Where the hell is Hortense, anyway? That woman's always keeping me hung up. She's fifty goddamn minutes late." He glanced at his very thin gold watch.

"Maybe she's at a PTA meeting."

"Pee Tee Asshole meeting!"

"You aren't bothering me."

He slung dark glasses across the bridge of his nose and became an expressionless stranger with no eyes to read.

"*You're* bothering *me*," he said.

"Well," she drawled, "if I am...I am."

She got up and went into the living room. She had been home all day and the place was a litter of papers and magazines. Her bed, visible in the next room, was unmade next to Hortense's with the covers and pillows in order. She went to the record player, shuffled a stack of records, found one and dropped it into place.

"La la la la." She sang with the music as she closed her eyes and moved in languorous circles. She knew he was in the room with her now. She had seen a cat watching a sparrow, tense and hungry and dangerous. The bird had dared fate by swooping and fluttering until it was mirrored in those yellow eyes. She swooped and fluttered.

She threw her arms above her head and yawned, her skimpy sweater hitching up and revealing her skin. Still she kept her eyes closed. If she stumbled she would stumble blindly. If she fell she would fall far.

His arms encircled her from behind.

"Let's just do it, baby." His hands rose to her breasts. They moved on them slowly. "Let's just play fuck the fucker."

Bad dreams followed good times, she knew that, but she wanted to know what she didn't know and right now. Right this minute. She didn't turn around to face him. She merely stared out at the late afternoon sun shining through the windows Hortense had washed on Sunday morning.

"Don't talk to me about it afterward," was all she said.

They knew they had forgotten to close the bedroom door when they heard a resounding crash from the living room. Eunice, dazed and wet-mouthed, stared past Booker at Hortense. A package had fallen from her arms and she stood in the middle of the room looking right at them.

Booker rolled off Eunice and onto his feet in one swift motion. He stood like an antlered buck staring down the muzzle of a shotgun. Hortense raked him with a glance from head to toe.

"She's crazy," she said, "so that makes you an even bigger shit."

She took off her coat and threw it on a chair behind her.

"Put something over that damp dick and get in here." She swung her attention to Eunice, who sat bolt upright, shielding her nakedness with a copy of *Time* magazine.

"You'd better go take a douche and stay out of my way for a while."

She turned then and went into the kitchen and ran herself a glass of water. It was lukewarm and brackish. She sipped it slowly, as if she had nothing else on her mind. After a moment she sensed Booker's presence. He was behind her, fingering his warm-up jacket and staring at the tops of his Adidas sneakers. She let him dangle

186

while she rinsed the glass and broke a dead leaf from a geranium plant.

"*Say* it and lemme outta here!" he yelled, goaded by her impassive calm.

She set the glass down carefully and walked by him into the living room. He had been mortified in the past by that unseeing, unnoticing passage. She had stepped over him drunk in the bushes. She had ambled around his inert bloody body when he had been beaten in a fight. She had sashayed past him as he lay caught in the sticky embrace of a prom queen in an empty gymnasium. Always with her nose in the air. Always with that delicate disdain stiffening her nostrils as if something were rotting directly beneath them. Now she was settling into a comfortable chair, plumping a pillow behind her back, lighting a cigarette and smoking reflectively. He charged after her and stood splay-legged in front of her.

"Yeah, yeah, yeah!" he shouted in mindless defiance. She merely glanced at him.

"It's your fault, goddamn it, you cold-assed righteous bitch." Shame made him sputter. "You've hauled me around by the ear ever since I was seven years old. I had to smoke behind the fuckin' barn. I had to drink behind the fuckin' barn. I had to jack off behind the fuckin' barn because I was afraid of you. That's right, Mama. Your fishy eye has been on me from the day I first saw you. You've been whacking at me with a big stick long enough."

"You finished?"

"No," he wailed. "This was no big deal, Hortense. I went for a dip, that's all. That's all it was."

"You're either a child," Hortense said, "messin' his pants whenever he feels like it or you knew what you were doing. It doesn't much matter which because you're out of my life either way. *Repeat.* Out of my life, Booker. That means don't call me when you're hangin' on the ropes. You can't lean on me, lay me, or love me from here on in. You'll notice I'm not screaming, I'm not crying, I'm not calling you names. I'm just shoveling the dirt in on you, Booker, because you're dead."

He was almost hopping now in his frenzy. "God, Horty, what're you doing to me?"

The other side of the coin came into view. Hortense teaching him to read, Hortense holding his hand at his mama's graveside in the rain, Hortense murmuring love and truth in the dark.

"Get your perfidious black ass out of here," she said quietly.

He had fallen from the tree. She had pelted him with apples and driven him from Eden.

Eunice showered for an hour before she crept into the living room to see how far she had fallen from grace. She had scrubbed herself so fiercely, washing her hair, her ears, her buttocks with such flagellant thoroughness that now she wore a drowned, mangled look.

Hortense was rigid in her chair, had not moved. She was sorting her emotions, balancing anger against reason, wrath against an inclination to yawn in the face of it all. Eunice made herself as small as possible, curling herself into a tight wary knot in the least comfortable chair in the room.

She knew instinctively that tears would not appeal and that contrition would get her nowhere. She relied instead on those ancient links between women who defy men even while they succumb. Hadn't they both raged against appetites which had led them to doubtful beds and dubious ends? Hadn't they both smiled mysterious smiles as lovers heaved and panted above them and their minds fled down cool corridors of thought as chaste and manless as a nunnery?

Just understand, her glance told Hortense, and I'll get off scot-free, because you see the absurd humor in it.

"I like you a lot better than Booker," she declared emphatically, "and it was just simple cunt itch that got me in this mess. You're my best friend, the best I ever had and worth three dozen of him." A tick began to pulse in her left eye, a nervous flutter which beat whenever her character was under scrutiny. "I always spoil things," she added wistfully.

"I'm not surprised by any of it." Hortense got up from her chair and walked the room, her hands clasped like a headmaster behind her back. "You stole my earrings when you first moved in with me and took money out of my purse. You're a liar. You cheat at backgammon. You're greedy. You always take the biggest lamb chop and the largest slice of cake. You weasel out of your fair share of the work and the only emotion you know is self-pity."

"It's all true. So true."

Hortense threw her hands up to silence her. "Just shush," she commanded and continued to prowl about the room. Eunice felt a rush of unease. If the jury was out too long she would be hanged. She knew that.

"Think of the good laughs we've had." She scuttled to bolster her case. "And you've said

189

yourself a thousand times that I have a cheerful disposition." There was no response. She saw herself scattered to seed. She gnawed on her thumb and wondered if she had any real charm for anybody.

"Horty?"

"Girl, just let me be. I'm thinking this over."

"You're responsible for me," she insisted. "You are. Without you around you know that I get dippy and do crazy things." She muttered an inward prayer that she had hit pay dirt. Hortense was maternal in a cranky, unwilling sort of a way. It was her best chance. She got up and trotted after her, getting underfoot in the process. Hortense paused and putting her hands on her shoulders shoved her down on the couch.

"You're more trouble than you're worth."

"I know."

"I don't like slyness," she snapped. "I don't like sluts."

Eunice wiggled like a child grasped by an angry mother's hand. She chewed a strand of hair, sucking on it noisily; she shifted from one buttock to the other; she flounced, flopped and fluttered. Hortense stood over her with unwavering severity.

"I haven't heard one word of sorry out of you."

"Well, God," Eunice cried, "if that's what you want I can apologize till I'm blue in the face. I'll start right now." She drew a deep breath. "I'll put saltpeter in my food," she offered. "I'll be as sexless as grass. I'll take the padding out of my bras and be ugly. Anything you say, Horty. Anything at all."

"If you hadn't lost your job," Hortense told her, "you'd be out on your ass, bag and baggage."

Pardon was finally in view and yet Eunice found herself vexed. To be kept on as a charity case was merely to be tolerated. She wanted more than that. She wanted either mortification, punishment, Sturm und Drang—or reconciliation, preferably accompanied by a tearful hug. Hortense had no sense of drama. If she was going to be coldly practical there would be no heat in it at all. And no fun. She gave her an impudent look.

"I can always move into the Y.W.C.A.," she said. She meant to draw her out and see where it led, but it was a match tossed into dry grass. Hortense flared.

"I catch you lapping up and down my man with a tongue like an anteater and you have the brass to sit there and look put-upon! They wouldn't have you in the Y.W.C.A. They wouldn't have you at the city *dump*."

Eunice made a hasty retreat.

"I just meant I wouldn't have anyplace else to go. I haven't got any money."

The plain truth, plainly spoken, put out the fire. Hortense sat down beside her, shaking her head. "Next you're gonna tell me you'll have to sell apples on the street corner. Shit." She pulled a cigarette out of her skirt pocket and let it hang, unlit, from her aggressive lower lip. "You're no damn good to me. You've lost me my childhood buddy and the best fuck I know."

"He'd come running back if you'd let him."

"I won't."

Eunice never dealt in absolutes. She was slightly in awe of people who drew lines and slammed doors. Possibly it was because she had no dignity to affront, no pride to humble.

"But you love him."

The word seemed weightless and trivial. It moved Hortense not one inch.

"I don't like him." She snapped a match on her thumbnail and puffed on her cigarette. "And when I don't like somebody, they ain't got a prayer."

Eunice shriveled under the cold blast like an oyster touched with lemon juice. "What about me?" she asked as meekly as she could manage.

"We'll see about you."

There wasn't much comfort in it, but Eunice drew hope and wrapped it around herself like a tattered blanket. Hortense would doubtless make life hell. She was not sentimental and she had ample experience with erring children. They got rapped on the head and cracked with a ruler. They were made to see the error of their ways. Well, there was nothing for it. She would have to clean Hortense's drawers and cook her those sandy grits she loved for breakfast. Penitence might be good for her once she got the hang of it.

7

STELLA KNEW the jig was up the moment she saw
the nurse with red hair and a temper to match in
close conference with the dog-faced doctor. She
had marked them for the enemy ever since she'd
been coming here. She was usually in and out
without a word to anyone, collecting her fee and
out onto the street before they noticed her. Let the
others pause for the nasty lemonade served in
paper cups with the seeds still floating on top. She
would give herself something a great deal nicer
than that. It was usually a whiskey toddy
pleasantly warmed and drunk slowly, not to revive
her but to make it last. She watched them with
their heads together and heard the nasal whine of
the girl accusing her.

"This is twice in two weeks, doctor. I don't know how she's gotten away with it."

She lay back and stared at the ceiling, making an airy pretense of whistling. Nothing much came out of her but breath hissing through her teeth. Never mind. She squeezed on the rubber grip and urged her blood through the tube into the glass jar attached to the bed beside her. Pity she couldn't turn a tap and have it rush out and be done with it.

She planned her day after the snippy girl stuck a piece of tape on her and let her go. She would have an idle stroll along the sea front and find a windless corner to write a line or two on the scrap of paper in her pocket. Then the promised toddy and then perhaps a bench provided by a considerate mortuary on a corner with the traffic hurrying past in a noxious-smelling but soothing stream. She liked the spectacle of people rushing to and fro on their frantic business while she sat like an island in their midst. The tapestry she wove in her head could be made anywhere, but it pleased her to let it form in the bickering noise of the street. Wordsworth could have his host of bloody daffodils. She was content with Mercury Monarchs and Impalas with their garish metallic paint.

"I am speaking to you."

She let her head loll to one side and took the least possible notice of the starched girl at her side.

"Yes," she said haughtily. "What is it?"

"The doctor wishes to speak to you as soon as you're finished. You must not leave without seeing him."

She disregarded her and watched her blood drip like falling red petals and marveled at its rich color. If that's what was coursing through her veins she would live to be a hundred and confound them all. She speculated on who might be lucky enough to be transfused with that lovely ruby elixir. Who knows? ... she might be transmitting some of her gifts along with it and some pale aborted girl or a sad student with a failed kidney might begin to dream dreams and rampage out of their daily rounds.

She was fussed with and then freed. The hands which pulled her upright were unfriendly. She peered woozily about her and patted her tangled hair into further disorder.

"My hat," she demanded. "I came in a spectacular felt hat."

"It's where you left it." The girl pointed it out as if it had some kind of unpleasant life of its own. Stella plopped it on her head and bowed majestically.

"The doctor is waiting for you," the nurse said in a doomsday voice.

Stella lurched past her on unsteady feet. "They better pay me," she warned as she passed, "or I'll come back and drink the goddamn stuff down again."

The doctor sat tapping a pencil on the desk before him. The rapping warned of a short fuse and even shorter shrift. He beckoned her in but made no motion toward a chair. Tap, tap, tap, and then he was launched on a tirade.

"We've checked on you. I have the records right here before me. We know what you're up to."

She took the chair without an invitation. The smell of sanctity and self-righteousness was making her lightheaded.

"I never said I was a volunteer." Stella's glance

pierced him through. "It says quite clearly you can volunteer or you can get paid. I'm one who gets paid. Under other circumstances I might be more generous and donate my blood, but in my position it's quite impossible. I might add that the blood you're getting is very, very blue. I am distantly related to the Cabots of Boston and there was a senator in the family somewhere."

The doctor thrust a muzzle toward her. Yes, it was a muzzle; with that wispy beard and those sharp little protruding teeth it could not be called anything else.

"You've been sneaking in here twice a month, lying about your name. It's quite clear that you are recklessly disregarding our rules about the number of times you may give blood—no oftener than once every eighty-four days. We have had experience with drunks before."

Why, the silly little cur was all but snapping at her. She buttoned up her sweater the wrong way and got to her feet.

"Don't be an ass," she told him. "Alcohol kills germs. I never intended my vital fluids to be passed on to prigs or Puritans. I only wish to save an interesting life, if any. Label me one hundred proof and pump me into somebody who knows a good thing." She made for the door. "And hereafter," she offered as a final threat, "I'll go where I'm appreciated."

She would really have like to stop and use the ladies' room, but she felt it the better part of wisdom to take the money and run. The woman in charge handed her the bills with the tips of her fingers. Stella riffled through them and handed back a torn and taped dollar.

"They won't take them like that at my watering hole," she said in elegant measured tones. "Dig up another."

"Really!" The woman behind the desk flung another bill in her direction.

"Thanks very much." She examined the disapproving face before her. "You look a bit peaky. Why don't you help yourself to a corpuscle or two?" She was out the door on light feet before she could be answered.

Most of the afternoon went in an unimpressive bar on the boardwalk. It had a beery smell and was none too clean, but there was a booth and the barman was properly morose and silent. Stella established herself so she could see a blue slice of sea through the open door and composed herself to work. It was not precisely a meditative process. Harshly she rummaged through the baggage of her life, ferreting out the moments of fate and passion, terror and delight. What had been the look on her mother's face as she died? What curses had her grandfather flung at age as he walked, bent double in the little shuffling pilgrimages he took to buy the cigar that finally choked him? What was the knotted meaning in her sister's mutterings as she shattered in a midlife breakdown? Sighs and whispers. She had cocked an attentive ear to them all. Not for her the raunchy celebration of sex so fashionable with younger writers. No hysterical accusations flung at life enclosing one in glass jars. No, she addressed herself to bad smells and clenched fists. She sifted through ashes and smoking ruins. She braced herself against floods and cataclysms of all sorts, the more Biblical the better. Crossed wires, missed trains, false starts, broken promises, swindles, the grim reaper, the power and the glory. She had a word for all of them.

By the time the sky darkened and the six o'clock news mired the world in traffic accidents and shootings, suicides and revolutions, she had written four lines of a sonnet she totally approved of. She had also consumed a fifth of bourbon and one hard-boiled egg in case an ulcer lurked somewhere in her gut. She paid her blood money for the booze, told the barman to cheer up as life was indeed a bowl of cherries, and sauntered into the dusk.

Marina One was ablaze with lights. Gas torches flared as if illuminating some ancient Hellenic rites. She flet a pleasant kinship with the rest of the tenants as they tanked up to get through the night. It was always the same. The men emptied their pockets on their bureaus and tried to stuff the day's troubles into the hamper with their socks and shorts. The women cried tears induced by charcoal smoke and ennui. They would huddle in the recreation hall after dinner like refugees, dancing cheek to cheek or playing quarrelsome bridge for stakes they could ill afford. Some of the women who worked would have their hair done in the beauty salon, hoping the Clairol color and the careless curls would lead to good sex and sleep without Seconal. To this end hi-fi's blared throughout the complex, salads were tossed with and without garlic, assignations were arranged with a minimum of small talk and life went on and on.

There was a man in her apartment. She never locked her door, for there was nothing worth stealing. She saw him through the window as she approached. He was gigantically tall; he over-flowed her stiff kitchen chair. He appeared to have a huge brindle beard and a great jutting nose, presented to her now in profile.

She stood speculating before her door. Bill collector? Not in that horse-blanket plaid jacket. Distant relative? Her line had pinched patrician faces and were generally undersized. Reformer, sent by an interested friend? She had none who gave a damn about her habits. Lover encountered in a run-down hotel, long since forgotten? She had kept to herself for some years now—at least that's the way she remembered it. A lawyer with a legacy? She thought not—he didn't look munificent. Rapist, robber, Hebrew scholar?

She barged in, swinging her handbag as if it contained a blackjack.

"Who are you and what do you want?" She felt it sensible to get right to the point.

"My name is Caleb Crown. You should know it."

"I don't."

Her ignorance of him did not go down at all well. He had been interviewed and photographed and widely quoted. He was used to being accosted in the street and supplicated on the telephone. He was annoyed. "I am a publisher," he said, "of the best writers in this country. I am famous for discovering and nurturing talent. I pay poorly, promote brilliantly, and eight novels of note are dedicated to me in gratitude and affection. Where have you been that you don't know who I am?"

"Out of town," she said.

"Your friend Henry Dillon is in my stable. He must have mentioned my name to you."

"Stables are for horses. No, he hasn't."

"I've made him rich."

"I'm sure he's done the same for you." She dismissed discussion of Henry peremptorily. "Very well, you're a publisher. What of it?"

He pulled his beard and glowered. "Henry thinks you're gifted. He says you may be a genius."

She shrugged. "A tired word."

His look was that of a man whose nerves were being rubbed by sandpaper. "He asked me to look you up. I have done so, though I'm not sure to what end." He wheezed irritably. "Why do you live in this garish place like an eccentric crone with a kitchen table and one chair?"

Stella hitched out of her sweater and removed her hat. "It's furnished with words," she said in perfect possession of herself. "I am a poet. Poorly paid and advertised not at all."

"I know who you are," he huffed crankily, "or I wouldn't be here. And you're drunk," he added abruptly. "I can smell you clear across the room."

"You smell drink because I've been drinking. I am never drunk. People often ascribe capacity to the Irish. I am not Irish. I hold my liquor without any help from ancestry. What do you want with me?"

He stood up, groaning from his long sit. He had an almost Falstaffian girth, but it sat firmly on his frame.

"Turn some lights on," he commanded. "And some heat. I detest this California chill that comes with night."

She shrugged and flipped the light switch. He had fine ruddy skin and eyes of almost sinister intelligence. He advanced on her and inclined his head to get a better view of her.

"You're not much to look at," he said emphatically.

"When I'm at my best I'm better than average," she retorted without ill will. "I'm simply not vain. I have an excellent constitution and energy to burn. Staying power is all that counts in my line."

"Not for people who have to look at you."

"I didn't ask you here, did I?"

"But I am here. Well, never mind. Do you eat at all or do you just drink?"

"I eat lightly and drink heavily. Why? Are you going to invite me to dinner?"

"Well, I want to talk to you. It might as well be over dinner." He rubbed his arms and shuddered. She did not know whether to ascribe it to cold or distaste. From the way he was scrutinizing her, rumpled hair to scuffed shoes, she felt it was more likely distaste. As she meant to get a really good bottle of wine out of him she let him squint on as long as he liked.

"It's a mistake to judge a book by its cover," she remarked, leaning against the table. She left the chair for him in case he should want to sit again.

"I'm a very entertaining talker. Are you a good listener?"

"No. *I* like to talk."

"We'll take turns." She tried a smile on him. He did not return it. He kept looking about as if he had found himself in a puzzling maze. She felt obliged to see what he saw.

It was a perfectly good room. It had windows and doors. It had a lumpish bed in the corner and plenty of paper and pencils. She was fond of pencils and bought them in all colors by the dozen. They were quite pretty, really. The walls were blank, of course, but art quickly exhausted itself, in her view. Had she dusted lately? No. Well, dust swirls had a puffy grace, blowing here and there across the floor. Had she flushed the toilet? Certainly! She was a lady. What else did he expect from a woman with eternal verities on her mind?

"I can't take you to a decent restaurant looking like that, no matter how brilliant you are. Do you have another dress? A washrag? Some face powder? A comb?"

She folded her arms akimbo and glowered, annoyed finally. "You'd better tell me your business right here and now. I have no time to waste primping."

He hooted at that. "Primping! You look like you've been in a coal mine for a month. See here. I have not eaten since lunch and that was only a lettuce leaf and three small shrimp. I am a big man. I am a hollow man. I don't want to talk business until I've dined. Come along or not, but I have something to say to your advantage."

He smoothed the old-fashioned chain which lay across his belly, hauled out a weighty gold watch and scanned its face.

"I'll come back in an hour. I'm punctual to the minute. Don't keep me waiting."

He moved his bulk to the door. "You have remarkably limpid eyes," he said and lumbered away.

Stella marshaled her forces like a good general. It was as obvious as the nose on his face that Mr. Crown was devoted to the pleasures of the flesh. He had not garnered that girth by dainty picking, and his last remark to her about her eyes hinted at other appetites as well.

She determined that she would serve herself forth as appetizingly as a suckling pig with an apple in its mouth. One had to give to get.

She examined the contents of her closet with a critical eye. The old brown skirt with the safety pin holding the waist was in tatters. Two sweaters were clearly the victims of moths and time. She threw them aside and dug deeper. There was a gray dress with a sagging hem and the forlorn remains of peasant embroidery, but it too had seen better days. One pair of slacks with a gaping hole and a Japanese kimono completed her wardrobe. She considered the blouse she was wearing. It might do if she found a brooch to hold open the neckline, but the lace collar was torn and if truth be told it did smell a trifle high.

She rummaged in her drawers, flinging aside her washed-out underclothes. She found a silk rose as faded as the last one of summer and held it coquettishly to her bosom. Ghastly. She tried sticking it in her hair. Worse. The only jewelry yielded by further search was a paste pin with a stone missing, and a George McGovern button. She thought of going naked, with her pubic muff in proud curls and a Venus smile on her lips. She liked herself best stripped to the buff, with her hair hanging in a tangle, but it would hardly do to be as honest as all that.

She decided to bum off Nell. She had been vaguely aware of elegance in her clothes and they were both tall. She scurried off like a determined pack rat.

Nell opened the door to her insistent rap.

"Hello. Isn't it too chilly for you to be out without a coat?"

"I'm here to borrow one," Stella said. "And a dress and shoes and lipstick."

Nell grinned and stood aside. "Come in."

Stella loped past her and turned to make a comparison between them. She had bigger tits than Nell, that was immediately apparent, but she could leave buttons open wherever necessary.

"We hardly know each other," she began, "but this is an emergency. You can say no if you like but I'll regard it as very unfriendly if you do."

"Then I won't. What's the occasion?"

"A man is taking me to an expensive dinner. The poor dolt doesn't know how expensive, but that's beside the point. The point is I've got to look human. What do you own that would give me an air?"

"Anything would be an improvement." Nell was tart.

"You pick. I don't really give a damn."

Nell led her to the bedroom. Stella saw at a glance that she had come to the right place. This one had a sense of style. There were flowers on her night table and a silk robe thrown on the bed. The pillow slips had lace and the books were leather-bound. She forgave her the luxury because of the books. There were a lot of them. Nell paused at the closet door.

"I'm not prying," she said, "but just what effect are you after? Girlish, soignée, seductive, horsy? I must say I'm surprised that you're making any effort at all."

"He's rich," Stella confided. "And powerful. He can do me a world of good."

Nell studied her. "It seems out of character."

"Strategy," Stella said. "A glimpse of boobs

204

goes down like candy with all of 'em."

Nell dragged out an armful of clothes and dumped them on the bed.

Stella wriggled out of her dreadful garb in a flash. She wore nothing underneath. Her body was beautiful, strong, as pure as Greek sculpture. Her neck was dirty.

Nell sighed and sank down on the bed. "You do yourself a great disservice," she said. "You're really a pretty woman."

"Balls." Stella snatched up a beige dress and held it under her chin. "Is this a good color for me?"

"No. It makes you sallow. Try the yellow."

Stella found it and pulled it over her head, ripping the seam in her haste.

"Damn, it's too small."

"Try the green, then."

Stella wriggled into a clinging green jersey and settled the folds around her hips. She minced to the mirror and pursed her mouth at the reflection. "I wouldn't burn the topless towers of Ilium, but it isn't bad, is it?" She turned awkwardly to see herself from all sides.

"You look very dishy." Nell leaned on an elbow, amused.

"This, then, and thank you very much. What over it?"

Nell tossed her a white coat. Stella flung it about her shoulders. There was just the suggestion of preening now as beauty triumphed over beast.

"My God," she said staring. "Maybe I'll just stay at home and make love to myself."

Nell took her firmly by the arm and marched her into the bathroom.

"This is soap," she said picking up a scented

bar, "and this," as she turned on the tap, "is water."

"I intended to bathe all along," Stella said sulkily, "since it's an occasion."

"Do."

She thrust a jar into her hands. "Deodorant." She picked up a bottle. "Perfume."

"Sweat is sexual." Stella thrust them both away. "It arouses *me* every time."

"There's no accounting for taste," Nell said. "Sit down and let's see what can be done about your hair."

Fifteen minutes later she had just gotten the snarls out. She tried piling it on Stella's head, tucking it behind her ears and finally decided to draw it back severely to show her noble brow. Stella fidgeted throughout.

"Enough. Enough. I'm far too good for him right now."

The two women returned to the living room, Stella clutching her loot. "There's one other thing."

"Don't hesitate," Nell said dryly.

"A drink. To bring the roses to my cheeks."

Nell selected her second-best Scotch, took a water glass instead of crystal, poured sparingly and handed it to her. Stella flopped on the couch, threw her head back and closed her eyes.

"You're a good sort," she said.

"I want the clothes back," Nell countered, "after you've had them dry-cleaned."

"You shall have them." She opened her eyes again. "I saw the table set for one. Are you between men or off them?"

"Neither. I'm just enjoying an evening alone."

"It can't be easy for you with men. You're intelligent. Proud. Maybe even arrogant."

"How is it with you?"

"Me?" Stella thought it over. "I like a good time in bed. I don't want to be bothered out of it. Men don't like that."

She swallowed her drink in two gulps. "The better friendship is with women. I had a fine friend once in my youth. She had a mind as sharp as an ax. And wit. And character."

"Are you friends still?"

"She died of cancer at twenty-nine. I have all her letters. They're as good as Swift's."

Stella held out her glass. "One more to see me into my bath."

Nell shook her head. "You'll drown in it if I do."

"Yes," said Stella getting to her feet. "I like you. I may take you up."

Nell laughed. "You'll wear out my clothes and drink my booze. I'm not sure I'll allow it."

Stella looked at her shrewdly. "You'll find we have things to say to each other. And in due time, you'll be able to boast of knowing me. I'll be famous. Get in on the ground floor."

"I'll consider it."

Stella started to go and then bethought herself. "Shoes," she cried. "I can't go in these brogues." She held a foot out in front of her.

"You're out of luck. You're at least a size nine. I have small, aristocratic feet."

"Who has boats to fit me, then?"

"Try Jake."

She put her arm through Stella's and urged her

207

out. Stella held back one last time.

"Jesus," she cried, "what if we fall into bed tonight? I haven't a nightdress fit to be seen."

"Glory in thy nakedness," Nell told her and put her out on the doorstep like a reluctant cat.

When Caleb arrived and saw her done up in her borrowed finery he confined himself to an approving nod and muttered, "That's better."

She was a little put-out. She had been quite dazzled by the sight of herself in the sea green dress a dryad might have worn. She thought very well of the way her hair swirled, and her legs seemed to her to be extremely handsome. She had managed to get some shoes from Hortense, and they gave her a swaying walk that was quite Italian and sexy.

She made of their crossing through the gardens to his car a kind of regal progress, putting her nose in the air and holding his arm as if he were a consort. It gave her satisfaction to see Jake poke his head out of his door and take notice of her, and one or two other tenants around the barbecue seemed visibly impressed.

She was even more imperious in the restaurant, following the headwaiter to their table with condescension and hauteur. It had become a kind of amusing game, one she had never played before, and by the time he had ordered her a vermouth cassis (she had wanted Scotch but to no avail) she felt she might well be Queen of all the Russias.

"So money buys all this, does it?" She looked at the white linen and the perfect rose on the table. Then she hitched around in her chair and surveyed her fellow diners. They were a classy lot, no doubt of it.

"Come now," he said peering over the huge

menu. "Don't play-act. There's nothing naive in you at all. If you had been diligent in your work all these years you might will have had all the high life you could handle."

She bristled at that. "I work slowly because what I produce is perfect of its kind." She snuffled and touched her nose with the damask napkin. She had forgotten a hankie. "There's no way I can be hurried. None."

He made no reply to that. He adjusted his glasses to peer at the hand-lettered bill of fare. A waiter had appeared on silent feet and stood by his side with an air of subservience.

Caleb asked his name.

"George, sir."

"Very well, George. Tell me when the sole was caught."

"Today, sir."

"What time?"

The waiter shrugged. "They get it every morning."

"Then we'll have it. And watercress salad dressed with walnut vinegar and oil, haricots verts done no more than three minutes, and I will see the wine list."

"I hate fish," said Stella.

"I am dieting. It would be self-centered of you to gorge in front of me." He tucked his napkin into his waistcoat and looked like a stern Victorian father. Stella downed her aperitif, swigging it like a sailor.

"That's to be sipped," he admonished her.

She sneered at him. "Ah, you're one of those who make a fuss about food and drink. Get it down, get the benefit, and get on to other things is the way I look at it."

"Primitive point of view." He nibbled at a piece

209

of Melba toast, studying her all the while. "I have plans for you," he said, crunching toast. "Good sensible plans."

Stella lifted an eyebrow. "You understand, don't you, that while I look years younger, I'm forty. I have plans of my own."

He beckoned the wine steward. "Batard-Montrachet seventy-one and not too chilled, please." He turned back to her. "Very well, you're forty. You look it, by the way. You've published two slim volumes of verse by an obscure little West Coast company which also turns out party books and map folders. Harold Bloom doesn't know who you are nor does Stephen Spender or anyone else who should. It's my business and has been for thirty years to bring new people to light. That doesn't necessarily mean you will have a wide sale. It does mean critical attention for your work and care in bringing you along. It means notice of you in the *New York Times*. It means judicious advertising and dignified promotion. It means a discerning editor to watch over you and keep you from flagging. Are you listening?"

Stella pushed aside the rose so she could peer at him closely. She did so, leaning her elbows on the table.

"Go on."

"It's obvious that it's recognition you're after. You can have it. You should have it, it's your due. I'll see, to the best of my ability, that you get it."

"Who do I have to kill?" Stella was leery.

"You have to accept a modest advance and commit to a reasonable delivery date. I am fairly lenient about that. I understand you cannot whip your Muse, but I will expect you to drink less and write more. Our books are beautifully designed and printed. If you work hard and in good faith, in no time you will have a cult, your picture in a news magazine, looking untidy, and an inflated sense of your own importance." He patted his mouth with his napkin.

"How *much* money," demanded Stella.

"I'm a fair man. I have a reputation for it. You won't be swindled."

"I've been sucked up to before." She leaned back in her chair and looked at him combatively.

He maintained his calm. "You're not easy to deal with, are you?"

"Yes, I am," she said promptly. "Think of a sum of money to offer me and then double it." She took the dregs of his drink and sipped it with nice restraint.

Caleb folded his arms. "Now see here. I cannot put Midas' gold in your pocket. We do not enrich our Sapphos, our Emily Dickinsons, our Amy Lowells. I would be happier if we did but such is not the case. You must content yourself with a laurel wreath."

Stella flared. "I know your ilk," she trumpeted. "Try paying your plumber one cent less than twenty bucks and hour and see what happens. Try offering your *garage* mechanic a laurel wreath. You'll get a monkey wrench up your ass is what you'll get!"

"You'll get a small advance," he retorted. "Growing smaller by the minute."

"Perhaps I'll get a better offer from someone else." She took on the sharp look of a fishwife haggling over the price of haddock.

"You'll get the best you can command from me," he said shortly.

He watched the waiter with a critical eye as

dinner was ceremoniously served. The fish was laid open, the bony skeleton whisked rapidly aside, steaming butter spooned with care. The waiter lingered as if he would like a taste of the dish himself, but a look from Caleb sent him backward to the kitchen.

They were alone again. Caleb looked at his plate a moment and then pushed it aside.

"You're damned difficult," he said, "and you've spoiled my appetite."

"You need to lose weight," she said. "There's too much of you."

The hint of a smile came into his eyes. "So. You've taken notice of me, have you?"

"You're not easy to miss."

"Stella," he said, "I find you quarrelsome and suspicious and churlish, but your work is splendid. You'd do well to put yourself in my hands."

She looked at the crisply curled fish on her plate. She looked out the window. She looked at the main chance.

"I'll sleep on it," she said.

A bottle of wine was brought in a frosted silver bucket; two glasses were put before them, glacially misted. She perked up considerably at the sight and decided to be charming.

"Are you married?" she asked.

"Widowed. I've been alone five years. I'm a man who likes to be fussed over. I haven't adjusted to solitude."

She conjured up a vision of his wife, a mothering, serving presence. She doubtless embroidered house slippers for him with his monogram emblazoned in red silk and read aloud to him in a high thin voice. She saw her placing a gout stool and offering milk white breasts to his weary head.

It made her chuckle aloud.

"Something amuses you about my bereavement?"

"You're over it," she said. "You wouldn't have that great belly if you weren't."

"She was a sweet woman. Not bright, but very spiritual." His eyes met hers with a sardonic gleam. "And you? Are you involved with anyone?"

"Free as a bird." She rested her chin on her hand.

"I'm sixty years old," he said, frowning at her. "And you're a handful. That's plain to see."

"Well," she taunted, "if your fires are banked, they're banked. There's nothing I can do about that."

He grasped her wrist then, and not lightly either. "Don't prod, my dear," he warned. "This old turtle can still stick his head out of the shell and snap." He let her go and picked up his wineglass, tasted, chewed appreciatively, drank.

"I like a contest of wills. But I like other things more. I like tenderness and good will toward my bed partner. I'd rather dry tears than cause them. I would like someone to understand the autumnal melancholy I sometimes feel in the midst of happiness. I would like someone skillful enough to remind me of my youth. I would find all kinds of ways to show my gratitude."

"I turn on my side and go to sleep," said Stella.

"Perhaps you have—to date."

"Well," said Stella, "we're not going to decide anything here and now."

"That's to come," he said, calling for the check. She sat in nonplused silence all the way home.

Over her protest that she could perfectly well find her way to her own door (hadn't she done it blind drunk a hundred times?), he insisted on seeing her up. She paused halfway up the stairs to remove the shoes which by now pinched the life out of her. She listened, with a certain malicious interest as they climbed, for heavy breathing from him, but he went up like an antelope.

"I won't ask you for coffee," he said, "because you probably don't have an uncracked cup to serve it in."

She thought it over. "You're right. I haven't."

He took her hand and held it in his. "Now then, my dear, think over all I've said. I'm staying at Henry's for a week or so. I'll want your decision before I return east." He patted the hand he held and returned it to her. "Have you your key?"

"I don't lock the door. That's how you got in in the first place."

He clucked disapproval. "You live very recklessly."

She gave him a sly smile. "You don't."

"You're the worse for wine," he said, "and I'm a gentleman." He stroked his jaw and fixed her with a long look. "Give me every credit for restraint. I'm very unsettled, looking at your pretty mouth."

"Talk!" she sniffed.

"When I was a boy," he said soothing her, "I seduced the Irish maid in my father's house. I remember shucking off my clothes on the stairs, so great was my haste. My father found us on the landing, rolling about the floor in transports of youthful high spirits. I remember him coming out of his room with a pince-nez on the bridge of his nose. He had on a Sulka dressing gown. I don't know how long he stood there, but finally he spoke to me. 'Caleb,' he said, 'this is not appropriate.'"

He patted her shoulder. "I think he might have said the same thing now."

He started away and then suddenly turned back. "It occurs to me that you haven't said thank you for the very expensive dinner I bought you."

She shrugged. "I don't bother with formalities."

"It's not your manners I deplore. I'm already aware that you haven't any. It's something else entirely." She did not encourage him to go on; he needed no encouragement. "You must come down from the heights, Stella, and move among us. Admit to a common humanity. It's sometimes humbling, but what of it? It's healthy to be able to say thank you. It's pleasant. It's openhearted. You've been surly too long, I think. *Try* saying it, whether you mean it or not."

"It wasn't even a very good dinner." She showed him the stubborn set of her jaw.

"Come, come." He urged her like a recalcitrant child. "You smiled during the meal. You may even have laughed. Yes, I think you definitely laughed. I remember admiring the whiteness and the evenness of your teeth. You enjoyed yourself, admit it."

"I don't deny it"—she flounced—"but I don't intend to make a fuss about it either."

"Stella, Stella," he said, "you mean to win the war, but you've lost the battle. You're almost smiling now."

"Oh, hell . . . if you're going to go on and on about it. Thank you for the dinner." It was begrudged all the way.

"A crack in the dike," he said, and he beamed at

215

her. "I'm pleased."

She sulked. "What's Henry's number if I want to talk some more?"

"He's a modest man. You'll find him in the book."

The look in his eyes could not be read in the dark. He stood there as if he had all the time in the world and wanted it spent near her. A night bird sang. Someone in the apartment above slammed a door. Diana Ross, on a record, sang of disappointed love.

"I imagine," he said, "that you sleep on your back, with your arms flung above your head."

Stella pulled the pins that held her hair. It fell about her shoulders. She was tired of being done up.

"Either come in or go home," she told him.

He merely smiled and turned, moving away through the dark, his footsteps heavy and measured on the creaking wooden steps. She went to lean over the balcony to watch him.

"Look where you're going," she called, "or you'll end up head over ass in the swimming pool."

He looked up at her, a corpulent Romeo to her raddled Juliet. "I can see very well in the dark." He waved and was gone.

Stella woke before dawn to think him over. She got up, padded into the kitchen to fill a wineglass and brought it back to bed, hoping its fumes would open her eyes and clear her mind. The cat occupied the warm hollow she had left. She tossed it out and settled in with the blankets drawn to her chin. She didn't particularly like what she was feeling. Her encounter with Caleb was like a mote in her eye she was unable to blink away.

The cat came back and tried to make friends. It purred against her breast.

"Scat," she said. "I don't intend to settle for *you*." She sipped the wine, but it tasted cheap and raw on her tongue. At her age she had to do better. She put it aside and watched the dawn lighten the wall opposite her. Somewhere in her mind was a hazy catalogue of men. They were shadow figures, one notable for his red suspenders and the bandana he wore to bed, another for the sea chanties he sang in her ear, a third who was blind and felt his way with wicked fingers. She realized now that she had never really spoken to any of them. Indeed, she had wanted it that way. She valued her mind over her body. She had never shared her thoughts.

She picked up the phone and aroused Henry's entire household.

"My God, Stella, it's five o'clock in the morning. Caleb is fast asleep and so was I." Henry was definitely cross.

"Then you're missing the best part of the day. Let me talk to him."

"This is outrageous."

"Put him on."

She heard cursing and stumbling away. Then Caleb was on the line.

"I don't see you as a madcap, Stella," he said coldly.

"What are you doing today?" she queried, thoroughly unchastened.

"I am going to visit my mother in San Diego." His tone was even shorter.

"I'll go along. I like the drive by the ocean."

"She is ninety years old. You're too much for

her. You're too much for me. I'm standing here in my bare feet. I'm chilled to the bone. I'm annoyed, Stella."

It was a long drive, she thought, holding the phone away from her. At the end of it she would know more.

"Sleep is death," she said. "Pick me up at nine." She hung up before he could reply.

Her back ached. Bed became intolerable. She dragged on her old Japanese kimono and headed for the sauna. She used it more than any other tenant in the building, but then no other tenant had so much sauce to sweat out of his system.

Steam rose over the warm pools. The early morning light had a pearly sheen. Water stood in the cups of the hibiscus blossoms and rusted the frames of the deck-side chairs. The frond of a palm tree crackled dryly in a small lifting wind. She padded on, enjoying the damp concrete underfoot. She had obstinately waded in puddles as a child.

Jake was naked in the sauna, stretched out with his eyes closed. A towel had twisted off his body and lay on the floor. Stella stood in the doorway and looked. She envied him his taut flat belly and his handsome feet with their straight toes. Hers had bunions. Yes, everything about him was nicely made and placed. Very nicely.

"Jesus." He saw her and sat up. "This place belongs to the men from six to nine-thirty. What the hell are you doing up at this hour, anyway?"

"I've come to get rid of the poison." She sat on the bench next to him in a companionable, confiding way. He hitched over to make room.

"The way you keep staring at it," he said, "I'm afraid it'll fall off." Then he grinned, picked up the

218

towel and knotted it around his waist. "Well," he said to her, "as long as you're here, stay."

"Ach, my mind's a thousand miles away." She sat back and listened to the hissing of the steam.

"Who was your fat friend last night?" He closed his eyes again. She told him only the facts, reserving the feelings for herself. He knew Stella of old. He let her hide them.

"If anything comes of it," he warned her lazily, "you have to start paying rent."

They were silent for a while, enjoying the opening of their pores and the lassitude the heat induced. She wondered if she should discuss Caleb with Jake. She knew he had had a long career of amorous adventure; what could he tell her about running before the wind without peril, what of crossing the finish line first, with pennants flying?

"Jake?"

"Hmmmm?"

She thought better of it and backed away.

"Nothing. Never mind."

In the long run she knew she would submit to no opinion but her own, anyway.

And what did she think of this other one, this great galumphing bear of a man with his Brahmin mind and his sonorous piss-elegant voice? There was sex in it somewhere. She had felt her hackles rise like a cat approached by a tom. She had felt an odd familiar tingle in the tip of her nose which always occurred when she was horny. And she had speculated boldly about him. Did the gallantry drop away when he lowered his well-tailored English trousers? Did he know a string of obscenities of Elizabethan roundness and rarity? Did he, looking into the last quarter of his life, lash himself to perform mightily—or did he rest on garnered laurels?

Another thought nagged. Did he mean to pack her into a new and unfamiliar mold and turn her out, altered, for the worse?

She recalled disturbing words: discipline, sobriety, responsibility. She balked at each and every one. There was some kind of bargain he meant to drive with her, she knew it. Well, he'd have to get up early in the morning to best her. She hadn't made her way this far, penniless and just slipping past her prime, without knowing her way around.

"Open your eyes and look at me," she told Jake.

He opened one.

"Would you say, my age and condition taken into account, that I'm attractive? Think of me, mind, tarted up and reeking of perfume. Holding my blue-veined breasts in my hands and lifting them toward you." She turned her beet red face toward him as if he were Paris at his judgment of Beauty.

He was prompt in his reply and not very flattering. "I've seen better. I've seen worse."

"I agree. But tell me plainly. Would you throw me out of your bed? Would you invite me in in the first place?"

He scratched the furry patch on his chest and reflected.

"We'd never even come close. I don't know whether that's because I've known you for ten years without laying a hand on you or because you're a rummy."

He leaned over and patted her flank. "I'd have to proceed platonically with you, sweetheart. No hard feelings."

"I couldn't seduce you under any circumstances whatsoever?" She pressed him like a shyster lawyer cross-examing.

"Jesus, Stella, what's with you?"

"Yes or no?"

"No." He wiped his brow. "No," he said again.

"Fair enough."

He was cross. "You want to open a can of peas?... Okay, I'll open it. I'll tell you what isn't attractive, Stella. What isn't attractive is the way you corner a man. It wouldn't kill you if you came in at an angle once in a while. Everything with you is head on."

"Why are you uncomfortable?"

"Because I love you," he said grumpily, "and I don't like this conversation a helluva lot."

He was right, of course. It wasn't necessary to be graded like a prize heifer for the soundness of her carcass, the size of her udders, the tonality of her "moo." She knew who she was. She always had.

He tried to make amends.

"Come take a shower with me. I'll wash your back."

"No, the booze in me is only half boiled away."

He lingered. "Stella," he said.

"Yes."

He grinned. "If I was alone on a desert island. Okay?"

"Better than nothing," she retorted, and turned her back to him.

Caleb had borrowed Henry's beautifully kept Lincoln Continental and had transformed it into a Dutch still life with gifts for his mother. A garden rake stuck out the back window, a flat of yellow pansies bloomed like scraps of bright yellow velvet and a bag of potting mix evoked deep woods, moss and harvest.

Beside him on the front seat was a brown paper bag neatly rolled down to reveal a dozen green pippin apples still dewed with water, ready for crunching should his impatient appetite overtake him.

The attire of the bon vivant had been replaced as well. He wore an elegant but faded shirt open at the collar and a hat of ancient vintage, battered, stained and utterly rakish.

Stella, in her shabby gray sweater, looked like a tramp he had obliged with a ride. She too wore a hat, black, squashed and tugged over one eye, giving her a sinister look that, together with dark glasses and a drooping cigarette, might well have led to her arrest had she been standing on a street corner.

He handed her into the front seat and she caught a pleasant whiff of soap and shaving lotion. He was obviously a man who tended himself with care. He had a morning freshness of manner as well, energetic and confident.

"Now, then," he began, snapping her seat belt for her, "I drive very fast but very skillfully. I would appreciate it if you did not squeal or call out warnings or jam your feet into the floorboard. I have been driving for forty years without a single unpleasant incident of any kind." He settled himself comfortably behind the wheel. "I will say further that I'm as nice as pie about stopping for calls of nature. No problem there. However I will not stop at souvenir stands or antique shops. My late wife was addicted to them and I vowed on her death never to indulge another woman in that way."

"You talk a lot in the morning, I see," Stella said, rolling down her window.

"My dear," he said, swinging the car into the traffic without looking, "at my age I feel the need to get it all said." He narrowly missed a boy on a motorbike and had a rude remark shouted at him for his trouble.

He tore onto the freeway and from that moment Stella began to review her life like a drowning woman coming to the end of it.

It was a ride of such surpassing recklessness that it became almost exhilarating. They sped along as if pursued by the hounds of Hell. Caleb loved the horn and used it with gusto. A matron, patting her bouffant hairdo and idling along, was raucously honked out of their path. A diesel truck was beep-beeped into the slow lane with an arrogant crescendo. He blasted out warnings to Greyhound buses and Winnebagos. Stella reasoned that since the landscape consisted mostly of mean little housing tracts and shopping centers it was just as well to have it all skim by in a blur. When she spotted a black and white highway patrol car she held her tongue. Since they were not dead amid strewn wreckage it was obvious that Caleb was the darling of the gods. They would certainly not be arrested for mere speeding. They were not.

Caleb further narrowed the odds by turning away and digging into the bag beside him for an apple. He offered one to her. The wind rushed through the car and tore the hat from her head. It sailed away out the window and was lost.

"That's my best hat!" she protested wrathfully. She had often flung it over garden walls, but to lose it like this was another matter.

"Unbecoming," he replied, maneuvering the car into a space almost too narrow for it.

"I expect you to pay for it!" She was shrieking now over the din, the wind, the honking, the traffic.

"Certainly."

Stella began to feel cheerful. She had discovered nerves of steel on this harrowing journey, unaided by even one nip or tipple. The smell of oil and exhaust and hot pavement bothered her not at all. She loosened her collar and rolled up her sleeves, admiring the delicate tracery of her veins. She thought of flinging all her clothes out the window and riding Highway 5 like a soaring bird in the company of the eagle who was Caleb. Perhaps there was something aphrodisiac in jouncing along like this. The warm sun spilled in on her and confirmed it. Yes, she would like to pull off the road and take another kind of ride, astride the man next to her.

A boy and girl passed them in a car painted with a fiery streak along its side. The girl nuzzled into the boy's shoulder; his hand cupped her breast, proving with bravado that he could do two things at once. They were indifferent to the whole world. Stella turned around to stare and met the boy's sleepy look. He made a kissing motion into the air which she took to be directed at her. She waved back jauntily. Caleb accelerated and left them behind too. She regarded him with possessive eyes, but he looked straight ahead, munching one apple after another. She made a humble pleasure out of watching. Such gusto. Such concentration.

"Let's turn off and ride by the ocean." He snapped his directional signal too late and was grazed by an enormous van. They rocked down the off ramp and came into the quiet of the road by the sea.

She offered mild praise. "Well. We got off alive."

"Churlish drivers in this state. Shameful."

The sea was a spoiled blue, dulled by kelp and oil spill, but there were sailboats with immaculate sails and fields of tomatoes showing red and green on the palisades overlooking the water's edge.

The contest appeared to be over. Caleb slowed down and pronounced the landscape very pretty indeed.

"Stop," Stella commanded. "I have to go into the bushes."

He complied with alacrity, skidding fifty feet or so to the brink of a ditch. He came around and opened the door for her and promised to turn his back until she called out.

It was a ruse. Stella had the kidneys of a camel. She walked off into a grassy meadow, waited a suitable length of time and then sat down, searching warily for poison oak before she did so.

"Come out here. You can see a fisherman on the beach."

He walked briskly toward her, as if stubble and rock were his native habitat. She noted that big men often move with grace. He surveyed the scene like a Spanish explorer coveting the sweep of land before him.

"Splendid," he said. "Really splendid." He remained standing over her.

Stella showed herself to advantage. She lay back, clasping her arms behind her head, displaying aggressive breasts and availability with one and the same gesture. She knew her eyes darkened with desire. She opened them wide so that he might see. She was, she thought smugly, an odalisque—overlooking, of course, the soup stain on her skirt and the hole in her stocking.

"Ah," she murmured, looking up at him. The little sigh promised pliability and yielding. It got her exactly nowhere.

"Stella," he said with instant comprehension of her purpose, "copulation in the grass at our age is out of the question. In the first place, there are ants. They are crawling on your skirt this very moment. In the second place, I require bedsprings to assist my weight. In the third place, I am expected to breakfast at my mother's house and she mustn't be kept waiting. Lastly"—he held out a hand to pull her up—"there are two small boys standing on the ridge behind us, waiting to see a comic turn. I can't speak for you, but as for me, I cannot make love to laughter."

She snapped her head around and saw the audience, sly-faced and watchful. She put her finger in her mouth, pulled and produced a horrendous grimace. The children fled. She scrambled up.

"I know a cheap motel near San Diego," she said.

"Why cheap? I'm rich."

"It's what I'm used to." She walked ahead and seated herself in the car again. He got in on his side but left the key unturned in the ignition.

When he spoke it was calmly. "It's childish to rub my nose into it," he said. "When we do have a night, and we will, I think we owe ourselves every comfort. The comfort of clean linen and tender beginnings. Whatever is used in your life you can keep to yourself. I'll do the same. I look forward to it," he added and started the car.

They drove for half an hour or more in total silence. When he spoke again it was to brief her on the coming visit.

"My mother is a socialist," he told her as they drove down a shabby side street, searching for her house. "She voted for Eugene Debs and insisted that my father do the same. She was arrested in Selma at the age of eighty, not only for marching for civil rights but also because she bit a piece out of a policeman's ear. My father adored her but died young from the strain of living with her. She had too many opinions for a harmonious married life. She is the reason I married a timid soul, as far a departure from her as possible, a mistake I will not make again."

He slammed on the brakes. They had stopped before a white frame house of no distinction, standing in a garden which redeemed it in a flurry of roses and blossoming lemon trees. A shutter had torn loose and sagged beside a window. A broken cane chair furnished the porch. A green and yellow parrot squawked invective in a cage: "Fuck you, fuck you." His mother made an appearance in the doorway, a tiny woman, old but unwasted, the size of a child but invincible.

His face lit up at the sight of her. "She has lost her glasses," he said, almost to himself. "She probably sat on them. Mother!" he called and rushed from the car to embrace her, leaving Stella to manage for herself.

She saw him swing the woman from the ground and waltz her down the path, causing her to cry out sharply and demand to be put down instantly. He gave her a final approving shake and a smacking kiss that appeared to rock her off her feet. She pushed him away and peered toward Stella. The car was too far distant to satisfy her curiosity. She tottered toward it with remarkable speed.

"Come out," she called, and Stella obeyed. The woman thrust out her hand and shook Stella's with enthusiasm.

"I'm glad you've come," she began. "I have much to say to you. Before anything else I wish to tell you I consider you an extraordinary writer. Radical. Militant. Angry. Everything any woman of sense would be. Come in and have coffee."

The inside of the cottage spoke of a persevering spirit. The oak kitchen table had been scrubbed to whiteness by an energetic hand and the worn pink and gray linoleum had been mopped and waxed diligently. The kitchen towels, hand-embroidered with cheerful maxims, were all folded the same way and hung neatly to boot.

The stove top was clean. One would look in vain for a spatter of grease lurking in the burners. The chipped kitchen tile had been tended by a battered toothbrush standing in a glass; the counter had been given the gleam of well-cared-for dentures.

Stella was blind to her own surroundings but eagle-eyed in her observation of others'. She took in the beauty of the lily blooming in a jelly jar. She saw the sweet potato sending forth its pretty shoot of green in a cracked majolica pitcher of swirling brown and yellow. She sensed, in the faint lingering smell of cinnamon and nutmeg and mace, that Christmas cakes had been baked here, wrapped in fine white linen napkins and offered as

228

gifts. Tea had been brewed here as well, probably strong to bitterness and sipped in the deep silence of early morning. Smiles had been offered in these rooms, and courtesy, and certainly the grocery boy or the day maid had gone home feeling subtly cheered, though they may not have known why. She was pleased by the sight of a violin and a music rack with a score spread open upon it. She saw a deck of cards laid out in a game of solitaire, family pictures in silver frames, a dog dish on the floor, bottles of French wine and, astonishingly, a clay pipe packed and ready to smoke on a table. She saw, sitting opposite her, a kindred spirit.

"The scones are just out of the oven. There's real butter. I hate margarine, I don't give a damn what they say about it. There's jam—those berries are from my garden. I'm full of thorns from picking them. There are no eggs. I'm allergic to them."

Caleb took his place after holding the chairs for both of them. The old lady ate heartily, nodding her head as if she were in accord with her own light hand with pastry and the excellence of her coffee. She dispensed the food lavishly, and when they were served she treated them to a show of emotion which was equally ample.

"I'm glad you came," she said briskly. "I've been lonelier than usual lately. I've taken to talking to myself and the dog and I find that disturbing. I was going to call you long-distance to find me the services of a good young analyst at the college here. I don't want to drift into senility just because there's no one interesting to talk to."

"Bosh," said Caleb. "You don't want a companion, you only want ears. Ears to fill up with your political palaver and what-have-you." He buttered his scone heavily, defying his arteries.

His mother turned to Stella. "Men are dense," she said. "He doesn't understand that old age is exile. Exile from ferment and creativity and sex and anything else that counts for much. You agree?"

"I'm not old," said Stella, "but I'm willing to be warned."

"Sensible. I knew you were sensible. I said so."

Caleb beamed at his plate, letting them decide between them what life was all about. He took a kind of harem pleasure in the empathy he felt between them; it made for a pleasant meal and good digestion following. Mrs. Crown left him to himself while she talked on.

"I want to speak of your work," she said to Stella.

Stella took this as her due and leaned back in her chair, ready to be praised.

"There are black holes in space," said Mrs. Crown. "Your poems look into them. I won't read them at night because they disturb my sleep. But I enjoy being terrified by day. At my time of life nothing is worth reading that doesn't send a chill down your spine. He," she said, indicating her son, "is a romantic. He likes books with happy endings. Like his father. His father," she added with a dry smile, "was an indulgence of mine. I should have married a labor organizer."

Caleb rose and patted her white head. "I'm going outside to put up chicken wire around your vegetable garden. The rabbits eat better than you do. Perhaps you'll be kind enough"—this last to Stella—"to dry the dishes for her. She makes me do it as a rule and I don't enjoy it."

He turned sideways to squeeze through the narrow kitchen doorway and went off whistling.

"Where did you get my book?" Stella queried. "Were there a lot of them on sale? Was it marked down?"

Mrs. Crown took her measure. "I won't lie to you. I bought it for twenty-five cents. You went unsold, you see. You were on the remainder shelf. Booksellers are quite ruthless."

Stella shrugged.

"No," Mrs. Crown said emphatically, "you mustn't let it go. You have to demand. Demand of yourself. Demand of others. When you get where I am all you can do is assent."

She rose, gathering up the dishes with the careless ease of a carhop, and stacked them in the sink.

"You've just met Caleb?"

"This week."

"What do you make of him."

"Nothing yet. Well..." She hesitated.

"You'd like to sleep with him. Almost all women want to. It's odd... he's gotten quite pudgy in the last few years. Perhaps it's nostalgia. Women see him as a great kewpie doll. He isn't."

"I never played with dolls," said Stella. "Tell me, what can I expect from him?"

"Almost anything you want, providing you don't wheedle. He takes positions on principle. His own are very high. He was charming to his wife. He's not ashamed of sentiment. You mustn't hector him or cheat him or he'll toss you down the stairs on your bum. I'm pleased he's my son. What else can I tell you?"

"How can I get him in bed?" Stella said, licking

the jam spoon.

"How should I know? We're not oedipal in this family."

She tossed Stella a towel. "Do dry these. I hate having dishes stand about in a rack."

Stella did as she was told, lazily dabbing at plates and cups as if she didn't know how. They worked side by side. Through the window Caleb could be seen bending and stooping at his work. The garden was laid out in neat rows of lettuce and beans and a flower thrust here and there for frivolity. He might have been a figure from an illustrated book of hours, a peaceful big-bellied peasant. He paused to wipe his forehead on a monogrammed Irish linen handkerchief. The peasant image vanished. He called to them. "Come sit outside. I'd like company."

The two women went out of the house and arranged themselves on the wooden back steps. Mrs. Crown steadied herself with a fine dry hand laid on Stella shoulder. When they were seated Stella had a strange urge to lay her head in Mrs. Crown's blue cotton lap. It was a fleeting moment. She had not been a loving child, but somewhere there was a remembered caress she sought again.

She sat up straight instead and stared ahead of her. She refused to be lulled into bathos by the sight of an old lady taking the sun. Next it would be priests or shrinks.

"I'd like a glass of wine if you have such a thing," she said.

"Oh," said Mrs. Crown, "so that's the way it is."

Obligingly she scurried into the house after Stella's drink. She was out again in a moment, brandishing a handsome green bottle and a glass.

Caleb's sensitive ears caught the pop of the cork. He paused, raised both a hoe and his voice.

"No, no, no, none of that!" he called. He lumbered to the porch, shaking his head. "The sun is out, things are growing, we are here to enjoy nature. If you wish to drink, bend over the garden hose. Meanwhile, come out into the patch and work up a sweat."

Stella's eyes fastened on the bottle as Mrs. Crown held it uncertainly, wavering between hospitality and doubt.

Finally she set it down. "I'll give it to you with lunch." She was conspiratorial in her tone.

Caleb leaned down to Stella and pulled her upright. "You have the pallor of prison." He grasped her face and turned it to the sun. "I like dark, gypsyish women. Let's turn you into one." She was trundled down the garden path and a rake was thrust into her hands. She dug her heels into the dirt like a mule and glowered at him.

"What kind of goddamn silliness is this?" she snapped.

"Sunshine and exercise are healthy for you. I am preserving you for posterity."

"You want a peon to clean up your mess. That's what you want."

He paid no attention and shoved her along the row of runner beans. "Look at you, woman," he said. "Here is a world of good smells and birdsong, tender buds and green shoots. Try to be in harmony with it. And rake thoroughly, there are snails."

"I thought you were a city man or I would never have come with you." Stella made wild swipes with the rake, destroying everything in her path.

233

He crouched ahead of her, weeding with quick sure hands.

"Submit nicely," he told her. "Give yourself to it, and I will take you wading in the ocean. I will make ham sandwiches with sharp mustard and we'll have pears and cookies and all the wine you can drink."

"I have to go to the bathroom." She was as stubborn as a child in her determination to outwit him.

"You don't. You went on the road."

"I feel faint."

"Flop backwards, then; the earth is nicely turned behind you." She swung the rake around her like an armed samurai, decapitating a dahlia as she did so. He let her fulminate while he examined a ladybug in the palm of his hand.

"These are said to be lucky. Shall I give it to you?"

She turned an angry back to him. He came close, all gentleness. The little insect was carefully deposited on her shoulder. "Make a wish," he said.

She rounded on him. "Very well. I want a boilermaker. Right now. *That's* my wish."

He was despotic but kind. "Finish the row, Stella, and I'll let you off."

Something in his manner, a kind of paternal tolerance, deflated her. She felt foolish. She gathered together a little mound of snails. Then another. Not one escaped her. She began to enjoy it, to anticipate her reward. She even bent double to search under the leaves. Death to the intruders!

"I've got the little buggers," she called triumphantly. A bee stung her.

"Goddamn sonofabitch!" she howled, jumping

on one foot, then on another. "Look what you've done now. I'm poisoned."

He pulled her hair up and examined the mark. Then he moistened his finger with saliva and applied it. "Stand still. You're not Cleopatra. It's not an asp. You'll live."

She wrenched free of him and marched toward Mrs. Crown, whose face was pursed with sympathy. The old woman put an arm around Stella and led her into the house, making motherly noises about men and what eternal fools they were.

Stella had two drinks for her trouble and was on her third when Caleb came in from the garden. His mother stood holding a bottle of Scotch, warding him off. "Don't say a word," she cautioned.

"I'd like some of that myself. In a glass. With ice." He went to the sink to wash the garden loam from his hands while Stella moaned behind him. "You're a big baby," he said.

"No, you are," his mother corrected him sharply. "This woman has heard the music of the spheres. And you have her pulling weeds. It's ridiculous."

"Listen to your mother," said Stella, feeling somewhat better for the drink. "Always listen to your mother."

He smiled on them both and laid out plans. They would all go to the beach. He would, if he could still fit into them, wear the bathing trunks of other years. His mother would take her umbrella and a blanket and he would make a splendid lunch. If they found a secluded spot Stella was to pin her skirts up and join him in the water. He would lave her neck with some. The salt would sooth the sting she suffered and cheerfulness would prevail. He

235

was already rummaging in the refrigerator. They were swept into compliance.

Mrs. Crown's sun hat had been fashionable in nineteen twenty-six. It had been refurbished some years ago with a ten-cent store rose. Sitting upright, presenting her patrician profile to the sea, she recalled Renoir and summer days lost in time. Beside her a picnic basket made the air odorous with garlic and cheese and fresh-pulled scallions from the garden. A rain-stained volume of Eliot lay open in her lap. She was sleeping, overcome by the sounding sea and the finger of sun which had found her under the pink umbrella.

In the water Caleb breasted the waves, thrashing and ducking, rolling and snorting like a playful dolphin. His gray hair curled tightly against his head; the gray patch on his chest matted. He became a Triton roaring at the sea and sky in a delirium of pleasure.

"Good, good!" he shouted to Stella. She stood at the water's edge, her skirt clasped gingerly in her hands, suffering the waves to lap her toes.

"Ugh," she said.

A jellyfish tumbled through the shallows and lay at her feet, a translucent blob shifting this way and that, a pale relic of life. She discredited its simple beauty and that of the trees cresting the hills and even the shattered remains of the ivory-covered shells on which she stood. Either nature or the morning Scotch was giving her heartburn.

"Ho!" cried Caleb. Now he rode the foamy crest of a wave, tumbling through it like a sea beast, showing his teeth and flailing his arms, battling the rush of water.

Stella regarded the bluish chill of her flesh and said nothing. He thrashed toward her. In his vigor he seemed to loom over everything in sight. He exhaled power.

"Glorious, glorious," he cried. "Isn't it glorious, Stella!"

Stella lifted one foot like a wounded crane. "I'm turning to ice," she said coldly.

Suddenly, wordlessly, he snatched her up and bore her out to sea. She gasped as her clothes were drenched through and through and gasped again as they submerged into a roaring green world. It was a whirling vortex of light and dark, air and choked breath, struggle and surrender. Wind or song or blood beat in her ears. They rolled over and over, clasped together in a mating of contortions and outcries. Good Christ, he was out of his trunks and into her in one writhing motion as the sea tossed them up and down. Her legs straddled his waist, barely meeting behind his girth. Fluids of all sorts became her element. She was alive. She was dying. She was filled to the brim and emptied. She clung like a child, a woman, a whore. Finally, he cradled her in his arms, made feather light by the buoyancy surrounding them. They rocked in the deep like two survivors of a shipwreck delighted with life.

"I surprise myself," he said, and kissed her throat.

"God Almighty," she cried out. "I feel tuned like a fiddle."

They came softly to the side of Mrs. Crown, whose hat now dipped over her eyes. She slept on, oblivious of them as they lay side by side on the sand. They might have been medieval tomb figures, so still were they, so joined.

Stella stared up into the empty bowl of the sky and wondered at herself. Her mind slept, she was all feeling. Could the rotund man next to her have caused this strange unsettling afterglow that left her as limp as a stroked cat? Could he have imposed himself between her and her certainty in one damp encounter? If so, she did not know herself. And if that was true it needed looking into. It was permissible to lose her purse or her bus ticket but certainly not herself.

The afternoon passed. Daylight fought dusk with streaks of pink and orange and blue. A somber edge of gray lowered the temperature and chilled the sand. A man came onto the beach with a rod and a line to cast into the darkening sea. He set a folding chair down with care, then a galvanized bucket, and stood with his hands on his hips, staring at the ocean, as if he at last commanded something worth having.

Mrs. Crown stirred and awoke. Caleb opened his eyes. Salt had dried his skin. He looked as if he had been altered in the water into some encrusted creature of the deep. Civilization had not produced him. Tiny fish had flipped gossamer fins and slid past him, staring into his eyes. He had risen out of waving sea grass; he had surfaced through streaming bubbles, bearing a conch shell aloft.

"We'll all be stiff as boards in the morning," he said, coming with a groan to his feet. "Let us head for liniment and hot baths."

He gathered them up, blanket, basket, umbrella, and shooed them to the car. Stella trailed after him in silence. She felt herself in the presence of myths. Would she freeze into a Daphne Laureola and twist

238

roots into the ground, while an amorous god snatched a last embrace? Would she be impaled on Neptune's fork and be waved as a trophy above his hoary head? She sneezed violently. She would catch cold! She hurried after him.

No one seemed hungry. Mrs. Crown turned on the kitchen light and heated canned tomato soup, which they sipped from mugs, sitting around the table. Stella's damp clothes had been hung on the wash line outside to dry. She wore an old dressing gown of Mrs. Crown's, a dainty Edwardian garment of ecru lace and faded silk. It gave her an unbuttoned, languorous air, as though she had just stumbled from bed and dreams of unbridled sensuality.

"I think I'll play the violin," said Mrs. Crown. No one disputed her. She went to the music stand and dragged it close, so she could see without searching for her glasses.

She played Mozart with labored sweetness, closing her eyes and trembling to the music like a reed in the wind. A moth flew in the window and beat around her head, as if her white hair were a flower it could not resist. In the middle, she stopped.

"I'm tired," she said.

Caleb scraped back his chair. "Into bed with you."

She dropped the bow. It had become too heavy to hold. "Leave the cups; I'll wash them tomorrow. Come back sometime." She threw the invitation at Stella. "I like you."

Her son came forward to embrace her. He wrapped her in his arms until she almost disappeared from view. Stella saw her white thin hand on his wide back, patting him as if he were an overgrown baby hanging over her shoulder.

"Send me books and candy," she ordered him. "Be happy."

He would not let her go. He showered warnings and admonitions on her. "Lock your door. Don't leave the iron plugged in. Put the rubber pad in your bathtub before you step in. Don't smoke your pipe in bed. I love you."

"Yes, yes, yes, yes," she said, and looked imploringly at Stella. "Take him away." She yawned widely, rudely.

"We're going." Caleb motioned to Stella.

"Your dressing gown." Stella began to peel out of it.

"Keep it. Put your sweater over it in case you're arrested for speeding. I'll iron your clothes and send them to you, although they really belong in the ash can."

Stella was reckless. "Throw them out." She wanted to say more. "You have style," she told the old woman, and that was as far as she went by way of thanks.

They walked slowly through the garden. Caleb seemed reluctant to go. He glanced over his shoulder, and when the light went out he sighed audibly. Night jasmine bloomed richly on the night air. He tore a leaf from a plant, crushed it, sniffed his fingers. He wished to take something tangible from the place. The life inside the house was painfully ephemeral. He sought Stella's hand.

"She's very old," he said.

Stella did not know how to comfort. "She'll outlast both of us."

240

"My resources come from her. I'm not ashamed to say it."

"I get along on my own," Stella said, stung with unworthy jealousy.

He put a heavy arm around her shoulders. "That is over," he said.

Stella huddled on her own side of the car, erecting a wall of silence behind which she examined the day. He drove at a terrible clip and now she wanted to call out and implore him not to cut her off in a tangle of blood and crumpled steel from the satisfaction she meant to have out of him. Or would it be better to be snuffed out and never have to weigh the price of surrender, because that was the pill to be swallowed. Nothing less would do. Surrender.

"Stop at the first motel," she said suddenly.

"Are you tired?"

"No," she said. "I want to see if it was a fluke."

8

NELL'S OWN PHYSICIAN was named Douglas
Stuart Colin MacFarland, and each and every
name appeared sprawled in a bold legible hand on
his prescriptions. He was a friend of her grandfather's and had looked after her in his dour
Scottish way from her twelfth birthday on. He had
told her about menstruation and about sex with
great clarity and no nonsense, sitting on the edge
of her bed with his large hands clasped in his lap.
She was not to be frightened, he told her, about
blood or about men. Nature's plan included both
and nature was sensible and often beautiful. When
she was ill she quite looked forward to his coming,
hanging out the second-story window, searching
the street for his battered car. He would roll up,
waving a greeting to her, while his radiator boiled

over, leaving a dark stain on the drive. He timed his visits so he could have breakfast in the kitchen and quarrel vociferously with her grandfather about gardening and man's fate, manure and manners. Often, when she lay flushed with fever, she had been forced to wait till they settled a question between them, and if he lost a point he would storm into her room with a black face and lecture her on clear thinking while he thumped her chest and peered down her throat. On those occasions sticky bottles would emerge from his worn leather bag and malodorous doses would be poured into a monogrammed soup spoon and thrust into her gagging mouth.

There had been hot summer afternoons when he felt lazy. Then he would draw up her dainty wicker chair and arrange himself in it and keep her wide-eyed and headachy as he told her that for a skinny stick of a girl, she had a good mind and should put it to use. He had no children of his own and so it was that he fastened himself on her. If she excelled she was in favor. If she failed he relegated her to an early marriage and drudgery and mediocrity.

When she was fifteen and told him she was going to be a doctor, he gave her a twenty-dollar gold piece, which he considered magnanimous and overly indulgent, but he was pleased and moved to be generous. Her grandfather shared her grudgingly with him only because he had seen her safely through diphtheria, measles and hives brought on by sexual frustration before she took her first lover.

Now he was approaching his seventy-fifth birthday like a rampaging bull, energetic, angry and not to be trifled with. He saw his practice in the front rooms of his home, a plain frame house in Santa Monica. The smell of oatmeal porridge hung over his consulting room like wet flannel. His bookshelves were jammed to overflowing with tattered volumes of Robert Burns and Milton and Victorian novels of obscure authorship. There were no medical texts. His memory was a matter of pride with him. All he needed to know about medicine was recorded in his head somewhere between lyric poems and Gothic romances. A rubber plant with engorged leaves grew to horrendous proportions in the corner of the room, dust settling over it in a ghostly gray film. The temperature was kept well below sixty degrees, causing patients to shiver with chill as well as fear at his pronouncements. He had been born to a cold climate and believed in its efficacy. Sunshine spoke of Paradise—in his view, there was no such thing. Hell, by all means.

Nell had come to him for her annual physical. She dressed in the large tiled bathroom, wondering what the doctor looked like afloat in the claw-footed tub, lying on his back. She noted a long-handled brush and a cake of yellow soap. There was no sybaritic lingering here. Doubtless he dug into his ears and scrubbed his toes, searching out lurking dirt like a zealot. Amused by her own curiosity she slid open a drawer. There was nothing in it but a comb and a jar of liniment.

"What are you doing in there?" His voice was impatient. "I wish to speak to you in here with your clothes on. You can primp later. Come out."

She hesitated, hearing a familiar note. It was the voice he had used in her girlhood to tell her she had an inflamed ovary, an abscessed tooth, a deep cut. It was the voice of anxiety.

She paused to use her lipstick, hating the feeling of it caked on her stiff mouth. She wiped it away and saw that her hand was shaking slightly.

"Well, woman?"

"Keep your shirt on. I have to use the toilet."

She stood in the middle of the bathroom, the white tile glaring all around her. She remembered now a strange scowl on his face, a frown which brought his heavy brows together and made him look like a prophet of doom. Where in the examination? Her mind raced back. She remembered how his hands passed over her, paused, moved again.

She opened the door.

"Take a chair." He waved her toward one and waited only long enough for her to settle into it.

"You've got a lump in your right breast," he said bluntly. "It has no business being there. How you missed it yourself I'll never know. Surely you caution your patients to examine themselves monthly. You're careless. Negligent. Stupid." He paused, agitated. "I want you in the hospital tonight. Saint Joseph's. I'm not a Catholic, but the nuns there are used to my ways and don't speak back to me. I'll do a biopsy first thing in the morning and if it's malignant I'll want to operate right then and there. You're a doctor. I needn't mince words." He pulled off his glasses and closed his eyes. "I don't suppose you go to church," he said.

"It appears to be too late now," she answered.

He rose to his feet and clumped back and forth across the room. His shoes were stout and worn, the shoes of a workingman. He bought them in the

Army and Navy Store and wore them till they cracked.

"It surpasseth understanding," he said bitterly. There was lamentation in his voice. Divine goodness had been challenged.

She had seen the disease often enough, identified it, prescribed for it, treated it. She had saved some patients, snatched them away, found them reprieves and acquittals, and she had lost others—weary old women, no longer willing to struggle, disbelieving men in their middle years, wasted young boys, bewildered girls. And now it was her turn. Would she lose the breast, lose both? The lymph glands, the muscles of her chest? Would she burn under the radiation treatments, suffer nausea and dizziness, lose her hair? Would she live?

"I'm going to smoke," she said, rummaging in her bag. "I know you disapprove but I'm going to anyway."

He held a light for her. "You needn't hang onto yourself in front of me, you know."

She glanced up at him with mocking eyes. "When I'm apprehensive I wet my pants. I've done that already."

He let that go with a deprecating wave of his hand. "It's nothing to be ashamed of. I've wept. At a sad ending. Over a woman... I've tended you since you were a wee thing. You can howl if you like."

She heard his voice echo across the years. Spit. Cough. Open. Shut. Breathe in. Breathe out. Little did he know what would result if she did as she was told now. Howl? She would wail like a banshee. She would flood the room. Anger burned in her.

The goddamned random idiocy of it happening to her. She had only begun to make choices in life. I'll have this. No, thank you, to that. How dare fate hurry her? She wanted age with its eccentricities. She wanted time to squander. She searched for invective, not tears; for sticks and stones to hurl. How could she ever have soothed those patients she had condemned, with their x-rays and cardiograms lying before her on her desk? How could she have offered rest and diet and pills and potions? Rage, *rage* at the dying of the light. Dylan had said it all with sublime boozy brilliance. Dignity had no charm for her; patient submission even less. Oh, how she would exhort those poor souls in her care now. Drink, carouse, climb the mountain, ford the stream, take, flee; fate is gaining on you. Indeed, she wept, for the men she hadn't loved, for the places she hadn't seen, for articles left unbought, for municipal bonds falling due in midlife, for sunsets, for honors never to be bestowed for flights to distant stars never to be undertaken. She had meant to learn French. To go to Africa. To dye her hair red, to win a Nobel Prize. And what in lieu of all this? A harp, a narrow grave, a sudden ending. Damn, damn, damn.

"I'll give you a drink of Scotch. I was saving it for Christmas, but I'll spare you a glass. A small glass."

"Parsimonious as usual," she said. "No thanks. I'll take your dose the way you've always given it to me. Unpleasantly." She glared at him ferociously.

"You're not dead yet," he snapped.

"I'm scared. That's worse."

"I think you should try to be brave," he said sternly.

"Who's watching?"

"I am."

"I don't intend to bother, just for you."

He went to sit behind his battered desk. There was a jar of hard candy in front of him. His teeth were quite rotten, but he refused to give them up. He pawed through them, found a lemon drop, unwrapped it, sucked greedily. Then he recollected himself and held one out to her.

"Douglas," she said impatiently, "don't give me one of your damned lemon drops. Give me a fighting chance."

He crunched the sweet fiercely. "I am not God," he said, "but I am a believer. Better a man of faith holding the knife. Cling to that."

Nell was reminded of the steaming broth he had spooned into her during girlhood illness. Taste this. All will be well. She had doubted then. She doubted now.

The wall clock ticked heavily behind her. The newsboy thumped the paper on the front porch. She sat brooding, examining the possibilities with cold precision. She looked straight into the face of death sitting in his corner. I'm too choice a morsel for you, she thought. Had she not been tangled in a weedy creek and surfaced to life and sunlight? Had she not survived the exploding firecracker, the Asian flu, a burst appendix, a broken heart? She would be damned eternally if she would go with docility into those bony arms. Centered in her, somewhere in the recesses of her soul, was a rock, a weapon. She stretched to her utmost. She had it in hand.

"I'll tell you what pathologist I want. It's my hide. I don't want any mistakes."

He took her wariness with bad grace. "I don't

make any. I've got plenty walking around to give testimony to my skills."

"I'd better be one of them."

A faint burr came into his speech when he was annoyed. "You can get another opinion. It's your right."

The sick have no rights, Nell thought sourly. No choice. No appeal. Numbly they submit.

"I want two days. Then you can have me."

He was outraged. "Out of the question. What for? Are you a gambler as well as an atheist?"

"I want to make love to a man while I've got two breasts to show him. I don't intend to make amends or make a will, just love. All day and all night, Douglas."

He shuffled the papers in front of him, swung around in the ugly oak chair he refused to throw out, rubbed the end of his nose. He was disapproving but curious.

"How will you keep your mind on it, girl? I wonder at that, with the sword of Damocles hanging over the bed. I should think there'd be more comfort on your knees."

"Why, I may be there, too," she said, "but not in prayer."

He was stern, but a faint smile washed across his face. "I understand you well enough. Don't think I don't. I've had some offer themselves to me, here, on my examining table. I swear on the Testament, should you doubt it."

"And?" She taunted him.

"What do you take me for? I understand the younger fellas take that kind of advantage these days. I prescribed a sedative and sent them on their way."

250

"Their loss."

"Hah." He was silent a moment, watching her moodily. "Another woman would ask a hundred questions of me. You know the answers, of course. Still...if there's anything I can say that will help..."

"Say it's all a mistake."

She saw his eyes fill up as she gathered her remaining strength to cross the door. She felt like a jointed doll moving clumsily at the pull of a string. She would suppress the tremors if it killed her on the spot. She very nearly heaved on his worn carpet with the effort. The door handle was at last within her grasp. When she spoke again her voice was sullen and aggrieved.

"Remember not to bill me," she warned him. "I'm a member of the club."

She fled to her grandfather's house; she would gather courage there, recover herself, be steadied. Among the things stored in the old man's heart would be a remedy for this day; what was dark would become bright and what was fearful would become acceptable.

She noted with surprise the beginnings of a Japanese rock garden near the fence. The rocks were arranged with some charm, but the whole thing had a tottery, insubstantial look, as if it were not intended to last the week. It drew her close with its strange, climbing shape, so at odds with the daisies and the snapdragons and the full-blown roses. It had a gay and careless air, as if someone in the house had been taken by a whim and rushed out to pile stone on stone. Above it all, tied to a green garden stake, was a paper kite, a gaudily colored fish with one large watchful black eye, roundly staring. It breasted the currents of air, bobbing, floating, puzzling the birds.

This could not be the work of Mrs. Keitel; the housekeeper kept her duties as narrowly defined as she dared. She hated and feared nature. Her nose reddened with allergy. Her sparse gray hair snaked into ugly disarray with the slightest breeze. She never set foot outside except to air the blankets or beat the rugs, and then she was darting and furtive, as if she were stark naked, whacking away at the carpets with a kind of fury. Most days she kept to the kitchen with the green blinds half pulled and a dishrag wrung out and hanging limply over the sink. There she made endless cups of watery junket or embroidered pillow cases with sprays of flowers in muddy colors.

It was too early for dinner, but Mrs. Keitel sat by a cold stove eating corn flakes out of a chipped blue dish. A glass of water and two soda crackers on a plate made a picture of Spartan self-denial. There was no book propped open before her, no newspaper, no distraction. Her mind was as dry as her dinner, her eyes fixed on the empty wall opposite.

Nell stood in the doorway observing her. Someone in Mrs. Keitel's past had made a point of proper mastication. A tyrannical aunt, perhaps, interrupting a silent meal to admonish her to eat without haste. Slowly, slowly, she munched the corn flakes, thirty little chews per bite, pause, thirty more. Her mouth was open and Nell could see the nasty pulp she was making of it, shifting it from side to side.

Mrs. Keitel sipped her water, patted her lips. She would rinse the two plates and the glass and walk

up the backstairs and remove her clothes, and, in a
faded nightgown, with her hair braided and all her
prayers said, she would lie on her single bed,
daylight still suffusing her room, waiting to sink
into dreamless sleep. There need be no resurrection
for her, Nell thought grimly; there had never been
any life.

"Is he home?"

Mrs. Keitel put her spoon down and turned her
head stiffly, startled. "Oh. It's you."

"There's no dinner cooking, I see."

"No." Mrs. Keitel was sparing of speech.
Speech, like food, was not to be wasted.

Nell was used to the obstacles the woman
strewed in her path. Where is the needle? Where it
belongs. Where is my sweater? Where you left it.
Who ate the last slice of cake? You know as much
as I do.

"I'm not feeling well," Nell told her. "In fact, I'm
quite tired and cross, so please tell me where my
grandfather is and why there's no dinner for him."

Mrs. Keitel was not to be budged. It would be her
way or not at all. She remained stonily silent.

"If you muck around with me," Nell said, her
temper rising, "I'll take that bowl in front of you
and upend it on your gray head."

Mrs. Keitel was now pleased. The blood was up,
the lines drawn. She had never liked Nell and she
meant to show it at every opportunity.

"You'd better see to him, is all I can say," she
remarked darkly.

Nell hurried from the kitchen toward the broad
flight of stairs, a flutter of panic taking her breath
away. The terror begun in the doctor's office
widened. He was ill. She had let two weeks go by

without calling and that meddlesome old woman had let him decline and fail. He had a cold. He had fever. He had worse. She nearly tripped in her haste to get to his room.

He was on the balcony, cutting the hairs out of his nose with a little curved scissors. On the bed lay a new gray suit, a striped shirt, a silk tie the color of a dove's wing. Beside them, ready to be taken up and clapped on his head, a fine new Panama hat. The air was rich with limewater. He turned this way and that, snipping, studying his reflection in a hand mirror, and then, thinking himself unobserved, he strutted a step or two.

He had taken her once as a child to see a parade. She remembered a white-haired old man, very tall, baton in hand, legs kicking, leading a band down the street. He was that very figure now, chest thrown out, legs straight, and God knows what his cock was doing. She saw instantly that the jaunty figure before her could not be involved in her fate; he had taken new life from some mysterious force and was no longer what he had been. He had turned off the path leading to his grave and was bounding through leafy woods with cloven hoof and the hairs of his nose nicely disposed of. He was a bright plant pushing upward. She was a weed. Her bones would bleach and burn. His would dance a jig.

"Look at you," she said with some resentment. "What in God's name is this?"

He favored her with a wide smile, a little bow from the waist. "My dear."

Her tone was faintly accusatory. "You've got a new suit. It looks expensive. It looks tailor-made." She rushed on, discomfited by his smug look of

254

pleasure. Gray suits. Silk ties. He must be spending money madly. His business of course, but on whom? And why? She saw polish on his shoes. Wasn't that a flower on the bureau, waiting to become a boutonniere? He'd never worn a flower in his life. Where was his brown jacket with the hole in the lapel? Where were his scuffed bedroom slippers? Who had cut his beard to make him an Edwardian dandy?

He came into the room and patted her head on the way to his dressing table. He took up two ancient silver brushes and stroked his hair into a fine mane. A cowlick refused to lie down. It stood above his head like a small horn, confirming him as a satyr.

Nell sank onto the bed. Who was this man with his own buoyancy, his own happiness? She felt stiff, quenched, alone.

He picked up his trousers and hauled them over his skinny haunches, and then, with his accustomed delicacy, turned his back to zip them. The shirt followed and the tie, knotted with a flourish.

"I cut quite a figure, don't I?" He solicited her approval.

"And how."

But he saw that she was less than pleased. She had never liked surprises and he was not given to them himself, in fact. He sat beside her and took her hand.

He began an explanation, speaking to her in the low soothing voice which had once called her out of closets and lured her down from rooftops and the dangerous high branches of trees. It was the special voice, the sweet voice, that had imparted lore and fantasy, had told stories bringing her safely to the edge of sleep, had explained and reasoned and reassured.

He had found himself, he told her, flirting with melancholy. It had come strangely. She knew how he savored a peach, the song of birds, the music of violins and water. Yes, she knew. It had all left him. The fruit untasted, the birds voiceless, the music stilled. He had kept to his room, watching day follow day, with his heart growing heavier as each one passed. He ceased to read. No other voices could speak to him as they once had. There were no occasions to celebrate. His clock ran down. His very heart slowed, he could feel it. Why hadn't he called her? Because even in his waning he knew he must resolve it for himself or he would end in the bleak country of dependence. He would not go there willingly, to be pacified with puddings and lap robes and little walks, clinging to someone's arm. He had done something quite daring instead. He paused to take up a cigar, bit the end and lit it with a silver lighter she had never seen before.

"I went looking for a woman," he said, "and I found her." Yes, he said, he'd been quite deliberate about it. He had been reading a Swedish novel, taken from the library at random, when his thoughts became too black to be borne. It was about an old man, like himself, who fell in love. In that moment before all feeling finally declined, he fell in love.

And it was a merry falling too, full of fondling and jokes.

"I was quite stirred up reading it," he said with a smile. "Desirous, yes, desirous. It was very heartening to me. I thought, here is an old man like myself, gifted with a second life long after he has any reason to hope for one. Here he is thinking of soft breasts and soft eyes and more than that, seeking them out. Well, I thought, if he can do it, so can I. No need to be timid. So I laid plans."

He saw Nell rapt with attention, her mouth ajar, as it had been in the past when he spun a tale. The room had just begun to darken. The two of them were reflected like shadow figures in the mirror, silvery, vague, close. Nell took a pillow and hugged it to her, listening.

He had gone to a concert in the city. It had been a rainy afternoon, a soft Irish rain, hardly enough to dampen his coat. There was Chopin on the program, romantic to begin with. He had bought a good seat and sitting next to him, with a profile of Roman elegance, was a lady. Not young but not old either. He could even recall what she wore. A white blouse with a cascade of ruffles, lovely shoes with buckles that shone in the dark. He wasn't sure about that, but he saw that she had narrow feet. Perhaps the buckles were only in his mind. She had remarkable ears, not tiny but ever so slightly pointed, and it made him think of fauns to look at them. He had begun with a little dodge, telling her he had lost his program. She had shared hers. They talked. How exciting it had been to flirt again. How many years it had been since the last time. They had taken tea afterward, and as the hours passed too quickly, dinner, and then a stroll past empty office buildings to a park where a drunken young fellow offered them a sip from his bottle in a brown paper bag.

They had listened to a fiery evangelist and a weary revolutionary. A minister with wild eyes exhorted them to be saved. A girl with long hair strummed a guitar and berated fate and men in a high keening voice. They had eaten ice cream cones, both favoring vanilla, and sat on the grass to finish them. He had held the handle on the faucet for her to drink. They had seen the moon, a bright sphere above them, and had been hustled for money by a dark and dangerous boy. Adventure, adventure.

They had arranged to meet again, and lo and behold, she was bookish and clever and nothing had so solaced him as the sound of her laughter. Life was eased of its burdens. They had, he told her triumphantly, gone to bed together. The old, he observed, must not be turned out to pasture. They must lie down in one. With a lady with gray hair and long legs and fine ankles and fine wrists. He fell silent then, deeply peaceful.

Nell looked at him intently. Yes, she saw the shape of the affair, the balm, the giddy joy. What a marvel that he had heard the mermaids singing their last song before closing time.

She got up and walked to the window. The curtain blew inward against her cheek. In the dusk the kite with its colored fish flew like a bright banner. They must have put it there, the two of them. To mark a gain against time. It rose and fell, rose and fell. She heard him stir behind her, jump to his feet, examine his watch.

"My goodness, I'll be late." He swept up his hat and strode toward the door. He turned then, to look at her across the room, outlined by the blue light against the window. Beyond her a tree bloomed white. She seemed very far away.

"Did you come for any special reason?" he asked.

"No."

"We'll visit next time, my darling."

"Yes."

He went out.

Nell bought a bottle of Scotch and headed for Stella. She knocked on her door and heard a bellicose voice shout out.

"I'm not at home!"

"Yes, you are. Let me in."

Stella peered out at her with the look of a bear prodded from its cave.

"It's you."

Nell held the bottle aloft. It made an immediate difference. Stella stood aside and waved her in. The room was a shambles, close, hot, dark. Stella wore men's pajamas. Her feet were bare, her glasses pushed up into her hair. Nell picked her way through the strewn books and papers, lifted the cat from the chair and sat in it. Stella remained standing; she offered no greeting.

"Call it forced entry. Call it whatever you like," Nell told her. "I felt like talking to you."

She set the bottle down on the floor. Stella swooped it up and read the label. "If this is meant for me you can talk all night long."

She padded into the kitchen for glasses. Drawers were pulled, cupboard doors slammed. There were mutterings, table silver was emptied with a clatter on the floor, there was an outcry as she stepped on a fork. "Shit!"

Nell saw two huge baskets of fruit rotting on a table. The banana skins had turned quite black, the apples were shriveled, one orange, half peeled, had fallen to the floor. Under its pink bows and yellow cellophane the fruit had turned to garbage.

Stella stood at the kitchen door, squinted at the label on the bottle, worked the cap free. She filled the two glasses she had found and was at hers before she came back into the room.

"This is lovely drink," she said, and handed the shorter measure to Nell.

"What's all that?" Nell indicated the baskets.

"Ah, that. A man sent it. I've got one hanging around, you know." She seemed to ponder the fact with some astonishment. "Are you surprised?"

Nell knew Stella would not be easily deceived. Stella would bite the coin to test its worth, would throw a lie in her teeth. Respect kept her honest. "Yes," she said.

"So'm I. I don't know what it will come to. He spends money on me. Calls, send presents. That fruit." She sniffed disdainfully. "I hate fruit. It's all core and peel and seeds. If it would ferment into something useful it would be worth having."

"Is *he* worth having?" It was good to wander away from herself into gossip.

Stella scratched her nose, grew wary. She hunched her shoulders, narrowed her eyes, fidgeted. "One day at a time for me," she said. "Then I'll see where I'm at."

"He might get away."

"Nobody wiggles off my line," Stella corrected. "If they're gone it's because I've tossed 'em back into the sea."

When the forces of women gathered, Nell thought, Stella should be at their head, mounted, armed, a powerful arm flung forward in defiance, promising victory. Her banner would be blood red, her mind white hot. Yes, she would draw them from their kitchens, snatch them from the bridge games, summon them from the tennis courts and the golf courses, from the psychiatrists and the beauty parlors, and the day would be hers. Nell very nearly cheered aloud.

The liquor coursed warmly down her throat. Stella threw herself into a chair, her feet planted, her face incurious, in no hurry to sound her out. In the shadows she seemed like a great stone totem, solid, ugly, impervious. Her prominent veins stood out on her forehead, her heavy gray hair hung loose around her wide and bony shoulders. She was a sight.

"There's a damn mosquito in here. I hear it buzzing." Stella sprang to her feet, grabbed a magazine and stalked the room, swatting at the walls. "There." A tiny spot of blood appeared among the other stains.

"Snuffed out," Nell said, swigging. "I hope we don't all go like that."

Stella's gaze bored through her like a drill. "That's a dark remark and you have a dark look about you. If you have something sticking in your craw, spit it out. You have a chance of being understood here."

"It won't go away by talking about it." Reticence was an old habit with Nell. Turn it this way. Turn it that. Work it out for yourself.

"That's a ninny's attitude," snapped Stella. "That's what's wrong with us in this country. A tight lip and a tight asshole. It's the purest shit. Look at nature, woman. Warts, scars, cracks, fissures, slime, green fungus, boiling gasses, poisoned wells, toads and warthogs, the lame, the halt, the blind. It all hangs out to be seen. Nothing hidden. Out in the open where you can deal with it. Tell me or don't tell me—but set it out in the landscape. It won't be bigger than any other mess you see before you. And that's all I have to say."

"I doubt it," Nell said, but the knot inside unraveled by at least one thread, perhaps two. Canonize Stella, she thought, the fiery prophet of the possible.

"Well." Stella hefted the bottle. "Let's get on with it. You've interrupted my work as is."

"I brought the bottle, don't forget."

"It doesn't entitle you to all that much."

They drank on, both silent, each with her own thoughts. A pleasant flush began to go through Nell...and more. It erected a barrier around her that nothing could penetrate. Nothing at all. Down demons. Away threats. She poured another for herself.

"Here, now, don't get ahead of me." Stella held out her glass and guided Nell's hand until she got it filled to the brim. She's piggish, thought Nell. She could see her shoving her way to the head of a line, grabbing the only vacant seat on a bus under the nose of a crippled old woman, taking the first piece of candy out of the box. Oh, yes, that great lout of a woman was doubtless a bully in school, jumping for the volleyball, shouting to be heard above all others. It was remarkable how precisely personality came into focus with a tot or two or three.

"We should eat something," Nell said.

"I don't see why."

"Neither do I." They bumped heads as they both made a lunge at the bottle.

"Manners," Nell admonished.

"Go ahead then, if you're going to swill."

"Hoity-toity," said Nell, and helped herself first, leaving only a drop or two for her hostess. Stella stared sourly at the dregs, heaved to her feet, disappeared into the bathroom and emerged with another bottle. She plunked it down between them. "That is not tap water, for your information. Keep it in mind."

They made hefty inroads with the first pouring. Nell felt a cheerful buzzing in her blood. When had she been drunk last? At her high school prom. Yes, that was it. The quarterback on the football team had tried to get into her pants under the stairs and she had hit him with a copy of Milton. Give me back the hour, she thought dreamily, and you would have your due, you great, hulking, pimply boy. And when else? By herself when she was thirteen. Solemnly. Experimenting. She had ended up naked in the backyard, running through the sprinklers while the gardener called on the saints and debated raping her.

"I'll have a bit more," she said.

Stella poured grudgingly. "I'll freshen mine too." The bottle wavered now over the glasses. Nell reached out and steadied her hand.

"You're spilling."

"You moved the glass."

They drank on. Now the warm dark was as soothing as an embrace, the smell of rotting fruit strange and wonderful. A street in Rome had smelled like that. Had there been a man in the doorway? Had she said yes to him or no? Had she ever been to Rome at all?

"Have you ever been to Rome?" By now she had slid to the floor. Her head rested on the seat very near to Stella's lap.

"Do you think I'm made of money? How would I get there? Why would I go? I get pinched on the behind here. In the Safeway market."

"It's not the same, you dolt." She has no soul, Nell thought. She's a tunnel closed at both ends. No, that was not fair. Looking at her, upside-down to be sure, but still, studying her, she had a sad maternal air. Weren't they the best of friends, drinking the night away? I like her, she thought, and she must like me as well. We're both clever. We achieve. Achieve greatly. Hurrah for the two of us. The great achievers.

"Why are you lying on the floor?" Stella asked.

"Is that where I am?"

"You're a sloppy drunk. You give way." Stella was very superior. "You'll notice that I am bolt upright in this chair."

"You're listing," Nell told her, "way over to the left. If you don't know that, you're drunker than I am."

Stella straightened. "If I go to the bathroom will you swear on your honor not to take another drop till I come out?"

"Certainly."

"I'm going to leave the door open all the same," she threatened, and made for the bathroom. Nell rolled over on her stomach and saw her majestically enthroned on the toilet seat.

"Kings often received their courts while sitting on the pot. Did you know that?"

Stella's voice was haughty and seemed far away. "Information of that sort is of no use to me."

She rose, flushed and walked carefully back into the room.

"You didn't wash your hands. You could spread hepatitis."

"Mind your own business." Stella seated herself again and took up her drink.

Nell drained hers. How safe, how cradled she was. How big and brave. She was full of wonder at it. While she mused Stella had slipped yet another good slug into her glass.

"Your health," she said.

"Ah," Nell replied, reminded. "That's what I came about."

Stella leaned down to peer at her. "You look all right to me—and if you aren't, put it out of your mind."

"Of course. Nothing simpler."

"Yes." Stella was firm, brooking no disagreement. "I intend to live to be a hundred and beyond. That's my intention and let no man meddle with it." She burped loudly.

"How are you going to manage that?"

Stella rose to her feet and declaimed, as though facing a huge, unseen audience. "Once, when I was a girl, and God knows that's a way back, I rode on a roller coaster."

"You were speaking of living to be a hundred..."

Stella roared on. "A roller coaster, lifting up into the sky like a big colored snake. I didn't have the price of the ticket but I meant to ride. There was a small boy standing there with a fistful of tickets. His father had bought them. I think the man hoped the boy would be thrown off and dashed to pieces. He was a nasty boy with a nose running snot and

265

mean little eyes. I said, 'Give me one of those tickets, sonny. If you use them all yourself the fun will go out of it.' He said something rude but I grabbed one out of his hand and before he could do anything away I went." She raised her glass above her head.

"Sweet Jesus, what a ride. The women screamed. The hairpins flew out of my hair. My heart popped out of my mouth. Everybody clutched the bars in front of them or clutched each other or simply clutched. One girl got hold of the hair on her man's chest and you could hear him yell for a mile. We were jolted and thrown and thrown and jolted and up and up and then we were at the very top. The people below were little pepper specks, sprinkled about, that's all they were. Then came the second before the last plunge. You know how a hawk rides the air, hovering? That's what we did. And then we hurtled down, the wind singing and screeching, the breath torn out of us, we plummeted like a rock. Then's when I made up my mind. I said, remember this, Stella, my girl, because this is the way you're going to live your life from this day forward, up and down and banged around and thrills all the way."

"You could have fallen off," Nell said, now flat on her belly, her head resting on her arm.

"I didn't," said Stella, "as you can see, if you're still able to see at all."

Nell didn't answer. She had passed out, quite peacefully, where she lay.

Just before dawn she awoke, every muscle crying in outrage. Stella, her head thrown back, her mouth wide open, snored loudly. The cat made its morning toilet, licked its paws with a darting pink tongue; then, tail held aloft, approached her, sniffed, backed away, offended. She yawned, groaned, dragged herself to her feet. She went to the window, raised it and stuck her head out into the first light. A hummingbird trembled above the Copa D'Oro, beating its wings in nervous flight. A small scruffy dog lifted his leg and destroyed the grass, then scrabbled with his forepaws to make amends. Birds began a busy chattering; a truck rumbled heavily in the street. The yellow eye of a flashing signal paled before the rising sun.

Nell knelt by the sill and let herself be washed by the air. She meant to accept this day with calm, but a nagging thought discomfited her. Patients frequently died in the early hours of the morning. She had been at their bedsides, sleepy, awed, helpless. She had lowered eyelids over sightless eyes with her own hand and wondered: Had they resolved to keep the sight of an unblemished sky? Had they come to some final truth that needed no confirming by the passing of another day? Had they cried out as they went: test me no longer?

Stella stirred, hawked, coughed. Stella, comrade beside the fires as they burned low, stalwart, breasting the wave at her side as it engulfed her. Bleary, blowsy sister, wake and brace the troops. But she merely shifted and slept on. Nell left her to it, closing the door quietly behind her.

Jake collided with her as she passed his door. He had come thrusting through it, loaded with fishing gear, swaddled in oilskins, clumsy in heavy boots.

"Oof," she said as she slammed into his chest. She knew by his rude robust air that he had been up for an hour. He had showered. He had shaved. He had eaten a huge breakfast, moved his bowels, made his bed. He had doubtless sat under his desk lamp sorting through the bright flies that now adorned his hat and jacket, giving him a raggedy peddler's look. He would skim the sea, plunder its depths, listen to the clamor of the gulls and be very pleased with himself. Let others go their lunatic rounds, he would have this day, rare and fine and exactly to his taste.

A lure grazed her cheek and something, she couldn't tell what, entangled itself in her hair. "Turn me loose," she cried.

"Don't wiggle, you'll only make it worse." She felt his deft fingers in her hair. "Damn, stand still." She heard his rod clatter to the floor. He swore. "This'll teach you to come lurching home, swacked, at the crack of dawn."

He freed her and held her away to look at her.

"I was drunk," she said. "Awfully drunk."

"Do you any good?"

"A world of good."

"You look like hell," he observed pleasantly.

"I do, don't I." She patted her crushed dress ineffectually. His gray eyes questioned how she passed the night. She let him speculate for a moment and then put him straight. "Stella and I tied one on. If it had gone on much longer I suppose we might have gone off and enlisted in the navy together."

He gathered up his gear. "Something must have got your wind up. I have time to listen."

She sagged against the wall then. Her head hurt, her stomach was sour and unkind to her. Dutch courage, she saw, was shortlived. I have time to listen. So say the faceless priests in the dark of the confessional. But a line forms behind you and the stories are old and often heard and nobody stays with you to the end.

"I'm a good sailor," she said. "Take me with you."

"I'd like nothing better."

She hurried for a jacket, made a call to her exchange, pleaded illness, arranged for the young Korean doctor on the floor above to cover her and put out of her mind the awful speed of time.

They bought enough groceries for a trip to China. Nell thought of cold bird and wine picnics out of fitted wicker baskets from Abercrombie & Fitch while he grabbed peanut butter and Heinz sweet pickles and potato chips and chili peppers. As he moved up and down the aisles, dumping doughnuts and strawberry soda into his cart, she saw him as a boy, in brown cords and torn sneakers, stoking up for a summer day by a pond or a stream or in a cave dangerously hollowed out of a hillside. It would seem the coarse appetite of youth had never left him. Ice cream sandwiches, that awful icy vanilla mush tucked between spongy chocolate layers, followed to complete the repast. She suggested apples and cheese. He threw in a dozen apples and a wheel of cheese with the lordly gesture of a gourmand.

Still, he was in touch with something, with this lunatic shopping, because she began to have the stir of excitement from her own childhood, when she had stuffed herself with Mallomars and maple nut fudge, washed down with a drink of warm water from the garden hose. All that sugar burning in her blood had sent her under the house with a neighbor boy and their kisses had been peppermint and carmel and astonishingly carnal for their age.

She was curious to know if they solved the same mysteries at the same moment in life. Had he wandered into a garage and found, in the depths of the galvanized tin ash can, one of those soft paper books, bound with string, with smudged, inky, erotic couplings flowering on every page? Had he sat in the garage, knees to chest, with the smell of leaking gas from an old Packard choking him, and turned those pages with their entwined figures, every orifice gapingly revealed, and marveled at the astounding agility? Had his heart pounded as he sat, flushed and unhungry at the dinner table, deaf to conversation, wondering how they did those things and what the sensations were that accompanied them? What was the child like before the man and why did she care?

"Do you like baked beans?"

"Love 'em."

"Will you eat them cold out of a can with a spoon?"

"Of course."

What if she had met him then, at twelve or thirteen, when she was thin as a slat and rude and forthright? He would have appeared in her life, suspicious and unsmiling, to watch her at a distance. He would have moseyed closer as he heard her fiery debates in the school auditorium, defending the Scottsboro boys and Sacco and Vanzetti, or seen her drive her first car recklessly into the school parking lot. He would have vied with her in classes and slouched by her silently in the halls. He would have appeared on her doorstep without invitation and argued hotly with her for weeks about euthanasia and Hemingway, before he grabbed her and kissed her without permission, jamming his tongue into her mouth, both their chins wet with spit, ignoring a cold sore in his passion. They would have been scrappy and abrasive; he would have wandered off after a softer girl. He would have wandered back.

"You're quiet." They were riding toward the boat slip.

"I'm speculating about you," she said. Her head lay against the back of the seat. She felt peaceful and lazy.

"Go ahead."

"What kind of a boy were you?"

He thought it over. "I guess I was a handful. Big for my age. Short fuse. Mistrustful—worried that someone would sneak up behind me or try to sneak one by me. Hungry for girls. Nothing special."

"Were you smart?"

"No, dumb. Illiterate. I'm a late bloomer. Never read a book till I was twenty-one. As it is, I'm only down to T for Tolstoy."

He turned around and groped for a poplin windbreaker on the back seat. He tossed it to her. "You'll need it on the boat."

She took off her jacket and pulled it on. It smelled of stale smoke and baby powder. Is that what he used, baby powder? She told him she fancied herself in men's clothes. She had worn her grandfather's yellow slicker to school, slinking along in its ample folds, feeling slim and supple and sinuous. She had looked grotesque, there was a snapshot bearing witness, but she had been happily unaware of it.

He told her that if his windbreaker made her feel slim and supple and sinuous, she had better keep it. What were her other peculiar crotchets?

She would tell him later. They had arrived.

His boat had no name. It was anchored among the *Deirdre*s and *Annabella*s and *Spindrift*s in austere anonymity. He expected her to lug her fair share and she did so, trotting back and forth from car to boat, storing the bundles neatly as he directed. A girl, belly exposed in a pink bikini, watched her from the deck of a nearby sailboat. Nell went back and forth. The bikini-clad girl turned to toast on the other side.

Finally, sweat trickling down her back and all stowed to Jake's satisfaction, he pointed out a seat.

"There's some chop out there today. How good's your gut?"

"Cast iron."

"All right. But if it doesn't hold up, puke downwind. I keep a clean ship."

The motor thundered to life and they were off, bucking the waves, a bronco ride on the back of a skittish horse. Nell turned her face into the spray, posing like a figurehead, but only until the curl left her hair and her mascara streaked darkly under her eyes. Then she grasped the railing and wondered about the sagacity of this entire venture. He pointed to a gull overhead that raced with them out to sea. Lovely, she mouthed, not meaning it. She stared down at the water. The waves were Botticelli scallops, white lines curling in folds of foaming green. The wind cried around her. Jake spun the wheel and stared ahead. Land receded. She speculated on shipwreck. Life on an island. Life in company with him. Would there be conversation enough for eternity? He cut the motor.

They drifted alone at the far edge of the world.

She soon saw that Jake intended to go about the business that had brought him here. He had pulled on a gray woolen cap fuzzy with loose threads and was now deeply engrossed in baiting his line. He had come to fish and she was expected to fend for herself. She was like that, too; when she sat over a book or wrestled with the writing of a paper, she barely tolerated the presence of anyone else in the room, would offer the merest grunt by way of acknowledgment.

"My Uncle Tyler Cooley expressly left me this rod in his will," he said to her suddenly. "He left half a million dollars to a Mexican lady he was fond of, but he left me this rod."

He seemed disposed to reminisce. Nell encouraged him.

"A favorite uncle?"

"Never would have gotten to my manhood without him."

He told her then of the man who had given him his first taste of whiskey, his first Havana cigar, his first conviction that life was worth living. He had made a fortune in auto parts before he was thirty-five and had devoted the rest of his short and colorful life to having a good time. He liked Jake because of all his nephews, and he had seven, Jake kept his counsel and did not pick his nose in public. He would send an airplane ticket for him, first-class, and Jake would fly to Montana every summer, getting off the plane more than half drunk, having had two cocktails and a bottle of wine with his lunch. His Uncle Tyler would meet

273

him in an old yellow Stutz Bearcat and they would go up to his lodge, where there was nothing but thick steaks and cold beer and time. His uncle would wake him at four in the morning and give him coffee laced with Old Grand-Dad bourbon and they would get in the car and bump down empty country roads till they came to a stream. They would put on old rubber boots that smelled as if someone had died in them and stand in the icy water and talk and fish.

There was usually more talk than fish but that was all right with Jake. Uncle Tyler was a great talker. His view of life, which he expounded in a whiskey-raw voice, was that it was meant to be a pleasing business. That meant the company of decent men and bad women. It meant saying what you meant to anybody, high or low, and never, on any account, selling yourself in return for a dirty buck. There were things he approved of and things he didn't. He didn't see why you shouldn't kiss a man if you had reason to love him. He often kissed Jake, a great wet smacking buss on the cheek, and Jake never wiped it dry in his presence either. He believed in giving to the poor but if they said thank you he screeched to a halt and never did it again. He didn't think any man should be beholden to any other. He hated Republicans and said so at a lot of dinner parties. He loved his old mother to distraction and sent her all kinds of beaded dresses and high-heeled shoes from Helena, which she was unable to wear, but she was buried in one of the dresses because he insisted on it. He bought Jake his first woman, a nice girl who waited table in a café, and he waited outside to see if it came out all right. He wrote him a letter every week of his life and enclosed a twenty-dollar bill, with directions to squander it any which way he wanted. He died of a ruptured spleen two days before his forty-eighth birthday and Jake had wept so inconsolably that they had sent for the family doctor. He felt his Uncle Tyler would have been glad of the tears. He loved a show of genuine emotion.

"I think you take after him," Nell said.

"I do, I do," he said and went back to his rod.

She left him alone. She found a spot free of gear, and wadding his coat under her head she stretched out at full length. The wide empty sky, the wide empty sea, they suited her. The very vastness rebuked fear. If death meant a restoration to this kind of harmonious infinitude it could be faced. The thought no sooner came than she was instantly annoyed with herself. She had not come here to test life against mortality. She was here with an attractive man. She was in her prime. She was aware of desire and curiosity. She would most certainly see how it all came out in the end.

She shucked her shoes and stockings, rolled up her shirt sleeves, gave herself to the sun. Jake hoisted himself onto a stool. She noted a tear on the seat of his pants. He had applied a neat patch, but it was just wide of the mark. He wears blue shorts, she observed, the color of this very blue sky. How well he matches. The boat rocked. Small waves tapped like gentle fingers against the sides. Everything became beautifully simple. What is beyond human power is beyond it. White clouds rolled overhead. She slept.

When she awoke she was alone. She sat up, frowning, her skin prickling with sudden fear. He was not in the bow. She scrabbled for her shoes, unable to see clearly with the light stabbing off the water. She peered down the hatch, but it was black below. A curious red haze seemed to hang before her. She blinked.

"Jake? Cooley? Where are you?"

Silence.

"Where the hell are you?" She cracked her shin against a metal box. It was some kind of joke. She was annoyed.

"Jake!"

He emerged from the hatch. "Yo."

"Where were you?"

"In the head."

"Ah. I just woke up. I saw myself abandoned out here . . . drinking seawater . . . going mad." She saw the sun was much lower on the horizon. She must have slept for hours. She felt dazed, dry, out of sorts. He showed her two black bass, mouths agape, lying rigidly on a bed of ice. "Dinner."

"Not if I have to cook them."

"You don't. I will." He studied her flushed face. "You've had too much sun. Let's go below and get a salt tablet into you." He herded her down the steps into the narrow space below. There were two bunk beds, stacks of old magazines, a picture of Fujiyama in cold solitary beauty taped to the wall. There was a littered table, the smell of brine. She sat down and rubbed her eyes with her fists. He handed her a large tablet and a glass of water. Dust motes floated in it. He sat opposite, watchful. The tablet stuck in her throat. She choked, coughed, beat the air with her hands. He leaned across and gave her a solid whack. Eyes swimming, she nodded thanks. He resumed his place. Why the sharp blow between her shoulder blades should have done it she couldn't imagine, but quite suddenly a vivid explicit sexual image crossed her mind. She was, in a moment, sensitive in every part of her body. In heat, she thought, give it its name, in heat, spongy, willing persuadable, in a hurry. In another moment, she speculated, I will be peeling him out of his shirt and pants. Image followed image. There was biting, scratching, licking, a whole marvelous and expert tangling, slick acrobatics, anointment with oils, the shape of his mouth here and there and bloody well everywhere. It had to be sunstroke.

"Wash your face and come topside." He started up the stairs. "I'll fix you a peanut butter and jelly sandwich."

Hah, she thought, comfort me with apples—and with sandwiches and candy bars filled with stale nougat and rancid nuts. Well enough, for now. She combed her hair a different way that pleased her. She sprayed scent behind her ears and then, somewhat absently, between her breasts. If he should find his way there, surprise, it would smell of lilac.

They had a silent and altogether greedy meal. She found she was starved and made way with the better part of what was in the basket. He lit his customary cigar and filled the air with smoke as he puffed tranquilly.

"You're an interesting woman," he began. It was a statement, not flattery. "No commitments. No marriage How come?"

What could she tell him that might be edifying? That she was an only child of long-dead parents, that she had been petted and cosseted by a doting old man? That she was impatient and self-sufficient and judgmental, even arrogant? That she was often pleased in bed and rarely out of it? Dared she insult him by telling him that most men were irrelevant, guilty, frightened, foolish? Dared she let him see the scope of her demands where men were concerned: wit, good sense, good sensibilities, firmness, fairness? And how could she, at the same time, let him know the delight she took, how very much she liked his sex? How pleasingly sentimental they could be, how fond, how faithful. How unpetty and unpatronizing.

"I've been badly spoiled," she said. "I'm not proud of it but I'm afraid it's the truth. I took prizes in school. The best home-raised rabbit. The best drawing of a cow. The best chocolate fudge cake made from scratch. Moreover, my teeth came in straight while others wore braces. The boys with the bluest eyes always asked me out and presented me with gardenias which cost them half their allowance. I could ride a horse bareback and jump a high hurdle at close to six feet. I was proposed to twice before I was eighteen; one of them went on to be a Superior Court judge, the other buys guns in West Germany and sells them in Brazil. I made Phi Beta Kappa, even though it was a matter of pride with me never to crack a book till finals, and my chemistry professor fell wildly in love with me and was prepared to desert a wife, three children and a mistress." She paused, ruminated. "I think it must have all gone to my head. Too clever by far, too fond of myself to live. What can I tell you? Narcissus loved himself."

"Never met your match?"

"I probably did. Too smug to know it."

He tore the top off a soft drink can with his teeth

and drank deeply. "What's your body count to date?"

She made an impatient movement. "Are you asking me about my love affairs?"

"Change the names. Protect the innocent."

"You won't learn anything. God knows I didn't."

"It's not important," he said. "I'd handle you differently, anyway."

He gathered up the sandwich wrappings, the bottles, the paper napkins, and stowed them neatly in the basket.

"Well, we've dawdled along for some weeks now," he said. "Don't you think it's time we moved this relationship along one square? Isn't it time we got into bed and grappled with each other? And it doesn't have to be a bed, Nell—I'd willingly lie down with you on a cornhusk mattress or in the tall grass. The bulge in my trousers would do credit to an adolescent boy at a burlesque show. You're thorny, bright and troublesome, but I consider that the final riddle of you lies between your legs, and I'd like to solve it."

Why hold back, she thought? Have me today, have me tomorrow, the day after is up for grabs.

She offered a warning. "You realize, don't you, that there'll be two of us in that bed. I wake early and I study my partner."

"I'm at my best asleep," he said.

She liked the prospects. Couple and grapple. No holds barred. Each in his corner, sweating, primed. Sound the bell. Shake hands. Mix it up and carry off the trophy to prop open the door. And if he won on points? Why, he most likely would put a large, bare, emphatic foot square on her stomach and proclaim victory to all the world. It was a narrow bed that waited below and it was a narrow beginning, but why not?

Then she hesitated, remembering what she knew and he did not. Very well. She would see how tough he was.

"Sit down," she said, patting the place next to her. "I have something to tell you."

The anesthesiologist was a bustling little man with hands so cold they gave her goose bumps. He called her "Doctor" respectfully and stared disapprovingly at her pretty lavender nightgown, as if he considered it inappropriate for the occasion. He gave her a shot to make her sleep easily through the night and then shifted from one foot to the other as he searched for a pleasantry to offer her. He came up with a weather report. It was going to be hot the following day. He'd heard it on the radio. And smoggy. He was allergic to smog.

She told him that as she was going to be asleep for most of it, it didn't really matter, did it?

No, he told her, it really didn't. He hesitated before leaving. He was going to play golf the next day; he would hold good thoughts for her.

"I trust it won't throw your game off," she said.

"No, it won't," he said. He left her.

A little black nurse with a high saucy behind and huge tilted eyes came in to write up her chart. She lingered to offer solace and confidences while Nell's eyes grew heavier. Her mama had had this surgery a year ago and she was off in Texas with a new husband and feeling just fine. Of course, the Texas fellow knew her mother had savings bonds but she didn't really think that's why he had proposed. He had a three-legged dog, he said, and he was used to there being some parts missing.

Nell observed that she might have to find a fellow like that for herself, if her luck didn't hold.

The little nurse said that any man who was worth shit wouldn't be the least put off.

"What's your name?" Nell asked her drowsily.

"Serena Alice."

"I'm glad you're on duty on this floor, Serena."

Serena concurred. Nell could have gotten one of the big nurses who were bulldykes. There were two around here and they were mean, mean. Their back rubs were more like beatings, and they plopped the old ladies on cold bedpans.

She plumped Nell's pillow and Nell caught a whiff of potent perfume and something else.

"Serena," she said, "you've been smoking a joint in the ladies' room."

"You can't do this job on your own legs. You need a little extra boost."

Serena whisked up a glass and gave the bed a crank or two. "I'm down the hall if you want me. Just ring and I'll come." And Serena floated away, a stoned Florence Nightingale.

Nell burrowed under the blankets and thought about Jake and what a rare old time they'd had. It had been like love in the middle of an old and comfortable marriage. There had been lots of talk, easy, unhurried, good-natured talk. He would like to see her happy. She had only to tell him what it took and he would find the means to provide it. If she liked a garden, he would plant it. Rings for her fingers? He would adorn her. Let there be no sadness kept to herself, no fear of growing old. He wanted to take a hand in all her troubles. In return she had only to learn to play bridge and allow him to smoke his cigars in bed. If she agreed he would proceed to put her picture in his wallet.

And he, she had inquired, what would he like?

He would like to have her on a bed of fallen maple leaves, red and gold ones piled deep. When his Uncle Tyler had gone off to make love to his Mexican housekeeper in the upstairs bedroom on a resplendent brass bed crested with angels, Jake had wandered up in the hills. He had lain under a maple tree, looking down at the darkened windows, and had vowed that when he had a woman of his own he would make love on those prickly leaves, and if the ticks got him it would still be worth it. To date he hadn't found a lady willing; they preferred hotel suites at the Hilton.

In that case they were made for each other, she responded. She had crawled under the dark green shelter of a mulberry tree and clasped the boy who delivered for the cleaners ardently in her arms, trying to get him to touch her nipples, but he was a Seventh-Day Adventist and scared to death to do anything but take the barrette out of her hair. It seemed plain that they would have to find a forest and roll from tree to tree in remembrance of things past.

Oh, Jake, cheerful lover, who had scratched his belly afterward and floored her with his avowal that, one tit or two, she suited him better than any woman he'd ever come across.

Only mean it, she thought, and they can cut off my head.

She was deep in a turbulent dream in which she was hurtling toward an unyielding wall, certain to be shattered on impact, and she struggled to free

282

herself, thrashed and fought and strained to surface again, dimly felt clouds dispelling, swam up out of darkness to find Douglas leaning over her bed and whispering, "Benign: I threatened to leave the church if it weren't. Apparently He heard me— He could ill afford to lose me."

Her voice was thick, her mouth parched, the ordeal still reverberated along her nerve ends. "I'll always be optimistic, from this day forward," she said. She was too exhausted to say more, but she reached for his hand. He grasped it and held it.

"Go to sleep," he told her. "I have five other patients to see."

"Stay a while," she said groggily. "Stay..."

"What a lot of trouble you are to me," he told her as he settled back to watch over her. She closed her eyes. There was no pain any longer; the vista was wide and green and consoling. She was shepherded by Douglas, holding her fast in his large, calloused hand. She slept.

It was rather like an unseasonal Christmas. Jake had contributed a lively myna bird that called "Good morning" and "Do you like San Francisco?" over and over again. Hortense and Eunice had wandered in bearing an old Sinatra recording of "My Funny Valentine." Stella came lugging a jug of California burgundy, having already opened it for sampling. It was she who made the toast, lifting her glass to Nell, who again sat tucked up in her own bed in her own apartment, with its sliver of the Pacific Ocean visible from the window.

"To narrow squeaks," Stella said, "and I'm glad it wasn't me."

The ladies lounged around her bedside, sipping

the wine, sharing Nell's reprieve, each silently thanking her own guardian angel that the ordeal had not been hers. Still, it had brought them closer and they were keyed up and noisy, getting drunk, getting sentimental.

"God," Eunice said, gulping her drink. "It makes you stop and think."

"Women get all the shit," Hortense announced loudly. "Menstruation, menopause, mastectomy, melancholy. God's a man. There's no damn question about it."

"Don't be a complaining fool," Stella said. "We outlive them, we outfox them, we outclass them. We have to suckle them at the start and lay them out at the end. Fathers, uncles, nephews, lovers, they've had their heads in our laps from the Madonna to Marilyn Monroe. I pity the poor buggers. I salute us." She swirled the wine in her glass and splashed it down the front of her dress.

"You'll never get that stain out," Eunice said in a slurred voice, sitting on her spine, hugging her knees, pondering her fate. What if it had been she?

She would never have survived it like Nell, all steel nerves and cool self-control. Sleeping pills for me, she thought, handfuls, washed down with diet Cola, thinking of her figure to the last; and then blankets of striped carnations and a handsome young preacher hastily summoned and a eulogy selected at random for those who die early. She very nearly wept for herself then and there. As soon as she left she would call Harvey. She would be very, very nice to Harvey, so that when fate stalked her he would be there to ward it off with his strong freckled hands.

Stella passed among them refilling the glasses.

Hortense put her palm over hers. "No more for me. I'm getting bluer by the minute." She tossed off what remained of her drink.

"You ought to call Booker," Eunice said sharply. "That's what's bothering you."

"You ought to button your big mouth," Hortense flared.

"Can't we get drunk like ladies!" Stella bellowed. The other two subsided. Stella glared at them and continued, "Our friend here went to the edge of the precipice. She has been hauled back. I rejoice for her. Now either *rejoice* or get the hell out of here!"

Eunice held out her glass. "The trouble is," she said, "this thing has got us all thinking. My mama's dead and so is Hortense's. Yours, too," she said, pointing at Nell, "and I don't know if Stella ever even had one. We're all thinking who'd come running if we needed them and how long would they stay? We're just neighbors in the apartment house."

"More than that," Nell said.

"Just neighbors in an apartment house," Eunice repeated dolefully. She wandered off into the kitchen looking for ice. The wine was warm, probably because Stella kept the jug between her knees. In any case, she hated warm wine.

She cracked ice cubes out of their tray and found she was feeling terribly sorry for herself. Nell's close call had triggered long-buried memories and emotions; that period when she had first come to town, lugging her favorite picture, "The Dream of Saint Ursula," under her arm, looking for work, making endless applications, standing in long lines at the unemployment office.

She was in the little apartment by the steam room then, and one night she had come home from her latest fruitless foray, turned on the gas oven, put her head in it and waited for Saint Ursula's jazzy little angel to show up. She remembered the shock of the explosion, lumber and light fixtures and plaster raining down on her head, and the big black girl from across the way grabbing her by her underwear and hauling her out, all the while yelling, "What the fuck have you done, what the fuck is this!" She had taken her to her own place and chewed her out for the rest of the night and kept her on. She'd been there ever since. With Horty. Of course, she paid half the rent now, she wasn't a charity case. But she was some kind of a case; that much she admitted to herself.

She returned to the others as Nell shifted wearily in her bed and said, "I'm going to throw you all out now. I'm drunk and tired. Thanks for rallying around..."

"Don't leave your dirty glass," Hortense directed Eunice. "Put it in the dishwasher. And take mine."

She came to Nell's side. "We're all glad you got off."

"I know you are."

"God," Stella cried impatiently, "next thing you know we'll be bawling and kissing each other and forming a goddamn sorority. I'm taking the rest of this wine with me. I've got a long night to get through."

She lurched toward the door with her finger hooked through the handle of the bottle, bearing it over her shoulder like a lumberjack on a spree, off to her lair.

Eunice emerged from the kitchen and followed her. She paused in the doorway and informed them that from now on she was going to burn the candle at both ends, seeing how easily it could be snuffed out.

Hortense offered her a parting shot. "You've used that candle for everything else, honey. You might as well start burning it."

Eunice thumbed her nose at Hortense, blew Nell a kiss and departed.

Hortense lingered. "You want the light out?"

"Yes, please."

She snapped it off. The two women were silent in the dark for a moment.

"Tonight I miss my mama," Hortense finally said. "Tonight I'd like to sink down by her chair and feel her hand on my head and hear her say 'Child' to me. I could always feel the callus on her hand she got from chopping wood and hoeing."

She continued then in a low murmurous voice and Nell saw, as she spoke, the muscular, tough little woman Hortense longed for. She had kept a lump of sugar lodged in her cheek for as long as Hortense could remember. She popped it in with her morning coffee and kept reserve lumps in her apron pocket. Hortense thought as a child that the reason they went into her cheek all day long was to sweeten her words as they passed through her mouth. She had written her daughter every week, half a page only, but words that were pithy and comforting. There was often a lace doily slipped into the envelope, or a pot holder or dried herbs or a river agate.

Once she had called long-distance from Texas, bringing a mayonnaise jar full of nickels and dimes and quarters into the phone booth so she could talk to her heart's content. It had been her one and only long-distance phone call, and she hadn't said much except that the garden was full of slugs, that she had planted a mess of sweet peas, that the tree frogs kept her awake at night. Only after the operator had warned her that her time was up had Hortense heard her call out over the hundreds of dusty miles that separated them, "I love you, Horty."

She had died two weeks later.

"The trouble is," Hortense said, "I've grown up but I don't believe it."

Nell heard her close the door quietly behind her. She drew the blankets up to her chin and stared through the dark.

She thought of them all, the departed ladies, and of herself. She thought of them borne along on a surging stream, moving swiftly, clinging to a frail raft; here one slipped, there one flailed; catch me, hold me, bear me up; a hand stretched out, a hand clasped. Would the waters close over their heads? Was the shore too distant?

The myna bird asked if she liked San Francisco, and when there was no reply, asked again.

9

HENRY DILLON stood at his study window and looked down on the top of Alice Dillon's head as she scurried about the garden below, exhorting the men stringing lights into the trees to be careful not to break the branches. A dove cooed, balancing her shrillness with its soft reiterated cry. She scurried here and there, tugging the pastel cloths into place over the many little tables set out on the lawn, dropping a nervous hand on the flower arrangements, shifting them just out of line so they no longer had the perfect air the florist had sought. Henry saw with some dismay that the predominant color of the decorations was pink. Alice ran to candy colors. He never knew whether it was an attempt at gaiety or if she were colorblind. It was most likely the latter. She was not good at festivities of any kind, and although there were any number of services for her to command she insisted on tending to every detail herself.

Grimly she awoke that morning to have a cross meeting with cook and the gardeners. Her brow furrowed with headache as she ate her abstemious breakfast of dry toast and a half a cup of tepid coffee. Then off into the garden to stare around her, blinking at the showy flower beds. She would not allow them to be cut, so the table arrangements were the stiff little knots of flowers she ordered for every occasion, jammed into their baskets with wires and decorated with satin bows more appropriate to funeral designs than a dinner party under the stars. Moreover, she would not use the good china, a pattern of surpassing ugliness she had ordered when they were young and poor, buying one piece at a time like a miser accumulating a horde. It was white Lenox with a heavy gold band and there were crystal goblets to match. Henry, who loved Italian pottery and wine drunk from thick green glasses, had shuddered at her choice even then, but he was gentle with Alice's delicate sensibilities and for years had pushed the pale and creamy food she favored around on the plates he abhorred. The caterer had supplied the tableware for the party.

Below, she fluttered. She had a peculiar paleness in the morning, as though the night had drained her. She never resorted to cosmetics, so that in the bright, sharp sunlight she had a ghostly look. Dear Alice, poor Alice, the two designations had juggled in his mind from the day they had married.

Her little dog bounded out of the house and

followed at her heels. Henry had given it to her as a birthday gift, thinking, as he matched the small yapping animal to his small anxious wife, how often dogs resembled their masters. Ashamed of the thought, he had tucked a diamond bracelet in its collar. Alice never wore it, but the dog had been a huge success. She had a tiny sleigh bed made and it was kept in their bedroom. The dog's snuffling often kept Henry awake. It would not eat unless Alice put the food in its dish and when they traveled she carried it with her in a ventilated box, warning stewards and pursers that if anything happened to it they would answer to her.

He had told her he wanted a fete by Watteau in honor of his friends Caleb and Stella. He had envisioned a beribboned and dainty picnic, perfect grapes and pears heaped on the tables, Mozart softly played under the trees and the other middle-aged and corpulent guests moved by the joy and lightness of it all, wandering along the mossy paths hand in hand. His plays often incorporated such a scene to the delight of the ladies who packed the matinees year after year. If he had not feared undoing Alice altogether it would have been something more Bacchic, with wine fountains and folk singers and silk pillows strewn on the grass. But Alice was not up to that. She had even been dubious about the fairy lights in the trees. They drew gnats and mosquitoes. She would, he knew, come down to the party smelling faintly of citronella. Mosquitoes attacked her fiercely and raised great red welts on her transparent skin.

"It looks quite nice, darling," he called down to her. She squinted up at him, shading her eyes, frowning.

"I don't know." She looked about her, as if she were, somehow, at the wrong address. "What if it rains?"

"It won't."

"If you want to talk," she said, "please come down. I have a sore throat. I can't shout."

The sorè throat he had anticipated. Sometimes it was a slight fever, a pain in the lower back, a sense of giddiness, but something always overtook Alice when a party was planned. Her little dog yapped. It hated Henry. Alice scooped it up in her arms, kissed its wet nose, whispered into its silky ears. Henry, watching from above, thought ruefully that he had never had such treatment at her hands. How dry her kisses were.

"We've ordered far too much food," she announced.

"We can afford it," he said with mild humor.

She did not respond. She took everything he said quite literally.

"Please come down, Henry. I want to go over the guest list again."

"We've done that several times, my dear."

There were only three people of their acquaintance she felt comfortable with, a slightly deaf and rather eccentric old aunt of hers, an elderly and effeminate lawyer who lived alone and grew orchids, and a young, angry and very ambitious Hollywood writer who sat at her feet and told her she was the only lady in a world of cunts. She permitted the word because in her heart of hearts she believed he was absolutely right.

The rest of their wide circle she viewed with disdain, keeping an exact count of the number of times she and Henry were invited to dinner each year in return for her own hospitality, as well as of Christmas cards, birth announcements, congratulatory wires and gifts. She knew precisely who had given the silver bonbon dish she had seen on sale in Beverly Hills, stacked by the dozens in a window. She knew if the candies sent from New York were stale and reposed in someone's drawer, to be dragged out and presented to her as a hostess gift. She knew when the needlepoint pillows went to others and she received a machine-made monstrosity hastily purchased in Spain. Her chilly thank-you notes went out on heavily embossed stationery from Cartier's written in a large, hysterical hand: Henry and she had been pleased to receive the donors' gift. Since they had not seen them in six months, a year, for quite some time, she had not been able to express her appreciation in person. She hoped their families were quite well. Had their son recovered from his divorce? Was their daughter finding herself at last or was she still unheard from in Saudi Arabia?

Woe to the senders of these tokens and mementos. Alice, sitting stiffly in their drawing rooms, heard every nuance, registered every hastily concealed pain. She saw the sleepy eyes of the gangly son of the house nodding from the poppy. She heard the high-pitched quarrel carried on in far reaches of the upper floors. She saw the tears, just dried, in the wife's eye; she counted the host's drinks. Had Henry been privy to all she knew his plays would have come far closer to life.

Henry met her in the garden, draped an arm around her.

"Don't overtire yourself," he said. "I want you to enjoy yourself tonight."

She shrugged off the remotest possibility of it. "I don't really see why we're doing this. The most Caleb has managed for us in New York is dinner in a restaurant. This all seems very extravagant to me. And what we'll do with Stella I'll never know. She'll probably come in a thrift-shop dress with liquor on her breath. I cannot believe for one moment that Caleb has any interest in her at all."

Henry led her to a garden bench too recently painted to sit on with comfort. He tested its sticky surface, sighed, sat down, pulling her down alongside him.

"I don't know why I should tell you this now, my darling, but it's so long ago. I was never really attracted to Stella, but when I was a boy I thought of asking her to marry me."

A large butterfly danced by. Alice followed its flight. She did not wish to hear what he was saying.

"It's not her beauty, if she has any at all. It's the wonderful working of her mind. Stella at her best is like some glorious fun house, full of mazes, bright with mirrors and distortions, frightening, amusing. Don't you see that?"

"I haven't thought about it," said Alice. "And why tell me all this now?"

He patted her hand. "Only to explain why Caleb is tempted."

She turned to him and he was struck with the sharp and pointed planes of her face. "If you were a true friend," she said, "you'd dissuade him before it goes any further."

Not I, my good and faithful Alice, thought Henry. In his mind's eye he had followed the course of the affair from moment to moment, like a putto in an Italian painting, peering down from the green foliage of the trees at Mars, sprawled on his back, while naked Venus, barebosomed and self-satisfied, watched him in his surfeited sleep. Oh, the beauty of it, autumnal love in the rich golden light of late afternoon. Impede it? Thwart it? Never!

The party was almost over. The remains of small cold Cornish game hens were left on the plates. Wine stained the tablecloths. The musicians, tired and chilled, played what they hoped was the last waltz of the evening. Two waiters moved wearily, speaking softly to each other in Spanish. A young actress fretted in the driveway over the loss of an earring. She went down on all fours pawing in the leaves, cursing, accusing. A film producer waited for her with the motor of his car running, striking himself in the chest where a strange pain had persisted all evening and muttering, "Don't quit on me now, you sonafabitch" to his rebellious heart. In the kitchen the catering crew packed away the petits fours and the pastry shells and imported chocolates to feed to their children. The cook quarreled loudly with a waitress, who burst into tears. Crab shells and lobsters left off ice made an odious smell. The drawing room was already darkened except for two young men who made promises to each other in the shadows; they were overheard by the houseboy who sniggered, causing their hasty exit.

In the garden Stella nursed a drink and brooded. The evening had been long and dull. Sometime, hours back, the wife of a director, a woman with a sad and ravaged face, had placed a hand on her knee, and then on her thigh. She had silenced the conversation with her loud announcement that she was not Sapphic—but could steer the lady to those who were. The table was made skittish; the talk after that veered nervously into tennis matches and recent operations. Pride of place went to two open-heart surgeries. They had the gruesome accounts through dessert and into coffee and brandy. Now they were all departed, the felonious businessman, the actress with the pronounced tremor, the musician with a disfiguring birthmark on his cheek, all gone to Valium and prayers or to tense all-night wakefulness.

Stella glared across the lawn at Caleb, collared by a film director who clutched his arm and proposed a ruinous arrangement with one of his writers. He droned on and on, his manner hectic, his accent Hungarian. Caleb's head, she could see, bobbed like a mechanical doll's. Kick him in the shin and come and get me, thought Stella, I've been too long at the goddamn fair.

She hadn't wanted to come in the first place. She had sulked and balked, but Caleb had been implacable. Henry had wished to bestow some kind of bounty on them and he was an old and valued friend. Poor Henry had few occasions for ceremony in his life. He had been passed over by the Pulitzer committee. He had never stood before the King of Sweden to be lauded for his contributions to literature. He had graduated from a correspondence college in his youth so there had been no cap and gown, no sonorous baccalaureate address. His opening nights were spent sitting beside Alice in hotel rooms while she vomited and begged him to let her buy a farm in Oregon where she could live in peace. He had seen Caleb's passion for Stella. He wished to scatter flowers before them, to have music played sweetly in their hearing, to give them his catered food and his best wishes. They had arrived early and stayed late.

Stella sipped her wine. It had tasted tannic and unpleasant at the first of the evening; now it seemed mellow. Perhaps they'd gotten to the good stuff at last. She slipped out of one shoe, scratched where a belt buckle bit into her flesh, slid down in her chair until she looked as limp as a rag. A cloud covered the moon. The night had a threatening empty blackness. Gone the reckless laughter. Gone the silken dresses and the flash of jewels. The rich cigar smoke hung stalely in the air. The pianist lifted his hands from the keyboard in a violent fit of coughing. The last horn wailed away into silence. Stella's head felt heavy on her neck, her lids heavy on her eyes. She had not said a dozen words all evening beyond "Yes, more" to the doe-eyed young Mexican waiter with the crucifix peering from under his shirt and "I haven't been to a movie since *Rin Tin Tin*" to the insistent and pimpled film critic who had sat at her right. She felt rust in her throat and gloom in her soul. She was certain she would have a head cold by morning. A moth plummeted into a dish of puddled ice cream. She lifted it out on the end of a matchstick; she peered closely to study it; she burped aloud. She drank on.

Alice emerged from the house and looked this way and that. She raised a nervous hand to her hair. The strings of lights began to be extinguished; pop went the green, pop went the pink. The musicians looked like figures cut from black cloth. Now she spotted Stella and wandered toward her, trailing a scarf behind her, a wavering flutter of blue chiffon.

"Stella?" She peered through the dark, leaning forward a bit, uncertain, hesitating.

Stella grunted.

"Ah, you're all alone." She sank heavily into a chair at her side. Across the garden Henry stood seeing the last of the guests out, bidding them good night in a jovial tone that was neither weary or diminished by the lateness of the hour.

"They've trampled my lawn," Alice said dispiritedly, "and nobody liked the food."

Stella tipped her head back and stared into the star-studded sky.

"The tower of Babel," she said reflectively. "Much said, nothing meant. Why do you do it?"

She heard Alice's shallow breathing. One day she would have sarcoidosis or a dark patch on her lungs. She was, Stella thought, fated to come to a miserable end.

"Why?" Alice pondered the question. "Henry loves people. They love him."

"Vultures." Stella was impatient. "Fools. There was a man at this table wearing a diamond pinkie ring and a gold bracelet. I wouldn't piss on him if he were on fire. Perfect idiot."

"Yes," said Alice, "I know the one."

"Erect a barricade," said Stella. "Dig a moat."

Alice didn't seem to hear her. "Once," she mused, "we had a party here for two hundred. I remember I had a swan carved out of ice. And nothing but white flowers. White begonias, white carnations, white lilies. There was a senator here and a Russian dancer and a blind duchess whose male secretary cracked walnuts and popped the meat into her mouth for her. He said his fingers were often bitten but he was well paid. They were all here, that night. Right in the middle of it I went upstairs, put on my nightgown, braided my hair and got into bed. The windows were wide open. I could hear the laughter and the chatter and someone singing lieder. They never knew I was gone." She brushed the crumbs from the table into her hand and folded a soiled napkin with care. "It's strange," she said. "As if I didn't exist."

She looked away. Caleb and Henry now walked arm in arm near a flowering hedge. Water splashed musically into a pool. Stella pushed a wine bottle toward Alice.

"Have a drink," she said. "Drink gives you presence when nothing else does. You'll come into being fast enough after you've belted a few."

"I'm not allowed wine. I have an ulcer." She gave Stella a pale smile. "I'm sure you guessed that."

"I could see there was something gnawing," said Stella. She felt misgivings as soon as the words were out of her mouth. She felt there would be a rush of confidences, confessions, complaints—and the hour was late.

Alice selected a chocolate from a silver dish at hand and nibbled at the sweet with little rabbit bites.

"If I were you," she remarked thoughtfully, "I would run away from Caleb before it's too late."

Stella sipped wine and looked impassive.

"Yes," Alice went on, "I would run away. You ought to listen to me, Stella. I've been an appendage to a man for thirty years. I've heard people say of me, 'That dark little woman is the wife.' The 'wife!'"

She clasped her hands, put them in her lap, then on the table, then against her flushed cheeks. "When I was eighteen I studied art in Paris. I went there quite by myself with a portfolio and presented myself to a great teacher in his studio. He had a fearsome reputation for savaging people, but he looked at my drawings and said get warm underwear and come here and study with me. I had the most wonderful winter of my life, all chilblains and timidity, but I worked... oh, how I worked and at the end the teacher bought one of my canvases for his own collection." She ate another candy, gulping it down fiercely, as if, like her life, it must perforce be swallowed. "It all ended when I married Henry. There was so much to do about Henry. I had to find him tax exemptions and a barber who could cut his hair the way he liked it. I had to put up lugs of strawberries to make jam because his mother did that and he liked home-made jam on his toast. I designed his study, the furniture and the curtains and even the pictures on the wall. I had his suits made and got pregnant the moment he said he wanted a child." A night wind ruffled her hair, revealing her broad brow, the furrows etched there.

"I joined the causes he believed in. I had my face lifted before I was forty-five because he had a young secretary with no lines at all. I sat beside him during interviews wearing proper little suits and heard them ask him about his work. They asked me what my favorite color was. There was a profile of us done once in a national magazine. They quoted Henry as saying that life was an art

300

he was trying to master. They quoted me as being fond of children and English tea."

"Well," Stella said gruffly, "I'm sorry for you. It's not right. It's not just."

"I've always thought I disliked you." Alice touched her pearls with delicate nervous fingers. "But just tonight, when I saw you sitting out here so stubborn and dauntless, I realized it was envy. My goodness, Stella, we might have been friends all these years and I could have learned how you do it."

"I'll tell you now," said Stella. "Give no quarter. You can't cleave a rock unless you're God and even He hasn't tried it with me yet. No quarter, Alice. Write it on a piece of paper and stick it between your boobs, and when you falter, haul it out and read it aloud. Defend what you are. Live for it. Die for it." She flung out a hand for her glass. "Now. Is the wine all gone or could I have a sip for the road?"

"The wine is finished," Alice said. She looked around the disordered garden. An umbrella sagged and flapped, flowers wilted, fine ashes blew through the air.

"It will take me all day tomorrow to put things right," she said. "Do go home now. Henry is cross if he doesn't get enough sleep."

"Henry again. Always Henry."

"Yes," she murmured, "and you'd best be careful about Caleb. His last wife embroidered house slippers for him. Just think, Stella—petit point house slippers."

Before Stella could reply Alice called across to the men, her voice high and thin on the night air.

"The party's over," she cried. "All over."

Caleb flatly refused to bed down in Stella's apartment. He was, he said, mortally offended by her lumpy bed, which he insisted would serve only for the mortification of a nun in penance. He demanded his comfort. Moreover, though he did not wish to insult her, he had to point out that her place was none too clean. He took her instead to a seaside hotel. She had sat silently by his side on the way from the party, her chin sunk on her chest, saying little.

She had, in fact, confined herself to two questions. What had he been talking about with Henry? And how many days had he left before his departure?

He was more than willing to tell her about his conversation with Henry. It had, of course, been about her. Henry had made solicitous inquiries as to his emotional state; he had responded enthusiastically with his new-found sense of well-being. He had told Henry that they, he and Stella, would turn out wonderfully. He expected, he told Stella, that she would do her part.

Stella did not smile. She felt, in the sullen early-morning hours, that he was swaggering. Inordinately proud of himself. Smug. She wanted nothing to do with happiness. She had another purpose.

"When are you leaving?"

"Far too soon. In three days." He drove recklessly, one hand on the wheel, the other stroking her hair.

The hotel loomed before them, a big pseudo-Spanish pile, looking as if it had been built yesterday and would not last till tomorrow. Stella hated the sleepy attendant with his Ruritanian uniform of red and gold. She hated the dapper elevator attendant, who had big horse teeth and a sallow yellowish complexion. Everything seemed false and fabricated. She slouched after Caleb to their room like a captive concubine, shuffling her shoes, her eyes downcast. She felt an inch from death. It was too much wine, but nobody could have told her that. She knew death when she felt it.

There were flowers in the room and a basket of oranges and a pile of sandwiches, cut thin.

Caleb moved about swiftly, leaving her standing by the door, still in her coat, still drooping and unwilling. He opened a window, patted the bed, lit the lamps, every gesture claiming the room for his own. He even paused to pull a daisy from the floral arrangement and tuck it into his buttonhole. Stella watched in wonder. He was turning the place into a goddamn love nest.

At last he came toward her, grasped her hand and drew her into the center of the room, where the huge chandelier rained a hard light down upon her. He pulled her free of her coat and tossed it on the bed. He took her face between his hands and studied her.

"Worse for drink but very lovely."

"I'm not going to look like a houri at this hour in the morning." She spoke fretfully. "Which bed do you want? I'm going to fall in mine right now."

He would see about that later. He left her standing and went into the bathroom. She heard water being drawn into the tub. She remained rooted where she was, too tired to move, feeling captive, hostile.

"Stella," he called, "come in here."

God, she thought, if he has any water frolic in

mind I'll kill him. She appeared in the doorway, her face looking sharp and impatient. The tub steamed with hot water, frothed with bubbles. He had his sleeves rolled up. His cheeks had turned a beautiful cherubic shade of pink.

"Off with your clothes," he ordered cheerfully.

"I'm in no mood for water sports," said Stella. "I'm awash with wine and dead tired, so whatever you have in mind you can just forget."

He shook his head, took hold of her and unbuttoned her blouse.

"Do what I tell you," he said pleasantly, "and be quick about it. The temperature's just right."

He'll have me wallowing like a porpoise in there, and then Christ knows what next. She shucked her clothes, leaving them pooled at her feet, and stared at him with cold eyes.

Without a word he scooped her up and deposited her in the depths of the tub. Then he lifted up her mane of hair and piled it atop her head. He bent toward her and she felt his sucking, biting kisses raining on her, and just as she shuddered at the sweetness of it, he was at her suddenly with a soapy face cloth, scrubbing ferociously where his mouth had just been. Be damned if he wasn't cleaning her ears, peering into them to see that the job was well done. Next his hands cupped a breast, lifted, caressed. He murmured something about great ripe apples and took a nibble to see if it was truly so. He fancied apples. The other breast felt his tongue as well. He lathered her bush, twisted its tendrils into peaks and curls and then stood back to admire the sculpture he had made with suds. He lifted a foot hidden in the green depths, held it aloft and nuzzled the instep against his cheek. And then to work again until she was as clean as a hound's tooth. Stella bobbed and turned in his hands like a rubber doll, astonished. Then out she came and was enveloped in a huge towel and dried from head to foot. Caleb groaned a little with the exertion of it all but went at it with the dispatch of an English nanny. Then off they marched to the other room, the cool air washing Stella's body, and the bed was turned down and she was slid under the sheets and warmly blanketed.

Then he undressed himself, depositing each article of clothing with particular neatness on the chair by the bed. A second later he disappeared and there were gargling sounds and snortings and snufflings and he was back, turning off the lights, raising a second window to the breeze, which ruffled his hair into white foam. Big and sturdy, he loomed at the window, making some sort of quiet communion with the night. Stella felt very still and suspended as she watched him. She felt foolish and wise at the same time, and for once, quite speechless. He came to her side, nudged her to make room for him, and then he was stretched out next to her, his girth making the bed sag and creak.

"Ah," he said.

Excitement rose in Stella. She put her hand between his legs, stroking, encouraging; the soft bud became a stalk.

"So you've come to life, have you?" His voice was loud and amused.

"All that warm water," she muttered. "What do you expect?"

"Well, my dear, tonight I have other needs."

Stella's ears pricked up. If it was to be anything athletic she would have none of it. At his age he needn't be too imaginative.

His encircling arm pulled her close to him, her head bumped against his broad shoulder.

"All safe... all serene. Dear Stella." She felt his chest rise and fall with quiet contented breathing. "Now I think we should find each other out. Tell me about your childhood and if I'm not fast asleep by the end of it, I'll tell you mine."

Stella struggled upright. "You want to *talk?*"

"You are too detached, my dear," he said. "Exchange of confidences binds. Connect me with your twelve-year-old self, and you shall have me as the roguish boy I was. Backwards from middle age we go. Begin."

Stella rolled away on her side and pounded her pillow. He could have her from the front or from the back or standing on her head, but she was outraged at this other surrender.

"I'm a private person," she remarked huffily, "and we'll get along better if you remember it."

"Tosh," he said. "You're a stingy person, parceling out your favors with a little leg here, a little backside there. I want more than that. I mean to have more." He settled himself, pulling most of the covers off her to envelop him.

She was suspicious. "Why should I tell you things you can use against me?"

"In the first place, I won't use anything you tell me to hurt you. In the second, people who are intimate must be vulnerable to each other. It's an act of trust."

In the dark Stella smiled a fierce and ominous smile. "I slept with the parish priest when I was thirteen," she trumpeted. "And very good he was, too."

"Unlikely if not untrue," said Caleb firmly.

"I stole money. From my father's pockets. From my mother's purse."

"Of little interest." Caleb was not appeased.

"What then? What?" Stella was becoming flustered, hot, uneasy. He probed like her dentist.

"The first poem," he said.

Stella thrashed, flung out an arm, gave him a glancing blow.

"On toilet paper." She laughed suddenly. "The whole bloody family was in the house on a Sunday morning. Bikes were piled up on our front porch. My aunts were sitting on their fat bottoms, shelling peas for dinner, the men swilling beer and talking shop, and I went to the bathroom and locked the door and sat there writing in blue ink that came through the other side of the paper. God, masturbating was nothing to what I felt then. Nothing. I came out all red and splotchy, with tears in my eyes. I think one of the aunts thought I'd been diddled by a cousin and had gone in there to wash it away. The next day I read it and it was the worst drivel you ever saw. I tore it to bits and stuffed it down the drain. Then I reasoned that inspiration in a smelly bathroom had been the cause of its being so terrible. So I waited till the feeling came on me again and I hiked off into the woods in search of beauty. A farmer, out hunting woodchucks, nearly blasted my head off with his shotgun, and I ran home, wetting my pants with the close call I'd had. No poem from that, I can tell you. Then I decided that the whole thing was a mystical experience and I went to church after the

307

last Mass was said, and it was dark and cold and I knelt down and put my scrap of paper on the floor, and by the light of the guttering candles I scratched out something. Then I waltzed into the confessional, lit a match, and just as I was being transported by my own genius the priest popped in the other half and asked me what I was up to. Poetry, I told him, and full of pride I shoved it across for him to read.

"He said it was sheer doggerel and as he was young and a Jesuit my heart turned to stone. Later, I decided he was just jealous. Not much poetry in what he had to do day after day. I never stopped trying after that. Before I was deflowered. After. When my mother died. When I was put in jail for lifting a bottle of bourbon from the grocery store. And other occasions which are none of your business."

He was silent.

"Caleb?"

By Christ, he was asleep, the damned inquisitive bastard was sound asleep. Stella thrust herself against his bulk, left a kiss in the hairy tangle of his chest and closed her eyes.

Stella sat in a chair, swinging her leg up and down in a fretful motion. A run laddered her stocking from her ankle to her knee, she noticed. She bent over, moistened her forefinger with spit, and stopped the unraveling threads. When she looked up again she saw the secretary behind the desk watching her curiously, trying to place her in the hierarchy of the clientele: was she a stripper in trouble, an abandoned wife, a litigious hooker? Caleb, seated next to her, cleared his throat.

"Let it be," he said. "I'll buy you a new pair as soon as we're finished here."

Stella slumped in her chair. The secretary answered the phone, chanting the firm's name in a bright, lilting voice: "Keller, Keller, Keller and Wainwright—good afternoon."

Caleb lit a cigar. When the girl was free again he questioned her pleasantly: "He knows we're here?"

"He'll just be a moment. He's finishing a long-distance call."

Caleb nodded and folded his arms.

The door opened then and a small man rushed out to them, energetic, precise, pleated folds under his eyes, a pince-nez bobbing on a ribbon against his chest, extending his hands in greeting.

"Forgive me, forgive me." He clasped Caleb in a warm embrace and beamed at Stella. "Do come in, come right in." He ushered them into the room behind him, standing aside with a little half bow to Stella.

His office was huge, and though sumptuous it contained small, homey touches: an old-fashioned muffler hung behind the door even though it was nearly summer, a striped one, yellow and white wool, surely uncomfortable, sure to scratch. The remains of lunch were on a table, a spiral curl of apple peel, shiny black seeds, a little pearl-handled fruit knife; and a glass of mineral water respirated, tiny bubbles breaking, a ring of lemon floating on its surface. A frugal lunch, the lunch of a man with a monkish view of life, moderate, close.

Stella clumped inside deliberately and dropped into the first chair at hand without waiting to be asked. She stared boldly around her. She avoided offices at all costs. No good, in her opinion, was to be got out of them. If you did find yourself in one there was always a dentist with a drill lurking there, or a doctor with dire warnings. Lawyers, with their ponderous legal tomes and their welter of closely written documents, were the worst of a bad lot.

She hiked herself up in the huge leather chair, revealing a badly soiled slip and three inches of thigh, and she glared first at Caleb and then at the tidy and compact little man behind the desk, who offered a tidy and compact little smile to match his appearance.

"Stella, my dear, this is Moses Keller, my close friend of forty years. He flourishes as the green bay tree. He is the father of six sons, and his second wife is often mistaken for his daughter, a thing that makes him proud as punch."

Mr. Keller rose and bobbed at her. "A pleasure, a genuine pleasure." He beamed. "So gifted, so talented, such an accurate ear, such soaring, confident flights. 'Ode to Hymen,' 'Cantos for a Long War in Southeast Asia,' 'The New Lysistrata.' I know the product, you see."

He sat down again, shuffling a few papers with small, rapid fingers, his smile slowly disappearing, as if it might somehow interfere with the serious business at hand.

Stella was not encouraging. She made a sniffling sound that might or might not have acknowledged him. Mr. Keller began to have an anxious look. He washed his hands dryly, rubbing one over the other. Caleb had extolled a glorious woman to him. This one looked as though she carried a concealed weapon. Perhaps not concealed. Her eyes, flashing at him, were dangerous and quite out in the open. He lined up paper clips on the neat surface of his desk and waited. Caleb went on.

"He's drawn you an excellent book contract at my request. I've looked at and found it to be in order. Moses loves the written word."

"I aspire dimly myself." He permitted himself a small chuckle.

"Confess, Moses. There was a bad novel in your twenties."

"Well, fortunately for all, the law is my first mistress."

Stella thought blackly of liens and foreclosures, of suits and countersuits, of quitclaims and summonses.

"He works for you," she said flatly.

"He does indeed." Caleb smiled.

"Well," she said harshly, "that's where the shit hits the fan."

Mr. Keller unbuttoned his jacket, revealing a damp shirt and a heavy gold watch chain. He felt as if he were baring his bosom to an asp. He should, he reflected, have left this one to his son, Anthony. Anthony defended radicals and lettuce growers, murderers and child molesters. He longed for Anthony. Anthony, alas, was cruising the West Indies to quiet his ulcer and deepen his tan.

Stella lapsed into a stony silence. She took in the Georgian desk with cold and calculating eyes, the silver inkpot, the French paperweight. She carefully noted the Morocco bindings and the fine view from the lofty window. She saw the framed photograph of the stiffly coifed woman, whose neck was encircled with perfectly matched pearls and whose look of satisfaction bespoke, at the very

311

least, well-trained attack dogs, steam-heated greenhouses, efficient housemaids, obliging young lovers.

And beside her sat Caleb, puffing on his cigar, admiring the ash that grew at its end; shrewd and merry Caleb. An image rose in her mind. The two of them, Moses Whatsisname and Caleb, frock-coated, sly, laying out walnut shells before her and urging her, as they manipulated them cunningly, to tell them where the little pea lay. Is it here? No? Then here? No? We seem to have fooled you.

She peered at them from under her heavy brows. Not so fast. They'd have to rise early in the morning to swindle her. Fleecing? She knew all about fleecing. Hadn't her daddy, resplendent in his straw hat and his flowered bow tie, sold off Florida real estate sodden with seawater to unsuspecting widows in the twenties? Hadn't he seated himself on their front-porch gliders with colored folders in his hands, extolling beautiful sunsets and inimitable views? The sky is light till ten o'clock and the sea stretches to infinity, somewhere or other, dear ladies. Yes, he had drunk their lemonade, squeezed just for him, and palmed the seeds with ever so much finesse, blowing them with such a refined little phut into his curled palm, and he had patted their hands, he intended to buy himself, right next door, perhaps; he would grow petunias and fish from the pier as the sun sank in the West, verily burned itself out as it sank in the West.

Hadn't her Uncle Ed, with the cowlick and the bulbous nose, run for the state senate on money which came to his house in thick white envelopes bearing no return address? She had seen him many a summer morning with his beefy arm draped around an innocent in the barber shop, murmuring promises into an ear sharply outlined by a fresh haircut. And her cousins. Christ's bleeding wounds, her cousins. George Harris and William Benjamin, sandy-haired and blue-eyed, nails short and clean, deodorant under their armpits, their private parts talcumed, alike as two peas in a pod. Why, they had gone through agricultural college on the friendly poker games they got up in the neighborhood, one dealing with a flourish while the other signaled by a little obbligato of coughs behind his hand. Not to mention her brother Valentine, who leaned on his butcher's scale with a scabby elbow while he smiled at his customers and inquired after their health with a gold-toothed grin; charging for bone and gristle he'd gotten rich. And the lesser felons, second cousin Harris, who signed his father-in-law's name to checks, and David Allen, who stole his mother's tea service the night before he went off to the navy. What a family of thieves. But they had made her wise to the game.

Try me, lawyer, she thought wickedly, just try me.

"This is a standard contract," Mr. Keller told her soothingly. "Nothing very complicated. It includes, of course, the terms of the advance as well as the entire royalty structure. The territory of publication, both hard-cover and soft-cover, U. S. rights, English-speaking rights, foreign rights, the usual indemnity respecting privacy and defamation, stipulations covering accounting procedures and an agreement to negotiate in good faith, which really amounts to no more than a first look, on your

313

next book." He ventured a smile at her. "Everything is clearly stated in plain English. We try not to obfuscate in this office. Still, if anything puzzles you, just draw it to my attention. I'm here to help in any way I can."

Stella thrust out her jaw. "The lawyer who gets my business," she said, leaning forward in her chair pugnaciously, "has an office over a drugstore. You have to walk up three flights of stairs to get to it and when you arrive it's about as big as a rabbit hutch. It has a battered wooden desk which he bought secondhand thirty years ago from a junk shop. It has a chair. Just one. Anyone else in the room aside from him has to stand. He answers the telephone himself, if he feels like it. If not, not. He's worn the same suit as long as I've known him and that's an age and a half. It's dark green. That may or may not be the color—I personally think it's mold. He doesn't own a car; it's shanks' mare for him, rain or shine. He brings his lunch in a brown paper bag and it's usually a peanut butter sandwich and a brown-spotted banana. That's *my* lawyer."

She leaned back and folded her arms across her chest. Caleb was watching her, his mouth pursed thoughtfully.

"Is there some particular point you're making, Stella?"

Stella waved an arm about, encompassing the paintings, the conference table, the gleaming walnut bar, the walls of books.

"Somebody," she said, feeling snippy as hell, "paid through the nose for all this."

Mr. Keller looked to Caleb in alarm. "I don't understand," he said weakly.

314

Caleb puffed, puffed again. "I believe Stella is questioning your probity, Moses," he said. He turned a chiding gaze on her. "I'm sure you appreciate that it would be insulting for me to vouch for Mr. Keller any further than I have. I'm sure you see that, Stella."

Stella laid on the scourge, flailing right and left. "You speak for him. He speaks for you. Humpty and Dumpty. It looks like I'm the only disinterested person in sight." She rummaged in her bag, found a handkerchief, blew her nose triumphantly.

Mr. Keller rose on his short legs, his face scarlet. He reached for a glass of water, which he swallowed in long, nervous gulps.

"This is extraordinary," he said aloud to no one in particular.

Stella leaped to her feet and stomped back and forth across the room. "It takes me years to make my poems," she said vehemently, "years of tyrannical work. I'm not giving them up, not a line, not a word, not a strophe, till I strike a bargain that suits me right down to the ground. I'm not one of those idiots who'll sell their souls for a fig." She shook her head to emphasize the point. Hairpins rained down.

"...My dear Miss..." Mr. Keller struggled to interrupt her, but she charged on, plunging, rearing, neighing.

"I'm not finished with what I have to say." She rounded on Caleb, included him. "It'll take more than a romp in the hay or my pants hurled off the Palisades or peaches out of season or lobster cocktails or suites of rooms in hotels with twenty-four-inch television sets; it'll take bundles and

315

stacks more than that to get me into camp, don't think it won't."

Mr. Keller needed to go to the bathroom. Mr. Keller wanted to go to the bathroom. "Would you excuse me just a moment," he said to Caleb. "I won't be a moment."

He scurried out. The door closed with a little click on his agitated back. Stella stood fuming in the middle of the room while Caleb tapped his ash calmly into the tray before him.

"Well, well," he said. "Apart from your customary paranoia, your profoundly held conviction that the entire world wants to cheat and abuse and hoodwink you, could you explain what you're up to? I'm at a loss myself."

Stella flounced one way and then another. "I'm not delivering myself up to the unknown put together by the unscrupulous. There's nothing hard to understand about that!"

"No," Caleb said mildly, "not if you're dealing with charlatans. As it stands, however, you are dealing with me, your devoted admirer, your intimate friend, as well as with an honorable and upright attorney at law. Or perhaps not." His voice grew steely. "I'm not patient with your shenanigans, Stella; with tantrums of any sort. You will either sign this contract with me or you will not. That's up to you. But what is not up to you is the apology you will offer my friend. That I insist on. Moses and I go back a long way, as far back as Harvard College. He was best man at my wedding, his eldest son is named after me. His name is stainless, his reputation unsullied." Caleb paused for a moment. "Now. Whatever offense I may have taken at this unseemly display I will overlook. You

316

need not say you are sorry to me, though it would be graceful of you if you did." Again he paused, but Stella remained mute. "I believe," he continued, "that there is a fountain pen on the desk. Your signature is required on all three copies. In ink, my dear Stella, not in blood."

"Not so fast, not so fast!" Stella cried, snatching the contract from the desk. "I'm going to crawl over this line by line, with my own legal counsel looking over my shoulder. The one I told you about, the *honest* one above the store. If we're satisfied, we'll be in touch with you."

Caleb reached into an inner pocket, withdrew his wallet and extracted some bills from it. He held them out to her.

"Take a taxi home. I will speak to Mr. Keller on your behalf. It's clear to me that you don't know how to say you're sorry. Good afternoon, Stella."

Stella grabbed the papers and stormed out, crying that a retreat was not a rout, not by a long shot. She marched toward the elevator, her face flushed, nostrils flared with anger. She had never been bested in a horse trade yet. She wouldn't be now.

Stella lay in her bed, her arms behind her head, a glass of whiskey balanced on her belly. Papers were scattered on the counterpane, an ashtray overflowed and spilled onto the sheets. She had not bothered to turn on the lights; her thoughts were better suited to glum darkness. Not that she was given to introspection. She had little or no patience with self-analysis, self-evaluation; deeds done needed no excuses, those undone even less review. When she was off balance for one reason or another, and those times of doubt and misgivings were rare, she treated herself to a good bottle, drunk slowly. On occasion she ground her teeth violently, she cracked her knuckles—a sure sign of unease with her. Do it or don't do it, get over it, get done with it—this was her litany, recited in a voice thick with liquor, taken in solitude. Remorse was a soppy, ashen angel, weeping crystal tears from empty eyes. Fuck it. If she set her foot on the wrong path she would climb it to the end, briars, nettles, stinging weeds notwithstanding.

She reared up, swung her feet to the floor, grasped the bottle and lurched to the mirror. She scanned her reflection. Why, only look, it was a face to turn heads still, it had character, it was a rare old face. She lifted the bottle in a toast. Some number of cells died suddenly in her brain at that moment; the earth sloped, dizziness made her unsteady on her feet. A breath from an open grave rose damply in her nostrils. She dismissed it; it was merely hunger, she hadn't eaten. Phantoms and beasts came out of the forest when five or six meals were forgotten. Had she breakfasted? That was millenniums ago. No, she had not. She had been in Caleb's bed, legs splayed out, empty-headed, replete, like any other prisoner of love awakening to the toastmaster, to the laundry, to the morning soap opera. Caleb?

The very name became a target. She stormed through the room, sweeping up the papers from the floor, bringing them up before her shortsighted eyes, yelping aloud in rage. A contract? It wasn't rich enough for her gifts, the conniving bastard. What did he think she was, a fire sale, a rummage

318

sale, a bloody flea market? She peered at the papers, muttered, dropped them underfoot and ground them under her heel. Back to the bed she went, sloshing the blankets with the open bottle. She knotted a pillow under her head, made ugly faces at the ceiling. Caleb. Caleb. He was a plug in the spout, that's what he was. A cork, shutting off that whirling, swirling outpouring of the unconscious that was her real self. What had she to do with languishing and soul kissing and soft stroking and secrets? Christ, what had she been up to? She wanted her old hard self back again. Make way, clear the streets, curb your dogs, Stella is abroad in the land. Yes, she wanted to walk the beach and be deaf to the enormous roar of the waves, be blind to the sun. She wanted her own landscape, the rocky, boiling, stormy country where she alone ruled. Caleb, the shepherd. Caleb, the spoiler. He had cut her down with a scythe: she was no longer grass springing greenly from the ground, she was hay, dry, baled, bound, fodder for cows.

A heavy tread sounded outside her door. There was a muffled pounding—muffled because her head had ducked under a pillow.

"There's a plague in here," she called out in a booming voice. "Move on!"

The knocking became insistent. Outside, Caleb's voice was raised in command. "Don't keep me standing here, Stella."

"Who is it?" she inquired in a la-de-da voice.

"Stella, be quick!"

She gathered her sweater around her with a majestic gesture and crossed the room with mincing steps, bare feet slapping on the floor, ending with her ear against the door. "Yes?" she said. "You wish to see someone?"

She heard his impatient grunt. "I'm too old for this."

Her combative face appeared in a narrow crack. Her eyes, narrow and mean, swept over him. "You've got on an Alpine hat," she accused, "with a red feather in the band. Disgusting." She flung the door wide, staggering backward.

He removed the offending hat and came inside, striding past her to toss it on the couch. She pursued him aggressively, put her face up to his.

"Slave trader!" She spat the word at him and then grinned, pleased with herself.

He grasped her by the arm with a rough hand, dragged her across the room and threw her down on the bed so hard that she felt something jar in her spine.

"You are drunk and foolish," he said with utter coldness.

Stella was very grand, gathering herself up with what she considered immense self-control. "If you are going to take that tone with me," she announced, "I will have to show you the door."

He loomed over her. "Any other man," he said, "would slap you silly."

"You dare!"

"Don't tempt me."

She sniffed.

Then she reached up and waggled a finger under his nose. "You'll never get me up on the block. Never." She pulled her lip up, showing her teeth. "Sound teeth." She thumped her chest. "Sound of wind." She tapped her forehead.

320

"Sound, sound, sound of mind." She rose, ducked under his restraining arm and made for the kitchen, stumbling in the dark. The light from the refrigerator lit her face as she peered into its depths. "Rat cheese," she said petulantly. "There's nothing but rat cheese."

Caleb was beside her in two strides, taking her by the shoulders and shaking her. "I won't have this," he said emphatically. "I will not have this!"

She flounced free of him and then, crouched and ferocious, she fought back. "Damn you. I'm finished with you. Heaving your great carcass on top of me, shoving and pushing and humping. And there I am like an idiot squashed beneath you, and yelling for you to do it some more. And all the while my mind is blank. *Blank*. You great prick, you've shrunk me. You've diminished me. There's nothing in my head but burst grape skins, fish scales, skeletons. A night with you and I'm nothing. An inane smile, soft eyes, puddles. Where's the thunder? Where's the lightning? What am I doing whispering in the dark into your cauliflowered ear? You're just a man. I've had 'em by the dozens, had 'em and gone on my way with a hay and a ho, and thank God I don't have to see your hairy backside again. You want me to be a soft gray mouse in your pocket. You want me to be a sweet child and sit on your lap with your hands cupping my dumpling buttocks. You want to stroke my hair and twine it around your fingers. Tame Stella, Stella on her back, Stella in love. Not for me!"

Caleb's roar shook the windows. "Silence!" Anger ripped over him in waves. He was a mountain of hot ash and lava, thrusting up out of an earthquake. He stomped toward her, all his great bulk aquiver with rage. Stella inched back a step or two. Caleb advanced, a clenched fist raised before him.

"You are a greedy, willful, destructive, monomaniacal and totally intolerable woman! I can only ascribe my having anything whatever to do with you to the onset of senility! Any twenty-dollar whore in any flophouse is your superior in every way. You say I've stolen your divine fire by making love to you—as insane a display of ego as I've ever encountered. What smarts here, my girl, is not your banked fires but the price I put on them." He took hold of her and shoved her angrily before the mirror. "Look at yourself—drunken, lazy, self-indulgent, the hide of a water buffalo. The Muse has gone elsewhere, has she? I don't blame her. Who would want to live in your company? The laurel crown on your unwashed hair? I don't think so."

He picked up his hat, put it on again, snapped the brim. Stella watched him, her mouth slack in astonishment. The eagle had swooped and pecked out her eyes.

"You're going?"

He almost smiled at that. "Indeed I am. Before we get to sticks and stones."

"Go on, then," she cried hotly. "I don't care."

"You will," he told her sternly. "But it will be far too late."

She hung out the window, watching his retreating figure. Far too good for him; she was far too good for him. But *wait!* . . . He was out of sight.

10

HORTENSE THOUGHT with longing of the little
buggers from John Muir Junior High School. She
had transferred away from there to Leland
Stanford High after principal Harry Saul had
cornered her in the cloakroom late one rainy
afternoon, the other teachers gone, all the children
gone, custodians gone, and had kissed her wetly,
crying that his life was a ruin, that he was growing
older and less and less sure of himself with every
passing moment, that only she of all the people he
knew could lead him in his progress from morbidi-
ty to bliss, starting right there and then on the
dusty floor scored with the heel marks of ten
thousand kids. She had retrieved the glasses that
fell from his high-bridged nose and were nearly

crushed underfoot in his amorous frenzy, had observed the shiny and scaling bald spot on his remorsefully hung head, and told him to piss off. He saw that he had misjudged her, saw the possibilities of disaster if she talked, clasped his hands in a fervent and doleful appeal for her silence and wrote her a glowing letter to take with her.

And so she had been six weeks at the high school. It took sheer brute strength of will to get from the first class to the last. She acquired it, but only at the cost of the first strands of gray in her hair and a coarse and hoarsened voice. She carried a can of hair spray in her pocket to ward off attack and learned to leave her jewelry at home. Someone, with the light, quick touch of an accomplished cutpurse, had snatched a gold chain off her neck as she bent over a drinking fountain. She had been goosed at the same time. She had admired the dexterity but deplored the loss. She had also had pornographic notes of almost dazzling lewdness left in her box. She had been, in her passage through the halls, tweaked, fondled, massaged, and tripped. Summer had not come a moment too soon.

Now it was bust-out day. The kids packed the halls, butting into each other, jiving, lounging against the walls, the boys with the sassy looks of little bulls, in their bright blue and yellow and poison green satin shirts, the girls with apple-hard buttocks straining their jeans. The Hondas and the Pintos with rust-raked fenders waited outside, stacked with surfboards and cases of illegally purchased beer. There was grass artfully concealed under hub caps and blankets and sun cream and AM-FM radios. There were knives, short-bladed and wicked, and a bone-handled razor or two. There was Vaseline and K-Y jelly and Trojans and a few sexual oddities made in Mexico and purchased by the boldest for use on the most innocent. It was summer, sand up the crotch, lust in the heart, larcenous. Long, hot summer.

Hortense swung down the hall to a chorus of whistles and rhythmic poundings. Every undulation of her hips was greeted with appreciative cries, yelps, wolf calls, yips. Some of the girls, those who subsisted on Fudgsicles and Coca-Cola and ran to fat around the middle, watched her sullenly: surely, on her sleek black skin there had to be a blemish like those that spotted their faces. One of the more reckless youths, who felt the brush of her hand as she cleared a path for herself, was transported into a fantasy so carnal it made his ears ring, his eyes water.

"Yeah, okay, fine, swell." Hortense plunged through them. "Just take it easy." She made the door of her classroom, only to be stopped by a muscular brown arm thrust in front of her, barring her way. He was a big galoot with pretty blue eyes, bad teeth and nerve.

"Baby, baby," he crooned. "I don't eat nuthin' but chocolate."

She slapped him away, riffled a pack of report cards she carried under his nose.

"These'll take the hubba-hubba out of you, hot stuff," she said. "You are F for failed, baby." She unlocked the door and was propelled into the room by the bucking mass behind her.

Someone had written "Summer Sucks" large upon the blackboard. She left it unerased and took her seat, pounding on the desk with a book until the babble subsided. In the back of the room a guitar twanged. Hortense wiped the offender out with a single dark glance.

"Okay," she said. "Before everybody rushes off to get V.D., parking tickets and polluted, I have something to say. I've had you in this class for six weeks and this is what I've concluded: there's no hope for you kids. Let me repeat: no hope, none."

There was a growl and a catcall. Hortense banged the book again. "Shut up. You need to hear this and you're going to hear this. This school was vandalized three times this semester. Three. Once with fire. Once with water. Once with an *ax!* Six merchants in the neighborhood were ripped off to the tune of two thousand dollars in shoplifted goods. Only two people in this class can fill out a job application in halfway literate or even legible English. There are enough crabs among you to start a cannery. Three of you are pregnant and nine of you have been aborted more than once. One of you slashed the tires on my car. Three of you have been arrested for drunk driving. One of you jumped your mama and damn near killed her. Four of you have helped yourselves out of my purse every Friday afternoon like clockwork. What I'm trying to say is—get out of my sight—and if you're not in the slammer, I'll see you next fall."

A cheer rose. A willowy, silky-haired girl in elaborately embroidered denims came forward, holding a bouquet of wilted daisies in front of her. She tendered them to Hortense with a melting smile.

"These are for you, Miss Washington, from the class. We all got up the money for it. Maybe some of it was stolen, like you said, but everybody contributed. It was like, man, we just love Miss Washington. I mean, we all got it on with you, even if you do chew our asses out more than any other teacher in the school. And we all feel we learned a lot from you. You ask any kid and he goes, 'Yeah, she's got it together, she's in the right space,' so what we want to say is have a real cool summer, and keep the faith." She thrust the rank flowers into Hortense's hands, jiggled so the boys in the front row would know she was not wearing a bra and took her seat.

Hortense held the flowers under her nose; then, with a weary sigh, she chucked them on her desk, first leaning forward to retrieve the condom tucked neatly among them. She held it aloft for all to see.

"You kids have real class," she said.

"We was just funnin', teach."

"Yeah, it's a joke, unless you got somebody you wanna fit it on."

Foot stamping and cheers greeted the last sally.

Hortense held up her hand, raised her voice. "If more of you used these things the world would be a healthier, happier, cleaner place." She flung it away disdainfully. It was neatly fielded in midair and pocketed.

She held up the report cards. "All right. Line up for the bad news. C's, D's and F's are as far as we go in the alphabet."

Moments later they were gone, filling the air with whoops, spilling out of the yard and into the streets, wild, free.

Hortense waited until the din receded. She meant to empty her desk drawers, return the textbooks to the library. Instead she sat, resting her chin on her hand, staring through the dusty windows at the cars stenciled with swastikas and other obscenities. Summer.

Summer was Texas, lying in a torn hammock with a water-stained copy of *Pride and Prejudice* bleeding blue onto her cotton dress, slapping at mosquitoes, digging out chiggers, struggling to keep the cool and witty presence of the nineteenth century in a backyard littered with dog turds and chicken feed.

It was climbing past the No Trespass sign, up a swaying iron ladder, to drop into the reservoir tank with the name of the town in white paint on its side, wearing her pink bra and rayon panties, to slide into the dusty water and float on her back and stare up into a sky the color of dirty linen.

It was squeezing jelly bags tied to the loop of pipe under the kitchen sink, while the gnats hummed in the air and the juice and sugar boiled to thickness with soft plopping sounds on the stove. It was peach ice cream with slivers of the fruit crushed in it, eaten on the back porch with a sticky-handled spoon, the night sullen with lightning, heavy with humidity. It was going into town where the drugstore signs flashed with every other bulb burned out and cowboys lounged against the buildings, shifting tobacco wads, waiting for the Western movie to come on. It was standing in the bus depot, where an old man blew his nose between his fingers and stared at her as she read the names of other places and composed farewell notes in her head. "Mama, I'll send for you. If I end up where it's cold you'd better think twice about coming, but I'll never do real good unless you're someplace close."

Summer was Booker. Booker, rattling over the backcountry roads in his old Chevy, held together with baling wire, boasting his head off about how he could take Tony Trabert or Ken Rosewall or Dennis Ralston if he could ever get out of this shit-ass town and do something besides deliver milk for the Alco Dairy. Booker, putting his cheek against hers and asking guilelessly how much she had saved; sister, he had said, I need dollars; he had to get away, away from the two cracked cement courts in Ida Hays Memorial Park on which grass and weeds sprouted; he needed coaching, pros to play against, proper courts with night lights so he could practice around the clock. Lend me your dollars, he had begged, so I can ankle on out of here.

"We're going together." She had been flinty. "And you're getting up your share. If you start living off me now, you'll live off me from now *on*."

Booker. Suddenly she wanted Booker. Ted Todson waited for her instead.

Hortense was used to dealing with men. She was harsh and dismissive with sexual advances unless she was really interested, canny and sharp-tongued if business was involved, and impatient and unyielding on almost every other level. The belly-pinching years had made her jealous of her time; it was not to be wasted. Her life with Booker had suited her. It was she who had begun it when they were children, winnowing him out from the sea of eager adolescent boys who had longed for her, hauling him into maturity after her like a dawdling puppy pulled on a leash. She had hatched him. She had shaped him. She had made him her own. She was bored by the probings necessary in other relationships with men, the slow, sensuous evaluations, the fencing, the parrying. Bored! She scorned the humiliation of being appraised, being judged. Banter wearied her. Flattery embarrassed her. She got her bearings by direct confrontation. It did no good to nibble her ear. Those who had succeeded with her, and there had been a few aside from Booker, had laid it on the line; they were rewarded with laughter and consent.

Ted Todson got off on the right foot.

"I wanted to see you again. That's why I'm here. I wasn't just passing by. I tracked you down."

He was waiting for her in the yard as she came down the steps of the auditorium. The school was deserted, one lone, gangly boy stuffing baskets on the court in the distance, the hoop loose and chattering faintly with every shot.

She noted that Todson had not bothered to shave, that he wore unbecoming pants with a pleated waist and a shabby jacket. He motioned to his car parked by the school fence. It was old and unwashed.

"Come take a ride with me," he said.

Hortense thought of Booker. He was out of her life and had been for weeks. He knew of old that she was not easily appeased. He knew her wrath. There had been no sign of him. Coldly, she had dismissed him from her mind, replacing him with work and halfhearted domesticity. She had painted the kitchen, relined the drawers, oiled the sewing machine. She had read a history of England, *The Decameron,* a cookbook. She had lain awake until morning, watching television, nursing anger. Eunice had made herself scarce, staying out most nights. Jake had shared his dinner on one or two occasions. She had gotten drunk once with Stella. She had gone shopping with Nell. For the rest, she had seen some bad movies, made herself a skirt, polished furniture, repaired an alarm clock. She had taken cold showers, clamped down on her sexual fantasies to the point of obliterating them, except in her dreams, felt resentment. She had stopped just short of self-pity, distracting herself with new records, an expensive house plant, a chocolate cake consumed to the last morsel in solitary gluttony.

The sudden appearance of Todson made her wary. When vulnerable she was more cautious than ever.

"Let's just hold our horses a minute," she said, coming to a halt in the middle of the yard. It was hot. Her dress stuck to her back. The kids had tired her. She was cross.

"Just what do you want with me exactly?" She hitched up her school satchel under her arm and regarded him steadily. That level gaze had caused passion to die in a score of men.

"Can we talk in the shade?" His hand cupped her elbow. She found herself walking beside him, glancing at him sidelong. A dusty red-pepper tree cast shadows on the ground. He leaned against it, watching her. She stood with a hip thrust out. The book satchel smelled rankly of old leather.

He seemed to be in no hurry to explain, stooping to pluck a blade of grass which he chewed on for a moment or two while she grew uneasy.

"Well?" she demanded.

His reply came smoothly. "I got a helluva kick out of watching you handle Booker that day at my house. Looking down your nose at the house, the tennis court, the whole layout. Climbing up that hill, your back like a ramrod . . . I half expected you to turn around at the top and give us all the finger."

"If you're looking for a put-down," Hortense told him, "you've already had it from me." She fished a cigarette from her pocket, snapped a match on her fingernail before he could get his lighter out.

"I run a big ad agency," he said. "Lots of clients. Lots of accounts. You've been bad for my business."

"I've got nothing to do with your business. I got nothing to do with you."

"Wrong." His smile was wide. "You've taken my mind off it. I sit in conferences and I wonder about you. I'm supposed to be thinking about dog food and cold cream. I've been thinking about you. So here I am."

"So here you are," Hortense said. She was not encouraging. He hunkered down under the tree. It was the move of a man totally at his ease. Hortense felt too tall and awkward looking over him. He squinted up at her.

"Your nose is shiny," he said.

"That's 'cause I'm sweating." She was huffy. "You're making me sweat with all this sucking around. Listen, mister," she went on impatiently, "this is my vacation. My vacation started today. I'm going home and put my feet in a bucket of cold water and I'm going to turn on my electric fan and eat ice cream. I'm gonna do the *New York Times* crossword puzzle. From what I can tell, you don't fit in *no*where."

He was not rebuffed. "Come have a cup of coffee. I'll tell you the story of my life."

"Let me tell you," she said. "You're white. You're married."

She did not wait for his reply or for anything else. She turned and walked away from him. It was a long way back across the school yard and she traversed it without looking around. It wasn't necessary to look around. She knew he was still there.

The apartment was stifling and musty. She opened the windows and rummaged in her closet for an old and voluminous housecoat. She took off her clothes and walked naked into the kitchen to take some meat from the freezer, returning to pull the robe over her head, leaving the top buttons open to expose her skin. She padded around the house, watering plants, thinking. She was not beguiled by Todson's account of his attraction. His pursuit of her had a kind of annoying arrogance. Still, there was a disturbing tug and pull in her. It came, she thought crankily, from not having had any lately, from the hot, still day, from walking barefoot and undressed through the silent apartment. She was suffering a self-imposed chastity. Booker's been in bed twenty times since we broke up, she thought darkly, thrusting, reaming, getting his dick wet, restoring his self-esteem. She knew Booker. He would never let his fires die into ashes. Son of a bitch, he would haul 'em. Damn Booker. Damn men.

Her front doorbell rang. She moved heavy-footed to the door and shouted through it.

"Who is it!"

There was no answer. Suddenly, she swung the door open. She glowered.

It was Todson, almost obscured by a bouquet of flowers.

"I used to sell books from door to door," he said. "It conditioned me never to take no for an answer." He moved past her into the room, into the kitchen beyond, flowers in one hand, searching for a vase with the other.

"These need deep water. Have you got a big vase? A bucket?"

She flounced after him, pausing in the doorway to watch him in disbelief. "Hey!" she cried. "Hey, what is this?"

"Persistence." He put the flowers in the sink, pushed the stopper in, ran some water. Then he turned to her and grinned. "Come on, let's be friends." He brushed past her into the living room, took a chair and crossed his legs indolently. There was a hole in the bottom of his shoe.

"Hortense," he said, "I like you. I like you, Hortense. I haven't said that to a woman in years."

She edged back into the room, sighed, sat down. "So?"

"I think at this moment I'd rather get into your mind than into your bed."

"You're not going to get into either."

"You know, I was brought up by a woman like you," he said lazily. "My father died when I was a kid. He had a Mobil gas station in Portland, Oregon. My mother took it over. I can see her now, in some kind of a printed cotton dress with gloves on to protect her hands from grease, standing in that station, pumping gas, wiping windshields, selling tires. She had a high, fluty voice, a society voice they used to call it, and she'd stand there asking truck drivers if they needed their batteries checked as if she were inviting them to a ritzy tea party. She never gave a nickel's worth of credit to anybody, not even the local minister. She had me print up a sign saying 'Cash Only, No Exceptions.' One night a punk kid drove in and tried to hold her up. I was in the back, scared shitless. I saw her pick up a tire wrench and brain him with it. He dropped like a poleaxed steer. He was still out cold when the police came." He paused and thought about the past a moment. "When it rained she wore an old flowered garden hat. Christ, she was a sight. She put me through Oregon State College, and if I ever fell below an A average she cut off my allowance. Once I went three weeks on Wonder bread and Hershey bars. I couldn't drink, smoke, spit, fuck or swear till I left home, and the day I did I cried like a baby."

Hortense drawled in reply. "I'm sure she was something else, honey, but if you're looking for your mama, pass by me." Her voice got flat. "I think you'd better do that anyway. I'm black clear through. Black skin, black soul, black disposition. And where men are concerned, black's my favorite color."

He looked at her for a moment, sitting across the room, pugnacious and implacable. "Booker wants a job from me," he said without inflection.

"Is that right?" She smiled, but it was a smile that did not reach her eyes. "Well, if Booker wants a job with you, let *him* kiss your ass for it. He's on his own these days. Dumb move," she added tartly.

335

"You almost had me going, what with your mama and all."

"You're right," he said. "It was dumb. Dumb, because it didn't work."

Foxy, Hortense thought. Admit your errors. Take defeat gracefully. But keep the eye contact. Don't press. She grinned at the expertise, finally amused.

"All right," she said, "you've got your foot in the door. Just one of 'em."

He sat back, satisfied. "One's all I need."

Todson's offices took up the top floor of a high-rise building on the edge of Beverly Hills. He looked down upon Spanish villas and lavish ranch houses, a Rolls-Royce agency, an expensive sea food restaurant. Lights spread below like tilled fields, here dark, there bright. Potted trees and flowering plants banked his terrace. A small stone cherub spat water. French park chairs evoked Paris.

He walked her through the premises, stopping at the refrigerator in the middle of a well-stocked bar. "Have some fruit juice, carrot juice, celery juice, spinach juice. I keep all the tonics. I take all the pills. Faulkner said there was a pill for every ill except the last..."

She shook her head, no, thanks; he remained standing for a moment, his head cocked to the side, absently jiggling some change in a pocket. "I find that friends of mine are beginning to keel over; men just fifty, or a couple years older, are dying like flies all around me. Where are the three score and ten we were promised?" He shook his head, bemused. "I've walloped the world—now I'd better live in it a little."

He led her on, throwing doors wide so that she might see how he provided for his staff. There was a series of rooms, all well appointed, containing hand-rubbed walnut desks. Jars of sharpened pencils were placed neatly beside sleekly designed Italian typewriters. Wastebaskets were conspicuous and copious—apparently he allowed for mistakes. There were water carafes and good pictures, piped music, footstools, humidors, silent wall locks. Nine to five had been made as painless as possible, ulcers were mollified by decor.

His own office abruptly reversed the concept. The desk was ugly varnished wood, scarred by burning cigarettes, stained, littered. There was a badly reproduced print of Michelangelo's *Creation,* God's outthrust hand instilling life into Adam. What inspiration he drew from that she could only surmise. The Supersalesman charging the supersalesman? There was an old mohair couch, a battered coffeepot, an ancient Underwood typewriter. There were no family pictures anywhere. The light source was fluorescent tubing, a hard hot light that suggested interrogation.

He saw by her sour look that she was not taken in. "I'm the Clarence Darrow of the advertising world—sloppy but shrewd."

She shrugged.

"You're right, it's all deliberate. Brings me in on people's blind side. It hasn't hurt business." He paused a moment.

"You're a smart girl, Hortense. It fools a lot of people. Last spring *Playboy* had a profile on me: Todson, a man in touch with his roots, Todson, manipulating the public in a frayed shirt. Hell, there are a dozen handmade English shirts hanging in that closet over there, three dozen more at home. I have my shoes made by a cobbler who takes a year to deliver a pair. I've got a Porsche motor under the hood of my Dodge. I own a block of real estate on this strip. And so on and so on."

"Uh huh," Hortense said. She shifted to get comfortable in the cracked leather chair. He sat across from her, enjoying his revelations, a magician pulling cards from his sleeve.

"It's all a sell—a hard sell or a soft sell." His tone mocked his own duplicity. "I got to this town in forty-nine. I had twenty bucks in my wallet, a duffel bag with some clean shorts, a nickel pack of gum in my pocket and larceny in my soul. I got off the Greyhound bus at eight o'clock in the morning, headed for the Beverly Hills Hotel, checked into a suite with a patio, went to the barber shop, charged the haircut, went to the pool and looked around for a lady who could foot the bills. And there she was, a hundred and twenty pounds, just over thirty, divorced, chainsmoking, drinking vodka for breakfast, as easy to knock off as a sitting duck. She's the present Mrs. Todson. She's a nice lady with loose screws, cold feet, big heart, and she's learned, after all these years with me, to take a somewhat ironic view. I've been reasonably faithful, I've doubled her money, I've left her alone, except for one weekend in Acapulco which produced my daughter and separate bedrooms thereafter for us. The business works, the marriage works. I'm bored." His grin was mirthless.

Hortense yawned visibly. She didn't bother to pat it. "You call that a hard-luck story? You had twenty bucks? I had a dollar. One green folded-up dollar stuck in the waistband of my panties. I had the clothes on my back and they'd already been there two years. No nickel gum, no nickel anything. I checked into the Y.W.C.A., in a room with an alcoholic getting over a six-month binge, a religious nut and a girl with the worst acne I ever saw. I walked thirty blocks to the employment office with my teacher's credentials in a manila envelope and got put to work at McDonald's frying hamburgers. You know that sign they've got up?— eighteen billion hamburgers sold? Well, I fried seventeen billion of 'em. It took me three years to get a teaching job. You want to know what's under the hood of my Ford car? A Ford motor, with a burned-out transmission and a leaking fuel pump. You know what I've got in my closet at home? Moths. My shoes cost six ninety-eight and I got 'em at Sears." She rose to her feet abruptly. "What am I doing here trading true confessions with you, anyhow?"

"We're getting to know each other," he said.

"You're bad news," she answered irritably. "I know it in my bones. You come at me one way, then you come at me another. When I was ten years old I got hold of a string of firecrackers. There was a nice little old man lived next door to us. He said, 'Child, don't mess with those crackers,' but I went right on and put a match to them. They went up in blue fire and I got good and burned." She shoved up a sleeve and rubbed the old, puckered scar. "Well, I ain't ten anymore and I don't play with fire anymore. So you can ride me home or put me in a cab—but I'm going."

He groaned and shook his head. "Hortense," he said, "you're a pain in the ass. Grow up. There's

some kind of attraction between us. Maybe it's
because we're a couple of carpetbaggers, but
whatever it is, it's there. We'll probably both get
over it. If not, we'll do something about it. Now if
you want to go home, I'll take you."

Hortense snorted. She was piqued that he
discerned willingness, however faint. "Mister,"
she said, "I run a little fever now and again when a
pretty man passes by, but it don't mean nuthin'.
You're just a little fever, about ninety-eight point
nine. I'll take two aspirin and you'll be gone."

"Maybe."

They left it at that.

The restaurant was dimly lit, partly to obscure
the bad food and the small portions and partly
because the management was convinced that low
wattage encouraged an atmosphere appropriate to
clandestine meetings. The fact that women met
there more often than men was stubbornly
overlooked. So it was that the ladies fumbled
through plates of creamed something or other and
drained their pitifully meager daiquiris. There
were added insults. The bread was always slightly
stale, the tab inordinately large. The waiters were
rude to single women and unspeakable to those in
pairs, going on the assumption that only men
could be sufficiently bellicose to demand attention,
malignant enough to make life trying for them.

They did not mess with Mrs. Todson, however.
She snapped her fingers under the nose of a
majestic maître d' and made her wants known in
her harsh and aggressive voice. She waved a ten-
dollar bill in the air, rather like a trainer creating
an obedience situation with a small dog. It was not

340

discreetly palmed or surreptitiously handed over; it was brandished.

"If you expect to get this," she announced, "I want a good table by a window, a waiter with clean fingernails and the speed of a whippet. I don't want anybody to hover or ask me how I'm enjoying my meal. There's no possibility of that in a place like this anyway. I'm expecting a young woman to join me. Don't keep her hanging around when she arrives. She's black and impressive, so you can't miss her. I want a cup of coffee as soon as I'm seated."

The bill was held slightly out of reach, but with a small lunge the man had it in hand.

"Leave it to me, madame," he said. "You'll be well looked after."

"I am," she answered. "That's why I can be as rude as I am."

She took her seat at the table and stared out at the waves lapping the pier. She did not like water; it was not her element, unless it was to be found heated in a Jacuzzi.

Hortense spotted her across the room, her elbows on the table, her nose sunk into a steaming cup of coffee. She threaded her way through the tables with her long determined stride and stood over Mrs. Todson until she looked up, blinking with her wide gray eyes like an awakened cat. The ashtray smoldered with half-dead butts. Hortense was late. She had agreed to come when Mrs. Todson had phoned much too early in the morning, with the burr of sleep or whiskey still in her voice.

"Let's have lunch, Miss Washington. A real old-fashioned ladies' lunch. I've got a lot to talk over

341

with you. It's about you and Ted. Now listen, before you get rattled. I liked you when I met you. I still do. I just think we'd better put our heads together. Could you come to that crummy Tiger's Lair at the beach? The food's lousy, but it's dark and my neighbors aren't likely to show up there."

Hortense had done little but acquiesce to the place and the hour. She had wrestled with herself on the question of dress and then thought to hell with it. A black sweater and pants would do for what was bound to be a hair-pulling number. A touch of vanity made her add a silver chain. She did not wear lipstick. The perfume was for herself. She never went without it.

She slid into the chair opposite Mrs. Todson and pushed the cutlery out of her way.

"Okay," she said, "I'm here."

Mrs. Todson thrust a strong dry hand across the table. "My front name's Gail. Can I call you Hortense?"

Hortense returned a firm grip. "Nobody's stopping you."

"Do you want a drink?"

"No."

"I've had two already. Then let's order." She pulled a pair of heavy-rimmed glasses from her bag, stuck them on and peered at the menu. Hortense set hers aside unread.

The waiter appeared with marvelous alacrity and stood, pencil in hand, ear inclined.

"Yes, girls, what'll it be?"

Mrs. Todson bestowed a long, insolent stare upon him. "We're not girls," she drawled. "We were once but not anymore, alas. The fact is, I would have considered you overly familiar at sixteen."

The man nodded silently, a little shaken, and she became brisk again. "I want a patty of chopped meat, rare to the point of cannibalism. I want one sliced tomato. Sugarless tea. Forgive me"—she turned to Hortense—"but what I eat is so nasty I want to get it out of the way as quickly as possible."

Hortense gave her order. The waiter sped away.

The two women took each other's measure, Hortense over the rim of her water glass, Gail as she struck a match to her cigarette. It was a hasty, furtive and totally accurate appraisal, each of the other.

She's tough but not bitchy, probably easygoing until riled. She's stood up well against time. She won't take any shit. She's probably dished plenty in her time. She smokes too much. Some part of her defenses don't hold up. I bet she's never cried. That ring she's wearing is my salary for a year. She's had her nose fixed. So mused Hortense.

She's nobody to mess with. She's smart but skeptical. She'd probably blister you if you crossed her. She's had to fight for every inch of her life. She has beautiful eyes. She's never retreated from a situation. She doesn't suffer fools gladly. Her figure is good but she could lose a few pounds. Thus Gail.

Hortense plunged first.

"He has the hots for me," she said bluntly. "I've seen him twice. We haven't gotten near a bed. I don't know if I'm to blame for any of it or not. He didn't get any invitation—but maybe I give off a smell or something. I don't like him much. Sometimes you don't have to like them much. I don't want to mess with your life; I don't want

343

to mess up mine. I'm not going to tell you I'm ashamed or anything like that. When I'm ashamed it's over a big issue. That's all. That's all I've got to say." She leaned back in her chair, one arm draped over the back of it.

"Very nicely put," Gail said. The waiter set their plates before them; blood was pooled around the meat patty.

"Lovely," she said. "Raw meat is my dish today." She tucked into it with gusto. When she spoke her mouth was full; her manners were not elegant but they were individual.

"The trouble is not with us, as I see it. It's with men. Maybe they're pricks because they've got pricks. I don't know. You're younger than I am, with more energy and more stamina. I don't want to get into a fight with you over Ted. I do want to hang on to him because I've got most of the kinks worked out of my marriage—believe me, there were a lot of them. You stay around for all those years and you raise up quite an edifice. There's a daughter, two houses, cars, boats, a terribly complicated tax structure and a cold-eyed view of what you both are. In our case, not much.

"He's probably told you we don't live together. A woman would have kept that to herself. But that's neither here nor there. Ted's after you. And lady, look out when Ted's after you. If you were my best friend, and he's knocked off a couple of those, too, I'd warn you about good old Ted. You're not, so you're more or less on your own. What I will tell you is that he's given Booker a job. He's going to want to be thanked for that." Her gray eyes were the color of stone. "He takes a lot of gratifying," she said.

The waiter sidled up, bearing coffee. The women were silent as the cups were filled.

"Dessert? We have German chocolate cake, a lovely lemon mousse, ice cream."

Gail waved him away. "Just go get the bill and add it twice before you give it to me." She held out her cigarette case to Hortense. Hortense shook her head.

"I'll leave him be," she said slowly. "The only thing is Booker. I'm finished with Booker but I don't want him hung out for bait. He's as weak as boiled spaghetti, the fool. He thinks because he's got all those pectoral muscles and big white shiny teeth and curly hair that everybody loves him."

"You love him," Gail said.

"No, ma'am. I'm used to him."

Ice clinked in the water glasses around them. The ladies surrounding them at the other tables murmured to each other across the slowly fading rosebuds in the plated vases; they delayed the grocery store, the laundry, the car wash. They stole an hour.

Hortense stared into her cup and found herself far away. Booker stood against the barn wall, a chalk stripe marked above his head.

"Am I tall now? Have I grown now? Horty, look at the mark. Where's it at?"

"Five foot, dumbbell. You're a shrimp. A little shriveled shrimp. You ain't never gonna do nuthin' but bump your head on my chin."

"I'm gettin' bigger!"

"No, you ain't."

"Then measure my pecker. Why don't you measure my pecker?"

Gleeful laughter. And she had. And it was a

345

limp little worm. How crestfallen, his face, how diminished his dream of manhood.

"Listen, Booker, that's gonna get bigger. You don't have to worry none about that."

He had tucked it back in his pants, solemnly, silently. He had wandered off without speaking to her. She had stayed behind to erase the smudge on the barn wall. To put it higher, higher. They had never measured again. Sadly, she knew that he had never reached the mark.

"Hortense?"

She was recalled by Gail Todson, who had risen to her feet.

"I've got to run. I've taken care of the bill. Oh, hell," she added abruptly. "Why do I hang on? I used to be kind of a dignified lady. Let's hope I haven't made a complete ass of myself today."

Hortense gave a little. "Two cats in a closet aren't all that much fun—but you were all right."

The other woman nodded. Then she turned and walked away. Hortense noted with a smile that the tip she left was miserly, half of it in pennies.

The calls began shortly thereafter. Hortense would be roused from sleep by the phone ringing. It was often two or three in the morning when everything seemed at low ebb. Her heartbeat felt slow and heavy, her mind numb. Eunice, in the bed next to hers, groaned at the sounds, woke, swore vilely, slept again, so that Hortense was left alone in the sooty dark, listening to him. She hated being caught this way, sluggish, fatigued. She began to have the feeling that he never slept, that he was there somewhere in the city, in a room blazing with lights, staring out into the empty corridors,

346

talking, talking, talking. She saw the outlines of his hard face tight with determination. That his energy never wavered was as disturbing as the calls. He seemed to be telling her that he could pursue her endlessly, that he could pervade her life, night or day, night *and* day. At first she was mildly annoyed, then belligerent, then brusque. Finally, profane and furious.

Eunice, her eyes gummy and sunken, sat upright in bed and urged her on. Who the hell did this bastard think he was? What the hell was he up to? Where did the fucker got off, hassling her like this? Her high, nervous voice joined Hortense's in outrage. She began to see it as malevolent.

"Horty, he's crazy. Those big guys get like that. Let's disconnect the phone. I'm getting afraid of him."

Hortense dismissed her fears. Men like Todson saw themselves as a blind force of nature. Opposition was to be blown away, bowled over, bent or broken. It *was* a kind of insanity, come to think of it.

She told him so on the tenth call in the flat, harsh voice she used with unruly kids. There had been a curious silence on the line when she finished.

"Look," she said, "I don't know how all this got started but I'm stopping it. Cold."

"Are you?" His voice was low. She had to strain to hear. "Are you stopping it?"

She hung up on him, slamming the phone into its cradle. Eunice shivered, clutching the blankets.

"Maybe he's on something?"

"He is. It's called an ego trip. Go to sleep, Eunice. Forget it. It's handled."

In the following nights she found herself waking suddenly, listening. But the phone was silent. He had tired of bullying her. The thought of him brooding over the rejection was almost as unpleasant as the calls had been. Then she became impatient with herself. She was making melodrama out of a man's ugly conceit. Another woman might have been flattered. Still, his total silence weighed on her.

She took to rising early in the morning, pulling on a light sweater and making for the beach. Once there she ran, streaking across the sand with the wind at her back, hearing Todson's heavy, insistent voice suggesting, insinuating. She brought herself up short. It had to be put into perspective. He was merely a sulky, thwarted man, neither sinister nor mad. A schmuck. That was all. But she fled the house anyway, passing most of the day out on the beach.

It was there she came across Stella quite early one morning. She saw her, at some distance, in her shapeless cardigan and battered felt hat. She saw further, as she approached, that Stella was engaged in some kind of strange ritual. There she sat, on the damp sand, surrounded by a ring of stones, each weighting a fluttering piece of white paper. The whole world, Hortense decided, had gone crackers.

There was something huddled and limp about Stella that made Hortense suspect she had been there all night. "Hey, Stella," she called as she came up to her. "You up early or out late?"

Stella peered up at her. "How long have I been here? I have no idea."

Hortense hugged herself. "It's pretty cold. June, and it's freezing. What's all this?" She indicated the strange druidic circle.

"Those are blank pieces of paper," Stella growled, "weighted with rocks. They are symbolic of my present state of mind. Emptiness pressed down with stone. I'm blocked. Silenced. Constipated."

Hortense hunkered beside her. She saw, at close quarters, a pinched grayness in Stella's face. She recalled then seeing the blinds drawn over the windows of Stella's apartment for some days now. She had not seen her making her customary sallies to the corner bar.

"Are you all right?"

"Of course I'm not all right. I haven't written a word in weeks. Nothing'll come. I'm on a rack. I'm roasting over hellfire. Also, my slacks are wet from sitting on this goddamn sea-drenched strand."

"Then get up," Hortense said with admirable good sense. "Go home."

"Verse is my home," Stella said grandiloquently.

"You're a little sozzled, aren't you?"

"Comment on the obvious is boring."

Hortense sat beside her, pulling up her knees and hugging them with wrapped arms. The sea hissed at their feet. A sandpiper minced in front of them, leaving tiny perfect tracks in the sand.

Stella showed signs of age. Circles ringed her eyes like kohl, there was a sad droop to her mouth, the locks of hair blowing untidily about her face were as gray as her skin. The nails on her hands were jagged and broken. Her stomach growled

349

loudly. Hortense thought of a stray dog, skittish, abandoned. She felt a wave of pity which she knew Stella would despise.

"Are you going to sit here all day?"

"Yes." The reply was obstinate. "All this day. All the next."

"There's got to be another way to turn on," Hortense said. "You've got sand all over you. You look like a barnacle."

"I don't give a hoot about my appearance. That should be plain. A battle is taking place here. Here I stay till it's won."

She rooted around in her capacious pocket and came up with a quart of bourbon with only a drop remaining. She tippled daintily, closing one eye and crooking a finger as if it were a teacup.

Hortense watched her. She saw clearly that Stella could not be cajoled or comforted.

"Wanting is a bad thing," she said half to herself.

"Nonsense." Stella's voice rang out strongly. "When my desires go, the worms can have me and welcome. What doesn't work is *two* desires at once. That's what I'm plagued with. That's what I won't have."

She flung the bottle into the water. She had surprising strength; it sailed high and far before it splashed.

"What happened to the fat man?"

"Ah. Him. Sent packing."

"And you miss him."

"I don't waste time on thoughts of the absent." Stella's voice finally lacked conviction.

They sat side by side, like two harpies, Hortense thought, and the waves broke and receded in front of them. There seemed nothing else to say.

It was Saturday afternoon. The poolside was crowded; on every deck chair a body browned in the sun. Ice melted in Scotch, in orange juice, in diet soda. One young woman had abandoned the top of her bathing suit. The diving board cracked and resonated, a diver shouted as he hit the water, belly first. Laughter was loud, conversation continuous.

Booker took the stairs to Hortense's apartment three at a time, and when he came through the door he wrenched off his tie and squirmed out of his plaid jacket, flinging it away. Sweat had marked large circles under his arms and stood out in drops on his forehead.

She was at the sewing machine, wearing an old pair of slacks, a man's shirt, her hair a tight screw on top of her head. There were pins in her mouth which prevented a greeting, even if she had deigned to offer one. She didn't. She merely looked up at him for a while.

She saw the change in him. He stood before her hesitant and subdued, like a man rising out of bed after a long illness. The muscles in his back, in his neck, were bunched and tense, and he had a curious new gesture, his hand wandering to his mouth as if he wanted to stifle what he was about to say.

She knew Booker of old. When dismissed or chastised he had always visibly declined, sleeping badly, eating badly, peanut butter slathered on crackers, beer, ice cream bars, food snatched at random. It was as if he were saying: "See what's become of me, out of your care." She was familiar with that hangdog dejection. Once she had caught him stealing money from the poor box in church. He had nearly fainted at the flaying he got. He had cringed under her castigation. She had warned him darkly that he needn't fear God's eye—but hers. *She* was watching him. He had to deal with *her*.

He had that same look now, as if he still heard her thundered "Thou shalt not!"

"Well," she finally said, her voice cold, "look what the cat dragged in."

She saw his eyes shift nervously around the room. "She here? You alone?"

She continued to feed the cloth under the needle, paying him not the slightest attention until she was finished. Then she bit off a piece of thread, folded the blouse and set it aside.

"Yes, I'm alone. Didn't you have a dime on you to call, before you come bustin' in here?"

She took a sharp tone with him. In the past he had found that bracing, even comforting. It put him at the center of her attention, where, in his childish vanity, he insisted on being. He had often goaded her into severity. He liked her best in this role, chiding, warning, scolding. To come from that to her acceptance had always delighted him. Her scorching judgment was more pleasing than another woman's caress. He was proud of her inflexibility; it was as inseparable a part of her as her harsh laughter, her mocking gaze. All his life he had submitted to it with glee. You can't get around Hortense, no sir, no way. The fun was in the trying. She had her little susceptibilities and finding them out was sweet. Her cry of "Get off, Booker!" or "You quit that right this minute, Booker!" were the triumphs of his boyhood.

"I didn't have no dime." When he was uneasy he lapsed into the careless speech of long ago.

He sat down in the nearest chair, his hands capping his knees. The humble posture evoked other times. Hortense saw him sitting in just that way on the porch of his house, while the minister intoned prayers over his mother's casket. She had come outside, sick from the thick air clouded with the scent of lilies, sobered by the sight of the cheap pine coffin balanced on the kitchen table, pressed by the packed bodies, and had sat beside him, both of them swinging their bruised and scabbed legs over the side of the porch.

He had slept in her bed that night, clinging to her all through the humid hours till daybreak, the two of them plastered together, sticking together with sweat and the fear of death.

She tapped a cigarette out of a pack, popped it in her mouth, tossed one across at him. He didn't attempt to catch it, and it fell on the carpet at his feet.

"Well, smoke it or pick it up, one or the other," she called sharply to him.

"I'm not smokin' anymore. I quit."

"You enjoying life so much you want to live a long one?" She chuckled briefly at her own joke and slammed the cover on the sewing machine.

Booker sighed deeply. She was impervious to his sighs.

"You're lookin' fine," he said. "Real fine."

She was impervious to his compliments as well. She threw him a glance over her shoulder as she went to the kitchen. "It's lunchtime. You want something to eat or not?" It was an offer but coldly proffered.

"I'm not hungry."

"Well, I am." She hummed a little tune as she went. Let him see that both her appetite and her appearance were unimpaired by his long absence. "You want to talk to me, come in here."

She had her head in the refrigerator, dragging out bread, tomatoes, lettuce, milk, hugging it all to her bosom. He hovered in the doorway.

"Sit down on that stool. You're making me crazy, standing in the door like that."

She found herself thinking what a clutter some men made by just standing around, hands hanging, waiting to be pushed or pulled. He had annoyed her before when they made a bed together, often after sleeping in it, holding his section of the sheet limply in his hand until she directed him irritably, "Tuck it in, fold it over, miter the corner." He had always made a botch of tasks, cutting himself on tin cans, banging his thumb with hammers. He had stood over stuffed drains, unflushed toilets, burst pipes, with the same helpless air, until she had shoved him aside and done the work herself. Only in bed had he been the great athlete that he was.

She pulled out the breadboard and set about making the sandwiches, cutting the tomatoes in thick slices, spreading mayonnaise in swirls.

"You've got a lot of nerve showing up here. I said I was through with you. You must be hard of hearing or something."

"I heard you." Again the sigh.

She felt a stab of impatience. "Make yourself useful. Put out the mats and the napkins. Pour the milk." She ordered him about in a loud voice. Meekly he opened drawers and cupboards.

"Those are the wrong glasses. The big ones are for milk."

Awkwardly, he arranged the table. She watched him.

"You look like you've been eating standing up for a month. You're scrawny. Peaked. You still in your old place?" She managed to keep her tone disinterested.

"Yeah."

"Anybody ever clean it—or are you living up to your neck in dirty socks?"

"I clean it. Sometimes."

She slid the sandwiches onto plates, then shoved him out of her path as she put the food on the table. "Don't get under my feet."

She leaned against the sink and folded her arms. "Yes," she said, "you're real brave coming back here." Her nostrils flared with the possibility of a fray. "I thought I put you in your place once and for all. I don't remember telling you I'd changed my mind. I don't remember asking you to come over here. I guess you're just here on straight nerve."

He grabbed her then, held her emphatically. "Don't be so goddamned rough on me!"

She disengaged herself, as if she were brushing off a housefly. "Keep your hands to yourself."

Then she drew out a chair and seated herself at the table, looking up at him sourly. "I didn't make that sandwich to throw it out. Sit down and eat. God!" This last was a snort as he tucked his napkin in his shirt front.

"I would've thought by now you would've learned to put it in your lap. You're traveling with the high and mighty these days. You don't see them sticking their napkins under their chins like no baby's bib."

He snatched it away, crumpled it into a ball and threw it. Then he pushed his plate aside, his face heavy with misery. Shrieks rose from the swimmers outside. A voice wah-hooed, there was the sound of splashing.

"Why do you live in this goddamn place anyhow? A bunch of honkies lapping up booze and pinching fannies, potbellied old farts wearing their rugs into the swimming pool. Shit. They all make me sick."

He grabbed up his glass of milk and gulped it, leaving his mouth rimmed with white.

"Wipe your mouth," she said. "You've got a milk mustache."

He used the back of his hand. "A bunch of honkies," he said again.

"You're working for one, from what I hear." Hortense stared at him coldly.

He got up from the table and slammed the window shut, muffling the noise. He stood leaning against the pane, as if to cool his skin at the touch of the glass.

"Yeah," he said. "I'm working for Todson." He let a moment pass. "I've got my car outside. Let's go for a ride. I can't breathe in this goddamned apartment."

"Nope," she said. "I'm going to finish sewing my blouse, bake a pineapple upside-down cake, wax the kitchen floor, and then I'm going to lie down and take me a nice nap with the radio playing at my ear. After that I'm going out to dinner and a picture show. Can't go for no ride with you because my day's all taken up."

A strand of hair made a pretty curl at the back of her neck. She pinned it severely in place. He watched her closely. Her brows met in a frown, forbidding desire. She saw on his face that he wanted her and felt anger that he should. The spoiled little brat. Marching in here with his melancholy look. It gave her satisfaction that he was afraid of her. Oh, he had reason to be. She half wished that he had appeared in his old guise, with his wheedling charm, his certainty, his laughter. He might have brazened it out, won her around. Might have? He *would* have. Often he had persisted through her anger, placing a kiss lightly on her forearm, blowing his warm breath against her ear. She had a taste for his wiles but not for this damp supplicating air.

"I see you got yourself a new thin watch," she said contemptuously.

He mumbled an answer. "It was on sale."

"Uh huh. I see you got a new ring, too. Some other kind of sale, I guess."

"All right," he said harshly, "so I got a couple of nice things. At least I don't look like somebody's washlady."

She hooted at that. "You've rolled around plenty with this old washlady, boy. Not for some time, of course. And why would I care what you think of my looks? What you think of anything?"

He made a despairing gesture. "I didn't come here to fight with you. You just won't have it any other way."

He seemed so deflated she became less pugnacious. "If you're here to put the bite on me, I won't lend you money."

"I didn't come for money either."

She felt a pang of anxiety. "You sick?"

"No, I ain't sick." His voice was dull.

Her good will was gone as quickly as it had come. Booker was up to tricks. He had plagued her with them endlessly, a frog in her lunch basket, a mousetrap in her bed, lies, he knew all sorts of sly antics. He was concealing something now.

"You're up to something," she said sternly. "What is it? You'd better tell me right quick."

Booker swallowed with effort. "Todson wants you," he said. "I'm supposed to fix it up."

There was a moment's silence. Then Hortense shook her head as if she had not heard.

"Say that again."

"This is all coming from him. I'm just saying what he said." He fell still again.

"You mean you're just a dummy, sitting in his lap. Charlie Dumb McCarthy."

He struggled on. "I know he comes on strong, but that's the only way he knows. He's really crazy about you. He talks about you all the time. Wants to put you in a big apartment, a big car. Wants to fix you up with credit cards. Said to tell you whatever you want is yours. Said to tell you 'good times and hard dollars.' And if any of that made you mad, to say, 'Don't get mad, Horty, he's really sold on you, all the way.'"

He was finished. He stopped and gulped air. He did not look at her, but he felt the burn of her look on him.

"So," she said, "part of your job is pimping, huh? Well, well. Isn't that cute? If I'd known that's where you were heading I wouldn't have wasted my time teaching you to read and write and long divide. I could have just bought you a white fedora and some tight shiny pants and turned you loose on any street corner." She lit a cigarette, blew the smoke into the air, watched it curl away. "I wonder why he picked you out. Must be he saw what kind of work you would do best. Yes, sir, you're a nice-looking boy with a little bit of swagger and a little bit of style. Not too smart but that's all right. Smart would just get in the way. I expect he watched you sucking around him, kissing ass, tugging on your cap, and he said to himself, 'Why, this cream wants to rise to the top in the worst possible way. That makes him my boy. I'll just give this boy an office and a telephone with punch buttons and some papers to shuffle around, and when I've got him good and housebroken I'll send the little pup sniffing to fetch her.' And damned if you aren't here. Dropping turds at my feet." She made a clicking sound with her tongue. "Tsk, tsk. You've made a mess, all right. A nasty, smelly mess. I should rub your nose in it. But I won't. I think I'll just pick you up by the scruff of your neck and set you outside the door and close it and lock it."

He started to speak. "Horty—"

She held up a hand instantly. "I'll be doing all the talking right up till you leave. There isn't much more to say, actually. Except that this finishes it. It's in a box, the hole is dug, it's buried."

The finality in her voice made him frantic. "Horty, don't kill me. Don't. Gimme another chance. I'll quit the job. I'll shove his face in."

"I don't give a shit what you do. You can believe that, Booker, if you never believe another thing the rest of your life."

He burst into tears then, a child's snuffling and

bawling. She watched him as he leaned against the wall, his head buried in his arms.

"Stop that," she said. "Booker, stop that right now. It won't do you any good, you know that. Now go in the bathroom and wash your face with cold water before you leave."

"Horty," he cried, "I'm nuthin' without you."

"Nuthin' with and nuthin' without, baby."

He stumbled away from her then into the bathroom. She heard his tears for some time after.

Eunice knew Hortense of old. It would not do to offer her the slightest sign of sympathy; she would immediately infer from any gesture that she was to be pitied. She had a way of squaring her shoulders and setting her mouth which said all too eloquently that she was scornful of interference in her affairs. Plainly, her stance declared, I'll handle things myself.

The small African violet, damp in its pot, thrust into her hands, was as far as Eunice dared go. She would have liked something more dramatic, some little tableau, her arms around Hortense, Hortense's head inclined to her shoulder. She had always longed for an older sister, seeing her as someone perpetually lovely, combing and brushing her hair, presenting an image like her own in the glass, the same eyes, the same mouth. She dreamed of them sharing dresses, confidences, boyfriends, heartache. She had often composed letters in her head which were dispatched to imaginary farms, villages, distant cities.

"Dear Sister: I've enclosed a snapshot of me. You can see I've lost weight. The pin I'm wearing is the one you sent; I'm never without it. Do you like my blond hair? Oh, I wish we were together so we could have a good talk. If you were here, I know I would sit by your side and tell you all my troubles. Don't worry about me, though; I am well and will visit you at the first opportunity." And so on and on.

"What's all this in honor of?" Hortense bent over the rich purple bloom.

"A man was selling them on the corner. He had a terrible birthmark on his cheek and I felt sorry for him. Then he shortchanged me. It just goes to show you."

Hortense laid aside the book which had gone unread in her lap for the last hour. She took off her glasses. Her shrewd glance came to rest on Eunice, who looked away furtively.

"I think I'll get ready for bed," Eunice said, rising and darting into the bathroom, leaving the door open as she wiggled out of her clothes. Where they fell, they lay, to be kicked out of her path as she came and went, to be stumbled over by anyone less agile.

The subject of Booker lay heavily on the air. She had awakened the night before to find Hortense sitting up in the dark, smoking, staring into space, her face deeply thoughtful. She had wanted to say something then, but at night, in the dark, Hortense appeared even more formidable and unapproachable than usual. She hated not knowing where matters stood. Curiosity and fear of Hortense's wrath warred.

She returned to the living room and made herself like a little girl at Hortense's feet.

"Would you brush my hair for me? I have a migraine headache. I'm so tired."

Hortense took the brush from her and began the long, even, sweeping strokes.

"That's lovely." Eunice closed her eyes and rested her head on Hortense's knee.

"Horty?"

"Hmm?"

The restful stroking continued.

"Have you sent Booker away for good?"

"Yes. Away for good."

"I know you hate me to ask..."

"But you will anyway."

"Horty, you're my best friend. My very best. You've been so sad these last couple of days."

"I have the curse," Hortense said crossly.

Eunice twisted around so they faced each other. She saw with some shock that Hortense looked old, ground down, weary. She always suffered from lassitude herself, but to see Hortense like that was unfamiliar. It was frightening. Hortense, who always had such a current of energy flowing through her.

"Can't we talk?" Eunice implored. "Can't we?"

"We never stop." Hortense laid aside the brush, rose and walked to the window. She ran her finger along the sill. It was just as she thought. Eunice had not dusted all week and it was her turn. She smoothed her hair away from her face. She knew Eunice would persist until all was laid bare, every twist and turn of event, every pang, every remorse. She was like a child, tugging at her skirts.

"Okay," she said. "There's not much to it. Things between Booker and me were just getting old, I guess. He came back and tried to make it up. I'd had enough." Instinctively and from long habit, she continued to protect him.

362

Eunice listened intently to every word. It was important to understand about survival; you never knew when your own endurance would be tested.

"But you've known him all your life."

Hortense sat down heavily on a chair. "I guess you could say it took me all my life to know him." Her voice was dry. "I do now."

She sat with her legs apart, her skirt straining over them, her hands resting limply in her lap. Eunice had seen women in that posture waiting at bus stops, a day's hard work bowing their shoulders. Where was the other Hortense, the one who could sweep her up, make her see all kinds of possibilities? Oh, where was she?

"Maybe," she said tentatively, "maybe you were too hard on him. You know you can be hard, Horty."

Hortense scowled. "Watch out I don't turn it on you."

Eunice rushed on recklessly. "Maybe your expectations were too high. I don't see how you can turn your back on all those years. Look at all you invested. Look at all that happened between you. Why, I can remember as plain as plain your telling me how you went into J C Penney and got Booker some new clothes, so when he came up north he wouldn't be ashamed of himself. How you took him into a restaurant and ordered a meal for him and just a cup of coffee for yourself; telling him to cut his meat in bites before he stuffed it in his mouth, not to butter the whole piece of bread at once, to leave a dime for the waiter. You told me all that, Horty. You taught him his manners."

"Did I? That boy still picks up a steak bone in his fist."

"How can he do without you? How can you do without him?" she asked unhappily. Hortense and Booker had been a certainty in an uncertain world, a fixed star to be guided by. Eunice floundered. Nothing remained from her own past. Her emotional history had ended in two weed-covered graves: Here lies George Wilson, at Peace with Jesus. Here lies Helen Wilson, Heaven is her Home.

"How will we do?" Hortense echoed her question. "I don't know."

"You love him."

"Liking him cuts more ice with me—and I didn't." Hortense clasped her hands behind her head and suddenly laughed raucously. "I guess if I'd kept after him the way I was going, he wouldn't have liked me very much either. No, sir. We were gonna buck heads anyway."

Eunice was appalled. She saw that Hortense was beginning to regain her ground, beginning to recover. It offended her sense of the romantic. She allowed her tone to become aggrieved. "I don't understand you."

Hortense snapped back. "You don't have to, baby. I understand myself and that's enough for me."

"What if you end up alone?" It was the fear that threatened her and haunted her.

"Well, what if?"

"I'm afraid to be by myself. Why isn't it all right to settle for a little less than what you want? Everybody does. Everybody in the whole world."

"Don't talk everybody to me," Hortense growled. "I'll tell you about settling. Dust settles. Ashes settle. What's underneath is buried. You go settling, honey, you're gonna be in big trouble."

"Where are you?" Eunice couldn't resist the barb. "Just tell me that."

"Me? I'm young, I'm healthy, I got my own teeth. I'll manage. Now go to sleep—I don't want to hear your voice another minute."

Eunice got to her feet. She needed yet another reassurance. Now that things were finished between Hortense and Booker, might Hortense not pack up and go, might she not shake the dust of this place and take off?

"Will you be going away, Horty?"

Hortense shrugged. "I ain't settled on anything just yet. Why? You want my green coat? You've been after it ever since you moved in here."

"I don't want the coat."

She wanted Hortense. Hortense made her feel safe and protected.

"Are you going to stay up late?" She lingered in the doorway.

"I'll be along pretty soon. Turn the lights out. You left 'em on in the bathroom all night. You're running up our bills."

Hortense picked up her book, slid her glasses back on. "Go on, don't stand there staring at me. You aren't going to see anything happen by staring at me. I ain't gonna come out in spots."

"Please come soon. I hate to go to sleep by myself."

"Stop being such a baby, Eunice. Good night. And thanks for the violet. It gives me hay fever but thanks anyway."

Eunice blew her a kiss and disappeared into the bedroom. She sank down on her bed, hugged herself, feeling disconsolate, feeling tears in the offing. Suddenly she snatched up the phone and dialed rapidly. It rang two, then three, then four times.

"Hello?"

"Hello, Archer, this is Eunice."

She heard his dazed, sleepy voice respond. "Hello, Eunice."

"I know it's late. It's after eleven, isn't it?"

"It's twelve thirty-five."

"Is everybody asleep?"

"Yes."

"Listen, Archer, tomorrow's Sunday. Let's go to the zoo. We'll eat lunch with the monkeys. That would be fun, wouldn't it? Would you like to do that?"

"We go to church on Sunday."

"After church. Get the taste of it out of your mouth."

She heard a faint chuckle from him.

"I heard you laugh, Archer." She suddenly felt merry, elated, seeing already the jig and jog of tomorrow. "Don't tell me I didn't because I did. I'll bring lunch and meet you on the corner."

"Is my dad coming?"

"No. Just you and me, Archer. Just you and me against the world."

She could almost see the shape of his smile, curved, shy, pleased.

"Okay," he said. "I'll see you then."

Somewhere he had found a pair of dark glasses which all but engulfed his face. They were the ninety-eight-cent variety to be found on dusty racks in the back of drugstores. He had, in fact, bought them that very morning, with some vague

366

idea that they would make him look older and like an airline pilot. He had tried on several kinds, but most were too large, sliding down on his nose, and those that did fit made him feel giddy, the bright green and blue and purple lenses making everything waver before him. His final choice had been these, with pink glass, and now the world was the color of strawberry sherbet. He had kept them in his pocket, hidden from his grandmother, until he was well away from the house, and then popped them on as he approached his rendezvous.

Water from his hair dripped onto his collar. He had paused, cutting across the neighbor's yard, to wet his celluloid comb under the garden tap. He made a part down the center, felt with his fingers to be sure it was straight, slicked it down on both sides. His grandmother always combed it back from his forehead, giving him a peeled and naked look. He felt his way enhanced him greatly.

All else was in order, with the possible exception of his tennis shoes. They smelled. He knew that because he had sniffed them critically before donning them and there was definitely a rubbery odor emanating from them. He had scrubbed them hard with a bar of Lifebuoy soap, with the result that his feet now felt damp and cold.

When he saw Eunice coming toward him with her pretty, swaying walk his heartbeat accelerated and he felt a nervous desire to sneeze. He wished desperately that he had gone to the bathroom before leaving the house. He wished he had grown taller since he saw her last. He wished the awful pinkness before him would go away, the pink dog crossing the pink street to lift a leg under a pink tree; it was making him sick to his stomach.

She was by his side now. She wore a ruffled skirt and a large straw hat that swooped fetchingly low over her eyes. There were flowers scattered over her blouse, which was unbuttoned to show the cleft between her breasts. Little silver birds rose and fell there on a chain. She had added false eyelashes and he was dazzled by the feathery shadow they cast on her cheek. He wondered how they had come about—her lashes had been blond and stubby last time.

He shifted back and forth in his squishy shoes and waited for her to speak first.

"Hi, Archer," she said. "I love your shades."

"Hello, Eunice."

He felt her arm drop fraternally around his shoulder. "I'm parked around the corner."

He was hugged up against her hip as they walked toward the car. It made his shirt ride up and bunch under his shoulder blades but he didn't dare disengage himself to pull it down; it would, he thought, seem unfriendly, as if he were trying to pull free. He worried frantically lest his damp hair leave a blot on her blouse. It seemed to take forever before they arrived at the car. Dimly he knew it was lovely to be crushed up against her, to smell her talcum powder and feel her warm skin, but anxiety spoiled it: his hair, his shoes, the pinkness of it all.

"Hop in." He was turned loose and clambered in. The hot air in the car almost overcame him. His glasses slid slickly down his nose. He shoved them back.

Eunice rolled down the windows, flipped on the radio, tooled the car expertly through the traffic.

He found himself speechless, numb, searching for something to say. He sorted through possible topics, the weather, her appearance, wondering all the while why he couldn't just say he was glad to see her: that's what he wanted to say.

"Are you glad to see me?"

He jumped visibly. "Yes," he said, and then wanting to adorn it, to enrich it, he repeated: "Yes, it's nice to see you."

She took off the hat and flung it on the seat behind them. Now he remembered how wonderful her hair was, full of red glints and curled tendrils.

"I was beginning to think that it was out of sight, out of mind with you, Archer."

He was almost offended by that. How many nights had he gone sleepless while her face rose before him, obscuring the figure of Jesus in the print on the wall, obscuring the geometric pattern of the wallpaper, obscuring everything.

"I guess you've been pretty busy," he said, making an accusation of his own.

"I don't know where the time flies to, but it goes, goes, goes." She took a sidelong glance at him. "I lost your phone number, Archer. That's why you haven't heard from me. Yes, I lost your phone number and my car keys and an opal ring, all in one month."

He knew it was a lie, not even a very convincing one. "That's okay," he said.

"No, it isn't, baby. Listen, I've been going out with your father a lot. That's what it is. I'm out late. I sleep late in the morning. Then I get up and drink coffee to get started and go get my hair done and come back and watch the afternoon television shows...do you ever see 'As The World Turns'? You get hooked on that damn show, believe me; it's like eating peanuts."

"Well," he said defiantly, "I've done a lot of stuff, too. I made a vegetable garden in our backyard. Peas and tomatoes and beans. I made a model airplane from a kit. And a lot of other stuff."

He thought heavily about all the long afternoons sitting on the porch while his grandmother slept upright in a wicker chair, her mouth hanging open, little puffs of breath bubbling out of her. Once his father made his daily call to see how he was, there was nobody else to talk to, nobody to play with. He hadn't made a model plane at all. Or a garden either. You couldn't call one row of puny radishes that the snails got to and spoiled a garden.

"I got invited to a birthday party next door," he said, inventing it on the spot, "and I learned to dance. A girl taught me. There were more girls than boys there." He would have willingly gone on but he could not possibly imagine what might have happened next. "There was ice cream, too—Neapolitan—and two kinds of cookies." No doubt about that being lame but it was the best he could do.

"Sounds like you had a ball."

"Yes."

They had arrived at the zoo. Eunice took a huge lunch basket from the trunk and he pulled himself free of the sticky vinyl seat and followed her up a winding path bordered with trees. There was the smell of cut grass in the air and people had spread picnics out on all sides of them. Here a red-checkered cloth was flung, there a blue and orange beach towel. He saw quartered watermelons and big kitchen bowls of potato salad. He saw the shells of hard-boiled eggs and smelled milk just beginning to sour in the sun. Somebody blew on a silver whistle. A baby, plump and diaperless, toddled down the slope, chasing a pigeon which waddled complacently in front of him. A boy tipped oil in his hand and stroked and stroked it over the bare back of a pretty girl.

He was eager to know what they had for lunch, and apprehensive as well. He had only been to one other picnic in his life and that had been in the church basement on a rainy day. He could only recall the skin of a boiled chicken lying on the paper plate before him, with little hairs still springing from it, and rice pudding so slithery he could not swallow it for the life of him.

"We'll see the animals and then we'll find a shady tree and have lunch. There's turkey and meat loaf and celery and fudge brownies and oranges—and mint Life Savers so we can digest it all." She pointed ahead of her. "That's a good spot right there. Let's put the basket down so nobody else'll grab it."

She handed it to him and he scurried ahead, planting it under the tree as if he were claiming the ground for them and no other. He saw that there were ants swarming about, but he would have died rather than say anything. She had designated the place. Here it would be.

The aviary resounded to the staccato chatter of birds, lapwings and speckled pigeons, red-eyed doves, mousebirds; there were tiny hummingbirds in whimsical flight, spoonbills standing and sleeping, bearded vultures with black bristle beards, storks and saddlebills, African ducks, showing their rigid tails to females while pumping their necks full of air. Lost on Archer, behind his pink curtain, were the colors, the flamboyance of it all, the bitter greens, the sharp yellows, the dawn grays, until Eunice suddenly snatched the glasses from his nose. He almost breathed his satisfaction aloud. The world was normal again.

"Oh," he said as the rainbow flashed and glowed before him, "they're pretty."

He was familiar with one particularly loud and aggressive blue jay which lorded it over the sparrows in his garden, a noisy quarrelsome bird staring at him in disdain as he pulled weeds without hope from among his radishes. But never had he seen anything like these jewels hurtling through the air before him.

Eunice pursed her mouth and strange chirping noises issued forth. Archer saw, in wonder, a parakeet inching toward them on a bar, tipping an inquiring head, responding. A chill ran through him. It only confirmed what he already knew. She had special powers to charm. He looked around proudly to see if anyone had taken note of her feat. A small boy standing next to them lapped a dripping ice cream cone, and then blew a loud raspberry at the flock of birds nearby, scattering them. His stony glance at Archer said, don't worship false idols; I have powers of my own.

Archer hated the mockery. At that moment, tongued too far, the ball of ice cream toppled into the dust. Archer smiled, a little flush of pleasure staining his cheeks. So much for the heretic.

Eunice led him on, taking his sticky hand in her

own. He marveled at the warm dryness of her touch. Didn't she perspire, ever?

The baboons hunkered on cement blocks and displayed their mimicry of humankind. They smiled mirthless smiles. They scratched endlessly. They showed their red bottoms, looking over their shoulders with round, insolent eyes. They picked their noses, cradled their young and, in plain view, they mated.

Terror and fascination struggled in Archer. He found a spot on the ground and riveted his attention there, certain that the thudding beat of his heart was clearly audible. What shocked him was the openness of it all. He thought of how he undressed in the bathroom with the pale yellow light of the bulb overhead barely lighting his mirror. Nakedness was a forbidden and surreptitious thing in his grandmother's house. She was never seen in a dressing gown, never glimpsed in the slightest disarray. He was expected to hurry through his bath, wash down there and be done with it. What would her displeasure have been had she known how he gazed and gazed at himself in the soapy water? He often felt his throat tighten with something close to tears that no one else saw him like this, that no other hand but his own caressed or stroked. The cat licked her kitten, he had seen it. There was other mothering in evidence everywhere. So, he reasoned, there's that love and then there's another kind. He knew very little of either.

"Do you know about love, Archer?"

There, she'd done it again, dipped into his mind.

"We have Health at school," he said cautiously. "Mrs. McKinley teaches it."

She led him to a bench and settled on it with a sigh. She rummaged in her straw bag, took out a compact, a soiled powder puff, dusted her nose.

"What did they tell you?" she asked casually.

"About our organs. About babies."

"That's all?"

Her arm had crept along the back of the bench. Now it touched him ever so slightly.

He felt this conversation could only result in failure. What could he wring out of Mrs. McKinley's lesson? He saw her standing in front of the class, sternly dealing with their wretched curiosity, her pale, slightly bulging eyes seeing straight into the very depth of their depravity.

Yes, her look had said, you're a bunch of dirty little boys and girls, but I'll set you right. It hurts to have babies. They arrive by means of gross appetite and the subjugation of females. This goes here. That goes in there. It's an utterly ridiculous plan. I had nothing to do with it. Ever.

Surely his father had kissed his mother. Dimly he remembered embraces cut short at his appearance. It wasn't much to go on. Had there been anything else to refute Mrs. McKinley's account? Nothing he could recall.

He saw again the charts snapping down as the teacher unfurled them. There was a drawing of a baby in a womb. He had stared at it, thinking of himself attached to his mother in that way. Always with her, always inside her, carried wherever she went, night and day. Yes, he had been pleased by that part of it.

"There isn't very much to it," he confessed to Eunice. "You can hear it all in one period."

"Oh, yeah?"

He nodded. He hoped he sounded poised and

sure of himself. Would she laugh at him if she knew how baffled he was?

"Did you go to Health, too?" He made it a club in which they might have mutual membership.

"No, I never did," she said, "and I wish you hadn't either."

At once he had a presentiment that he would hear more, much more than Mrs. McKinley ever dreamed of.

She got up then and tucked his arm into hers. They strolled past the spider monkeys, the lion-tailed monkeys, the dusty leaf monkeys with their climbing games, their wrestling matches and their roughhouse play, the babies taking long, long leaps to cling securely to their mother's fur; past the purple-faced langurs, with the hair on their heads shaped into caps, hoods, bowls, fringes and other hairstyles. And all the while she talked about that mysterious business.

Away, caution. Away with Mrs. McKinley's charts. Now he followed Eunice through forests and glades where flowers sprang up in their footprints. He heard the thin, piping sound of Pan of Arcadia playing on a reed. He heard the hoofs of horses, bulls and goats, saw bronze masks brandished on poles, listened to the splash of water poured in libations, made out the faint rustle of the first sprig of corn. There were the sounds of a festival, lyre and lute, a glimpse of sacred prostitutes, and nymphs in a mossy clearing, punishing unresponsive lovers and stealing away young men for themselves. His own head rested on flesh that was smooth and milky and entwined in garlands. He felt like laughing at the clarity of it. It was so simple. So deep.

Generously, he forgave Mrs. McKinley her

ignorance. No one had ever trusted her enough to impart these secrets to her. He wondered if he should write it all down anonymously and leave it on her desk.

The murmur of Eunice's voice died away.

"Well, thank you very much for telling me," Archer said. "It was interesting."

"It should wait a while," Eunice concluded. "Just open a drawer in your mind and drop it in. Then when you're ready, you'll be ready."

Oh, soon, he thought. But then he saw that his head barely touched her shoulder.

He ate the picnic lunch with enormous appetite.

Harvey left early in the morning, tiptoeing from the room so as not to awaken her. He made a little ritual of arranging the breakfast table for her, orange juice, sugared breakfast cereal, the newspaper carefully folded and propped up at the entertainment page, for Eunice was not political, had no interest in sports, did not care whether it rained or shone. Sometimes he added a blighted rose, sometimes a geranium leaf. On occasion there was a note. "Would you like to eat out tonight?—I think it's too hot for you to cook." "Don't bother to defrost the refrigerator—I've already done it." "You looked so pretty last night— I couldn't stop looking at you." There were always two or three twenty-dollar bills discreetly tucked into the paper napkin, demonstrating his tact. The business of keeping a woman worried Harvey. He would have felt better about expressing his feelings in some other, more tender way, but he sensed that Eunice preferred the money. He waited in vain to be thanked.

He often stopped to lean over her in the bed before leaving the house, breathing cautiously, marveling. She was so flowerlike, so perfectly pale, so delicately wrought. The very air about her held a dying and delicious memory of perfume and bath soap. He resolved to quarter her in castles, to feed her caramels, to rub her back and plait her hair. He would command song for her. He would halt traffic so she might pass. He would deck her in brooches and speak to her in verse. The mere sight of her made him feel blessedly singled out and favored. He put it to himself that he was the luckiest man on earth.

And what of the sleeper? Beneath her shadowed lids, feigning sleep, Eunice could barely wait to have him gone. Barely awake, her mind was stuffed with grievances. She would chide where he would love. Must the shower go on precisely as the clock struck seven, to hiss and steam like a nest of disturbed snakes? Must he lather and shave and hum, all at the same time, with spirits so hearty her very toes curled under the blankets? What narrowness drove him to the same habits morning after morning? Why make the coffee first every time? Why not throw caution to the winds and squeeze the orange juice first? Might not some glorious experience result from such a reversal? ... Orange juice and *then* coffee? Think with glee of a bran muffin for a change, instead of a slice of toast, medium brown. Change your chair. Sit with your back to the wall clock so that time's tyranny relented. Watch the sparrows bicker. instead of reading the stock market report. Even wander in the garden, cup in hand, letting the dew fall lightly upon you as it does on bush and bramble. Run naked, for God's sake, to snatch up the morning paper and thrill and astound the neighborhood. Any or all of these, but go forward, I pray you, with a difference.

Fat chance. He made love in the same ordered way. First the apologetic crawl that brought him under the blankets with her. Had he hit her with his knee? She must excuse his clumsiness. Was his elbow in her eye? He was chagrined if indeed it were. His cold feet he could do nothing about. Then came the kiss on the neck, the kiss on the lips, the kiss on the breast, the kiss between the legs, all in the same careful manner, as if he were afraid of disturbing or awakening her. He hadn't yet.

At last the front door closed behind him. Quietly. A malaise fell upon Eunice. A mood of little pouts and sulky glances. She sat up, throwing back the sheets, naked, flank and thigh, and she confronted the day. Should she buy a large picture hat of Milanese straw adorned with a rose of palest cream? Should she seek a yellow scarf and bind it around her head to make of herself a harem lady? Should she paint her nails green and her mouth burgundy and astonish the lads in the park? Should she go without panties and try on shoes and see the face of the salesman color with confusion and lust as she hiked up her skirt and waggled her foot this way and that?

What was she doing here anyway? She belonged back at the Marina with Hortense, with terrible Stella, with cool Nell. Yes, it would be nice there, all of them sitting under the shade of the Italian umbrella, spooning Italian ices, pulling their thin dresses away from their moist skin, and talking in low, skeptical voices about all manner of things.

She wandered instead around the house, dust rag trailing from her hand like a limp ribbon, flicking idly at the furniture as she passed. What sense did it make to polish furniture of such hideousness, so dark and cumbersome, all yellow varnish and thick legs? Better to burn it in a consuming fire, replace it with a sand-colored Japanese mat and one fragile tulip in a glass vial. Flick, flick, and so much for that.

Well, then, nature. And so into the garden, to move peckishly among the few gaudy nasturtiums and the bowed hibiscus. Near the fence, knees cracking to bend and pick a tiny pansy of perfect blue, she heard a sigh. She stood tiptoe to peer over the garden fence, and there on the other side stood the young widow who lived in the house next door, wan and lonely. She was hanging the wash—a white nightgown, a white slip, a single white towel. She spent half an hour in desultory conversation with her and heard a lament that clearly echoed her own. The days were so long, so long. As she leaned against the fence and talked to the other woman, as the breeze carried their mournful conversation, they became sisters in ennui, kindred spirits.

"I'm going to paint the fence this afternoon. I hope the smell won't bother you."

Paint the fence, paint the Sistine Chapel, it's all the same to me, Eunice thought. "No," she said, "I'll be indoors. I think I'll bake a cake, a lemon surprise cake. The surprise will be if it turns out."

"Do you use a mix?"

"Betty Crocker."

"Save me a piece. I never bake for just myself."

"I will," she said tenderly, for now she felt sad and sorry for the widow who must eat cupcakes because she was alone.

"Goodby then," she called on her way back to the house, and "Goodby" she heard in return as she closed the door.

She had meant to stay only a week or so—Hortense was cranky, had told her to get out of her hair for a few days. Archer was to have come over for company, but his grandmother fell and broke her wrist, so he was captive in another house just as she was captive in this one. Sometimes they talked on the phone, comparing television shows, telling jokes. Sometimes she was met with an awkward silence at the other end of the line; then she knew he was not alone and did not want to explain her call.

Finally it drove her to serious housework. She found silver in a china cabinet, a Victorian teapot, an ornate platter, a candy dish with a fretted rim, and she piled them on a table. She imagined them coming as wedding gifts, the pot from Uncle George, who expected to be invited to Sunday dinner, the platter from distant cousins, who hoped to be asked to a leg of lamb, the dish because someone in the family had two of them. They were all tarnished now and set aside, along with the family ties that no longer bound.

She thought about polishing them. She changed her mind. They would only darken again. Why bother? She found a bucket and liquid wax and waltzed across the kitchen floor, whistling "Night and Day" through her teeth, swirling a mop over the dirt she had not swept up. She arranged the tin cans in the cupboard so that all the labels presented themselves in orderly rows, cat food, string beans, pineapple and peaches. She bathed the cat, who retaliated by scratching her. She turned the hose on the windows and swabbed them down with wadded paper towels, but it made her back ache so she left the inside for another time.

The closets intrigued her. She rummaged through the one in the spare bedroom, shoving aside old raincoats and abandoned jackets and umbrellas with broken handles and torn webbing. It was then she found the cardboard carton.

She lifted it down and sat on the floor, looking intently at pictures of people she did not know. There were pictures of Harvey as well, young and homely, staring stolidly at the camera, teddy bear, bat and ball, bicycle handles, pony's reins held stiffly in his hands; Harvey, older and sadder in an army uniform; sadder still in a blue serge suit with a white carnation, standing with his vivacious bride behind a mountainous wedding cake.

She even read his letters. They had been kept without much sentiment, bundled together carelessly and held by a thick rubber band.

Dear Helen,

We got to Paris yesterday but I didn't get to see much as I had a bad cold. I sent you a bottle of French perfume, which I can get at the PX at quite a good saving. Put some behind your ears and think of me. This sure is a beautiful city from what I've seen of it. I'm going to try to get to Notre Dame tomorrow and will send you a post card from there.

Best love,
Harvey

Dear Dad,

I guess I don't have to tell you about this place as you were here in the last war, but I thought you might like a view of Napoleon's Tomb. Thanks for sending me the baseball standings. I don't think the Giants have much of a chance this year. I've thought about what you said about my GI loan and I guess I will buy a house if we can find something Helen likes. I hope your shoulder isn't giving you too much trouble. Take care of it so we can get us some mountain trout fishing in when I get back.

Lots of love,
Harvey

Dear Mom,

I'm sorry my letter to you got lost, but the mail gets loused up all the time. I guess it's because it has to come from such a long way. I guess I did forget your birthday. I sure didn't mean to hurt your feelings and I'm sorry I have. I know you have a lot of worry about me being over here. I asked Dad to get you a new purse from me. He said you needed one. Maybe Helen can help you pick it out. Anyhow, many happy returns, even though late.

Love,
Harvey

Dear Helen,

It's a beautiful fall night here. The trees are just starting to lose their leaves. I took a walk along the Seine and you could see the moon in the water. It was beautiful. I thought about you and wished you were here with me to enjoy it all. Maybe if things go right we could come back here after we are married.

All my love,
Harvey

And then there was a journal, a cheap nickel notebook, the writing precise and minuscule:

"Sometimes I think about killing myself. I walked around in the rain all yesterday afternoon thinking about it. I don't know what there is to go back to there. I don't know what I'll be or what will happen to me. Not much, that's for sure. It's funny, I'm young, but I don't feel young. I feel a thousand years old, as if I know everything I'll ever know. The only surprise would be if I shot myself. I'm going to bring home a gun and put it away."

And the gun was there, in his bottom drawer, among the neatly folded T-shirts and boxer shorts. Eunice stared at it for some time, afraid to touch it.

This was Eunice's view of life: If you can still be surprised by events large or small you are all right. If something troubles you, hide it with two sweeps under the nearest rug and think determinedly of other things.

If the morning sun kisses your face it will be a good day, and an even better one if you find a safety pin and pick it up. Don't ever make decisions on Tuesday. Four-leaf clovers don't mean a thing, so it's folly to pick them and preserve them in lockets of gold. Far better if you pluck a hair from the head of someone you love for luck. Don't step on cracks in the sidewalk. Do make love in the moonlight whenever possible, with your pillow at the foot of the bed, even if it occasions some comment from your partner.

Always eat food from the sea in preference to food grown on land. The number three is very desirable. The number ten is to be avoided at all costs. You can see the outlines of your life in a teacup, but you are foolish if you accept it as gospel. Wash your hair out of doors; there are gamma rays that penetrate the brain and make you smart.

That was what she was doing when Harvey drove up in the new car. He hallooed to her from the rolled-down window and she lifted her dripping head, getting soap in her eyes which stung and burned.

"What?" she responded crossly. "What?...I can't see a damn thing!"

His voice was full of cheer and high spirits. "Come see what I bought for you."

She bound her dripping hair in a huge towel and swayed down the front path and there, spanking in the bright sunlight, was a white Buick with a shiny black top. He turned off the motor and dangled the keys in his hand, smiling widely.

"My God," she said.

"Power steering and power brakes," he chanted. "Factory air conditioning, AM-FM radio, white side walls, heater, and it's all yours, bought and paid for."

"My God," she said again. Now the soap ran down her back and a little chill followed in its wake. He leaped from the car and ran to grab her hand, pulling her into the street. Frantically she clutched at the towel. It fell away and her hair spilled around her shoulders in soapy, snaky ropes.

"Wait," she cried.

"No," he urged and pulled her along. Up went the hood so she could peer stupidly at the huge exposed motor. Up went the trunk so she could gawk into it. The doors swung back to reveal red leather upholstery which gave the whole interior a hellish gleam. Moreover, the key ring was a huge silver "E" and from it the keys dangled smartly.

He snapped the lights off and on. He pushed the radio buttons. He showed her how smoothly the front seat slid back and forth and how, if one wished to ruminate under some lovely spreading tree, one could tilt the passenger seat back, making it a kind of cushioned bed. And then there was the smell. That ineffable, unreproduceable smell of animal hides and lamb's wool, of motor oil and something else she couldn't define. Together they cocked an ear at the good stiff creak of the doors and the solid satisfying thunk as they shut them.

"It's gorgeous," she said, "absolutely gorgeous. Oh, let's go get Archer and drive down Wilshire Boulevard and blow the horn and get the jump on everybody at the stoplights. Let's do *that!*"

"Well," he said, "I don't know. I took off work."

"Call in and say you're sick. Say your daddy died. One day won't matter. It's the first brand-new car I've ever had in my entire life."

"I would have bought a Rolls," he said expansively, "but they didn't have any in white."

She hugged him in a crushing, exuberant embrace. "I'm going to learn to change tires and sparkplugs and everything. I'm going to wash it every day with baby shampoo. Oh, please, clean out the garage. It *has* to be parked in the garage."

He murmured assurances that he would, on

Sunday, right after breakfast; he would throw out all the old newspapers and the baby crib; he would hose it down. She made plans rapidly. She would bind her hair in a scarf and alert Archer that they were coming. They would spend the whole day, even till dark, riding around the city. She would drive past the Marina so everyone could see her. Hurry, hurry, she admonished him, so this most wonderful, most unexpected of days could begin.

She got Archer on the line and spoke so rapidly that for fully three minutes he thought he was talking to a madwoman.

"Who is this?" he kept inquiring plaintively as she babbled at him.

"Me, me, Eunice. It's white, Archer, it's pure white, like the driven snow. We're going all over town. Put on a nice shirt and comb your hair. I'll come by and beep for you."

"When are you coming," he asked slowly, "so I can be ready?" —

"Listen for the horn, honey. I've got to jump into my clothes."

In fact, she took off her clothes and stood naked before Harvey, her pink nipples pointing at him.

"You gave me a present," she said, "and I'm going to give you one. Stay right there."

She dashed away from him into the kitchen, flung open the cupboard doors, scrabbling until she found what she was looking for. Back she raced, clutching in her hand a large jar of strawberry jam. Harvey stood rooted to the spot, a little alarmed.

"Take off your clothes," she commanded. "Take off everything."

Mesmerized by her sure and authoritative manner, he did as he was told.

"I'm going to put jam on your cock," she said happily. "I'm going to spread this delicious goop all over you and lick it off again. Have you ever done that?"

He had not. Such a thought had never occurred to him.

"It's lovely," she promised him. "Lovely for you and lovely for me."

She removed the bedspread. No point in having to wash it afterward.

"Now," she said, "lie on your back. Don't be nervous, Harvey. You're going to be thrilled out of your socks."

He lay like a blind man, his eyes closed, experiencing her by her touch and by her breathy, excited voice.

"Isn't it nice?" she called to him brightly. "Isn't it nice, Harvey?"

He felt himself lathered, felt cool and sticky. The scent of strawberries recalled the peanut butter and jelly sandwiches of his youth. They had been made by his mother. He went limp with shock at what he was doing, at what was being done to him.

"Never mind, you'll be up again in a second," she said, enclosing him with her open mouth, and then, "Oh, I don't know which tastes better, you or the jam."

Her little cries of pleasure made him feel as if he were an item ordered from a menu. Then his whole being exploded.

"Oh, Christ!" he shouted at the top of his voice.

He saw her red, smeared mouth; he felt her busy tongue. His hands pulled at her hair, clamped on her ears.

"I can't stand it," he said. "Eunice, I can't, I can't!"

Nor was she through with him then, although he lay winded and spent on the bed, wondering idly if the seeds had caught in her teeth. He almost laughed aloud at that. There were two kinds, those of the berries and those he had spilled into her mouth.

"Wait," she whispered. "I'll show you some other things." She danced around the bedroom. "I saw this trick once in a carnival," she told him. "You had to pay a dollar to get in. A boy I knew said he'd pay my way if I would do what she did afterwards. Look." He saw with amazement a disappearing act. A tube of cold cream slid between her legs and was seen no more.

"Go after it," she whispered, and when he did she bit him on the neck and called him names that he hadn't heard since the army.

"The boys in high school nicknamed me the vacuum cleaner," she said solemnly, "which wasn't nice, but I guess not many girls have muscles down there like me."

He agreed. Fervently he agreed.

"Well," she said, "the rest will have to wait."

He burrowed his face against her belly. "Oh, Eunice," he said at length, "I want to give you the world."

"Okay," she said, "but let's go for a ride now."

They roared down the street toward Archer's house with Eunice at the wheel. She drove at full tilt, narrowly missing a mangy brown dog and a fire hydrant as she slued around the corner. Harvey, belted in and nervous, kept a weak smile on his face. He was already burdened by the lie he had told, calling into the store to say in an apologetic voice that there was illness in his family. He had coughed a series of little nervous coughs. He had spoken in a low tone. The clerk, upon hanging up, had winked at another clerk, and then had hurried off to make a report to someone higher up.

But the knot of guilt was gone as he careened along by her side. They were lovers riding the back of a white swan through the glassy waters of a looping stream. He heard the call of the meadowlark where there was none. He was a man bewitched.

"Hey," she shouted jubilantly as they approached Archer's house. "Hey, everybody, we're here!"

She saw the lace curtains part, making a little crack. She saw an old and sour face peer out at her. She stuck out her tongue. The curtains closed abruptly. Then Archer came down the steps, holding his hand aloft in a tentative wave.

"Jump in," she cried, "and away we go."

"Hello, Daddy."

"Hello, son."

"This is a nice car."

He clambered into the back seat, struggled with belts, secured himself, all the while staring around him.

"A nice car, a nice car," Eunice mocked feverishly, "is that all you can say?"

"It's a Buick," he added hurriedly, "with two hundred and five horsepower and a four-hundred-and-fifty-five-cubic-inch displacement. It gets twelve miles in city driving and sixteen to eighteen on the road, depending on your personal driving habits." He sat back nervously.

"Just watch my smoke" was her only reply as

they burned rubber and tore off down the road.

It was a daylong odyssey, broken by lunch in a drive-in because Eunice could not be persuaded to dismount her steed and eat at a counter. She confided to the carhop that the car was hers and just acquired.

"He gave it to me," she said, jerking a finger at Harvey, who immediately turned brick red.

"That's neat," said the little girl with the tight rump and a freckled, saucy face. "I love white cars. That's three hamburgers, no dressing, three Cokes, three fries, right?"

"What kind of a car do you have?" Eunice was not ready to leave the subject.

"I ride on the back of my boyfriend's Honda. It's making me bowlegged, too."

Harvey looked to confirm it. Archer scrunched down in the seat and looked uncomfortable.

She made dire threats to them if they spilled anything on the leather. She made them tuck napkins under their chins and eat their entire lunch bent over their plates. But she was mellow and magnanimous as the sun turned red in the late afternoon, bounteous and generous, for she let Archer drive.

They were out in the deep valley on a quiet street when the great moment came.

"Climb over here and try it out," she said, turning to look at him in the back seat.

Harvey protested. "Eunice, I don't think...he's too small to see over the wheel..."

She was adamant. "He's going to drive this car," she said firmly. "Are your hands clean, Archer? I don't want to get the wheel sticky."

He wiped them on his cords. "Yes," he said.

She hauled him over then, grasping his shirt in one hand and his crotch in the other. Then he was positioned in that hot and embarrassing place between her thighs, crushed into her soft bosom, and with his eyes starting and his breath coming rapidly he took the wheel between his hands. Stretching to the utmost, his foot found the gas pedal; the car moved.

"Stay on your own side," she whispered into his ear. "That's right. Turn a little to the right, a little, not too much, and press the pedal. Uh huh, you've got it. This kid," she said, turning to Harvey, "is a natural-born driver. Don't run into the curb, Archer. There's plenty of road in the middle."

They went around the block three times before the cop spotted them and waved them to the curb. Harvey groaned. Archer foresaw years in prison and tears filled his eyes.

"I'll do the talking," Eunice said. "You guys just button up and let me handle it."

The officer took a long time coming around the car, drawing out a huge pad of citations as he approached.

"Good afternoon," he said. He had bright yellow hair and a virile and energetic air. "Out for a little ride?"

Eunice took a moment to set Archer aside. Then she smiled.

"He's underage," she said, "and it's against the law, I know that as well as the next person, but we just got this car this morning and I thought it would be something he'd remember all his life if he was the first to drive it. I think memories are important—and he'll never forget this one."

The officer smiled at Archer, who had been

wondering if he could hold his breath until he died on the spot.

"How's it handle?" he asked.

Archer choked something in reply which sounded like "Fine."

"May I see your license?" This was directed at Eunice, who promptly emptied her purse in her lap. Among the hairpins and the cigarettes, the Tampons and two or three peanuts in their shells, she produced what he wanted and handed it over.

"And may I see the registration?"

Harvey hurriedly retrieved the slip from the glove compartment, cutting a finger on the hinge in the process.

"I'm sorry, officer. About the boy ... it was just a block or two."

The policeman leaned on the car window. He looked at Archer. Archer looked away and blinked rapidly.

"How old are you, son?"

"Nine. I'm nine." Was it a crime? He was sure it was.

"I've got a boy just about your age."

Archer tried to nod, but his head was immovable on his neck, frozen there.

"He rides a bike."

"I usually walk where I'm going," Archer said numbly.

"Yes," the officer said. "Old shanks' mare isn't a bad way to get around. All right, folks," he continued, "enjoy the rest of the day. Here's your ticket. You can handle it through the Automobile Club or if you want to contest it you can appear in Municipal Court."

Eunice flared. "You have a heart of stone," she said coldly.

"Yes, ma'am." He touched his cap and walked away.

"I've been arrested," Archer said in a stunned voice.

"No," Eunice said, "I have. But never mind. Put it out of your head. Nothing's going to spoil our day if I have anything to say about it. Ready?" She looked at the two of them. "Okay. We're off again." And they roared away, scattering a flock of sparrows into wild flight.

Sunset found them on the beach beside a smoking fire, eating hot dogs that were charred on the outside and cold and raw within. A fat man ran down the beach grunting, his belly heaving over tight blue shorts. A blond, bronzed boy emerged from the sea in a rubber wet suit and swaggered by them, carrying a surfboard high over his head. Newspapers and sandwich wrappings blew over the sand.

They were left to themselves, weary now, sand fleas swirling around them, conversation contracted to small remarks. Each of them felt the melancholy of approaching dusk. A woman came to the edge of the embankment above and called out crossly to the jogging man:

"Fred. It's time to go. Fred?"

The man ran on, as if in flight from the sound of her nagging voice.

Eunice made a mess of the meal, dropping the food into the fire, pulling it out again with cries of pain as she scorched her fingers. Sand gritted in their teeth, a cool wind blew away what warmth remained, the day wound down.

Eunice poked the fire with a stick. Embers shattered and fell into fragments. She waited for the moon to show, hoping that under its clear white eye some of the earlier intoxication would return.

"Let's go wading," she proposed.

Harvey hauled out his pipe and said he would just smoke if she didn't mind; perhaps Archer would accompany her.

Archer had been tunneling in the sand, but now the fragile bridge broke and the holes filled swiftly with fine white drifts. He was getting bored, he was getting tired.

He followed her to the water's edge, saw the white flash of her skin as she peeled out of her stockings and hung them around her neck. He did not care to remove his own shoes and socks; he had a crooked big toe and she would see it.

"Come on," she said impatiently. "What are you waiting for?"

The water was dark, inhospitable; what might lurk in it? "I'll watch," he said.

"Do what you want. I don't care."

But as she moved into the waves he followed, first tucking his socks carefully into his shoes, leaving them lined up neatly on the sand.

He hated the icy sting of the water. He wished she would hold his hand. Instead she stood transfixed, staring at the horizon.

"China's out there," she said.

His calf muscles knotted, his foot cramped. He did not care about China. A lone bird winged out to sea. He wondered if it would finally sleep on the water, wings folded, tranquil until dawn.

"I knew a girl who drowned once," Eunice said. "Her name was Nancy Ellis Quinn. She sang soprano in the glee club."

"That's too bad." He didn't particularly want to hear stories of death and disaster just then. But it was strange and startling.

"She got pregnant in the back seat of a car. Her family was furious, so she went to the beauty parlor and got her hair done, and then she went to the river and jumped in. They asked me to give the speech at her funeral, because I was her best friend."

"What did you say?"

"I said she was a lovely person with a lovely voice, and I said if they didn't want things like this happening every day of the year they'd better get hold of Marvin Bicker and scare the shit out of him, since he was always trying to get girls in the back seat of his car. The next day his father drove him to the post office where they had a marine recruiting office and made him join. He wrote me a nasty post card from Guam." She smiled brightly at Archer. "I fixed him," she said.

Archer looked up at her thoughtfully. Eunice as avenger was a stranger to him. "I have a pain in my foot," he said, backing away. "I think I'll go up on the dry sand and stamp on it."

She followed him and watched as he hopped up and down, trying to ease the cramp, arms windmilling to maintain his balance.

"Oh, sit down. I'll fix it." She grabbed his foot in her hand, spilling him backward onto the ground, and before he could protest she was leaning over him, loose breasts under the blouse swinging, alternately blowing her warm breath on his chilled foot and massaging the taut smooth skin over his thin calf.

"I'm fine," he said, red with embarrassment. "It's fine now, it's okay."

She hung on. "You've got awfully big feet for your age."

He tried to draw away, offended. He could say something about those great mounds hanging from her chest; he was simply too polite to do so.

"It embarrasses you to be touched, doesn't it?" Now she was more outrageous than ever.

"No," he said. He wished a huge wave would come and carry her out to sea, that she would drown like Nancy Ellis Quinn before his eyes.

"Yes, it does, and the sooner you get over it the better. If you crawl in your shell like a snail how is anyone ever going to know that you have tender feelings? How, unless you stretch out your hand and say, 'I'm Archer'? Do you want to be left at the post, while everyone else in the world goes prancing around, hugging and kissing each other? How will you ever get a wife so full of you that she lets the pot roast burn and the book fall out of her lap unread, just for the thinking about you? Throw out your arms, Archer, and the more who fall into them, the better. If you close them, you just hug yourself."

"I don't care," he said defiantly.

"But I do. Now give me a kiss. Here on the cheek—and I'll tell you if you'll pass muster or not."

She offered him her face. She smelled of brine and sweat and hot dogs. He pecked.

"Thrilling," she said. "Now let's go home."

He maintained a moody silence in the back seat until they drew up in front of his grandmother's house. He had things to think about and was prepared to leave them without a word, but his father gave him a look which clearly warned him that he was neglecting his manners.

"Did you have a good time, son?"

His mouth still burned from the kiss. How could that be called a good time?

"Yes," he said.

Eunice turned and grinned at him. "Want to give us another kiss?"

"I have to go now; I have to go to the bathroom."

"All right," Harvey said, opening the door for him. "Off with you."

He ran up the path, as if hurling himself into the house.

That night Harvey lay stiffly on his side, listening to the rumble of the pipes which followed each flushing of the toilet. Eunice returned to bed and lay beside him in silence. She heaved herself over on her stomach, twisted on her back again. The sheets rustled as she tossed and turned and flailed. At last she sat up abruptly and cried out accusingly at him: "Why did you want to kill yourself, Harvey? Why?"

He did not ask her how she knew. It didn't seem important. Perhaps that desire was always on his face for all to read.

"I've forgotten now," he said. "Since you came."

"I tried once," she told him. He took her hand and held it. She sank back on her pillow and they lay in the dark together.

During the course of the next few weeks Harvey presented Eunice with a red fox jacket lined in white satin, three thin gold bracelets, a ruby ring. She found herself in a state of constant excitement, running from the closet to her jewelry case half a dozen times a morning, draping herself in the coat before a mirror, adoring the fuzzy, tartish look it gave her. The clink of the bracelets sliding up and down her arm became her favorite sound; more than once she roused herself from sleep at night to hold the ring under the lamp and study it, like a drop of blood pricked from a finger.

She went to any length to please him. She chopped onions for fried liver, though she detested it, sewed buttons on his shirt sleeves, washed his back in the tub, made popovers. They wandered through the department stores at night, hand in hand, and picked out a new lamp with a pleated paper shade and a hunting scene encircling the base. They bought a reclining chair in leather, testing it first, she on his lap, giggling as they tipped this way and then that. They cleaned leaves from the rain spout, he on a ladder, she with her arms around his legs, propping him up to keep him safe.

She thought she felt the first stirrings of love. Not love, really, but pleasure at the sight of him, reading, smoking, balancing his checkbook with his tongue lodged in his cheek. She wanted it to be love, she willed it to be. It was reassuring to turn down the bed at night, to darken the house, to lie close, back to front. Breakfast at eight, dinner at six, bed at ten seemed like little barricades erected to keep her from wandering off. She'd been a vagabond long enough. Stay a while, she told herself. It's not the most exciting time in the world, but you've been off the wall too long.

So they played Monopoly under the lamp light and walked arm in arm in the rain. She cut his toenails and trimmed his hair where it grew ragged around his collar. They installed squares of kitchen linoleum on their knees. They canned a lug of peaches, Harvey fishing the bottles out of the scalding water, she peeling and stoning the fruit. They painted a bureau and stenciled it with field flowers. They pasted stamps in an album he had kept since boyhood and she marveled at stamps from Mozambique and Morocco and New Zealand. They had grown parsley in a window box. They invented names for each other which embarrassed him and made her laugh. He removed a sliver from her wrist. He fixed her watch. She bought him a terry-cloth bathrobe and pipe cleaners.

The visitor arrived just before ten in the morning. She always peered through the curtains when the doorbell rang. The papers were full of horror stories, housewives raped and murdered; only this morning, sucking in her breath and shaking her head in disbelief, she had read of a woman who had opened her door to an innocent blond child of fifteen with long ironed hair down her back who had proceeded to cut her and stab her in the very doorway of her home with a thin carving knife. She kept an ice pick handy on the drain board—though she knew very well she would have been unable to use it on anything but an ice cube.

But her curiosity overcame her and she opened the door to him. His hair was thin and lay in wide, parted strands, as if the comb he used had broken teeth. There was a light rain of dandruff spotting his lapels and a piece of white tape holding the earpiece of his glasses. A careless man, in a hurry.

"My name is Galloway," he said to her. "Charles Galloway. My credentials."

And he pulled a slick black wallet from his pocket and flipped it open.

Which transgression was this? She thought of parking tickets torn into bits and scattered into the wind, library books unreturned, cherries sampled from fruit stands, and then panic overtook her.

Many months before she had been in a department store, killing time. She had seen a red and white scarf, striped like a barber's pole, and had carried it out into the street to see if she liked it in the sunlight. At that moment Hortense had come by, blowing the horn at her, startling her, hurrying her. She had climbed into the car still clutching it. My God, it was just a dollar scarf; she wasn't a kleptomaniac, it was merely her inertia, her damnable vague, lazy way that made her drift off with it instead of returning it. She had never worn it, not once.

She paused long enough to concentrate on what Mr. Galloway was saying. He had removed his hat, was patting his forehead with a large and rather dirty handkerchief, was saying something about making an example of Mr. Medford in order to deter others, and suddenly she saw the shape of it all.

She grabbed for the doorjamb then and heard her own voice, high and babbling, one word tripping over another. They were just foxtails, she told him, not even good skins; the ring was just a tiny little stone, just a chip, hardly visible; the bracelets turned her arm green. He could have them back this very moment, oh, please, take them back.

Fate had found her, had dogged her, come around corners, tracking her, searched her out even in this miserable little cul-de-sac with its yellow sign which plainly read "Dead End." And Harvey, poor wheyfaced Harvey, who only meant to be kind. Well, she wasn't surprised. Everything in her life turned out this way. Dresses bought on sale unraveled at the seams, prizes in a Cracker Jack box were always tacky and made in Hong Kong, her snapshots faded, her hopes died. Harvey would go to jail and sit in the prison library and think despairingly of his lost life. She would write him post cards and come on visiting days with apples and they would touch fingers and cry.

Why, she thought desperately, hadn't she told him she would be content with a cuticle scissors, a hair ribbon, a shower cap! Spring would come with dandelions, summer with dry grass, fall with burning leaves, and she would be alone.

It's a test of character, she thought, to see what I'm made of. She resolved to be steadfast. She would not recriminate or scold, and if she wept it would be in the clothes closet with her face buried in his coat, unheard.

In the kitchen, with a lamb chop cold and greasy on the plate before him, he said only this: "Never mind, Eunice, it was worth it."

11

"IF YOU THINK it's outrageous, kindly do not say so."

Her grandfather stood before the full-length cheval glass in his bedroom, looking every inch the Edwardian dandy. Nell came to stand behind him, thinking that she looked rather handsome herself in her unaccustomed finery, flowered French silk dress, large picture hat, good pearls. She thought they might be taken for a pair out of a Henry James novel, living in some elegant watering spot, Bad Godesberg, perhaps, mistaken for royalty by Europeans and whispered about over teacups. Who is that distinguished-looking gentleman and that ravishing creature with him? Is it a liaison of disparate years? Is it sinister? Is it sanctioned?

"I think," Nell said, "that it's remarkable you're up to it."

She came around in front of him and gave his tie a firm tug. He batted her away impatiently.

"Don't fuss with me. I'm not the center of attention. It doesn't matter how I look."

"As I'm your only relative present," she remarked, "I would like to have a sense of family pride. Therefore, pull up your socks; they're slumping over your shoes."

She seated herself on the edge of his large, lumpy, dark bed. She had spent so many hours in this room, in tears and laughter, pique and rage. She felt it ought to be sealed off like a tomb, housing all the emotions of her childhood. But the old intimacy was slipping away. Today would end it. Well, her behavior would be exemplary. She was no longer of an age when she could thrust out her lower lip, allow her eyes to brim with tears, demand that she come first in all things. She rather wished that were not so. In the old days she would have stared at him defiantly, announcing in sulky tones: "I don't want you to." And moreover she might very well have had her way. Well, hey and ho for those days—they were no more.

She told him what a dashing figure he cut and wasn't it lucky that everything in the garden had come out in a rash of bloom. She wandered to the window to confirm it. The summer roses had a velvety look, and one or two bushes, unwilling to be merely pretty, were fiery red. The lilies were tubes of ivory, folded over themselves like fine, ancient parchment, the hedge a silver gray. She saw with a pang that he had left a book under a tree, its pages ruffling in the breeze. It might have slipped from his lap as he dozed there, aging and disorderly and familiar to her. She saw that he had

404

removed the old split cane chair. Had he thought it shoddy or did it recall his more sedentary days, when he sat in the shade and peeled figs and sought no company but his own? Now three gentlemen tuned their violins under the tree looped with ribbons, and there was a punch bowl centered on a white cloth, bobbing with summer fruit. There were a dozen gilt chairs standing on the lawn and a maid in a white apron and a cap and nurse's shoes to spare her feet.

Matters were slow and stately below. Two waiters, one young with a scampery walk, one old and shuffling, brought out silver trays laden with sandwiches, cucumbers cold and green on rounds of bread, shrimp curled pinkly, watercress and cream cheese. She saw the boy take a shrimp and cover his theft with parsley. She saw the wine bottles frosting in the huge tubs of ice and the cake, a virginal white and doubtless poisonous if it stood much longer in the sun. She scanned the sky and frowned at the ashen look of some clouds beginning to build up over the trees, but all in all it was festive, gleaming, a credit to everyone.

"What kind of present did you get me?" her grandfather demanded. He was finished with his dressing now and sat in a straight chair, as if he feared disarranging his finery. He smoked his pipe, puffs coming out as if his lungs were bellows.

"Something very expensive. Something you'll love."

"What? So far it's been cut glass ashtrays and salad tossers."

"Balzac. *La Comédie humaine* in blue leather, gorgeously tooled. I can hardly bear to give it up. I intend to borrow it back."

"Very nice. Can you afford it?"

"Not really. Still, you don't get married every day."

He held his pipe in his hand and looked at her in some wonder. "In a way, this vindicates my whole life...mind and body still good for something."

"Yes," she said, "you're a ripe old cheese, there's no mistake about that."

"What time is it? Do we have time to talk before they all get here?"

"Yes, plenty of time."

He beckoned her. "Draw a chair up close. Sit beside me."

She complied. He brushed ash carefully from his coat. It fell on his trousers and stayed there.

"I'm giving you this house," he said. "And its furnishings and the services of Mrs. Keitel—if you can stand her."

Nell pulled off her hat. She did not know whether she felt burdened or grateful, consoled or abandoned.

"Aren't you going to live here?" The house without him was inconceivable.

"We've decided on Frances' house—there are no stairs to make me wheeze. There's also her place in Provence—I may just get a beret and settle down there." The very thought seemed to infuse him with energy. "And drink wine and bathe in the blue Mediterranean. Is that goatish enough for you?"

"Yes, indeed. Randy as hell." She felt as if he had raced past her, hurtled a garden wall and disappeared.

"Hmm." He peered at her. "I know that look of yours. You're not pleased."

"Don't be silly."

"No, I see something's not right with you."

"Well," she said wryly, "it's just that I begin to see myself as a kind of Mrs. Havisham, shut up in a great house with cobwebs hanging from the furniture. Hanging on me as well."

She remembered the time when he had gone east to bury his brother. He had not wanted to take her on such an occasion, and she had stood in the depot watching the train pull away, lighted window after lighted window, gathering speed and rushing by her until she was alone in the dark.

His face grew stern. He wagged a long finger. "Nell, I won't have it."

"What won't you have?"

"You musn't cling to me. You may *not* cling to me."

"You're right, you're right, you're right," she said.

He went on, scolding her. "I don't believe in self-sacrifice. It's unhealthy, it's morbid. Now, look here. You'll have this house. You'll have some money from me if I don't spend it all, which, incidentally, I very well may. You're young and when you're not sullen, you're beautiful. You may wish to marry or you may not, but in either event, I want to see you behave with style."

"Go get married, why don't you, and leave me in peace."

"That's exactly the way I wish to leave you, my darling. In peace."

A murmur of voices rose from below. Nell craned out the window, glad of the interruption. "They're here," she said, "and some lady's slip is showing."

The violins swept into a waltz. The birds sang in

407

response. She rested her head on her chin and gazed down. "Dr. MacFarland's all spiffed up in a green suit," she said, and she thought: Why has everybody gotten so old? So old.

He came and stood beside her and he spoke in a softened tone. "There's Frances."

A gray-haired woman in floating blue lace waved and called.

"Hello, you two. It's time to come down. It's time, William."

They moved away from the window together. He did nothing ceremonious, he gave her no special embrace. He did not even touch her. But he did look at her under his heavy, winged eyebrows, directly, humorously.

"Well, granddaughter, will you give me away?"

"Yes," she said, and added to herself, if I must.

The ladies sat under the ilex tree, their heels digging into the grass. The afternoon sun was high and merciless, the cake had been too rich, but still it was a party and in their diminishing ranks there were so few occasions for celebration. So they drank the wine and looked across the garden at their husbands, those whose husbands were still alive, and wished the music would go on until dark. The bride's bouquet had been handed with a flourish to the oldest among them and she sat holding it carefully, while the white petals trembled and fell in her lap.

In the drawing room a few brave souls moved cautiously, heads inclined to catch the beat of the music, holding each other fearfully.

Dr. MacFarland was a dreadful dancer, but he loved to dance and would not turn Nell loose. He said the marriage of his old friend had so shaken him that he must without delay take his mind off it; he didn't know if he was embarrassed by this late-in-life mating, or jealous or abashed. Unnerved he was.

And so he grasped Nell by the waist and refused to let her go, pulling her tight against his tweed suit, swooping, darting and stomping with her in a lumpy, stiff-gaited waltz.

"Loosen up," he told her. "Give yourself to the music. *One,* two, three—*one,* two, three...

"Well," he said, "so he's off to a new life. It makes me wonder about mine. There's not much to it these days. My patients, of course, some of whom I've been treating for fifty years; that hasn't changed. And a few friends, those who have managed to survive; not many, one or two. We play bridge, quarrel over the cards, and afterward it's stale pound cake, weak tea and bed. If it weren't for Horace Walpole and Sir Walter Scott I'd be in serious trouble. I'm seeing a psychiatrist, you know," he said abruptly.

"I didn't. Whatever for?"

"Depression. Sleeplessness. Loneliness. I've come to a time in life where I'm left by myself, and I'm bad company for myself. It's costing me a fortune to be told in addition that I'm no good at relating to people, that I'm arrogant and judgmental. I knew all that before I went. Now I'm going to dip you back, so hang on."

Nell did, afraid that they would collide with the furniture. He was being rash the way he was tossing her about.

"Yes, it's quite terrifying to find yourself old and alone, and discover you have a bad character to

409

boot. We have terrible arguments, that mind man and me. I say it's because my wife up and died on me and he says, 'No, it's because you're rigid and repressed and narrowminded'... Am I?"

"Yes."

"Your grandfather and I have been friends for half a century. How do you explain that if I have no charm?"

"He has."

"So do you and it hasn't gotten you anywhere."

"Thank you very much. And look out—you're headed into that table."

He jarred her backbone as he swerved clumsily to avoid it.

"Look here," he said, "a while back you came to me in trouble. You were given a reprieve. What are you going to do with the life you got back?"

"Live it."

"How? I'm willing to listen, it's not too late to learn. You see, I have an open mind after all. I can take a new tack. Melancholy is a nasty business. Almost all my friends are dead—or have I said that already?"

"Not me. I'm alive and devoted to you."

"I'm too truculent for you. And you're too giddy for me."

"Giddy? I'm a serious young woman."

"Not so young. You're in your thirties. I know *where* in your thirties, too."

They revolved in the center of the room, spinning like a top, out of step with the music. People retreated to give them more room. He clutched her even closer and she pushed at his chest.

"Don't hold me so tight. Your jacket's prickly."

410

"Sorry." He moved back a bit. They danced on.

"I had an affair once," he announced with a slightly braggadocio air. "With my music teacher. It went badly."

"Really? Why?"

"I was young and fractious. She didn't entirely please me so I set about molding her. She didn't want to be molded."

"I should think not."

"How do you conduct those matters these days?"

"Hit or miss, the same as you did."

He was sweating alarmingly.

"Douglas," she said, "sit down and loosen your collar. You've overdone. I'll get you a glass of champagne."

She steered him to a chair, saw him settled into it, helped him with his knotted tie and then threaded her way through the guests, pausing to smile, to speak, to acknowledge good wishes. A woman in a violet dress with violets pinned to her shoulder in a damp clump seized her hand.

"William is remarkable. I think he's so brave to marry at his age."

"You're next, Mrs. Starling."

The woman flushed with pleasure and laughed nervously. "I don't know. Oh, I don't think so. Oh, I think not."

She saw her grandfather in the next room, sipping a drink, smiling, speaking to his friends; he caught her eye and waved to her over their heads.

She stopped a waitress and took two glasses from the tray. When she returned to him, Douglas was slumped in the chair, mopping his brow.

411

"That's warm work," he said, and he patted the seat beside him. She sat there, handing him the brimming glass.

"Have I depressed you with my problems? I think I depress everyone these days, except my cleaning woman, and she's deaf as a bone. Perhaps that's why she's exempted."

"I'm worried about you," she told him, casually placing her fingers on his wrist to feel his pulse.

"Getting old is very nasty. I tell you that so you'll make the best of being young. Are you making the best of it?"

"Well, I'm having a very nice time currently with a very nice man. We sleep together, which keeps me from being tense and unruly, and for the most part we don't get on each other's nerves. I don't know him very well. I'm not sure I need to or even want to. I'm a stubborn woman. I like having my own way. I don't want to be compelled to justify or explain anything I do. Most men won't put up with that. They needn't. I won't put up with anything less than that. So there we are."

"Women are fierce creatures," he said. "Far stronger than my own poor sex. I go to the old peoples' home, you know, to look after them. There are the ladies, bright as dollars, finger painting and making pots, eating with good appetite, and there are the men, staring into the air and plucking at the bed sheets." He drained his glass, gulping steadily.

"Whoa," she cautioned. "That's vintage. What's your hurry?"

"It goes down like water. No bite to it at all." He sighed deeply. "Piety," he said. "I'm left to my piety and constipation."

"They may be one and the same thing," she told him with a smile.

He ignored her. "I wish your old cock of a grandfather had stayed behind with me, that's what I wish. He'll never hold up, having to shine every minute, the way you must with a woman. You have to keep up to the mark with them, perform, they judge you very stringently. He'd have done better to stick with me. We were going to build a dovecote this summer; I've already bought the lumber and the wire. We were reading *Martin Chuzzlewit* aloud—I read aloud very well. It was my habit to come by here after the clinic and have a glass of something with him and sit out in that garden and read the better part of a chapter a day. And what of the fishing? Every Sunday, off the pier, with bait in the bucket and a bottle. I doubt if that woman will be able to put up with his chess game. I couldn't. But he was a good talker, your grandfather. He knew everything about Voltaire and quite a lot about that fellow Proust. Too effete for me. Still, you don't find a well-read man under every rock."

"Why do you use the past tense?" Nell asked. "He's still alive."

"Not to me." The old doctor scowled and then held out his glass to her. "Pour a bit of yours in there. I've got a terrible thirst from the dancing."

She obliged him.

"I'm weary of it all," he said tonelessly. "I don't notice things anymore. I have aches and pains. I have bad breath. I give people black looks. I sleep with the light on all night."

"So do I," she told him.

"But you're sure of the morning. I'm not." He

closed his eyes momentarily. "You'll have to drive me home. This drink has befuddled me."

She shook him lightly. "Douglas?"

"Yes, yes . . . what is it?" He made an effort to sit upright.

"I forbid you to be like this." Her voice was angry.

His huge head fell back against the cushion. "Do you indeed? Then I'll stay with that Viennese head meddler and struggle on." He seemed too weary to pursue it further. "They're playing a nice waltz. But I won't dance anymore."

Lucidity, she decided, comes afterward; after things are over and done with and one's time is spent asking how and why things happened in just that particular way. In the same way, she concluded that "lovers" was a foolish and inadequate designation for two people sharing bed, board and one bathroom. One is not wildly in love at seven in the morning when a man grunts and wakes beside you, smelling brackish and musty, and shows you his furred buttocks as he takes over the bathroom at the very moment you wish to use it yourself. One is not passion's slave at the breakfast table when conversation is monosyllabic and mundane, having to do with bacon and eggs and the stuffed-up garbage disposal. Nor is one blind to the whole world as small quarrels erupt about money or laundry or one's taste in friends.

It was true, Nell conceded, that she had lived cheerfully enough with Jake. Cheer easily maintained, she added, because little or no pressure had been put upon him. She yielded in small things. His cooking was better than hers. She admitted it

414

and ate his Irish stew with as much gusto as he did. He *was* neater, although she came to detest the way he folded a damp bath towel in exactly three quarters and let it hang sodden on the towel bar. He took his own sweet time at everything, love, talk, meals. She sometimes had the urge to prod him to the end of a sentence or the end of foreplay or the end of a crust of bread, but he was not to be moved from his deliberate pace.

He was not a rancorous man. He *was* a lazy one. She thought him prodigal with his time. An hour with the morning paper seemed excessive to her. An hour in the shower maddening. His day could begin at one o'clock as well as at eight in the morning. Hers began at six, confronted by a dozen decisions, a dozen appointments, a dozen put off to be met at the very first free moment. His sense of laissez-faire insulted her view that things must not be left alone just to happen, but she prudently kept impatience to herself. It seemed to her imbecilic to try to alter a grown man; futile as well.

She was kept from smugness by his view of her, which he expounded on with candor. He found her too tart, verging dangerously on the sour. Except in bed, where she was erotically complicated, her head ruled her heart. He found her authoritative about altogether too many things. He could damn well work the *New York Times* crossword puzzle as well as she. She often commanded where a request would have done the job. He would have preferred her to be moody instead of icy when displeased. All irritating but tolerable because he also found her witty and bawdy, generous and dashing, rarely, if ever, a bore.

They were rather like a couple driving down a

country road, in a pastoral setting, with a cow or two, a barn, a stream, nothing to impede or halt or endanger them. A pleasant, drowsy journey, with the possibility that one or the other might nod off.

And yet he surprised her. It came in the area of surprises—they were in bed. He sat up, stuffed a large, black cigar in his mouth, the first of the day, removed it to bite off the end, patted her flank and made a pronouncement.

"I had to get up to pee in the night three times last week," he said, "and that tells me something. What does it tell you?"

"You have prostate trouble," she told him.

"It tells me," he went on, "that I'm getting older. You remember my story about my Uncle Tyler?"

"A remarkable man," she muttered into her pillow. "What about him?"

"He died at forty-eight. Tomorrow is my forty-eighth birthday." He struck a match and puffed the foul smoke into the room.

"We'll have a cake," she said. "I'll buy you a handsome tie."

He waved her into silence. "I've come to a conclusion, and since it affects you I'm going to tell you what it is. I expect, at the outset, to come up against your tight-ass view of things, but I'll ask you for once to hold off and listen carefully to what I have to say."

"I only wish to remind you that it's Monday morning and I can't lie around in bed. But I'm listening."

"What's life about?" he asked her, shifting his bulk. "Don't answer, I'm going to tell you." He puffed again. The air was filthy now.

"It's about getting and spending and laying

waste our powers. It's about heart attacks and breakdowns and larceny of every description. It's about sharp practice, political villainy, sexual dysfunction. In the main it's shit, right?"

"Not in my view," she said, "but go on."

"I would say the major color is gloom. I would say we're walking a tightrope over a sea of excrescence. I would say if chicanery doesn't get us, the mortician will. The young are bootless, the old imperiled, the poor ever with us. The streets stink, the air reeks and I have a bad morning cough. Therefore," he said, "I have taken steps which my Uncle Tyler took before me, but far too late to save his hide. I am about to chuck it—and I invite you to come along."

She glanced at her watch and threw back the covers. "Keep talking while I brush my teeth. I'll leave the door open."

He sat on the edge of the bed, raising his voice over the running water.

"I've bought an island in Juan De Fuca Strait. It's got a house, a chicken run, a dock, an Airedale pup, four apricot trees and sanity. There's one other family living there. They're of Portuguese descent, Catholic, and have five lively kids. The mail boat comes over from Seattle twice a month. The captain is a pretty good storyteller and a fine drinker. There are any number of things to do on that island. You can watch the birds, grow herbs, whittle a soft stick and turn your mind over while sitting on a rock in the ocean. The fog is bad, the fishing is good. There's enough room so that if one of us gets a little ornery he can hike a mile down the beach and be out of the other's way. There's nothing to lose, everything to gain, and I'm putting this place up for sale tomorrow. In the main I love you, Nell, but with or without you I'm going to Juan De Fuca Strait."

She finished brushing and rinsed her mouth, carefully placing the glass on the sink. Then she came out and leaned in the doorway, looking at him.

"Well," she said, "in the main I love you, too, Jake, and I'm going to let you go."

He ground out his cigar and pulled at the end of his nose. "I mean it," he said. "I'm not fooling around here."

She came into the room and gathered up her clothes. He leaned back against the headboard and looked across the room at her with a lopsided grin.

"Just so long, Jake?" he asked her. "Just like that? You won't even think about it?"

"Afraid not."

"You think it'd wear out?"

"No. We'd probably get on very well indeed, flopping on the beach, sleeping in the sun, making mud pies." She smiled at him.

"Well, why the hell not? My Uncle Tyler was a happy man. And he never saw a soul except his Mexican lady, me, and the veterinarian. That man knew about living, I'm telling you. He had those misty blue hills in sight night and day. He took his bath in a river where he could watch the fish between his toes. He picked daisies in the meadow and put 'em on his dining room table in a soup can. He was an elegant man. A remote man. A smart man. And he would have been an old man if he'd started sooner." He paused. "Nelly, hang up your shingle and let's go dig earthworms. Come with me."

"Mmm," she said, brushing her hair and pulling it severely into place.

"What'll happen to you," he said shortly, "is you'll stay on here and keep on handing out pills. You'll get older and that sharp edge you've got now will get honed like a razor blade. A lot of men will come and go and you won't give a damn either way. Be my girl. Let me get two tickets."

She was dressed now. She put her keys and cigarettes and note pad into her purse. "What you say may all be true," she told him, "but who's going to take out the garbage?"

She went into the kitchen. He climbed out of bed and loped after her in his bare feet, stood in the doorway watching her as she poured her coffee.

"What does that mean?"

"Just that. Who's going to take out the garbage if we all head for the nearest island? Who's going to change the bedpans and the light bulbs? Who's going to sell potatoes? Aspirin? Diaphragms? Who'll drive the bus? Who'll mop the floor? Who'll teach the multiplication table? Who'll dance Giselle? Who'll make jelly and penicillin?"

She sat down and cupped her hands around her coffee mug. He stood disheveled and disgruntled.

"Somebody elected you, did they?" He glowered.

"Have some coffee, Jake. You sound cranky."

"You think if you turn off the stove the whole goddamn world stops cooking? Christ, lady, you've got a real ego going there."

"We can make it a fight," she said quietly. "I'd rather not."

"No. I'm not looking for a fight either. I guess you are what you do—and there's no way I'm going to get around that." He stood a while regarding her, shaking his head and scratching his belly.

"Are you gonna miss me?" he asked.

"Oh, yes. Are you really going?"

"You'd better believe it."

"Principles are fine," she said ruefully, "but you can't fuck them on a rainy night, can you?"

"But you'll stand on 'em?"

"I guess so."

"Well," he said.

"Well," she echoed.

They were already cut adrift, already embarked on separate journeys.

"If it thins out," he told her, "I can always be reached. I'll have to take a boat and take a walk and take a ferry, but I can always be reached."

"Providing the tide is right." She smiled at him. "Goodby, Jake."

"Nelly."

He moved forward to kiss her, to persuade her, to beguile her, but she was out the back door before he could get across the room, and he had only one leg in his trousers when he heard the short, sharp coughs and then the roar of her souped-up Triumph as she pulled out of the carport, late for her rounds and already speeding though she was still backing up, tires squealing as she turned and negotiated the narrow alley and then raced for the highway and was gone. He stopped, then, all thought of chasing after her leaving him, and he got all tangled up in his feet, hopping about like a crazy person until he fell back on the bed again, one leg still in his pants, one out.

12

STELLA STUDIED the photograph in the newspaper and concluded that Pritchard's features resembled her own except for his eyes, round eyes like bits of chocolate, dark and sweet.

She was faintly elated to discover that he was still alive. He was her brother, after all, and while she hadn't seen him since 1951, she was pleased to note that his hair was not white, that the passing of time had left him looking still boyish and full-cheeked.

His recent notoriety, if one could call it that, had to do with his raising the largest pumpkin in California. He was pictured with his arms straining around the huge orb, a proud smile on his face, as if he had unlocked some mysterious secret of nature.

Stella reasoned that if he had time to spend in his garden, his tiny, tense, religious wife must be dead. No loss. Stella remembered her scattering mothballs in every corner of the house and praying at the dinner table until the meal was cold muck in front of them. She had been a deaconess in her church and a wet blanket at home. Further, his son, who was a canny corporation lawyer in San Francisco, with a house near the Presidio and a French cook in his kitchen, regarded his father as a rube and had cut off all communication with him except for sending a loudly checked jacket, too large and unsuitable, as a Christmas present and his discarded English overcoats from Burberrys on Father's Day.

Vaguely she wondered why she hadn't stayed in touch with him herself. Of all her family she had always been fondest of Pritchard.

He had ridden her to school on the back of his bicycle with his strong legs pumping and the wind fresh and cool in their faces. He had saved the tinfoil in cigarette packages and had given her a large, heavy ball of it to weight papers on her desk. He had made her a swing from a piece of orange crate and a strong rope.

And so he had grown to mild young manhood, spending most of it tending the odorous mulch pile he cherished the way other boys of his acquaintance were beginning to cherish girls, feeding choice morsels of garbage, lettuce leaves and carrot tops into it until it was a dark, rotting syrup. He had a gulping, hearty laugh which rose above all other laughter when a joke was told. He carried old ladies' packages for them and refused the dime they pressed into his palm. He believed in a just

422

and merciful God. He watered his neighbors' lawns should they be out of town. He rubbed his mother's back and shoulders should she complain of headache. He never quarreled.

Stella hoped he had money. She knew he was industrious. He had worked at the same neighborhood hardware store for years, sweeping the street in front of it, waiting on trade, arranging rakes and hoes, trowels and garden hoses into beautiful patterns on the walls. He had bought the business when the owner died, crying inconsolably at the man's funeral, catching everyone there by the lapels to tell them that his boss was a dear, dear fellow and the world would not soon see his like again.

He was not a man to indulge himself except for Burpee seed catalogues and flats of bedding plants. He treated himself to a cigar only twice a year, once on his birthday, again on Thomas Jefferson's birthday. He admired Jefferson greatly.

He had always been tentative with Stella. Stella as a young girl, locked away in her room, lying flat on her belly, her hair uncombed, her gaze fiery and intent on a book, caused him to tiptoe carefully past her door, unless she required him to fix a light cord or repair her headboard so it would not wobble.

Bright women blinded him with their brilliance. In consequence he had married a dim woman, dim in color, dimmer yet in perception. He had never had a happy day with her.

Over the years he had sent post cards with cryptic messages so that his sister might not feel alone in the world.

"Cabbages as big as melons this year." "I'm wearing dental plates now." "You wouldn't recognize me anymore, I'm afraid." "My roses are the talk of the street."

Only once had she answered. "I'm working my head off. If anyone dies, my number if OLdfield 10404."

Once, when the gas company had shut off the utilities, she had thought of calling on him for help; but something had intervened, she couldn't remember what, and they had lost touch.

Now she had something in mind that needed cold hard cash, and there was no blinking the fact that she had worn out every source on this side of town.

So it was that she thumbed the pages of the telephone book and found him, Pritchard Carver, on Broadway, in Glendale, California.

To show Pritchard she respected his hard-won position in life she washed her hair and took a bath. She borrowed carefare from Jake, and taking a cheese sandwich to eat on the bus and a pencil and a piece of paper, she crossed the city to what remained of the bosom of her family.

She had to walk two or three blocks from the bus stop and her brassiere strap broke on the way, forcing her to duck behind a hedge and tie a knot in it. She didn't intend to appear in front of her older brother jiggling like a tart.

A little girl stood on the front porch of the house and inquired nasally what she was doing.

"Get off," Stella said.

The little girl stared.

"Get off, I say."

The little girl thrust one finger up her nose.

424

"This is my lawn. You get off."

Stella bared her teeth and the child fled.

Stella finished adjusting her underclothes and marched on, staring at the house numbers with a nearsighted squint. She suddenly recognized an old dark green wicker chair of her mother's on the porch. Her mother had rocked in it every night, staring into the starry sky, thinking her own thoughts. They all left her alone, accommodating that darkness which overcame her from time to time. Stella decided she recouped something of her life, gazing into the heavens on those solitary evenings. Sitting in this green wicker chair, which now had a hole in it.

She approached the house, smelling the turned earth. The gate was blistered and in need of paint, but beyond every care had been expended. The garden ran amuck with peas and tomatoes, stalky corn, squash in yellow curves, huge phallic cucumbers of a pale green. There were two figures in among the orderly rows of growing things, a scarecrow and a man, hoeing. They resembled one another. The man had a red bandanna handkerchief knotted around his neck and suspenders holding up his earth-stained trousers.

"Pritchard," she said, "is that you?"

He turned, and shading his eyes he stared into the street. "Yes," he said. "Who is it?"

She passed through onto the garden path laid out in stepping stones.

"It's your sister Stella."

The hoe dropped from his hands.

"Stella?"

"Don't gawk. I'm remarkably unchanged from my youth, so there's no need to gawk."

425

"Oh, my," he said, wiping the dirt from his hands onto his pants. "Oh, my goodness."

She slouched toward him, thrusting out her hand.

"Well," she said, "I'm tired and I'd like to sit down."

He winced at the sight of her, the shapeless dress, the odd necklace of seeds and beads, the cracked leather purse. The gray of her hair was too painful to look at. He blinked shyly and took her hand.

"Well, what do you know," he said. "Little Stella."

"Big Stella. Thirsty Stella. Hot Stella. Do we have to stand here? Your neighbor's peering at us from under her window shade."

He ushered her into his front room, hand under her arm. It was close and hot and dark. There was a three-piece suite of golden oak furniture, a stiff little oval picture of her father and mother on the fireplace mantel and the famous pumpkin resting on the hearth. There were no books. There was no air. She sat down and waved him into the chair across from her.

"This is remarkable," he said slowly. "You won't believe this, but I had a dream about you last night. Yes, you came to me in a dream, wearing a beautiful hat and carrying some peonies in your hand. I never have much luck with peonies. Not enough shade. You came into the backyard and said, 'Pritchard, it's ending. Hurry up and do something with your life.'" He paused a moment, and he shook his head. "I had beans for supper. They don't agree with me so that might account for it. Stella, my goodness."

426

"It's not the second coming of Christ, Pritchard. It's just me."

He drank her in. "You still have dark good looks, Stella. You always had those dark good looks."

"I saw your picture in the paper, holding that thing you grew."

"The biggest in the county. The biggest in the state."

"Is that what you've been doing all these years? Growing big things?"

"It's my hobby. You could say it's my hobby."

"Jean's dead, I take it?"

"Yes. I have her planted next to Mother and Dad."

"Planted?"

He nodded.

"Well. So you're alone?"

Her brother had a look of utter content. "I'm out in the yard from dawn till dark," he said brightly.

"You haven't got any money buried out there, have you? I need some money." She wasted no time. "I'm glad to see you, of course, but I wouldn't have turned up here like a bad penny unless I had something in mind, would I?"

As always he expected nothing; he was entirely forgiving. "You always did go your own way."

"Well, I can't *pay* my own way, that's the problem, Pritchard. That's the problem with sister Stella. I've come to put the bite on you."

His face saddened. He pulled a burr from his shirt and shook his head. "I've got my social security, and I get twenty-five dollars a month from my son's wife, who's a very decent girl. There's nothing else." He was embarrassed by his impoverishment.

"You owned the hardware business," Stella insisted.

"The bookkeeper stole it from me, bit by bit. Mrs. Adams. Of course you never knew her. Embezzled it all away. Never suspected her. Kept a lovely coleus on her desk. Grew ivy in the ladies' room in a water glass. I was very surprised at her, I must say."

She leaned back and groaned. "Damn," she said. "I was two hours getting here." Then she had a thought. "Papa's watch, his gold watch. You have that, don't you?"

"Why, no, John got that when he graduated from law school."

Her frenzied gaze rolled around the room. "You must have something somewhere!"

He was crestfallen. "There's only the greenhouse. I bought it after Jean died. To make up for everything," he said defensively. "It's out in back. Would you like to see it?"

"All right," she said irritably. "Show me the goddamn thing."

The gentle hiss of steam filled the greenhouse, taking the curl and the starch out of her. He led her along the rows of miniature plants, curled, green, tender to the touch. His voice, when he spoke, seemed prayerfully lowered, as if they had come into a sacred grove.

"Everything does well in here. Isn't it fine? No wind disturbs them. No insects. They can't be bruised or harmed. I call it 'The Peaceable Kingdom.'"

"It's hot as hell in here," she replied. "My armpits are running."

She stalked up and down the rows and then out

428

the door, leaving it ajar. He followed her, running to catch up with her rapid stride.

"Are you in trouble, Stella?" he asked anxiously.

"Never out of it," she said, walking on.

"I'll make you some lemonade." Now that she had come he wanted to keep her, he was unwilling for her to go again.

"With gin?"

"I don't keep spirits."

"I have to catch the bus," she said shortly.

"We've hardly had a talk. Father and Mother, Selma and Orville, Mattie and Tom, the twins, Alice and Eugene, John and his wife and their three children...there's so much to catch up on."

Yes, she thought, we could sit knee to knee, but my history would shrivel your skin and yours would bore me to death.

She paused to give him a kiss on the cheek. He smelled of fertilizer.

"Keep America green, Pritchard," she said, submitted to his bony hug and then pulled free.

"Come again," he said. "I'm always home. I'll pick you some peas next time."

Stella thwarted was Stella rampant. She tried, on three different occasions, to reach Caleb by phone and was told at his office, his club and his home that he was not available to speak to her. She had engaged in a heated conversation with his houseboy, beginning with extravagant claims of extreme need: she was starving, she was being evicted, she was ill. The houseboy remained unmoved, and was then treated to a string of profanity so Irish and archaic he thought her mad.

The lackey had hung up on her.

She had then composed a letter on her twenty-nine-cent pad in a bold scrawl, but she was dissatisfied with its tone, unable to strike just the right balance between imperiousness and reconciliation. In addition, she was certain it would go unread.

Thus it was that she sold the stove and the refrigerator out of the apartment, neither of which belonged to her, to a man she met in a bar, warning him that he must come late at night to take them away, no questions asked. The man was larcenous, mounted the backstairs after midnight with a seedy-looking companion, disconnected the appliances, paid her a measly forty dollars and went off into the dark, telling her that they were always in the market for transactions such as these.

Without further ado she gathered up her nightie, her toothbrush, her toothpaste, a fistful of pencils and a moldy rain slicker and stashed them in a large brown paper bag. She left a note for Jake propped on the kitchen table, saying she expected to return in style and that she would reimburse him handsomely for having made off with his property. She then stationed herself at the entrance to the Santa Monica Freeway, heading east, holding up a large cardboard sign which read: I AM ENTIRELY HARMLESS. KINDLY GIVE ME A RIDE TO YOUR FURTHEST DESTINATION.

She got no takers for the better part of two hours, sweltering and scowling as cars whizzed by her.

At last a diesel truck slowed, the driver squinted to read the sign and then stopped, throwing open the door to the cab.

"Okay," he said. "Hop in."

She clambered up with agility, deposited her greasy bag, the toothpaste having already squirted inside, and settled back with a sigh.

"Man is a wary beast," she said. "I've been standing on this on-ramp all morning. I'm Stella Carver."

"Joe Polanski. That's some sign you got there."

"The truth is not convincing or I would have been to Denver by now. How far are you going?"

"Salt Lake City."

"I'm agreeable to Salt Lake City. How far is it?"

"Seven hundred and forty miles. We ought to get to know each other pretty good."

She studied him. He was close to fifty, with a square, stubborn face, dark, bushy brows, intelligence in his eyes and the faintly pugnacious air of a man fending off the troubles of his life with brute strength.

"I'm going to tell you something at the outset so we won't have to deal with it later. I do sleep with men but not at random. I have a long, arduous journey in front of me and I'm going to need all my energies at the end of it. You may or may not have had that in mind, but I'd rather be clear at the beginning than have to tussle and pummel and knee you in the crotch at some rest area along the way. If that doesn't suit you, let me out at the next exit."

He gave her a sour look. "I've got all the women I can handle," he said. "One in L.A., one in Yonkers. Enough."

"You're not married?"

"Married in L.A., not married in Yonkers. Understand?"

431

"Certainly. Is it okay with you if I roll down the window? I'm boiling."

"Sure."

She did so and turned her face to the breeze.

Mr. Polanski was a man of discretion and rectitude. They rode in silence for almost an hour before he asked a question. "How come you didn't take a bus where you're going? Only the kids bum."

"I'm set on my course and I have no money. When I'm washed and combed I'm quite presentable. I have an engaging smile. I have a thumb. And, as you see, I'm riding down the road at this very moment." She was pleased with herself and smiled at him. "Determination's the thing, my friend, in every endeavor."

He was in accord with her. He liked women of substance, formidable women. He took a pack of cigarettes from his pocket, shook one into his mouth. "You tied up with somebody?"

"I'm involved. Neither tied up or down."

He struck a match under his nail and bent over the flame, keeping one eye on the rushing traffic. "How come he lets you tramp across the country? There're a lot of wild people roaming around, you know."

"He's not my custodian."

"Think you can handle yourself, huh?"

"Who but a fool would rely on anyone else?"

"You want to hear something?" he asked, turning in the seat and giving her a solemn look. "I told you I got two ladies I do business with? Each of those ladies has seen me blubbering in her lap and I ain't ashamed to say it. Last year I lost my job. I'm new with this outfit. A whole year I was out of work. First I thought, hell, I been working all my life, I got a workshop fixed up in my garage, I'll make a dog kennel or something like that. Two weeks later I was going crazy. Every day down to unemployment to see if they got anything. Every day reading the classified ads in the newspaper. Looking everywhere. Trying everything. Finally I took a mop and a pail and some of my wife's cleaning stuff and I went around knocking on doors, asking could I wash windows. I made eight dollars doing that. That night I was bawling in my wife's lap. The same back east with the other one. She was going to leave me and marry some car salesman. Same thing, cried like a baby. Don't tell me you don't need somebody. I need somebody."

"Two somebodies, it would appear," Stella said.

"Okay. I got a lot of emotion. It's the way I am. You want a cup of coffee?"

"I'd rather have a beer."

"At ten o'clock in the morning?"

"I never take anything stronger until lunch," she said primly.

"Ah-hah, I think I know about you, lady. I think I know about you." He wagged a finger at her. "I got drinkers in my family," he said.

"Splendid," Stella said. "Then you know how they hate to be meddled with."

"You want to get juiced, get juiced. Only I don't pay."

"I'll accept coffee. Coffee and toast. Perhaps an egg."

"Okay, I see how you operate. Breakfast on me."

The heat during the afternoon was intolerable. Mr. Polanski removed his shirt. Stella unbuttoned her blouse and took off her shoes. The landscape was oppressive; tire factories, bottling plants, anonymous stucco suburbs elbowed each other for miles. She dozed for a long time, her head back, heard herself snoring when they hit a bump and struggled awake. The hot interior stank of sweat and motor oil. The road seemed to wind before them endlessly, now cutting through brown hills stubbled with brush and pocked with outcroppings of stone. The truck was so large, the cab so high, that she had the impression she was flying over the highway rather than riding on it.

She knotted a handkerchief around her brow. It gave her a raffish and slightly drunken air. She found herself swaying with the movement of the truck. The heat had sapped her.

"I got some salt tablets in the dash. Swallow a couple—here's the thermos..."

She was limp. "I like dark, cool places," she said. They had slowed to go through the hamlet of Littlefield. She looked longingly out the window at the signs of various bars: Pete's, The Kick-Off, The Tap Room. The truck rumbled by and she stared out the window, imagining the cavelike interiors, seeing only blue neon scroll reading "Coors Beer."

She straightened again. She saw a brush fire in the hollow of a far-off hill smudging the blue sky with a sullen cloud.

"Look," she said. "The burning bush. God's voice next, no doubt."

She reached into her bag, withdrew her paper pad and fanned the still air against her fiery face. "I think," she said, "that I am going to faint."

Mr. Polanski took her at her word and thrusting out one arm he pushed her head between her gaping knees. Her face was within an inch of the rubber mat, fumes assailed her, her ears rang.

"I'm getting off the road. Sit tight."

The next she knew she was lying in a field with Mr. Polanski's jacket wadded under her head. A jack rabbit peered alertly at her through the gorse; the sky was bright white and cruel overhead.

"That's all right, that's all right," Mr. Polanski murmured, patting her hand. "You're okay now."

She came up woozily on an elbow, dismissing his ministrations. "Don't fuss, don't fuss."

She struggled to sit up, pushed her heavy hair back from her face, slapped sand from her blouse and her skirt. She felt the taste of bile in her mouth, grit in her teeth—she spat. Then she pushed his assisting hand aside and hauled herself up on unsteady feet.

"Let's move on. I've got this whole bloody country to get across."

"Wait a minute," he said to her. "We've got to work something else out. You passed out on me, I've lost a lot of time. Look, I'm not in the transportation-of-ladies business; I'm not even supposed to pick up riders, my insurance doesn't cover it. I haul freight for a mean sonofabitch who'll have my ass if this load comes in late. So what do you say?—we call it quits and no hard feelings."

She looked around her in disgust. "Well, if you're only going to think of yourself—"

He exploded. "Who the hell am I supposed to be thinking about, lady? I pick you up. I schlep you. I spend my own dough feeding you. You've cost me time. And now I'm supposed to apologize for trying to shake you off and get my fucking job done.

435

You're a pain in the ass, you know that?"

"You have a point. I'm just trying to get where I'm going, but I see the justice in what you say."

"I'll drop you in Cedar City."

"Very well. Cedar City. Whatever that may be."

But he stopped to give her one last meal in Cedar City, a tough steak curled in grease and a cheap bottle of wine. She left the meat untasted, put the bottle in her purse, grunted meager thanks and took up her place under a traffic light with her thumb stuck out. He waved as he drove by. She did not return the gesture. Hail and farewell, Mr. Polanski.

The car that stopped for her was a white Cadillac with gold hub caps and wheel spokes; the statue of a Remington cowboy welded to the radiator cap saluted the breeze with a Stetson held aloft. A sequined band down the side proclaimed it to be the property of Don Burden, The Texas Moonstar. The driver aimed the car so close to her she was forced to jump up on the curb, cursing him soundly in the bargain.

"Hayou," he cried in a merry voice. "Hayou?"

It took her a full moment to realize he was not hailing her but inquiring after her well-being. "How *are* you?" How was she indeed! Pissed off at being nearly run down. He flung open the door and beckoned her in, his hands fiery with gemstones. She saw another figure in the back seat, slumped under a huge, creased cowboy hat, a pair of elaborately tooled boots propped up on the seat in front of him. She noted, in passing, that the man's fly was open, but as he was fast asleep she was not concerned.

436

"Give you a lift, little lady?"

"Where are you heading?" she asked.

"Kearney. I got me a spread in Kearney. You riding or standing there?"

"I'm riding, thank you," she said, and positioned herself in the front seat, her disreputable bag in hand.

He looked like a fat child grown thin, not quite handsome but close enough to it, with a cocky air of self-satisfaction, as if applause resounded in the air about him, cries and whistles and little girls' shrieks.

He was instantly voluble. She ought to know him, he made that plain at the outset, because, hell, his records were on every juke in the country; they were played in France, in Australia, and the Irish Free State, too. That fellow behind there, sleeping on his tail bone, was Cal Everly, his lifelong friend, business manager and asshole buddy. They were good old Texas boys with two and a half million green American dollars stashed away in a Swiss bank. That brought them just about all the fucking and drinking and good times they could handle. He put a hand on her knee to punctuate his pleasure in living.

"Off with the hand," Stella said. "Pronto." She looked at him pleasantly.

The man whooped. "We got us a buckin' bronco here. Hey!" He swiveled his curly head around to the back seat. "Hey, Cal, wake up, we got us a smokin' pistol in here."

"I heard. I hate a big mouth on a woman." The voice from the back was gravelly with drink.

"What's your name, little girl?"

Stella turned to bend her coolest, blackest gaze on him. "My name," she said, "is Marie de Rabutin Chantal, marquise de Sévigné, more commonly known as Madame de Sévigné. That would be an accent acute on both e's."

"That's more handle than I got on my pump," he said.

"Also," she went on, "tell your friend in the back seat that I find him offensive; and, if you will, that his pecker is out for the world to see. Considering its diminutive size, its pallid color and general lack of tone, he would be well advised to put it back in his pants, as he only lays himself open to ridicule by displaying it."

She reached into her bag, took out the wine bottle and had a satisfying swig.

With a roar the man in the back sat up, stuffed himself back into his pants, yanked up his zipper and vented his spleen.

"What are you dragging that along for? Fucking old bitch with a bottle! Pick up something nice and round if you're gonna pick up. Shit, my dog wouldn't get up on her from behind!"

"Hell, Cal, she's salty, and I like salt on my meat. She's a whole shakerful."

"Well, I don't know about you, but I'm gonna gag her before I eat her. Take me to some quiet place and I'll show you."

Stella corked her bottle with an emphatic splat and turned to look at them both with an unblinking stare of profound and intense purpose. It was a moment before she spoke.

"If you touch me," she said, "I'll ruin you. I'll hound you and reduce you to cinders. I've never made an idle threat in my life. I'd do it if it took me thirty years. I have reservoirs of force, of vigor, of competence and potency that I haven't even begun to tap yet, and it would be focused on you two. That's the validity it would have. I'd come to the door of your house in Kearney with police and attack dogs. I'd find you through your secretary, your agent, your PR man, your music publisher, your booker. I'd come at you with lawyers, FBI men, security guards, Pinkertons, and a kitchen knife in my hand. If either one of you so much as touch me."

The one in the back seat shrieked, "Get rid of her!" and the driver replied, "Cowboy, she's gone!"

The car squealed and skidded to a halt, pulverized rock spraying over the hood and windshield. A high, wide plateau broiled all around them. The air was still, the road ran off to nowhere. She got out stiffly, slamming the door behind her.

The driver leaned over, speaking through the open window. "It's miles from anyplace, but you brought it on yourself. You could've rode all the way with us, with just one little stop on the prairie for fun, but have it your way."

"So long, amigos," she said.

They roared off, clouds of dust and stinging sand billowing back in her face.

She was alone. She knew there was life all around her, snakes, lizards, birds, beetles, kangaroo rats, coyotes; knowledge and intuition told her there was a plethora of life sharing this uniform and monolithic place with her. But she felt alone, she disliked the immensity of the desert under its clear, fading sky and the heat was making her ill again.

439

"This is a dangerous journey," she said to herself, aloud but undaunted. "And why not? All life is."

She sat down on a rock to wait. It was getting dark. She drank the rest of the wine just to pass the time.

The farmer who picked her up during the cold night hours was a brittle old man, frayed and taciturn, a man who would chop wood slowly, would bend painfully to retrieve a bucket, a dogged, unflagging man. The car was an ancient Pontiac, shock absorbers long since gone, front seat sprung, but he made no apology for it.

"You're between towns. It's pretty late to be out on this road."

She looked him over carefully. He waited out the scrutiny and then said, "You'll be all right with me. I ain't nothing more than I look—a dirt farmer."

He drove slowly, both hands on the wheel at all times, gripping it as if he held the reins of a skittish horse. He spoke only twice more. Once to tell her his destination, Rock Springs, and once to offer her a peach from an open bag on the seat between them.

He had a faint asthmatic wheeze which bubbled through the quiet night like a kettle on the boil. Stella found the sound comforting. She slept.

It was dawn when they approached the town. The old man shook her awake and took his hand away swiftly as soon as her eyes opened.

"Lady," he said, "I live down this road. I'd invite you to the house for a cup of coffee, but my missus is bedridden and don't like company. You can take

440

the rest of them peaches if you want."

She got out and paused a moment to lean in the window. "What's your name?" she asked.

"P. J. Walker."

"Well, Mr. Walker, you're a decent man to spend a night with. I can't say that occurs often in my experience. I'll take the peaches."

A young sailor on leave from a nuclear submarine took her from Rock Springs to Point of Rocks, and two little old ladies, one of whom crocheted in the back seat while the other chattered endlessly of her sister-in-law's bad cooking and her poor brother's destroyed stomach, gave her a lift from Point of Rocks to Rawlins.

An Indian laborer stopped outside of Rawlins to wave her into the back of his truck, where she rode wedged between a lashed-down cultivator and a panting, salivating, tail-thumping red setter, who sniffed her crotch and licked her face.

He took her to Sinclair, where she flagged down a young girl in pink plastic curlers, whose crying baby squalled and wet her lap all the long, tedious afternoon, while her hair grew wet at her nape and sweat trickled continuously between her breasts.

At Laramie a minister offered her a ride and half of his sardine sandwich. She gagged after one bite and hid it in her pocket, where it smelled rankly all the way to Pine Bluffs.

There she was picked up by a woman close to her own age, with a soft, cloudy beauty, good clothes, good scent. The car was black, air-conditioned, quiet. The woman's hands on the wheel were narrow, ringless, with short, unpolished nails. She could take her to North Platte, she told her, in a dry, inflectionless voice. Stella peeled off her

441

stockings, jammed her slicker behind her head, made a disorderly nest for herself. She edged toward sleep but was roused by the feeling that she was being watched in some disturbing, ambiguous way.

"Why are you staring at me?" she asked crossly.

"I'm sorry," the lady said.

Stella had no appreciation of prudence. "What's there to stare at?"

"You're a handsome woman."

"Handsome." Stella echoed the word flatly. "Ah. I think I see what I'm into here. My dear," she said, "I've lived a reckless, some even say a rash life. I understand appetite. I approve of it. I don't think, however, that mine is the same as yours."

The woman's grin was wide and engaging. "How quick you are," she said.

"Yes, yes," Stella replied, "there's no question that *I'm* quick. The thing is, how quick are you?"

"Very."

"Then you'll understand quickly when I tell you I don't go to bed with women. Some charming ladies have invited me to get over my obstinacy from time to time, but it's an experiment I've never made."

"There's a lovely inn in the country not far from here," the woman said. "Very cool, with beautiful rooms overlooking a garden. We could bathe and rest."

"It's bad manners to persist," Stella told her.

The woman put a gentle hand on Stella. "I would do nothing to embarrass you, nothing to startle you. You would hardly know you were seduced until you were."

"It's all right for school girls, I guess, to get up to

442

something with their gym instructors. But after fifteen it's narcissism. You might just as well look into a pool of water."

"Come look," the woman said, her touch moving lightly up Stella's arm. "Let's lean over the edge and look together."

Stella did not debate it. When they stopped to get gas on the outskirts of North Platte and the woman went into the washroom, Stella left the car and walked around the block out of sight, raising her thumb again. She did not wish to reproach or be reproached, judge or be judged. Nor did she care to romp with sloe-eyed ladies in flowered bed sheets. She just wanted to move on. She had a place to go.

A fairground operator took her to Kearney, complaining of business; folks didn't want to see cootch shows anymore; they were nothing compared to what they could watch in their downtown picture shows. There was a sudden wind and a drenching rain outside the city, thunderheads standing out sharply in the sky. She was driven to shelter under a tree, where a car packed full of amiable college fraternity boys found her and took her to Grand Island, shifting her boisterously from lap to lap all the way. A drunk endangered her life from there to Council Bluffs, hurling beer cans at fence posts the entire distance. She got lucky with a long ride to Iowa City in the company of a beekeeper who rented honeybee colonies to farmers who needed pollination for their crops, went on to Elkhart with a Boy Scout leader in short pants and knee socks, got lucky again with a sheet and pillowcase salesman for Wamsutta, horny and downhearted, who traveled six days a week, nine

443

months a year, and was afraid he would die all alone in a hotel room somewhere. He took her into downtown Scranton.

She spent part of the forty dollars for a cheap motel room, the rest on a good bottle of Scotch and two tacos. She filled a bathroom water glass, propped it on the tub, bathed, drank and schemed. She slept in a bed for the first time in three nights, restless and fitful, and was out on the highway again before dawn.

A stock clerk at Macy's took her the rest of the way, warning her darkly to put whatever money she had in her shoe, to buy a hammer and carry it at all times, not to ride in the subway, not to walk in the park, never, ever to get into an elevator alone; everyone was the enemy. He took her across the rest of Pennsylvania, across New Jersey, past the swampy, steaming junk yard of Jersey City, through the Holland Tunnel, and let her off near Times Square, calling a final warning that it was full of hookers and pimps and addicts: take care!

It was hot, the temperature at a hundred, the humidity near a hundred, the tar in the streets had begun to run, sticking to the soles of her shoes. Garbage cooked in green cellophane bags; the people looked pale and wet and cross.

She asked for directions, was ignored, refused to be ignored, accosted and collared five different passers-by before she was told which way to go. She walked forty blocks, scanning the city to see if it suited her. It did not. The buildings made the people Lilliputian, the traffic was an abomination, the Guggenheim was pompous, lacking wit, the Metropolitan might be possible, she would decide after she had been to see it. Windows were grimy,

444

pigeon shit ate the facades of buildings, motes blew into her eyes.

'The side streets were better. Window boxes bloomed, the houses had panache, there were signs saying "Curb Your Dog." She approved of that.

Caleb did well for himself. His was the biggest house on the street, brass doorknobs polished, tubbed trees perky, front steps swept, garbage cans lidded and labeled—Caleb's own general tone prevailed.

The houseboy was unaccustomed to the likes of Stella. She stood in the doorway like flotsam cast up by a turbulent sea and with hauteur undiminished said: "Tell him it's Stella and that I will not leave until I see him."

She pushed past the astonished young man and sat down in a gilt and red plush chair, legs out, arms dangling, looking about her. How immensely rich Caleb must be, how darkly opulent were the polished Jacobean chests and the bronzes in massive groups upon them. How acquisitive he was. She counted the Hellenic torsos—there were five, spotlighted. The floor had been laid for a Renaissance prince in Carrara marble, the stairway for ducal entrances and exits. She thought what the silver urns would bring in a pawnshop and pursed her mouth in a silent whistle.

Then she heard his heavy tread, and her gaze rose to the top of the stairs. And there he was. Her heart kicked in her chest, she heard a cry that must have been her own, and with the blood surging through her veins she ran up, taking the steps two and three at a time, and she flung herself on him. She slammed into his chest, very nearly toppling him backward, and she held him in a hectic, viselike embrace until his arms finally rose and encircled her.

"Well," he murmured into her tangled hair. "Well. And well again. What have we here?"

Smothered against him, the words spilled out of her. "I crossed the whole goddamn country. I want my book contract. I want my advance. I want my publication date. I want you," she cried.

He held her out at arm's length and shook his head. "The order of priorities is typical of you, my dear. But welcome." And he kissed her brow.

She clung to him like a barnacle. "Don't be a fool," she said with savage intensity. "I've been out of my head without you. No good to myself, no good to my work, mad with longing. All links broken. Punished. Stagnant. Sniveling. You have only to look at me to see the state I'm in. My God, man, I'm in love, and it's gall and wormwood and pain in every bone of my body. I can't work, I can't sleep, even drink's not what it was. You've ruined drink for me! It's grotesque, I tell you, what's befallen me. Words shamble through my head. What's a poet without words, you unfeeling prick! Am I nothing to you that you chop me down? Heal me, I tell you. Restore me!—Or roast in hell forever!"

"How daintily you woo me," Caleb said, letting go of her.

"I believe in plain speaking," Stella said. "I don't give a fig for pride or dignity either. I have to get back on my feet, that's all I know. I begrudge the time I spend mooning over you. I want you where I can get my hands on you. I want to be appeased and purged, sated, freed! I have to have you back."

446

"You figure very largely in that speech," Caleb told her dryly. "I appear in the role of a prescription, to be taken to lower the temperature, to restore the brain to clarity. A pill, in fact—a term of mild contempt used by my children to designate a fool."

"Must we stand here discussing it? I want to sit in a chair. I'm exhausted. Do you know what I've been through?"

He was immediately his old solicitous and courtly self, helping her into a room filled on all four walls with books, and where there were no books there were heroic portraits, battle scenes, Venus reclining, Venus and Eros. He rang for tea. He poured a good measure of Scotch into a glass and handed it to her.

"I've been completely miserable without you," he said quietly. He sat down behind a huge desk halfway across the room from her. "My heart has been quite broken. Don't accept it smugly as your due, Stella. You haven't earned my feelings. By right, you shouldn't have them. The truth is I can't withhold them from you."

"But you have," she cried hotly. "I abased myself. I humbled myself. I called endlessly. And paid for the calls, too. And where were you? Out to lunch. Out to bloody lunch!" She was fierce in her outcry. "*I* came to *you*. Further abasement. I've made a hegira to you, across this entire, benighted, franchised country. And damn—we're quarreling already. There's some best in me somewhere, Caleb; for God's sake bring it out."

"Come to my arms," he said softly. "Come to me, my wicked, my devious, my ungrateful Stella."

All that afternoon, while the light washed the

447

walls with gold, she lay across his lap, looking up into his wise and weary face. She felt torpid, as though she lay on a riverbed with waters moving gently over her head, fracturing sunlight and sky, dulling sound. She studied him idly, the stroke of his eyebrows, the long curve of his mouth, the lines that creased his forehead, his imperial Roman nose. But he seemed detached from her somehow, apart from her, a mythical figure, wine-clad, besotted, ravished with love and wine, a Bacchus, withered cherries hanging from his ears, trailing away from her through a green and darkened wood, retreating, vanishing, leaves closing after him. She called him back.

"Take me to bed," she commanded.

It was, she thought, waking some hours later, pure delight, like a pure ideal, to put aside her superior self and to melt into this great old man. He had awesome gifts as a lover, but beyond that she could sit in his shade a while, rest and renew herself. She prodded him awake.

"Don't sleep."

"You've tired me out."

"I've watched you sleep for an hour, you great whale. You're almost beautiful when you sleep. Though you bulge here and there. Put your arms around me and tell me something delectable."

"Well," he said, heaving himself up on the pillows, "we must decide what to do with you."

"Palaver? More talk? Let's just be, for Christ's sweet sake." She put her face against his huge belly. "How your guts rumble."

"Disquietude," he said, "as I see our future together."

"Why get your wind up? It's a piece of cake."

Stella was emphatic. "I'll function as I always have. You'll be the rock. All else will be hot flesh and straddling until you are too old for it. Then I'll spoon-feed you and rub whiskey on your gums and cosset you in every possible way."

"I shan't ask for that."

"What, then?"

"Time." He stroked her hair.

"Eons," she said. "We have eons. Put your hand on the small of my back. Just there. Your hand was made to fit where my spine sags."

"I am older than you, very much older."

She grew impatient. Matters were growing morbid. A small terror plucked at her and she staunched it with abuse.

"Don't try to weasel out of marrying me. Yes, I want marriage. The ring, the words, a settlement, everything. I didn't make this wretched pilgrimage for nothing."

"I have some say in it, I trust?" He looked at her with his dark, heavy-lidded eyes, his all-seeing gaze.

"You don't. You must have me. For better or worse." She flailed at him, pounding on his massive chest, hurting him. He caught her hands.

"Then I will. If I must, I will. Peace, Stella. I will have you."

She rolled on top of him, locked her legs around his, ground her hips on him, clutched, sniffed, bit, licked, tongued, kissed.

"Speedily," she said.

"Yes," he answered, looking over her head at something far away and unnamed. "Speedily."

They flew through the night back to California.

Stella lay curled up against Caleb all the way, lapping champagne in the first-class compartment, first from a chilled glass held aloft in a series of extravagant toasts, then sloshed jovially into her water tumbler, then slopped into her coffee cup, and for the last thousand miles or so drunk manfully from the bottle. She had to be assisted upon arrival.

It was too late to go to a hotel, so over Caleb's mild protest they went back to her apartment. It stank dreadfully of cat and mold. Stella had left food uncovered on the drainboard before her hasty departure and the result, after eight days, pits and cores, stems and peelings, was a pyramidical fantasy of rot.

"Never mind," she said, flinging open all the windows to try and stir the hot, motionless air. "It's just for one night. I'll put clean sheets on the bed."

She went to the linen closet. "One clean sheet, as I don't seem to have two."

"You have an incomparable flair for disorder. I thank God I'm a rich man and you need never do anything for the rest of your life but sit on a silk cushion and soil it. Is your bathroom fit to use?"

"The water runs. There's soap."

"If this were our first consummation," Caleb told her, "it wouldn't take place, that I can assure you. There, there," he added, "I love you, sloven though you are. Come kiss me."

She did so fiercely. "We'll darken the room. You won't see anything. There'll just be you and me, naked and amorous. Hurry up."

"I was hoping," he said dryly, "that you were thinking of bathing, too."

"Yes, yes," she said impatiently. "Tomorrow. I'll wash my feet."

"That's reassuring."

He took his bag and went into the bathroom. She heard him singing as the water ran into the tub. Hastily, she swept the clothes and the papers and the books under the bed, righted a lamp shade tilted at a crazy angle, killed a fly with her shoe and rummaged frantically for a decent nightgown. She found one that was stretched and faded and slipped it over her head. She lit a candle and stuck it into a saucer, so that the room had a pleasant, shadowed light. She tied up her hair with an old belt and arranged herself in bed with the air of an odalisque, or as near to that attitude as she could manage, with her gown sliding off her shoulders and the pillows lumped and knotted behind her, down escaping to float in the air each time she punched one.

He came into the room smelling baby-sweet, his hair neatly brushed and still damp.

"The candle's a charming touch," he said, and climbed in beside her. "May I blow it out? The danger of fire."

"Let there be darkness," she said.

They lay side by side, his hands composed and folded on the counterpane, on the clean sheet she had promised. Their voices were murmurous.

"You are my beloved," he told her. "I see what an excellent woman you are and I'm touched that you want to be by my side."

"You've unsettled me," she said, "but I don't care. I love you. Move your leg, please, I'm getting numb down one side."

"My love, my sweet," he said. "Ah, Stella, what

a maze you are to wander through, thorny, green, puzzling. What a delight. To be happy and amused, both at once, what man can say the same? You'll never want for loving, my dear, as long as I live. You may take that as a promise."

"I'll hold you to it," she said passionately. "To the very letter of it. Never another. Not a hand on a buttock. Not a stray thought. Only Stella. Ever Stella."

"Ever Stella," he agreed. "Now turn over and fit yourself against me."

"You're so fat," she said. "A mountain range."

"God bless you."

"He must," she said, and grasping him around his pillowy middle she fell asleep.

Caleb died in the night.

In the last moment he dreamed he was young again, with birds wheeling around his head and a sounding sea at his back. He seemed in touch with a special slant of wisdom that cast a mild and warming light over his entire life. He felt himself gathered in and made eternally cheerful. All that he had ever known or thought or read or championed or cared for was distilled like stones shining and clearly seen in water, and he regretted nothing.

Stella awoke, her eyes still gummy from sleep, to find him marble cold beside her, leaned over him, saw cessation in his face, saw that he was already on another journey.

Time passed as if she were apart from it, smothered in webs and in veils; it was figmental, preposterous. She was aware of the sound of her own voice, howling, of people in the room, crowds of people; Jake was there, Hortense, others, packing in, stampeding, surging. A siren shrieked, there were two attendants in white. For a moment she thought them murderous, storming at the body on the bed; one leaped up on him, mounted him, struck him with his fist on the chest, hammering him repeatedly. The action seemed manic, insane. She thought she saw a kiss bestowed; it was the other, kneeling at Caleb's head, mouth on his mouth, bellowing air.

She saw a narrow white cot trundled past her on squeaking wheels, saw the heavy body transferred to it, strapped into place; she moaned as it wheeled past her and stood to follow, savage, raging. Jake held her back; she struck him.

She felt the prick of a needle in her arm. Nell was there, leading her to the couch, settling her, covering her. It was unbelievable. She had been so smug with the certainty of life. Of health. Of continuance. Hers. His. Theirs. The knife stroke of it. So sudden and final. No recourse, no redress. They were going to grow old, be quarrelsome, accustomed, bound. She battled despotic sleep. She drifted.

So he had died on her. Without farewell, without ceremony, with no by your leave at all, he had gone out of the game.

I must make something of this, she thought to herself, because if I cannot, if I do not...For a moment she lost her train of thought.

Caleb, how you suited me. Suited me. How clever you were. How insinuating and rowdy, such a juicy plum. I never expected the likes of you, rolling into view like a great wallowing ship. You were a summer evening, soft air, zephyrs. And tart as

453

rind. Flavorsome. Erect and lascivious. Strong and stubborn and full of dignity as a parson. Chiding and corrective, willing me to be what I was not. Oh, friend. With your probity and slyness, your steely mind and courtly airs, your sumptuous tastes, your unabashed greed. What a fanciful man; how you nourished me, maddened me, made me laugh. How sweetly you forbore. Nothing base in you. All honor. God knows I never had one like you before. And God knows I never will again. Ah, Caleb. Fat prince.

At that, she cried aloud in pain, and Nell, dozing in a chair in the corner, came to her side.

13

THEY WOULD ALL remember the day in differing
ways, but each with the realization that the road
had diverged and that their lives would now take
other turnings. They wished to embrace each
other, to reinforce each other, to affirm they found
much to admire, each in the other. During this
hour they would smoke too many cigarettes, drink
too much coffee, cry, blow their noses and say
"What the hell" to fate. In concert and in
sisterhood it all seemed so much less threatening.

Stella had a new place at the top of the
apartment and Jake had made her a condition of
the sale of the building. She was to stay there as
long as she liked, and the rooms already suffered
the battering of her presence, with the familiar
litter rising on the floor and her gray cat spitting

nervously in the corner. She would not now, would not ever, care where she was. She went about her old business in her old way with one alteration only: she had given up drink for food and was already growing portly, short-winded and odorous from the peanuts and the chocolates and the crackers she carried in her pockets.

The ladies had gathered for breakfast, yielding the place of honor to Eunice. She had bought a new straw hat and smart red luggage which waited packed at the door. Smoke spiraled in the air, cups chattered against saucers, their talk rose and fell: what had been, what would be, arrivals and departures.

Hortense was acerbic and bracing.

"Just remember," she told Eunice, "no is a word, too. Use it once in a while. No, I won't sleep with you just because you bought me a chicken dinner. No, I can't give you any of my money. No, I don't mess with married men. No, honey, you're too young. No, mister, you're too old. No, you can't have my house key. No—no way. Think you can remember any of that?"

"No," Eunice said, grinning at her.

"I got to be crazy, letting you go off to Alaska."

"Let her go," Nell said. "She's a big girl now, Hortense."

"We're big girls—she's still a runt...Tell me again, Eunice. You got yourself a job *where?*"

"In a camp at the pipeline, outside of Fairbanks. You get a lot of money and big tips and opportunities. You *do,* Hortense, don't look at me like that."

"Uh huh. Opportunities."

"They have long nights," Stella said. "Can you get through a long night, child?"

"I have so far."

"Zonked on Seconal."

"I feel strong," Eunice said. "I honestly do. It's going to be a new life."

"It's the old life in a new place, you mean." Hortense was cranky.

"It'll be different," Eunice said with confidence. "I *know* it's going to be different."

"That's right," Nell told her. "Go around the next corner."

"Is that what you've got in mind for yourself?" Hortense looked at Nell with lifted eyebrows.

"For myself." Nell pondered the question. "Well," she said, "I don't think I care to live entirely on remembered bliss. I think as time passes I may very well come to admire a little compromise as a sensible and rational way to live. So... I think I'll take a teaching appointment at S.C. and write a paper on kidney disease—and seasonally, when the geese honk overhead and the leaves fall, I'll put in a long-distance phone call to Jake and we'll meet halfway, say in Sacramento, in a Ramada Inn in a room overlooking the parking lot. He'll bring me a quart of Washington blueberries, leaking through the wrapping paper. I'll bring him a box of cigars. He'll say I've gained weight. It won't be true. We'll take off our clothes and brush our teeth and crawl into a bed that vibrates if you drop in a quarter. We'll make love and talk and be full of good will. On Sunday morning, when it's time to go, we'll be irresolute. I'll leave a bedroom slipper behind. He'll forget his razor. We'll stand looking at each other. He'll say, 'See you on May Day; I'll bring fudge.' I'll reply, 'The kind with walnuts in it.' He'll call from a pay phone in Tacoma that night to say that the sun is going down and the sky is gorgeous; he just wanted me to know. I'll write him the next day to say miraculously my sinus condition has cleared; bless him."

She looked around at the women who were watching her, willing her to a conclusion. Eunice gnawed her lower lip fretfully.

"I hate to be left dangling. How will it end?"

"Not badly, I trust. Not at all badly." She turned to Hortense then. "And you?"

"Pay my money, take my chances."

They looked to Stella, seated in a rocking chair. They all thought of Caleb, that force, that presence, making grass on a plot green now with his bones and his marrow.

"Work," Stella said bluntly in the silence that fell. "Work, work, work and again work."

"I suppose you're through with men," Eunice inquired fearfully of Hortense.

"I haven't locked the door, but it sure as hell ain't going to be easy to get in."

Stella stared out into the bright blue day. "Speaking for myself, I am not bent on death and destruction. I say yes to life when asked."

They thought of what she said and were pleased by it. Each knew the excellence of it, fine spring rain, books, jokes, orgasms, poetry, hot baths, linked arms, tulips, children, the whole fine flourishing shape of it.

"I'll write to you all," Eunice said brightly.

"No, you won't," Hortense told her. "You'll forget to buy stamps. You won't be able to find the mailbox. You'll be in love."

"God, I sure hope so! Well," she said, looking at

her watch, "I've got to toddle."

She stood up and looked around with a tremulous smile. "Oh, shit," she said, "I'm going to miss you all."

"You're gonna miss your bus is what you're gonna miss." Hortense set her mouth. "Get someplace on time for once."

Eunice looked at them, Hortense, Stella, Nell, in the bright sunlight and her heart went out to each in turn.

"Will you be all right?" she cried.

Stella answered for them all. "The direction is forward," she said.

The bus depot seized Archer's imagination and turned it over and over again, like the time he had been caught in a wave at the beach, hurtled upside-down, seeing sky, sandy bottom, green rushing water. People were milling around, dragging suitcases in all states of repair, one with brown tape crisscrossing it, and some of the people sat on the hard benches and stared as if they were leaving life itself. He saw one old man drinking something from a bottle in a brown paper bag and another crying in the corner, his thin shoulders heaving—a moment of separation had undone him altogether.

The place was dirty, too. The very seat he sat on was littered and sticky and popcorn had been spilled and crunched under his new shoes. Every other moment a voice blared a destination or a departure in tones so harsh he could not make out a single word, and he watched Eunice anxiously, hoping her ears were sharper than his.

He excused himself and walked to the water

459

fountain, his mouth feeling like old socks from the excitement of it all, but the water tasted of rust and he saw what looked like a blob of mucus and was quite sure somebody had spat in the basin.

When he sat down again Eunice asked him about his clothes, inquiring if he really wanted to wear that celluloid clip bow tie and that green wool jacket all the way to Alaska. Wouldn't he like a nice, roomy T-shirt, which she could purchase at the news stall? They were going to an unbuttoned life, to the end of the U.S. Highway system, to the end of the road. No reason not to get off on the right foot.

He explained carefully that the outfit he was wearing had been his grandmother's choice, reserved in the back of his closet for funerals and visits to third or fourth cousins. The tie was, in fact, biting into his chin with its sharp edges, reminding him of his grandmother's last embrace and fiery caution: "I'm going to die soon, Archer, but I'll know what you're up to from the grave and beyond." This was followed by a kiss smelling of paregoric—and thus he had been relinquished and released from her care.

Eunice was already on her feet; a moment later she was back, unfurling a shirt that said "Win With The Dodgers" and a large pin reading "Digging For Gold Beats Gold Digging." She said she thought it was singularly appropriate, considering where they were going, and right then and there she whisked off the tie, the jacket, unbuttoned the shirt and stripped it from him, told him to hold his arms straight above his head—and the new shirt slid over him, ending somewhere near his crotch. The air blew on his body; there was room to wiggle.

"Thank you," he said.

Eunice flung an arm around his shoulders. "Isn't it goofy, Archer, the way things turn out?"

He acquiesced tentatively.

"We know your daddy has to be away for four or five years, and there's your grandmother getting her place in the old peoples' home, which she's had her eye on forever, and your mother moving to Tuscaloosa, in a house too small for any number over two. So guess who was left to take care of you? Me. After all the discussion and the long-distance phone calls your daddy said, 'Listen, Eunice, you and Archer get along swell and Alaska's part of the United States of America, the last frontier, and a boy ought to see that, so why don't you take him up there with you and put him in school and teach him to play poker, so when I get back he'll know a thing or two?'"

"Yes," Archer said, "it was a surprise."

"Yeah, in a way, but to tell you the truth, Archer, I had my eye on you from the beginning. I mean it could have come to kidnapping if all this other stuff hadn't fallen into line. I'm pretty determined when I want something, you know."

"Uh huh," Archer said. He looked at his shoes and wished they were two-tone brown and white instead of all brown.

"I for one," Eunice said, "think we'll have a ball. We'll go to a lot of movies and get a bowl of goldfish and learn to ski and look for whales in the ocean off of Captain Cook's Outlet. I'm good company, you know. I know fourteen different Polish jokes."

"I know some, too."

"That's what I mean. We both know a lot of jokes."

"Yes," Archer said.

"Okay, then."

They both fell silent while a woman's nasal voice urged everyone headed for San Diego to get a move on.

"Listen," Eunice said, "there's something else I want to tell you. When you're sunk, sad about anything, I'll know it. I mean, you don't have to put a smile on your face every minute of the day. I can tell when things aren't copacetic. You can even cry if you feel like it."

"No, I won't have to cry."

"No?"

"I enjoy your company," Archer said.

Eunice nodded. "Most men do," she said.

Their bus pulled in and it was announced. Archer carried both their bags and Eunice let him. He selected their seats and was willing to give her the one closest to the window. She let him have it. He asked her where the toilet was in case he needed to use it and she pointed it out and also showed him how the lights over their heads could be brightened or dimmed.

They put their lunch, cream cheese and pimento sandwiches, in the overhead rack and they put their heads against the little white doilies pinned to their seats. The air conditioning went on as soon as the bus rolled away and its hum made Eunice sleepy.

"When we get out in the country, look for the Burma Shave signs," she told him. "They're a gas." She closed her eyes.

Archer pressed his face against the glass to watch out for them. He looked northward and far, far beyond.

THE BEST OF THE BESTSELLERS
FROM WARNER BOOKS!

DAUGHTERS OF THE WILD COUNTRY   (82-583, $2.25)
by Aola Vandergriff
THE DAUGHTERS OF THE SOUTHWIND travel northward to the
wild country of Russian Alaska, where nature is raw, men are
rough, and love, when it comes, shines like a gold nugget in the
cold Alaskan waters. A lusty sequel to a giant bestseller.

THE FRENCH ATLANTIC AFFAIR   (81-562, $2.50)
by Ernest Lehman
In mid-ocean, the S.S. Marseille is taken over! The conspirators—
174 of them—are unidentifiable among the other passengers. Unless a ransom of 35 million dollars in gold is paid within 48 hours,
the ship and everyone on it will be blown skyhigh!

DARE TO LOVE by Jennifer Wilde   (81-826, $2.50)
Who dared to love Elena Lopez? Who was willing to risk reputation and wealth to win the Spanish dancer who was the scandal of
Europe? Kings, princes, great composers and writers . . . the famous
and wealthy men of the 19th century vied for her affection, fought
duels for her.

THE OTHER SIDE OF THE MOUNTAIN:
PART 2 by E.G. Valens   (82-463, $2.25)
Part 2 of the inspirational story of a young Olympic contender's
courageous climb from paralysis and total helplessness to a useful
life and meaningful marriage. An NBC-TV movie and serialized in
Family Circle magazine.

THE KINGDOM by Ronald Joseph   (81-467, $2.50)
The saga of a passionate and powerful family who carves out of
the wilderness the largest cattle ranch in the world. Filled with both
adventure and romance, hard-bitten empire building and tender
moments of intimate love, **The Kingdom** is a book for all readers.

THE GREEK TYCOON by Eileen Lottman   (82-712, $2.25)
The story of a romance that fascinated the world—between the
mightiest magnate on earth and the woman he loved . . . the
woman who would become the widow of the President of the
United States.

A Warner Communications Company

E BEST OF THE BESTSELLERS
FROM WARNER BOOKS!

THE KINGDOM by Ronald Joseph   **(81-467, $2.50)**
The saga of a passionate and powerful family who carves out of the wilderness the largest cattle ranch in the world. Filled with both adventure and romance, hard-bitten empire building and tender moments of intimate love, **The Kingdom** is a book for all readers.

BLUE SKIES, NO CANDY by Gael Greene   **(81-368, $2.50)**
"How in the world were they able to print **Blue Skies, No Candy** without some special paper that resists **Fahrenheit 451**? (That's the burning point of paper!) This sizzling sexual odyssey elevates Ms. Greene from her place at the head of the food-writing list into the Erica Jong pantheon of sexually liberated fictionalists."—Liz Smith, **New York Daily News.**

THESE GOLDEN PLEASURES   **(82-416, $2.25)**
by Valerie Sherwood
From the stately mansions of the east to the freezing hell of the Klondike, beautiful Roxanne Rossiter went after what she wanted—and got it all! By the author of the phenomenally successful **This Loving Torment.**

THE OTHER SIDE OF THE MOUNTAIN: **(82-463, $2.25)**
PART 2 by E.G. Valens
Part 2 of the inspirational story of a young Olympic contender's courageous climb from paralysis and total helplessness to a useful life and meaningful marriage. An NBC-TV movie and serialized in Family Circle magazine.

Please send me the books I have checked.

Enclose check or money order only, no cash please. Plus 50¢ per copy to cover postage and handling. N.Y. State residents add applicable sales tax.

Please allow 2 weeks for delivery.

WARNER BOOKS
P.O. Box 690
New York, N.Y. 10019

Name ....

Address ....

City ....State ....Zip....................

___Please send me your free mail order catalog